SPARROWHAWK

Book Four
EMPIRE

A novel by
EDWARD CLINE

MacAdam/Cage
155 Sansome Street, Suite 550
San Francisco, CA 94104
www.macadamcage.com

Library of Congress Cataloging-in-Publication Data

Cline, Edward.
Sparrowhawk. Book 4, Empire / by Ed Cline.
    p. cm. — (Sparrowhawk series ; bk. 4)
ISBN 1-931561-87-7 (hardcover : alk. paper)
1. Virginia—History—Colonial period, ca. 1600–1775—Fiction.
I. Title: Empire. II. Title.
    PS3553.L544S627 2004
    813'.54—dc22

Manufactured in the United States of America.

10 9 8 7 6 5 4 3 2 1

Cover painting "A Seaport" by Claude Lorrain, 1644
Book and jacket design by Dorothy Carico Smith

For Pam,
Vote for Repeal!
Ed Cline
17 Dec. 2005

SPARROWHAWK

Book Four
EMPIRE

A novel by

EDWARD CLINE

MacAdam/Cage

Dedicated to the memory of Wayne Barrett,
who was the first to discover this

"To hold an unchanging youth is to reach, at the end,
the vision with which one started."

Ayn Rand, in *Atlas Shrugged* (1957)

CONTENTS

PART I

Chapter 1: The Enigmas

A shallow man takes pleasure in being an enigma; an honest man finds the role unpleasant. To an honest man, foreknowledge of an expected calamity is a curse if he is naturally outspoken and wishes to give warning, but is constrained by a codicil of sworn secrecy. It puts him at a distance from others, who in turn are sensitive to his reserve. Foreknowledge turns him into an enigma. It enables him to prepare for a danger, while others are oblivious to it. Foreknowledge can lure a shallow man to feel unjustifiably superior to others, even contemptuous of them, allowing him to flaunt false wisdom in the garb of the unknown.

Jack Frake had sounded many warnings to the other planters, and this had already made him an enigma to them, and an unsettling, distasteful one. They knew what he thought, but could not understand why he thought that way. However, he did not feel superior to them, although he did feel a twinge of contempt. The contempt was involuntary, rooted in impatience rather than in foreknowledge. During the late war, he had spoken often and frankly about the likely consequences of a Crown victory. The others had chosen not to believe him.

"See, sir!" exclaimed Reece Vishonn in the gaming room at Enderly one evening early in November, when he had thrown a ball to celebrate Guy Fawkes Night. "Our fellows can give them a taste of it when they put their heads to the business!"

Several planters were present, and someone's idle remark about Sir Jeffrey Amherst's policies toward the Indians had sparked a lively discussion of the future of the frontier. The defeat of the Indians at Bushy Run and the relief of Fort Pitt in August were still fresh in their minds. Vishonn added, "I've patented some thirty thousand acres there over the mountains. Took stock of them before the French riled up the Indians. They have all the earmarks of good mining land, and contain more first-grade lumber than there is sand on the banks of the York. I'll be able to do something with them, once the army clears out the Indians, or arranges some sort of treaty with them."

"If it can," remarked Jack Frake.

"Oh, I've no doubt that Amherst can, sir. It will simply take time."

"Time? Yes, it will take time," said Jack, cocking his head in concession. "The only thing that will defeat Pontiac and his allies is the continued absence of the French, or if they fight the army on its own terms, which I think they did at Bushy Run."

Ira Granby frowned. "I can't decide, sir, whether you have slighted His Majesty's forces or not."

Jack shook his head. "I have not. The army is good at fighting other armies, on other continents. On this continent? Well, the French learned quickly enough that what might be sane tactics in Germany are suicidal here."

Ralph Cullis drawled, "Well, *that* did the French little good, sir. They were beaten everywhere, and roundly trounced here."

"At what price, sirs?" asked Hugh Kenrick.

Everyone but Jack glanced at him. He stood leaning back against a window bay, arms crossed leisurely. He seemed to be studying them all with a special interest. His appraisal did not include Jack.

"What price?" asked Vishonn. "What do you mean by that?"

"The Crown has accumulated probably the greatest debt in our history. How do you imagine it will be paid?"

"Indemnities from the French," remarked one guest. "They started it all. Let them pay."

Arthur Stannard, the British tobacco agent, volunteered, "War has always incurred debt, sir. And this was a mighty struggle. Concern for how the debt will be paid is irrelevant and a waste of time. The Crown will do what it must."

William Granby, one of the county's burgesses, said, "Better a formidable debt than encirclement by Papists and barbarians. You won't convince me otherwise, Mr. Kenrick. They were ready to drive us into the sea — the French with their crucifixes and muskets, the Cherokees and such with their war clubs, all of them making the sign of the cross as they butchered our women and children and destroyed all that has been accomplished here."

"Yes," echoed his father, Ira. "Better a debt than death."

Vishonn said, "Yes! Whatever our portion of that debt may be, I for one won't mind paying it!"

Jack and Hugh exchanged brief glances, and said nothing more. Vishonn and the others noticed the silent communication, and a question mark appeared in each of their minds. They were faced with two enigmas, one more perplexing than the other.

Jack did not feel superior to the others; he knew that he was, and that is a very different thing. He knew that he was a more complete man, better able to think and act than they, that his vision of himself and the world and what was possible to him were more secure, integrated, and potent than the haphazard, disparate, and conditional states he observed in other men.

He had never nurtured the habit of thinking of himself in relation to others. Once, however, the comparison did occur to him, during a discussion of this very kind. It flashed before his mind, unbidden by him, without an iota of vanity on his part, as a jolt of astonishing clarification, prompted by some lightning-like conclusion: He imagined himself a polished, gleaming column of marble, and the others, a sundry collection of obelisks of brick. It was a natural, inevitable, irresistible, and just comparison; he did not reproach himself for having thought it. Rather, he was amused by it, and had smiled then at the discovery; the others assumed that he was merely being cordial. But he was the marble — straight, tall, solid, with sharp corners. The others were of brick, some better mortared and more neatly troweled than their fellows, but whose parts could be removed and interchanged with parts from the others.

Bricks, even finely glazed ones, do not reflect light well; Jack saw nothing of himself in any of the others, nor sought it there. And he was too whole a man to think of the corollary: that the others could see themselves in the mirroring polish of his stature, that they saw the difference between themselves and him, and that what they saw caused them to feel humbled, afraid, resentful, and grudgingly deferential. And, somehow, unhappy with themselves. None of these things were they in the habit of acknowledging or contemplating.

Jack was too secure in the character and course of his life to dwell on the unbidden imagery. But the moment did help him gain an insight into the nature of the men who opposed or feared him. He did not often wonder about the motives and ends of others; when he did, it was only when their actions threatened to impinge on his own life. Then he was bothered by their own brand of the inexplicable. He could only suspect that beneath their refusal to credit him with a truth was a deeply buried admission that he was right. His awareness of his superiority also caused him to wonder why certain things were not obvious to men who otherwise had the capacity to see, but did not, or would not, see them. That sublime moment aided him in understanding the inconstancy of other men and why he felt reluctant to deal with them.

A man who merely feels superior craves the company of those who, whether they despise him or fawn upon him, acknowledge his superiority. Men of genuine superior virtue naturally hunger for the knowledge or company of their equals. There were few other men with whom Jack felt comfortable, who caused in him neither a conflict nor a sense of intrusion by their presence. John Proudlocks reminded him of himself when he was a youth, struggling to learn and to shape himself, even though the man was only a few years younger than he. Ian McRae, Etáin's father, seemed to accept him without reservation, as a man in whom he would entrust the person and happiness of his daughter. There were a handful of other men in Caxton — Thomas Reisdale, the attorney and scholar, was among them — in whom he observed shades of his own character or evidence of virtues he could admire.

The only other man who almost fully reminded him of himself — in stature of character, in a rigorous exclusivity of personal purpose, in scope of vision — was Hugh Kenrick. The phenomenon was a luxury Jack knew was possible to only a few men. He enjoyed this luxury because he knew that, regardless of the appraisals he made of other men, there was little measurable distinction between the self and what was commonly called the soul.

He recognized in that man a self that would never submit to malign authority; a self that was sensitive to the machinations of others, a self trained in the brittle, lacerating society of the aristocracy to be on guard against sly encroachments; a self that was proof against corruption, sloth, and violence; a self that recognized and cherished itself, and so was proud; a self that quietly gloried in its own unobstructed and unconquered existence.

A self very much like his own.

As Jack did not commit the error of believing that he was an ideal product of the Cornwall or Virginia poor, he did not believe that Hugh was an ideal product of the aristocracy. A man, after all, regardless of his origins, was responsible for the sculpting of his own soul. He could allow its shape to form by chance or the unprotested choices of others; or he could choose, for better or for worse, a portion of its image and content, or all of it. Poverty and privilege alike could be only temporary impediments to that task for a man determined to be independent. Wealth and comfort, poverty and hardship — these could be but mere excuses or artful blinds for abdicating the responsibility of that life-long duty to oneself. That duty was the only one Jack acknowledged. He could not remember a day or a moment in his life when it was not a commandment, one that he gladly obeyed.

He saw evidence that he was not alone in his estimate of Hugh Kenrick or his influence.

Early in December, John Proudlocks came one Sunday evening to the great house for supper and their usual chess game. He brought with him a heavy tome, Blackstone's *Analysis of the Laws of England*, which Hugh had given him as a gift. "I should like to hear what you think of this," he said to Proudlocks then. "That will be worth more than the crown and six shillings I paid for it."

"I have read Mr. Blackstone's book," said Proudlocks that evening to Jack over supper. The tome sat on the table near him, and he would touch it now and then as he spoke, as though doing so helped him organize and articulate his thoughts.

"That is, I have read much of it, those parts of it that were clear and not burdened with Latin. Now, all these laws, they are, as Mr. Kenrick said, the British Constitution. This Constitution, I think, is something like the stone face I saw once on the side of a mountain in the north, when I escaped from the Mohawks. It is mighty, and unique, and awesome, like that stone face. But, this Constitution — it, too, seems carved by nature, and not by men. I mean, these laws — many of them good and just laws, many of them as intricate as a spider's web, many of them more cruel than Algonquin law — they were made by men, but there is no —" Proudlocks paused to find a word "— there is no…direction to them. I mean, there *is* direction, but it is…chance." He shook his head in frustration. "It is almost as though the wind and rain and snows carved them, too, making some parts fine, leaving others rough."

Proudlocks paused again, and his face brightened. "These laws, they are unlike Mr. Kenrick's conduit. He drew that in his mind, then fashioned it. I think he had to know much before he could do that. I remember what he said, before he left, that the Constitution here was a great mass of precedents, of findings and decisions that turned over ancient traditions and old laws, and that it was all around us, like the air. Beneath them all I see the gift of chance. I mean, there is liberty granted in much of this book," he said, tapping the top of the tome twice with a finger, "but that was not the intention. Liberty was given life almost by chance, or accident. It was something that came with other purposes, but it could not be corrected, or denied, or taken back, or turned over, once it was known." The dark, handsome brow furled in judgment. "Liberty, I think, ought to be the purpose of laws, as plain and clean and straight as Mr. Kenrick's conduit." He shook his head. "I do not think that this Constitution is a final form of what it ought to be."

Jack smiled. One thing he enjoyed while listening to Proudlocks was watching his face as he spoke. As his friend uttered words, his expression registered the efforts of an active mind determined to choose the correct expression of a thought. "I agree with you," said Jack. "So will Mr. Kenrick, and Mr. Reisdale. You must tell them what you have told me, in the same words."

Proudlocks grinned. "By then, I may find better." Then he frowned. "They would not regard me as ignorant or presumptuous, Jack? I mean, there are many centuries of law discussed in Mr. Blackstone's book, and much wisdom."

Jack shook his head. "It was a fine commentary, John. Mr. Kenrick will be pleased to hear it, while I believe you will startle Mr. Reisdale. I have read some of his own commentaries on the Constitution. You have raised some issues which I believe should have occurred to him." Jack smiled in benevolent mischief. "You will clear some cobwebs from his head."

A few evenings later Thomas Reisdale came to Morland Hall to discuss the agenda for the next meeting of the Caxton Attic Society. Hugh Kenrick also came. Jack invited Proudlocks to repeat his perspective on the Constitution. This Proudlocks did, omitting his comparison of it with the stone face.

When he had finished, Reisdale studied the man over his bifocals for a long time. The floor clock in Jack's library ticked away the minutes, and puffs of smoke rose from Jack's pipe almost as regularly as the mechanical sound. Neither Jack nor Hugh had ever before seen the attorney in so quiet a state of thought; he usually had an answer or reply ready before another person had finished speaking.

Then Reisdale removed his bifocals and studied them for a moment. With a meditative grin, he said to Proudlocks, "This is true." With a subtle change in his expression, he regarded the man with a special respect. He glanced over at Hugh and Jack. "Perhaps," he said, "I have been too long immersed in the subject to mark the true shape of our Constitution. Like Jonah in the whale." Then he rose and began pacing before his companions. He nodded to Proudlocks once. "And you are right, sir. If our liberties are to be preserved, they must be the singular object of laws, and not a parcel of afterthoughts." He paused in thought for a moment. "But, good heavens! It's too logical, sirs! Why, if such a project were ever to be undertaken — well, the entire Constitution would need to be recast! No! There must be some accommodation for what *is*...."

The attorney began pacing again as he spoke. His companions could not decide whether he was moved by excitement or by agitation.

"But, no....No, sirs! I do not see it ever happening! Parliament would not consider the matter at all! That is, the only persons who could and would venture to compose a bill on that subject to be debated by a committee of the whole House, are *not* in Parliament — my correspondents there in London." Reisdale stopped to wave his arms and bark in a scoffing laugh. "Wilkes? The cider tax? The influence of the court party? These are nothing, these are but trifles, when one contemplates the terrible, riving crisis caused by doubts about the Constitution! We would endure a crisis greater than the Glorious Revolution — and one bloodier than the Civil War."

He shook his head in unbelieving desperation. "It's too logical, I say. Too...gravely imperative. Why, a recasting of the Constitution specifically to preserve and enhance our liberties would require that England shed both the monarchy and a corruptible Parliament! And who is more likely to light the fuse to *that* powder keg? Englishmen at home, or Englishmen here? *We are*, sirs! Has not the match already been struck? Have you heard what that rabble-rouser in Hanover talked a jury into doing? Pastor Acland came to me a day ago to ask me about the legality of the award. He said it was a slight to the Crown, and ought to be punished. I informed him that the Crown may not punish a court and a jury for doing their duty, for they were protected by the Great Charter. He did not like *that* logic, sirs! But, before you know it, that brand of duty will move us to petition Parliament to recognize our right to disallow, in angry reciprocation, every act it passes, and every decision by the Privy Council and the Board of Trade. Mr. Franklin's Albany congress would become feasible, and some congress of legislatures here would begin disallowing at their pleasure all the Crown's laws and directives!"

Reisdale, with open, pleading hands, turned from one fact to another. "Can you not see the progression to tragedy? Disallowance would lead to disobedience. Disobedience would lead to rebellion. Rebellion would lead to punitive reprisal! Reprisal would lead to...war." He shook his head again. "Yes, sirs! I see the logic in Mr. Proudlocks's cogitations. It is straight and unbranched and unaccommodating. That is where it would lead us. It is a horrendous logic, persuading us of a ludicrous conclusion." He paused. "But…if our liberties must be taken as seriously by legislators as we ourselves take them…then that logic is inescapable."

Reisdale stopped suddenly and slumped into his armchair. His companions noted the anxiety in his face as he stared at the floor, an anxiety that was almost tangible to them. "Oh, sirs!" he said quietly, in not quite a whisper. "All these years, I have been but a sweating baker, concocting mere political pastries in the oven of my mind, to be consumed in a single sitting, and then forgotten. My mind is now aflame and topsy-turvy." He glanced up at Hugh and Jack. "And you, sirs: What are your own thoughts on the matter?"

Hugh shrugged lightly. "The Constitution must be sheared of the monarchy, and Parliament reformed against the corruption of liberty, and begun afresh." He added, "Nothing is *too* logical, come what may." He turned in his chair. "Mr. Frake?"

Jack said, "Or, we must shed the mother country, to begin afresh — come what may." He paused. "Liberty must someday emerge from the caves in which she has dwelt for so long, and claim her rightful place in the full sunlight. I agree with Mr. Reisdale. That is more likely to happen here, and not in England."

Hugh looked with surprise at his friend.

But Jack did not notice. He was hearing another voice, that of a friend from long ago: *"Oh, Jack! Can you imagine it? No kings, and so no need for all the varieties of danegeld!…Oh! Wild imagination! Suppose our colonies in America did such a thing? Can you imagine them nullifying their numbing bondage? Revoking their oath of loyalty to the King? Not petitioning him for protection from Parliament? What an outlandish miracle that would be! The parable of the loaves and fishes is much more credible a tale!"* He smiled in memory of the man who had spoken those words, and of the boy who had heard them, and for a moment forgot the present and his company.

Reisdale sat speechless. The utterances of both men seemed to be necessary but contradictory ends of a logic that he would neither contemplate at length again nor speak with his own lips for years.

John Proudlocks only dimly grasped that something important — perhaps even dangerous — had just occurred. But he was observant enough to notice what Reisdale was too distraught to see: a schism between the masters of Meum and Morland Halls. He saw the confident, unyielding, but unconcerned sets in the expressions of the two men. He knew that both men had the capacity to act. He wondered now whether they had the capacity for violence in their convictions, for he was certain that they were both aware of the logic of those convictions, which could only lead to a clash between them.

He glanced at Mr. Reisdale. This man, he knew, was frightened by the prospect of violence between England and Englishmen here. This did not frighten Proudlocks; he had seen more violence and brutality in his young life than the attorney had in his fifty years. He glanced again at his friends Jack and Hugh. The prospect of violence between them did not frighten him, either. It merely made him sad.

After a while, the men spoke about the agenda for the next meeting of the Attic Society at the King's Arms Tavern. Reisdale and Hugh left for their homes. When Proudlocks made to leave for his tenement, Jack said, "Thank you, John. You have foreshortened our wits and much of what is to come."

Proudlocks nodded, and acknowledged the compliment with a simple "Yes." Then he added, "I will check the seedbeds tomorrow morning, and see if Mr. Hurry is ready to sow the barley."

*   *   *

Official copies of George the Third's Proclamation were sent to all the royal governors of the colonies. Lieutenant-Governor Francis Fauquier received his copy, sealed with the red wax of the king's coat of arms, long after most Virginians had read and discussed the edict and its implications.

In early January 1764, the day after the last bonfires of Twelfth Night had died out, the *Sparrowhawk* arrived in Caxton as dusk began to darken the waterfront. Captain John Ramshaw brought copies of the *London Gazette*, which contained the full text of the proclamation, to Jack Frake, and bundles of recent issues of the *Gazette* and other London newspapers to Wendel Barret of the *Courier*. Barret would reprint in his newspaper many of the articles he found in the London papers.

Ramshaw found the shop still open. After an exchange of greetings with the printer, he slapped a copy of the *Gazette* on the shop counter, and with a finger stabbed the front page. "This, sir, may deserve a special number of your paper. You people are being fitted for fetters."

Barret, a short, stocky man in his fifties with black, twinkling eyes that could swiftly change to pins of contempt, raised his eyebrows. "Oh? How so?" He bent to read the first page. "A proclamation? I see...."

Ramshaw also brought mail. Two large parcels of letters and newspapers were addressed to Hugh Kenrick from his father and Dogmael Jones, and one parcel for Jack Frake. Barret's shop also served as a post office for Caxton. The printer sent one of his apprentices to Meum Hall with Hugh's mail, and to Morland with Jack's. There was mail for the other planters and residents of the town and country, Ramshaw told the printer. His bursar would bring it up the next morning.

Hugh read the proclamation in the *Gazette* over his breakfast. Then he went to the stable, saddled his horse, and rode to Morland Hall on the narrow path that connected the two plantations. He met Jack halfway on it, heading for Meum Hall. They grinned at each other, and waved their copies of the paper in the air.

Then their grins vanished. "We were right, Hugh," said Jack. "There is no room for doubt now."

Hugh nodded. "The lion was issuant," he remarked. "Now it is rampant."

Three days later, a special edition of the *Courier* was sent to its subscribers. It contained the text of the king's proclamation, in small, tight print. It occupied the first and second pages.

Reece Vishonn was one of the subscribers. At Enderly, in his library, he reread the paragraph that proclaimed the closing of the frontiers, and sat blinking in a disbelief that eventually succumbed to anger. At last he could no longer contain himself.

He exclaimed, "Your royal will and pleasure be damned, sir!"

Chapter 2: The Dioscuri

"I am compelled by His Majesty's gracious proclamation to speak out of turn," said Reverend Albert Acland from his pulpit on the second Sunday of February, "and to depart, if only briefly, from our sacred liturgy, at my own humble discretion. I quote Matthew, verse sixteen."

He paused to note the passive, attentive faces of the parishioners looking up at him. His glance roamed over the men, women, and children who sat huddled together in the chilly confines of Stepney Parish Church. The building's wooden steeple above creaked and sighed with every winter gust that swept around it, and the constant draft through the windows and gaping holes in the mortar numbed one's feet and sent exposed hands and fingers to curl inside the warmest pockets of one's garb. It was cold enough that he saw his own breath as he spoke, his words as staccato bursts of vapor that dissolved in the air almost before he completed them.

All the great planters and their families were here this morning: the Vishonns, the Granbys, the Cullises, the Otways. All but two, though many of the tenants and servants of Meum and Morland Halls were present. He often wondered what *those* people thought of their masters, the masters who would not deign to set foot inside his church.

Reverend Acland knew what those men thought of him. Jack Frake despised him, so much so that he would not even register his contempt in the pastor's presence. That one was beyond redemption. But he had nurtured hopes for Hugh Kenrick. These were dashed one fall day last year, when he chanced upon that man outside of Mr. Rittles's shop in town. He had enquired, in an impartial, conversational manner, "Dear sir, why do I never see you at services, giving thanks to God and assuring Him of your devotion?"

Hugh Kenrick had looked at him with frosty amusement, then said, as though it was a chore to even bother with composing a reply, "Because, dear reverend, on Sunday mornings I perform that service in my library, by reading Mr. Locke, and Mr. Trenchard, and Mr. Addison, and books on the wonders of science and of the world. Currently, I am captivated by a treatise on human physiognomy, written and illustrated by a Dr. Leighton, of the College of Surgeons in London. He makes some interesting observations on how the subtleties of the skull's contours affect one's appearance." The planter had paused to smile. "Now, sir, if you possessed a particle of Jesus' benevolence, you would not doubt or contest that answer, but instead think: Ah! So, *that* is how this gentleman thanks God and expresses his devotion. He absorbs knowledge of God's wondrous works and those of his children. What need of him to sit in a cold pew, listening to me recite musty sermons, intone supplicating prayers, and lead a raucous congregation in the singing of musty psalms? Why, he is more virtuous than I."

Acland had been so startled by the answer that he forgot to be offended. He'd asked, hopefully, "Is that how you regard your absence, sir?"

Hugh Kenrick had shaken his head, this time with solemn amusement. "No, sir, that is not how I regard it." And in his expression the pastor saw the unmistakable, silent message: No man is the ward of my soul, neither my friends, nor my acquaintances, nor a ghost, nor, least of all, you, sir.

Reverend Acland recovered from the pain of the moment, and added it to his secret pile of resentments. This morning he had the satisfaction of seeing nearly a full congregation. The townsmen, traders, and artisans were well represented. The McRaes were here, too, and the Stannards, the Tippets, and even, for once, the tobacco inspector and bachelor, Richard Ivy.

Acland cleared his throat and continued. "'Lay not up for yourselves treasures of the earth, where moth and rust doth corrupt, and where thieves break through and steal; but lay up for yourselves treasures in heaven, where neither moth nor rust doth corrupt, and where thieves do not break through nor steal."

As he spoke, his glance rested in turn for a mere second each on the stubborn, petulant face of Reece Vishonn; on the stoic face of Ira Granby; on the tired, ironic face of Ralph Cullis. All three planters owned large tracts of land west of the Blue Ridge, bought years ago in speculative greed. His Majesty's recent proclamation rendered title to those lands nugatory. That was justice, mused the pastor, and God's justice, at that. Reece Vishonn, among all the planters in the county, stood to lose the most. This man had shown him the least sympathy when the Two-Penny Act was passed by the General Assembly, reducing the reverend's salary. This man, the most powerful voice among Stepney Parish's vestrymen, had more or less told him to be satisfied or be gone. This man, among all the men who sat on the county court, had blocked his initial moves to sue the parish for back pay, by persuading his fellow justices, on one hand, to recognize the Crown's disallowance of the Act, and, on the other, by assuring the pastor that a suit would mean years of costly litigation and the expenditure of more than the pastor had then or could ever hope to recover.

Reverend Acland had heard the grumblings of the planters over the proclamation. He took some satisfaction in the knowledge that they could neither settle those lands nor clear them, nor survey them, nor exploit them in any manner, except at the risk of armed conflict with either the Indians or the army. Nor could they sell those lands now, except to Crown agents, on Crown terms. Nor could they escape to them, except at peril of torture, death, and even slavery at the hands of the Indians, or eviction and fines by the Crown.

This morning, Reverend Acland felt emboldened to remind them all of their duties — of their Christian duties, and of their duty to obey the king. Religion, to the pastor, long ago became not so much a creed of personal salvation as an invaluable tool of vengeance on those who seemed to be more successful in living than he. His regular exhortations for humility, modesty, and states of grace in the eyes of the Lord disguised a malice which most of his congregation mistook for earnest righteousness.

Etáin McRae, later that morning over breakfast in the modest house that stood in back of her father's store, startled her parents with the observation, "If we are not to care about treasures of the earth, we should all become poor, and so have neither house nor clothes nor the means to support a church. There would be no church. Are not our treasures responsible for Reverend Acland's pulpit and fine vestments?"

Ian and Madeline McRae stared at their daughter, and were at a loss to answer. After a moment, Ian McRae cleared his throat and said, "Many teachings of the Church should not be taken literally, Etáin. They are exempt from logic."

Etáin frowned. "'Thou shalt not do murder' — that is plain enough," she said, oblivious to her parents' surprise. "And, 'Thou shalt not steal.' Though I do not believe a bishop would be able to explain to me why they are right commandments." The girl paused to rest her chin on a hand. "But what Pastor Acland said this morning, that was sophistry. If he meant it, then he should vacate his own house, and go about in rags, beg for food, and preach on people's doorsteps. What he said this morning, I thought was vindictive. He is a hypocrite. I think all ministers are hypocrites, whether they are English churchmen or wandering divines."

Madeline McRae, more cosmopolitan and worldly than any other woman in Caxton, could only reply, with a stern but gentle urgency, "Etáin, that is enough."

Ian McRae's mind simply choked on his daughter's words. He could not find any words with which to reply. He sat blinking at his daughter, more frightened for her than offended by her.

Etáin frowned again, and did not pursue the subject. In the back of her mind, as a measure against Reverend Acland's sermons and notorious piety, were the two men who were, to her, exemplars of moral action and worth. They were, for her, treasures of the earth, and she would not renounce them.

* * *

Lieutenant-Governor Francis Fauquier understood the intent of the proclamation at least as well as did the minister. Unlike that man, however, he possessed more than one particle, if not of Christ's benevolence, then of humanist concern for the edict's implications and for the grace of his colonial subjects. In February, after reading its velvety paragraphs and pondering their explicit meanings, he wrote to the Board of Trade, profusely praising the ukase on one hand, and on the other humbly contradicting his praise by broaching the issues which he sincerely believed that His Majesty, his Privy Council, and their lordships of the Board might not have given their full attention. He inquired about the status of all the legal settlers west of the demarcation line, in addition to the hundreds of thousands of acres of land that had been patented by individuals and land companies decades ago, on much of which taxes and quitrents had already been paid. Many of these patents had been granted by past royal governors and approved by the king, the Council, and the Board. In fact, he tactfully pointed out, both the settlements and the patents had been encouraged by the Crown's own policies. The new policy, he gently reminded his superiors, was truly a reversal, and could not be implemented without risking grave consequences or with any hope of success.

Fauquier was skittish, for while he felt it was his duty to raise the subject, he did not want to risk still another reprimand from the Board. Their lordships were not pleased, he knew, with his habit of signing acts and legislation passed by the General Assembly but to which had not been appended suspending clauses, which allowed the Board or Privy Council to nullify legislation they did not like. They did not tire of reminding him that it was not his prerogative to endorse such laws and thus violate their explicit instructions to veto any law sent up from the House of Burgesses and his Council that did not carry the mandatory suspending clause. And they were especially not happy with his practice of exercising his own judgment and defending both a clause-less law and his oversight by pleading the colony's extenuating circumstances in long, apologetic, and irrelevant discourses.

The Board of Trade received their delinquent governor's letter in late March, but did not read it until early July. In their tardy reply, their lordships offered no concrete guidance to Fauquier except to urge that he abide "by the obvious sense and spirit of His Majesty's Proclamation." The Board devoted many more words, however, to a request for an abstract of all patented land in Virginia from which quitrents — an ancient feudal levy on freeholders paid in lieu of service to a king or lord — might be drawn, to more accurately calculate such revenue due the Crown. The Board wished this detailed abstract to include all land patented, bought, and sold, together with names, dates, numbers of acres, and locations, from the founding of the colony a century and a half ago to the present.

Fauquier reluctantly, and privately, conceded to himself that their lordships were neither blind nor insensitive to the consequences of the proclamation, that they were indifferent to both reason and practicality. He balked at their request for the abstract, and instructed his deputy auditor and deputy secretary to compose memorials to the Board stating the difficulties of the task. He himself did not reply to the Board until late December of that year. In his letter, he stressed that the proposed project would take years to complete, that the colony's land records were neither complete nor wholly accurate, that the General Assembly would probably refuse to vote the funds for the project — or not enough — and that, in any event, the information sought by the Board could be readily obtained from the Auditor-General's office there in London, which contained the annual rent rolls and accounts of the colony. The Lieutenant-Governor derived some personal satisfaction from the circumspect reproach in his letter to their lordships. This was the limit of his rebellion.

* * *

Captain John Ramshaw, nominally an Anglican, rarely attended services. He reasoned that an angry sea was enough of a fear-inducing phenomenon without him having to be fearful of the Entity credited with its creation. He had fought and survived many storms, and after each one thanked himself first before thanking God. As he saw it, he had beaten Him every time, and charged to an imaginary account in His name every broken spar, shredded sail, and damaged cargo caused by a storm. This was the limit of his faith.

In February, he delayed sailing the *Sparrowhawk* to Norfolk so that minor repairs could be made on the vessel. He stayed with Jack Frake at Morland Hall. As a novelty, he attended Reverend Acland's service at the church. He, too, concluded that the minister was a vindictive man. When he returned to Morland, he said to Jack, "By God, I can tell you, that man has no love for his flock. He'd just as soon see them offer their throats to wolves as see them graze in the fields of purity, just as long as they submitted."

Jack smiled and put down the book he was reading. "I warned you," he said. Then he rose from his desk. "Let's have some breakfast."

"Speaking of wolves," remarked the captain as they waited for Mrs. Beck to serve them, "when I was last in London, I picked up much talk among the merchants there about some mischief they are up to. It seems that many of them have pestered the Board of Trade and other dens of thievery with demands that something be done about your money, these notes issued by the Assembly here that pass for specie. In London, you know, they are virtually worthless. And I believe our friends wish for a law that would require you people to pay all your debts and for laded goods in sterling."

Jack scoffed immediately and shook his head. "Not so much sterling flows through the colonies in a year that could keep Queen Charlotte in good service for a week."

"A week or less," chuckled Ramshaw. "Even so, they will demand such a law. I do not believe any of these fellows appreciate the disadvantages under which the colonies labor."

"If they knew, do you think it would make a difference to them?"

"No. Probably not. The navigation rules do not give you people a fair roll of the dice. They never will, never can. That is why smuggling and forged cockets are more profitable means of trade than 'fair' trading." Ramshaw grinned. "Does your friend Mr. Kenrick know how you remain solvent?"

"He suspects, but does not inquire." Jack paused. Mrs. Beck came in with a tray holding their breakfasts.

When she was gone, Ramshaw asked, "How does he fare?"

"His father owns a bank, and you know that he also has a busy commerce. Hugh is paid in specie — not necessarily in sterling — just as you pay me, in violation of another law. Otherwise, he would be in as great a debt as any of the other planters here." Jack chuckled. "Between us, he and I are largely responsible for any coin you may see changing hands in Caxton."

"He is a good and wise lad."

"And a friend." Jack took a mouthful from his plate, then said, "He has a friend in the Commons now, who has written him that there is also talk about removing smuggling cases from colonial juries and assigning them exclusively to non-juried vice-admiralty courts, and perhaps even trying defendants in London. And his friend reports talk of a stamp tax on documents here, and reordering the customs establishment."

Ramshaw cocked his head. "I heard the same talk. Jack, there are now twenty-six colonies in the king's dominion, but only thirteen worry their lordships, the gentlemen in the Commons, and the merchants." He sipped some coffee. "We've talked of this before, son. The proclamation is only an overture. I do not know how it will end."

"It can end in only one of two ways, John: capitulation and slavery, or rebellion and independence." Jack saw understanding in Ramshaw's eyes, not shock or dismay. He saw acceptance. He raised a hand and briefly touched his heart. "That is the logic of the matter. There will be no middle ground. The logic will not permit one. No Act of Settlement is possible here, though I know that many well-meaning men will believe it is. But we are either free Englishmen, or Americans, or whatever we choose to call ourselves when the time for decisions comes — or we are not free. Even should the king and Parliament and the Board of Trade and the merchants relinquish their hold on us, separation is inevitable. It already exists. Some here and in London sense it; others know it. Else, why would the king and Parliament and the Board feel it imperative to begin encircling us with laws and troops and boundaries through the ruse of colonial security? And should it come to rebellion, the logic of the matter will allow only two choices to those who possess the power to act against the colonies: a peaceful separation, or war."

Jack sighed, and shook his head. "John, I wish it were in my own power to hasten the business, to be done with it. But if the logic leads to rebellion, *that* must be made in concert with other men, and I must wait for them to see the logic and the wisdom of it. I own that if I acted alone now, this day, or next year, those same men would send me to the gallows, as Redmagne and Skelly were."

Ramshaw, at that moment, could not help but remember Jack when he was a boy of twelve and a batman for a master smuggler in Cornwall. He felt an odd paternal pride in the way that boy had turned out, as a worthy heir to his old friend and fellow smuggler, Augustus Skelly. He said, in a low, ominous voice, "Not all rebellions are successful, my friend. Look at the Netherlands, and Turkish Greece, and Ireland. And England itself. The history books are strewn with the bodies of failed rebellions."

"The likelihood of failure is not a good excuse for not attempting one. Perhaps we should not be thinking of rebellion, but of revolution."

Ramshaw leaned forward in earnest. "Allow me to play the devil for a moment, Jack, and put this to you: I agree that today, or next year, you would be condemned to hang for treason and strung from a pole near the race course that's just beyond the Capitol in Williamsburg. So, what makes you believe rebellion or revolution is possible? In Virginia, and Maryland, and New York, and Philadelphia, men continue to toast to the king's health. I have seen no evidence of rebellion in them. A talent for bickering, and for smuggling, perhaps. But for rebellion? No."

"It is there," replied Jack. "The Crown's likely actions will provoke it to action, in time." If men can rally to the cause of that Wilkes fellow in England, graver protests are possible here. I am as certain of that as you are certain of a storm at sea by knowing the nature of the clouds you see in the distance over untroubled waters."

Ramshaw nodded, then asked, somehow already knowing the thrust of the answer, "And if a rebellion happens, and it fails? Or if it ends the other way, without a rebellion, but with ignoble submission and slavery: What would *you* do?"

Jack shrugged. "Find myself a new maze of caves, perhaps west of the Falls, in the Blue Ridge, and carry on Skelly's and Redmagne's careers." He shook his head emphatically, "I will *not* live as a fenced-in 'subject,' John, permitted no lawful fences of his own against predators, lawful or otherwise."

Ramshaw regarded his young protégé with some admiration, and with some sadness. "Wisdom, son: You are rich with it, richer than a Spanish silver mine. But I don't envy you the burden of it."

Jack laughed. "Sometimes," he confided, "I don't envy myself for it. But when I am in such a desperate mood, I imagine the alternative — ignorance — and then the burden is not so onerous."

The captain laughed in turn. "Spoken without a shred of modesty *or* vanity! I don't wonder that the good minister in town detests you!"

Jack studied his guest with fondness. Ramshaw's hair was almost pure white now, peppered with the fading black of his youth. The weatherworn face was frozen in an unalterable mask of age, ruddy and beaten by countless gales and winter crossings of the Atlantic. "Every voyage is a lifetime," Ramshaw once told him. "So don't be surprised if I grow old faster than you — or not at all."

Ramshaw seemed to know his thoughts. He sipped his coffee, and said, "I plan to retire after a few more voyages, Jack, and enjoy my ill-gotten gains. When and where, depends on what those coggers and caitiffs in London do to the trade. You know that I have a house at Great Yarmouth, in Norfolk, and another I rent to a Scots merchant in Norfolk on the Roads here. You also know that I have acquired all the shares of the *Sparrowhawk*. When I retire, I shall retain some interest in her, but sail her no more."

It was Jack's turn to smile sadly at his friend. "You will miss the voyage, and the grand game with the Crown."

"True," said Ramshaw. "I will miss those things, and much more. Now, you are not my principal client here, but you are my favorite. I should not like to see you at the mercy of some law-abiding master or captain of the *Sparrowhawk*. I have some candidates as my predecessor in mind. But, as a ship's husband — and that would require a certain investment — you would have some say in her business and comings and goings." He paused when he saw his host frown. "I know that you are not as enamored of the sea as I am. But give it some thought through the winter, and we will talk again when I return in the spring."

Jack nodded. "This is not to be taken as an answer," he said, "but, after breakfast, you might do me the honor of showing her to me again. It has been some time since I last trod her decks."

Chapter 3: The Soloists

At the end of the one-week session of the General Assembly in January, Lieutenant-Governor Fauquier felt free to schedule a February concert at the Palace. Friendly and lively company, refined conversation, and music were his ways of escaping the tedious and often risky duties of office, a means of reminding himself that another, far more enjoyable realm existed over which the chores of empire had little influence. He planned, of course, to perform some numbers himself, together with other musical talents who lived in Williamsburg.

Among the latter was a young law student, a tall, red-headed, lanky lad who was reading law under the wing of George Wythe, the town's most eminent attorney. This fellow was not only proficient with the violin, but bright, argumentative, and affable. The Governor often invited him to the Palace to sup, to engage in provocative and speculative conversation, and to perform in the company of the town's other appreciative and enlightened residents.

His secretary sent invitations to the concert to many of these luminaries, and also to those in the outlying towns. Hugh Kenrick received one, as did Reece Vishonn and his wife. In his acceptance of the invitation, Hugh appended an unusual query: Would His Honor be gracious enough to work into his program some numbers performed by Miss Etáin McRae of Caxton on her harp? "Her impressive repertoire has lately been enlarged by the transcriptions for that instrument — in her own hand, mind you, for she can both read and write notes — of certain pieces of Handel and Gluck, never before heard in these parts. I will vouch for both her abilities and the pleasure they will bring you and your company."

The Governor, intrigued, feeling adventuresome, and hungry for the sound of a harp, acceded to Hugh's request, and letters were exchanged making the arrangements.

When Hugh visited the McRaes and informed them of the concert, the parents were stunned, excited, and anxious about the event, in that order.

When they had recovered, they expressed their gratitude. "If you are not careful, sir," said Madeline McRae to him privately, "you may win our deepest sentiments — and Etáin's."

Hugh glanced across the drawing room at Etáin, who was talking with her father. "That, Madam, would not be an unwelcome development."

Etáin, who was both excited and frightened by the prospect of playing before the colony's social elite, asked him, "But — what shall I play?"

Hugh replied, "Some of the new music I brought you. I have seen your notes and heard you play them." He told her what the Governor had agreed to add to his program. "But be sure to take some other music along, for I believe that you will so impress the company, they will request one or more encores."

And, so, on a cold Saturday morning in February, the McRaes in a borrowed chaise and Hugh on horseback wound their way along the frigid road that led to Williamsburg.

The concert that evening was a great success. In the newly renovated ballroom, Fauquier and other amateur musicians performed a sonata each by Corelli and Campioni, followed by a vigorous rendition of a Vivaldi cello concerto, his four hundred and thirteenth. In the latter, the Governor proved his virtuosity on the cello. At his guests' request, he performed a solo sonata by Domenico Alberti on the Palace's new harpsichord, and Peter Pelham, the organist at Bruton Parish Church, played a somber Chabron sonata on a chamber organ.

After a leisurely intermission, during which Fauquier treated his guests to a generous buffet, the Governor introduced Etáin McRae, "a young lady and prodigy from the fair town of Caxton on the York." For a hushed and quickly dazzled audience, Etáin, wearing her customary green riding suit and ribbons in her hair, played Handel's fourth *Coronation Anthem*, Gluck's "Dance of the Blessed Spirits" from his opera *Orfeo e Euridice*, and Boyce's *Hearts of Oak*.

To no one's surprise, the company requested encores. "I declare, sir," remarked Fauquier to Hugh, "this wisp of a girl could play the most ruttish tune on that harp and convince God that she was honoring Him with a hymn!"

"She has that talent, your honor," replied Hugh.

Etáin played her own transcriptions of a François Couperin concerto and a Telemann concerto, with the same reception by the guests. They would have requested more, except that the Governor saw that she was tired, and put no more demands on her.

Fauquier was so pleased with her abilities and with her reception by the company that he presented her with five gold guineas. He spoke with her parents and urged them to send her to London to take lessons — "not that she would need them," he assured the stupefied father — with a music master of his acquaintance, who taught children from the finest families — "I do believe that some time on a regular keyboard, together with a brush with theory, could only ensure her supremacy in the art" — and added that if and when they were amenable to the idea, he would be happy to write a letter of recommendation to the academy — "and perhaps even contribute something to the expense, if you are not averse to brooking a bit of disinterested charity."

"Thank you, your honor," replied Ian McRae, who managed not to stammer. Madeline McRae nodded gratitude and performed a brief curtsy.

"Of course," continued Fauquier, "I cannot guarantee that your daughter will return *here* for an engagement. As delightful as they are, I do not put on very many of these concerts." He glanced at the girl across the ballroom. Etáin stood by her harp in a circle of admirers. "But, you may rest assured that if I can fit her in at some point in the future, she will open the program, not conclude it."

"You are too generous, your honor," said Madeline McRae.

In the course of the evening, Hugh stepped outside to tour the Palace yard with its stables, coach house, and gardens. He heard a step behind him and turned. He was shyly approached by the red-haired musician who had performed with the Governor. He smiled at Hugh as though he were about to address a mystery, or a legend.

"You are Mr. Hugh Kenrick, I believe," he said.

"I am, sir."

The light from a nearby cresset flickered over an intense, freckled, eager face that seemed to be struggling with a question. Then the musician said, "I have heard that you freed your slaves."

Hugh grinned, uncertain whether he was being congratulated or accused. "I did not free them, sir, although that was the consequence, and the object of my actions."

"And you are the same man who built a device to water his crops, and persuaded his town to lay brick walkways along its principal street?"

"I am the same." Hugh did not wonder that his conduit was common knowledge, but was startled that the stranger regarded the walkways as a notable item of interest. It had taken the vestrymen of Caxton more than a year to approve of the idea. In exchange for the amenity, they had agreed to exempt Meum Hall from parish tithes for five years. But the refurbished kiln, under brickmaster Henry Zouch's skillful and productive labors, was earning Hugh more income. Much of the brick was not only being used to repair some of the great houses of Caxton and for the construction of new houses for Reece Vishonn's married children, but bound pallets of them were being loaded aboard coastal vessels for delivery to customers up the York River and on the James.

"You are a man of many radical parts," commented the musician. "You are also a planter, are you not?"

Hugh nodded. "Yes. I am master of Meum Hall."

"'Meum Hall,'" mused the young man. "'My hall,' or 'My home.' I like it. Someday, I hope to have a chance to name my own abode."

"A proper name for one's home deserves as much serious thought as the name of a child, or the title of a book." Hugh studied the face and figure of the musician, who seemed to be the same age as he.

"It is a distinctive name." The stranger paused. "I have also heard that you are the son of a baron, and the nephew of an earl."

Hugh said, "I neither advertise nor exploit those facts, sir."

"May I ask why not?"

"They are more a burden than a benefit, if truth be known. I have always striven to escape their influence."

The musician commented on the success of the concert, and praised Etáin McRae. The two men talked for a while on that subject. At length, Hugh said, "Although I helped her choose her music, it occurred to me this evening that Mr. Handel's *Coronation Anthem* seemed an inappropriate piece to perform at this time."

"I had not heard it until this evening," said the musician. "It is mainly choral, is it not?"

Hugh nodded. "With a proper orchestra. I heard it performed once in London, at the King's Theater, not long ago."

"Then it must have a libretto, a spoken leitmotif."

"Yes," said Hugh. "'Let thy hand be strengthened…Let thy right hand be exalted.' There are more lines that concern justice, mercy, judgment, and truth. Mr. Handel wrote it to celebrate the accession of His Majesty's grandfather."

"I envy you for having heard it in a true concert theater." The young man paused. "Why do you suspect it was inappropriate to perform at this time?"

Hugh studied his companion for a moment, then asked, "Have you read the Proclamation?"

"Yes, of course," answered the stranger. "Why, only last week, our host — well, he, and Mr. Wythe, and Mr. Randolph, we often play for ourselves on Tuesday nights, and talk of things — his honor commented on the Proclamation, in answer to some bold questions of my own. I am not at liberty to divulge everything he said about it, but he spoke...darkly."

"Has he had from London any intimation of new taxes to be laid on the colonies?"

The musician nodded and smiled. "Our host confided in me that some years ago, Mr. Pitt informed him that it may be necessary to create a special levy on the colonies, once the war was concluded, to meet some of the costs of winning it. Our host cordially advised Mr. Pitt that such a measure would be ill advised. The temper of Englishmen here — with which his honor is not only more familiar, but sympathetic to — would not long tolerate it, nor would their purses."

Hugh grinned pointedly. "That, taken together with the lyrics of the *Anthem*, could only cause me to realize that the *Anthem* was inappropriate."

"I see. Do you doubt the efficacy of the Proclamation?"

Hugh shook his head. "Not at all. What I doubt is its intent and purpose."

The musician narrowed his eyes in thought. "You and I are not quite of the same mind, sir, but near enough that I have enjoyed our talk."

Hugh nodded. "And I enjoyed your performance this evening. You must have had formal instruction."

"Thank you, sir," said the musician. "But, other than a brief introduction to the instrument by a tutor some years ago, I have had no formal training in the instrument. It was necessary to teach myself. I do not miss many notes, and am working to bring some spirit to my playing. It is not enough to merely play the notes of a composition. One must imbue them with some character."

"That is a sensible philosophy of music with which I entirely agree."

"I am fortunate that the Governor asks me to perform with him and his circle. It obliges me to aim for perfection."

Hugh was certain that his companion was not much older or younger than he, yet the other's manner toward him was that of deference to wisdom and experience. He was not sure he was comfortable in that role, but he was amused. They spoke again of music, pacing back and forth together in the Palace yard in the cold air that neither of them seemed to notice. At one point in their conversation, Hugh remarked, "I believe that a man ought to adopt some work of music as his private overture to the opera of his life."

The musician laughed and replied, "*That* is a unique and true observation, sir! But you must own that not so many men lead lives that would merit symphonic interpretation. I myself do not expect my own life to earn, on those terms, better than the tune of a country-dance. You see, I am planning a career in law, and my librettos would be limited to what I say in country courts and the General Court here, for my clients. And, if I enter politics, and run for burgess, I would not expect my overture in that respect to be more than a lullaby. However, that is the only contingency I would attach to your notion, sir, which is an intriguing one, worthy of a treatise."

Hugh scoffed lightly. As he said it, he felt foolish, but he wanted to say it. "Do not dismiss your future life so lightly, sir. You may accomplish great things. You seem to be a well-read man. You should recall how many great men in the past had humble origins and, at your age, nurtured humble, unexceptional estimates of themselves. I am thinking of men such as Mr. Locke, and many of the composers we have heard this night."

The musician said nothing for a while. Then he asked, "Have *you* chosen an overture for yourself, sir?"

"Not yet," said Hugh. "I have heard much great music, but none that has moved me to assign that purpose to it."

They were passing the rear entrance to the Palace ballroom that led to the gardens. A black servant came out then, came down the steps, and whispered something in the musician's ear. The musician nodded once, and the servant went back inside. "My apologies, sir," he said to Hugh, "but Mr. Wythe is asking me to join him and some other gentlemen to accompany the Governor in an impromptu performance requested by Mrs. Blair. Will you excuse me?"

Hugh chuckled. "Of course. But you have the advantage of me."

The young man looked shocked, and he blushed. "Oh! A thousand pardons, sir!" He held out a hand. "Mr. Thomas Jefferson, of Albemarle."

Hugh smiled and reciprocated the gesture. They shook hands. "It was my pleasure, sir. When I visit Williamsburg again — perhaps when the Assembly sits in the fall, and the theater here has a program of plays — we can continue our conversation."

"Yes. I would like that." With a brief bow and a last friendly smile, the young man turned and rushed up the steps and back into the Palace.

Hugh shortly followed him. Inside, Reece Vishonn took him aside and, in a low voice, said, "Sir, I did not know that you had so much influence with the Governor."

"Nor did I, sir. If I have any influence, it is addressed to his more reasonable side."

The older planter scrutinized Hugh for a moment. "I have heard that Mr. Granby, the son, has expressed a desire to move to his father's property up-country, to Frederick, and to vacate his seat in the Assembly for his county." He paused. "Have you ever contemplated a political career, sir?"

Hugh frowned, then laughed. "I can't imagine a drearier prospect than a political career, Mr. Vishonn."

"Well," said Vishonn, "I must agree with you there. I'd lief mind my fortunes than sit in a stuffy chamber listening to lawyers joust over little matters. That is why I have stayed out of it." The planter pursed his lips. "But I do believe the time is coming when, like it or not, a political career may become necessary." He paused again. "Do think on it, Mr. Kenrick."

Hugh did not think on it. That evening, in his room at the Raleigh Tavern, he took a sheet of paper and a pen and began making notes for an essay on the subject of a "life overture." But he could not concentrate. He would think of a point and begin to develop it, when the image of Etáin would again break his train of thought — the image of a poised, confident, resolute girl with ribbons adorning her mob cap and hair, weaving for herself and her auditors a world of unsullied beauty as her fingers flitted with graceful, symmetric energy over the strings of a harp.

Until now, he had not thought this could happen again. He did not encourage it. Etáin had looked at him many times this evening, especially while she was playing, her glance telling him that her music was meant for him alone in the crowded ballroom. He had merely smiled at her, permitting himself no more than the expression of happiness for her that a patron or benefactor might feel for the successful debut of a protégée.

If he had no rivals, he would not have hesitated to ask for her hand in marriage. But he could neither forget his rival nor her words of years ago. He could only ponder: I lost one love to a lesser man, and endured it. Could I bear to lose another to a better man, or to an equal? He glanced at the notes he had made on the paper, and asked himself: Will a somber dirge haunt the overture of my own life?

Two days later, driven by a desire for a resolution, and by a desire to see Etáin again, he called on the McRaes at midafternoon tea. He found her and her mother minding the father's store while Ian McRae was down on the waterfront on business. Madeline McRae said, "The *Galvin* from Liverpool has arrived, and Mr. McRae is expecting cargo on it." She sensed the object of Hugh's visit, and dismissed her daughter. "Go, *fille*," she said to Etáin, "entertain Mr. Kenrick, but first bring me a cup of Bohea."

In the parlor, Etáin seemed happy to see Hugh, and nervous. His calls always had a purpose, and their times alone together were rare and special. At the Governor's Palace, surrounded by so many people and immersed in social protocol, she had been able to spend less than a minute with him. She said now, laughing, "Mr. Vishonn told my father at the Palace that had he a spare son, he would order him to court me, so he could some day welcome me as a daughter-in-law!"

Hugh smiled as he watched Etáin fix the tea. "Mr. Vishonn would not have said that, had he been sober. I would ascribe his remark to one too many glasses of the Governor's sillery."

"Hugh!" exclaimed Etáin. "It is not like you to tease!"

"I was not teasing *you*, Etáin. Mr. Vishonn often decants his soul in direct proportion to his helpings from the punchbowl. You see, he asked *me* that evening if I would think of standing for burgess."

Etáin paused in her chore to study him. "That is an amusing thought — *you*, as a pompous burgess! He ought to have known better than to ask you that."

"He does know better," said Hugh. "However, it is an amusing property of wine that, depending on the volume of its consumption, it can either erase knowledge, or warp it with what appears to be true knowledge."

"Well, then you shall have none here!" said Etáin. She paused, though, and asked, "Unless you would prefer it to tea?"

Hugh shook his head. "No, thank you. Tea will be fine."

She finished preparing the tea, poured him a cup, and took a cup back out to her mother. When she returned, she sat down opposite Hugh and asked, as she fixed her own tea, "Have you so much idle time that you call today?"

"It is not an idle call I pay, Etáin," said Hugh. He put down his cup and saucer on the tea table that stood between him and the girl. "I…am anxious to know if you are close to solving your riddle."

The cup and saucer in Etáin's hands froze in the air. After a moment, she put them down, too, and said, with gentle regret, "No, Hugh, I have not." She saw the look of resigned acceptance of her answer on his face. She studied him for a moment with undisguised fondness. "You should know that the day after we returned from Williamsburg, Jack called on us, and he took me for a stroll along Queen Anne Street. Of course, he knew about our going to the Palace. Everyone in Caxton knew. Mr. Barret is to write a little item about the concert for the *Courier*." She paused. "Jack asked me the same question, Hugh."

Hugh cocked his head in surprise. "Prompted, no doubt, by disquieting jealousies of his own." He shook his head. "You see, Mrs. Vere came to town that day to find some cinnamon and oranges for the wine cake she knows I like, and saw the two of you, and, in the course of complaining about Mr. Rittles's prices, let drop that little complaint, too." He paused. "That is partly why I am here."

Etáin's expression of discomfort changed to one that was unconvincingly distant. "You both honor me with such worry, Mr. Kenrick. And I am presuming that you, as well, appreciate my dilemma...and know that I am not insensitive to your own...and to his...." She picked up her cup and saucer, took a sip of the tea, and rested the delicate porcelain on her lap.

Hugh knew that she was exerting a self-control that was not natural to her. He felt proud of her, and wished he could rise and embrace her. He saw in her eyes that she knew this, and would not protest if he did. But his impulse was arrested by the sight of her and the stature of the woman she was becoming. So he said, "Well, until you have solved it, I will press you no more for a decision." He added, "Neither Jack nor I has a right to."

Etáin nodded slowly, then said, "But, until now, neither you nor Jack has pressed me for one, although," she added with a brief smile, "my parents are perhaps as anxious as are you."

Hugh frowned. "Are you afraid to make a decision?"

Etáin shook her head. "I will not be, when I have found an answer." She studied him again. "Is it because you fear my answer, that you are anxious?"

"Yes, I own that it is that. It is, I think, the only thing I fear."

"Dear Hugh," said the girl, "you will not lose me, whatever decision I make. You must remember that as your rival is not a Boeotian, I am not a...sister of your Reverdy."

Hugh grinned in concession. He was pleased that she remembered their first conversation years ago, at the celebration ball at Enderly. It was then and there that, facing him and Jack Frake, she had first posed the riddle: Which of you is the north, and which is the needle? "I know that about both of you," he said. "It is always on my mind, as a reproach to my anxiousness." He paused. "Why can you not decide between us, Etáin?"

Etáin put down her cup and saucer. "Because you are so much alike in everything I think is admirable in a man, yet so different in your approaches to things. You are like twins. Together, you and Jack are my Gemini." She stopped, and then said, "But, there is a...flaw in one of you that I have not been able to ken, because I do not think it has manifested itself."

"A flaw?" mused Hugh. "I cannot imagine what that might be...in Jack. As for myself...well, I am as mortal as he. One of us is the north, and one the needle. Am I Castor, or Pollux? But," he sighed, "I am happy that we comprise your Gemini. It is no small honor you pay us, and some consolation to me, at least."

Etáin said, "Jack asked me those same questions, Hugh. And I gave him the same answers."

"It would be like him to ask them," remarked Hugh. "How can you know that a flaw exists in one of us, if you cannot identify it?"

"Because you both have done something, or said something, that seems to tell a distinction between you. I am not even certain that it is a flaw. And I have been unable to identify what it is."

Hugh sighed again. "Well, until you do, I suppose we shall conform to the story of the Gemini, and Jack and I consider you as our sister, Helen. There, however, the analogy of our Olympian myth grows skewed. There is no Paris to steal you away, and Caxton is no Troy."

He saw the fondness in Etáin's eyes dissolve to love. "That is one of your sadder virtues, Hugh," she said. She rose then, came to him, and bent to brush a hand lightly over his face. "I still have the penny you gave me at the ball. It will never be spent."

It was the first intimate evidence of her feeling for him. Hugh closed his eyes at the touch of her cool fingers and palm. He allowed himself to raise a hand, and pressed it against her unseen waist.

Etáin lingered for an immeasurable second, then stepped away. "I must go back to the shop."

Hugh looked up at her with loving gratitude. "Yes. You must." He glanced down at the tea service. "Thank you...for remembering our first encounter," he whispered.

"Thank you...for it," whispered the girl in turn. With a rustle of her skirts, she turned sharply and left the parlor.

Hugh followed her back into the shop a moment later. He exchanged a few words with Madeline McRae, and then left. He mounted his horse and walked it leisurely back to Meum Hall, somehow happy about his short time with Etáin, but only just then wondering what she had meant by his "sadder virtues."

* * *

Ian McRae returned to the shop near dusk. His wife and daughter both noted that he looked unusually dour. He said little, except to inform them that he had arranged to have his modest cargo — plows, hammers, nails, pewter dishes, tinware, kettles, muskets, and sundry household necessities, all specially ordered by his customers — drayed up to the shop the next morning.

After their supper that evening, he waited until Madeline and Etáin had cleared the table of the last of their meal, then took a letter from inside his coat and dropped it on the table. "*That* came today, on the *Galvin*. Sutherland and Bain are ordering me back to Glasgow, and instructing me to settle all the accounts here." He glanced at the shocked, attentive faces of his wife and daughter. "If I were not in arrears to the firm, I would resign and begin my own trade here, or in Norfolk. But I have been too generous in my terms with my customers, it would seem, and so I am in arrears, and we must comply." He paused. "Etáin, you may stay, provided you marry."

Etáin shook her head. "I am not ready to, Father."

Ian McRae did not immediately reply. "Well, perhaps by spring you will be," he said. "For by then, we must have sold everything in the inventory here and closed this place." He looked at his daughter with a sad but firm resolution. "If you mean to stay, my dear, you must be bold."

Chapter 4: The North

In Lausanne, Switzerland, near Geneva, young Edward Gibbon, on a restless quest for a history to write, contemplated a sojourn in Rome to study its past and its ruins. In Blackburn, Lancashire, James Hargreaves, a poor weaver, refrained from scolding his daughter Jenny for having, in the course of her play, overturned a spinning wheel, his chief mode of income, for the sight of it gave him the germ of an idea for a better way to work wool and cotton. And at Strawberry Hill, Twickenham, upriver from London, Horace Walpole, member for Castle Rising and youngest son of the late Earl of Orford, was preparing to publish The Castle of Otranto, a new genre of novel later called "Gothic." Respectively, these events comprised a major step in the evolution of the discipline of history, the beginning of the Industrial Revolution, and the debut of what would in the next century become Romantic literature.

Etáin McRae was as oblivious to these men and events as they were to her, yet her own ponderings were no less momentous.

That night she tossed and turned in her bed like a woman gripped by fever, made sleepless by the turmoil of her thoughts. Until now, she had enjoyed the luxury of time. This had been abruptly robbed of her. Now she must make one of two decisions: to return to Scotland with her parents, or to choose between Jack Frake and Hugh Kenrick.

The first choice loomed ominously in her thoughts. She imagined a dozen dire, vividly likely events that could end her life, or at least the possibility of her ever seeing the men again: a savage storm at sea that could sink her ship; a fatal error in navigation that could dash the ship on the rocks on the coast of England, a common tragedy; a deadly shipboard sickness; on land, robbery and murder by highwaymen; an overturned coach; a variety of catastrophic mishaps.... The prospect of going to England thus became less and less a portent with each stark, capricious nightmare, and the choice receded in her mind until it was a mere distant, abstract foolishness it was pointless to dwell on further.

She would not return.

That left Jack and Hugh.

She plumbed the depths of her soul, asked herself a hundred questions, and set up in her imagination a special ledger book such as she kept in her father's shop, with columns for pluses and minuses for each man.

But she found that all she could enter for both men were pluses.

In the end, she decided on her measure; she chose her north. Exhausted by the task — realizing ultimately that her decision rested on what she regarded as justice for herself — she fell asleep just as light began to touch the top of the holly tree beyond her window.

She allowed herself a few days to test her certitude. In her free moments, when neither her mother nor her father's shop required her presence, she spent time on her harp. Once, her mother heard her playing a simple melody that was somber but serene, a melody that seemed to mirror her daughter's recent mood. When she complimented her on it, Etáin said, "It is a Quaker hymn that I found in some of the music Hugh brought from Philadelphia last month. It is called 'The Right of Conscience.'"

"It is pensive," remarked Madeline McRae, "yet untroubled. Are there words to it? There must be, if it is a hymn."

"Yes, but they are not worthy of the melody, which is fine enough. One can attach one's own words to it, so that it becomes a private hymn."

Some mornings later, as Etáin donned her cloak and bonnet, her mother asked her what errand she was going on.

Etáin first finished tying the ribbon of the bonnet beneath her chin and the cord of her cloak. Then she faced her mother and said, "I shall not return to England with you and father."

"I see." Madeline McRae let her needlework rest on the shop countertop. She knew what her daughter meant, knew what had distracted the girl for the past few days, knew better than to inquire, and knew that this was all she would learn for the moment. She searched for a question to ask. "How…are you to go on this errand?"

"I shall walk. It is not far."

"Do you wish me…to accompany you, my girl?"

Etáin shook her head. "I must go alone." She paused. "I will return before midday. When is Father coming back from Yorktown?"

Ian McRae had gone downriver to see a tradesman about some goods the man had purchased on credit. The mother said, "Perhaps, tonight. If not, then by tomorrow morning."

"You shall both be pleased." Etáin leaned over the counter and bussed her mother on the cheek, then turned and left the shop.

Etáin walked up Queen Anne Street out of Caxton. She crossed the stone bridge at Hove Creek and turned west on the public road that followed the creek. The countryside was quiet, except for the lowing of cattle searching for forage, and the sound of an ax somewhere chopping wood. She met no one on the road, and was glad of it. The world and the morning seemed to be her own. She hummed the melody of the Quaker hymn.

She reached a narrow log and plank bridge; such a bridge crossed the creek to each of the plantations on the north side, from the Otway place to Cullis Hall and the eastern part of Queen Anne County. She walked passed that bridge; it led to Meum Hall.

She crossed the one to Morland Hall and followed the path that meandered through the fields, past the tenants' homes, past the cooperage and tobacco barns and the prizing machine. She found Jack Frake and John Proudlocks in the stables harnessing a cart for a trip to Williamsburg for supplies that were not to be found in Caxton. Both men were startled to see her, Jack, of course, more so than Proudlocks. She nodded to the latter, and smiled at Jack. Jack knew that only some extraordinary reason could have caused her to walk this distance, alone, so early in the morning.

He took her inside the great house, to his study. Etáin removed her bonnet and laid it on the desk, and undid the cord of her cloak. She said, "Father has been recalled to England by his firm. He must close the shop."

"I did not know that."

"The letter arrived yesterday. He and Mother will return in the spring."

Jack let a moment pass before he asked, "And you, Etáin?"

This time Etáin let a moment pass. She said, "You are the north, Jack. I will marry you, if you still wish that."

"If I still wish...?" Jack reached out and embraced her. They kissed for a long moment. Then they stood for another long moment, holding each other. Jack, his face pressed to her hair, said, "I...had not expected you to decide so soon...."

"Nor had I," said the girl. "Father said I could stay, provided I marry."

"I see." Jack held her shoulders and spoke to the face he loved so much. "Of course, you have told your parents."

Etáin shook her head. "No. Not even *maman*. Father is in Yorktown. I have told no one."

"Not Mr. Kenrick?"

"I will tell him now."

Jack smiled a cautionary smile. "He is not a needle, Etáin."

Etáin's face was serene. "No, he is not. Rather, he is the south."

* * *

Hugh Kenrick was in the field with Mr. Settle and Bristol, marking out sections for the spring planting of corn and barley, when Mr. Spears came from the great house to inform him of his visitor.

Hugh frowned in surprise, then said, "Have Miss Chance fix us some tea, will you, Spears? And see that Miss McRae is comfortable. I will come down shortly."

"Yes, sir," said the valet with a nod, and turned to hike back to the great house.

Hugh finished instructing Mr. Settle about the corn and barley acreage, then mounted his horse and rode back to the house. Inside, he put on a waistcoat and washed his hands before descending the stairs and crossing the breezeway to the supper room. He found Etáin admiring Westcott's portrait of his family. A tea service sat on the table. The girl turned to him as he came through the doors. "Good morning, Hugh."

"Good morning, Etáin. My apologies for having made you wait."

The girl did not immediately reply. She shook her head and said, "No, Hugh. It is I who owe you an apology, for the same reason."

"Wait? Wait for what?" He said it, almost mechanically, but knew instantly what she meant. He allowed himself some hope, and added, "You are forgiven, for whatever reason that may be."

"I have just come from seeing Mr. Frake," said Etáin. "We...are to be married."

This time, he allowed himself some time before he replied. And now it seemed as if a dooming eternity passed between each of their exchanges. Hugh remarked, "Yes...of course...." With a flickering, pained smile, he added again, "You are still forgiven...Etáin...."

"Thank you, Hugh." The girl sat down at the table and studied him for a while. The tea service was near her, but she did not glance at it. "I want you to know that...I do not esteem you any the less....It was a difficult choice....I am neither indifferent to you, nor fearful of you....I wish there existed a way to spare you the cruelty."

"If such a way existed, it would be a kindness…a worse cruelty," remarked Hugh after another eternity. He heard himself speak the words, but they seemed to have been uttered by another person. After a moment, he shook his head. "I am not privileged to enquire into your criteria, Etáin. And I hope that you will not think it vain of me for knowing how difficult a choice you were faced with. You know that I am a proud man. I know that I am not a Boeotian. If I were, a riddle would not have occurred to you."

Etáin smiled for the first time, but only briefly. "And *there* is one reason it was so difficult." She paused. "About my silly riddle, Hugh….Jack is my north. He always has been. I know that now. But you are not a mere needle. You are a different direction. I do not know how else to explain it."

Hugh shook his head once. "No explanation is necessary, Etáin."

"Then why do I feel that I owe you one?"

Hugh remained on the other side of the table that separated them. He leaned forward, resting his hands on the tabletop, and spoke almost as though he were scolding her. "You honor me with the feeling, but I beg you not to entertain guilt for your decision. That would distress me almost as much as it might you. You do not owe me an explanation of a private judgment, which should make you happy…. And I wish most earnestly for your future happiness…."

Etáin nodded. "You have paid me so many kindnesses, Hugh — the music, the concert at the Palace, your company, every moment since we first met, from that first ball, to this moment — and I hope you do not think me ungrateful."

Hugh straightened to his full height. "They were not kindnesses, Etáin. Remember that I am not a kind person. Nor were they bribes. They were, and will continue to be, expressions of my…feeling for you. If Jack will allow them — as expressions of affectionate friendship."

"I am certain he will, Hugh. You and he are almost brothers."

"An elder brother," mused Hugh to himself. For a moment, Etáin saw that he was lost in a thought of his own. In his face she saw a distant, sad irony. Then he began pacing. "When will your parents publish the banns?"

"Soon, I suppose." Etáin thought for a moment. "What moved me to decide, Hugh, is that my parents are returning to England — I mean Scotland — for my father's firm has instructed him to close the shop."

"Oh…?" Hugh paused in his pacing. "Well…I must see more of them before they leave. Well, that will leave Mr. Stannard the whole business, too...." He resumed his pacing. "Now, Reverend Acland is not likely to want to come so close to Jack in so intimate a circumstance as a marriage ceremony. He would probably refuse to officiate. And, I am certain that Jack would likewise not savor a proximity, nor wish him to have a hand in such an important event. Therefore, I shall write Governor Fauquier, and ask him to perform the wedding. He is, after all, the titular head of this colony's church establishment. Would you mind that?"

"No." Etáin smiled again. "You are generous, Hugh. I will ask Jack about it." Then she rose and put on her bonnet. As she tied the knot of the ribbon, she said, "I must go now."

"Yes." Hugh escorted her to the front door. He said, "My riding chair has been repaired. May I drive you back to town?"

Etáin shook her head. "Thank you, no. I will walk."

Hugh took one of her hands, raised it to his lips, and kissed it, lingering on it long after that gesture had been made. Etáin brought up her other hand and lightly brushed his face with her fingers. After a moment, Hugh released her hand. Then she turned and walked down the porch steps. Hugh watched her go along the path that led past the kiln and other out-buildings to the gate hidden in the far trees. He stood on the porch until her form merged and vanished into the early spring foliage.

He retreated to his study, and sat for a long time staring at the books on his shelves. Fénelon...Bodin....Locke....Harrington....Bolingbroke.... Not a single light among them could offer him a word of advice or a nugget of wisdom this moment on how to cure himself of the aching desolation he felt now, and which he knew he would feel for a long time to come.

I must congratulate Jack, he thought. But, not this minute.

A ray of sunshine briefly pierced the melancholy overcast of his soul, and he understood what Etáin had meant by this being one of his sadder virtues. Well, he thought, there is some dignity in grief — depending on how well one wore its mantle — but little consolation, and no resolution.

All he could see now in the unlit space of this study, glowing in the aura of his memory, were an angelic face and hands that played gracefully over the string of a harp.

Chapter 5: The South

Jack Frake agreed with Hugh about Reverend Acland. It made no difference to him, however, what other official presided over the marriage. He accepted his friend's offer to ask Governor Fauquier to perform the ritual. And so, on a sunny mid-April afternoon, a short, simple ceremony was held in the ballroom of the Governor's Palace in Williamsburg, witnessed by Etáin's parents, Hugh, John Proudlocks, and three members of the Council who happened to be there on colony business.

Outside the Palace, Hugh told Jack that he had business upriver at West Point the next day, and so was obliged to return to Meum Hall that afternoon to prepare for the journey. "Also, some of the bashaws in Gloucester have been pestering me with invitations to call on them, and I won't hear the end of it until I have knocked on a few of their doors."

Even though there was no hint of an ulterior motive in Hugh's words and manner, Jack sensed without thinking it why his friend was leaving Caxton, and said nothing. With a last shake of Jack's hand, and a brief, decorous embrace of Etáin, Hugh bid the wedding party goodbye and departed for Meum Hall, leaving them behind to celebrate the occasion.

From Meum Hall the next morning he rode to West Point, crossed by ferry the Pumunkey and Mattaponi Rivers, and rode back east along the opposite side of the York, stopping for a day or two at several plantations. His reputation preceded him, and the hospitality shown him by the owners — powerful men who owned far larger plantations than his own or Reece Vishonn's — helped him to forget, for a while, both Jack and the woman on whose bare shoulders his own hands would never have a right to rest.

At one point, on the riverfront lawn of an ancient plantation that was almost a town by itself, his host pointed to some dots far across the York. "That's your place, sir, if I'm not mistaken, and just up a bit from it, that's Morland Hall, your neighbor." The patriarch laughed and remarked in jest, "Why, we're practically neighbors, too, sir — after a vigorous row across the water!"

Some tenacious benevolence in his soul allowed Hugh to smile, not in response to the jest, but at the sight of one particular dot, in acceptance of an intimate, personal fact. "One of my sadder virtues," he thought to himself. But was it so sad a virtue? The circumstances were sad, he admitted, but not the virtue that allowed him to endure them.

* * *

Men who have lost in love will try many things to fill the melancholy void. They may mourn the loss until they are emotionally drained, and can feel no more, not even their love, or become addicted to the crushing disappointment, until they can feel nothing else. They may seek to erase the pain by indulging in plebian pastimes, such as gambling, horseracing, or other diverting panaceas. They may drink to distraction, or even to tragedy. They may allow their melancholy to swell into a maddening, unrequited obsession, or fester into a malicious envy or jealousy. They may grow permanently bitter, and so poison their capacity for love, murdering it within themselves. They may commit suicide, or vanish to another city or country, or grow so distant in the eyes of their lost loves and close friends that they become cold, unknowable strangers. Men may grow in that sweet hell, or they may shrink in its fumes and flames.

Rarer are the men who choose none of these remedies, but turn instead to a life-saving course of action. They redirect the energy and vitality of their souls to other passions, passions that share the wellsprings of their lost loves. They may redouble their efforts to improve and perfect their property, or hone the powers of their minds by immersing themselves in the wisdom of their time. Or they may go into politics, if they believe that this realm would benefit from their presence and participation.

Hugh Kenrick, exponent of the Enlightenment, veteran of the discipline of reason and proponent of its properties of salvation, did all these things. He wished to live, not merely to exist or survive. He did them, in part, in the unacknowledged honor of the person who would never grace his life or house as his spiritual partner.

He designed and had constructed atop a pine tower at the side of the great house a water collection tank in order to have running water inside the house and the attached kitchen, and had iron pipes installed with taps and basins in many of the house's rooms. He designed and had built an underground ice-cellar. He reduced the acreage devoted to tobacco — the market for the leaf had declined in Europe, at least temporarily — and planted more wheat and corn. His brickworks grew in reputation, and vessels called regularly at his pier to load pallets of the brick for customers as far away as Richmond and Fredericksburg. He journeyed to Philadelphia on business to see his and his father's agents, Talbot and Spicer, to see Novus Easley, and for pleasure, to buy books not carried by the printers' shops in Caxton and Williamsburg.

One hot afternoon, the summer following Jack Frake's marriage to Etáin, Reece Vishonn rode from Enderly to Meum Hall to broach again the idea of Hugh standing for burgess. Although William Granby could have retained the seat and probably won reelection even though he had already moved with his wife to Fredericksburg and another county, he had expressed no interest in continuing to represent Queen Anne County. And no one else had announced his candidacy for the vacant seat. With Vishonn was Edgar Cullis, the remaining burgess.

The planter and his younger companion found Hugh on the top platform of the pine tower, wearing a straw hat and a carpenter's apron that was heavy with nails, busy with another man hammering planks to the structure. Near the base of the tower were some thin, curved lengths of pine. Several workers were busy hewing and planing other lengths, while another group was engrossed in the task of fitting another length into a flat contraption that lay on the ground near the cooperage.

Hugh did not notice his visitors until the worker with him spoke to him. He waved his hat at them, then climbed down from the platform. He rinsed his face and hands from a bucket of water, then strode over to the mounted men. "Good day, sirs," he said in greeting. "To what do I owe this call?"

Reece Vishonn nodded, but stared back at the tower and the activity around it. "What is it you're putting up, Mr. Kenrick? A watchtower? Are you expecting Indian raids, or mischief by Mr. Swart?"

Hugh laughed, and explained the work that was going on. "…It's not so strange a machine, sir. There are several like it in London. Once it is assembled, we must treat it like a ship. We will caulk the seams inside and out, even though the tongues will fit into the grooves and the weight will help seal the whole. Then we must tar the inside wall as well, to prevent further leakage. That will give the water a slight taste, but they say tar water has medicinal qualities. But, see here," he said, as he showed his visitors around the cooperage, and pointed to the flat, oaken device that held a single curved plank. "This is an idea I've adapted from how carriage makers up north fashion continuous rims for their wheels. Once a plank is ready, and its tongues and grooves finished, its length is forced into this mold and allowed to set until it assumes the necessary shape....The tower vessels in London are rectangular, and their corners often spring leaks...."

Edgar Cullis squinted in thought, and asked, "But, sir, how is water to get into this receptacle?"

"By rainfall," answered Hugh. "The roof, or lid, will have three wide funnels to collect it." He grimaced. "Of course, I shall need to devise something to discourage birds from making nests over them." He nodded to a pile of iron pipes that lay beneath the tower. "And, once the receptacle is finished, we shall connect the pipes. I've prepared two rooms in the house and the kitchen there to link the pipes with the tower."

"Those are not *my* pipes," remarked Vishonn.

"No, sir. I purchased those in Philadelphia, as well as the brass taps and the basins. Porcelain basins, no less."

Vishonn shook his head. "You, sir, are a wonder. Who would have imagined that London plumbing would ever come to Caxton?" With an admiring glance over the tower and the scene around it, he added, "I shall have to look into constructing one of these for Enderly, Mr. Kenrick."

"When you are ready to, I would be happy to offer my consultations." Hugh waved his hat to the house. "Well, please come in, sirs. I shall ask Mrs. Vere to prepare some tea."

When they were settled in Hugh's study, Reece Vishonn stated his business. He knew that his host frowned on chitchat and idle talk. He and Edgar Cullis sat in their chairs, teacups in hand, and waited for their host's answer. The ticking of the floor clock was interrupted by the muffled hammering of the workers on the water tower.

After a moment, Hugh smiled and said, "I have pondered for some time the question of whether or not I could tolerate a stint as burgess — provided I am elected. And, yes, I am willing to mount the hustings."

Vishonn breathed a sigh of relief, as did his companion. "Your election will be practically guaranteed, sir. You have more friends in this county than you may realize."

Hugh frowned, and took a sip of his tea. He asked, "Why solicit me, sir, and not, say, Mr. Frake?"

Edgar Cullis chuckled, glanced once at his companion, then leaned forward and addressed Hugh. "I warned the gentleman that you would ask that question, Mr. Kenrick. Truly, I did."

The older planter by then had marshaled his thoughts, and cleared his throat. "Because, sir — and forgive me if I speak frankly about your friend, and mine — his views are too, well, *violent*. Written in stone, so to speak. I am in agreement with many of them, of course, but not all, mind you. However, there are many planters and freeholders here who would not agree with him on the quality of a leaf or ale, never mind any matter that concerns the Crown. I confess that I fear him, but only a little. Others, though, tremble at the thought of him speaking his notorious mind in the Assembly." Vishonn assumed an apologetic look. "*That* is why we have never solicited Mr. Frake's candidacy."

"But that is what the Assembly is for, sir," said Hugh. "For our representatives to speak their minds."

Edgar Cullis shook his head. "Pardon me, sir, but not at the price of repeated prorogations by the Governor, which surely would happen every time Mr. Frake rose to speak. And that would happen if Mr. Robinson or Mr. Randolph or Mr. Wythe failed to move for a censuring of him."

Hugh grinned in concession. "You have answered half my question," he said to the older planter. "And you have portrayed Mr. Frake as a kind of golem, when in truth he should be dubbed Gog to my Magog. My views are compatible with his in every aspect. Surely you know that."

Vishonn shook his head this time. "Not in every aspect, sir. Whereas you hold out hope of persuading the Crown of the value of these colonies — and of Virginia in particular — Mr. Frake seems resigned to the worst possible predicament, and is adamantly fatalistic in that regard."

"That is true, insofar as we differ about a resolution. But that is our sole difference."

"It is a difference that makes you a far more eligible candidate, sir."

"And a far more credible one," added Edgar Cullis.

"And now I answer the second half of your question," said Vishonn. He rose and paced back and forth before Hugh's desk. "It is through steadfast moderation that we have a chance to outflank and foil the forces that require our absolute obedience and observance of the Crown's laws. There is a coolness in your wit, sir, that has seduced many of us in Caxton. And it is cool heads that will be wanted in the Assembly in the future. The Assembly is at this time roughly balanced between men of Mr. Cullis's generation, and men of my own. Younger, hotter blood, however, is beginning to be returned by the counties, and these are impetuous youths who I believe would prefer to send fire-ships of rhetoric to king and Parliament over civil remonstrances and addresses. Their immoderate language could only invite reprimand and retribution."

Hugh put down his cup and saucer and thought for a moment. Then he asked, "If you believe that the Crown is of that character, why would you wish to clasp the hands of men whose first impulses are reprimand and retribution, and not reason?"

"We do not believe that all ministers are determined to bridle us, Mr. Kenrick," said Edgar Cullis. "It is unthinkable that all the Crown's men are hostile to the colonies, or are blinded by plain avarice. There are many in Parliament, too, in both Houses, who question the wisdom of Crown policies, past and contemplated."

Hugh's face brightened, for two reasons. He thought of Dogmael Jones, member for Swansditch, and the coterie of allies he had drawn around him in the Commons. But he said, "You are mistaken, sir, only about the ministers and members of Parliament being blinded by avarice. Most of them know full well the motive and ends of their policies." He had thought, too, of his uncle, and of Henoch Pannell, and Crispin Hillier. "Do not underestimate their determination to subjugate us, nor should you overestimate their capacity for civil persuasion. If they were so susceptible to reason and good sense, we should never know their names, nor feel the consequences of their actions, except if they wrote books on logic or music, or authored papers on anatomy or the best way to grow tobacco."

Vishonn cocked his head in studious concession, but which Hugh sensed was dismissal of an irrelevancy. He sat down again. "You are better acquainted with these gentlemen than we are, good sir, and we defer to your appraisal."

Hugh smiled again, and rose from his desk to pace thoughtfully behind it. Then he turned to his visitors, his eyes sparkling with mischief. "Here is a sample of a speech I would likely make in the House, sirs. Please listen to it, and then tell me that you still wish me to run for burgess."

Vishonn and Cullis glanced at each other, then nodded.

Hugh rubbed the palms of his hands together once, then spoke. "Does not the Board of Trade behave like another unelected legislature, so that we, the unenfranchised liege subjects of His Majesty, are cornered by both it and Parliament? Are not the Board and Parliament two horns of the Crown bull that, in turn or together, regularly gore us, so that the weighty beast can more easily grind and crush us beneath its hooves?"

Hugh paused to observe the reaction of his visitors.

Vishonn and Cullis regarded their host now with patent doubt. They stared up at him with wide, startled eyes.

Hugh waved a hand. "All magazine caricature aside — we are not represented in Parliament, sirs, and so cannot oppose and counsel the Board's nefarious depredations. We are unable to box the ears of their lordships who sit on that Board by proposing in the Commons that their arrogance be rewarded by censure and a reduction of their munificent salaries. Nor are we represented by anyone on that Board, for no prince or lord has originated in these colonies, no ancestral vassal from these shores ever joined with his *peers* to force King John to set his mark upon the Great Charter. Nor has anyone native to these shores ever been invited to sit on it." Again, Hugh grinned in mischief. "You must concede, gentlemen, that a Duke of Pennsylvania, an Earl of Massachusetts, or a Marquess of Virginia would be a nomenclature ludicrously alien to ears on both sides of the Atlantic."

He paused again, to allow the humor to register on the faces of his listeners. But their faces remained stolidly amazed. He resumed a grave expression. "And so, no British-American ever can or ever will be appointed to that Board, thus denying us a voice on it to caution the Commons against the reprobating laws passed there. Therefore, I move that this House appoint a committee to compose a petition to Parliament, or to a group of liberty-minded members of it, to make it an order of its natural business to discuss the begging necessity of colonial representation in that august body. For surely, sirs, there is room enough in that cramped chamber for a dozen or so more bodies! It is not so frequently attended by all the members that those guilty of habitual delinquency could object to a *colonial bench*!" Hugh addressed Edgar Cullis. "Sir, will you be so gracious as to second my motion?"

An inarticulate groan emanated from the burgess's throat, sounding like a hiccup. Reece Vishonn merely blinked.

Hugh chuckled. "Thank you, sir." He reached down and took a last sip of his tea, then sat down again behind his desk. "But, fear not, sirs. You know that in both Parliament and our own House, no quorum-approved measure is ever countenanced by vote without it first being dissected by a committee. And when good, unprecedented ideas are referred to a committee, they either suffer death in it, or are subjected to the unguent of *moderation*. It is a matter of unimaginative men faced with the inconceivable, the unthinkable, the unthought-of. Committees, I am told, by their nature usually settle for the familiar. If they are assigned the unenviable task of

how best to frame an unfamiliar measure — such as a formal protest
against an action of the Board of Trade, or an Order in Council, or a Parliamentary law — a committee must answer the question of which style of
protest would serve their purpose, yet not embolden the wolf lurking in the
woods that border their pastured minds. There are only two styles open to
them: the fire-ships of staunch outrage, or servile pleas for mercy and
amity. Should they risk provoking an immediate attack by disputing the
wolf's appetite, power, and purpose, or meekly grant him humble license
and leave to make unopposed forays to gnaw on our innards at his riskless
leisure?"

Hugh rose again to pace before his visitors, and spoke as though he
were thinking out loud. "Of course, the issue I cite here is a moot one. *Colonial* representation in Parliament is an inadmissible incongruity, and will
bedevil the man who attempts to champion it. The redundant, disabling
term in it is *colonial*. I would not fault the first minister or secretary of state
who expounded on the impracticality of the notion. Colonial representation is as much an oxymoron as a crutched horse. For, you see, the colony
that secured representation in Parliament would cease being a colony, and
instead be recognized as a county, or an extraordinary borough." He sighed,
and glanced at the worried expressions on his visitors' faces, though he did
note in them a dim comprehension of his point. "But what turmoil such a
prospect would cause in men's minds! Even the dullest members of that
body would be tossed and buffeted by squalls of thought! Why, Parliament
would be obliged to redefine itself, and in the course of that momentous
task, be forced to contemplate the abandonment of certain ancient and burdensome aspects of its character...."

Then he seemed to remember his visitors, and turned to them. "Well,
sirs, I hope that my rehearsal has not frightened you. Am I still your preferred candidate?"

Reece Vishonn, after a moment to recover from the onslaught of words,
nodded. "You are, sir. Most certainly. While you offered a brace of novel
ideas — some of which I have heard discussed before — you have proven
yourself a model of realistic moderation."

Edgar Cullis cleared his throat. "I agree with Mr. Vishonn. You would
make an excellent voice for moderation. You are able to convey the terrible
aspects of an ogre — or a wolf, as you call it — yet still communicate, to
those disturbed by it, what a fraudulent phantasm it is."

"A phantasm, Mr. Cullis?" replied Hugh. "Hardly that. Last week I received letters from my father and some acquaintances about the passage of two new acts."

His visitors sat up in their chairs with new interest.

Hugh said, "Obviously, news of their enactment has not yet arrived here. One act reduces the levy on sugar from six to three pence, but adds a number of items to the enumerated list — various spirits, cloths, and finished goods from regions not within the Crown's realm. It also removes from colonial courts all jurisdiction over customs suits and places it under a vice-admiralty court in Halifax, and the new rules governing the seizure of cargoes, landed or not, are harsh and laden with penalties. Further, this act virtually indemnifies customs officers from fault and liability, even in the event the vice-admiralty court finds that an officer is a notorious blackleg guilty of embracery."

"I was not aware of that act," said Edgar Cullis.

"Nor I," said Reece Vishonn.

"The other act, also passed in April, abolishes all colonial currency as legal tender to pay debts to merchants in England. Henceforth, all debts to them must be paid in undiscounted sterling."

"Bosh!" exclaimed Vishonn, his face flushing red. "Where are we to get such money? How many people here have even seen a piece of British copper or silver, let alone carried one in their purses? That is an *outrageous* expectation! We should all be reduced to living in hovels! We should not be able to establish any credit, ever!"

"This is true," said Edgar Cullis. He added, tentatively, "I am not happy with the interference with our courts, either. That constitutes an ominous presumption."

Hugh merely smiled again, remembering his visitors' sentiments on "moderation." He sat down again and idly twirled his brass top. "The letters also report that Mr. Grenville has been polling ministers, merchants, and even colonial legislatures about the feasibility of a tax on legal documents and other paper instruments, such as attorneys' licenses and bills of lading, and even newspapers, which tax would entail the purchase of a stamp to be affixed to the document in question. The implication is that any document that does not bear a stamp, would have no force in a court of law." He paused. "There's interference for you, Mr. Cullis."

The burgess, usually suave and composed, shot from his chair and sputtered, "That's...that's...that's an *extortionate* notion, if I ever heard of one!"

"Are you certain of this information?" asked Vishonn with incredulity.

"My sources are unimpeachable, sir," answered Hugh. "They are in a position to know the ministry's every thought and motion."

The floor clock struck four. Vishonn reached into a pocket and consulted his own watch. He snorted once in anger, then said as he rose from his chair, "Well, we shall need to talk of these events later. We will leave you now to finish your water tower. I believe the next step is to inform Sheriff Tippet of your intentions. He will write the Governor, asking for a writ ordering an election. When Mr. Tippet has received it, he will set a date for the poll, which will be posted on the courthouse door, noticed by Mr. Barret in the *Courier*, and announced at the close of each service by Reverend Acland. He is obliged by law to do that, you know. Very likely Mr. Tippet will schedule the election early in the fall, to coincide with court day here. In the meantime, you should cultivate the fellows who may vote for you. There are about sixty qualified electors in this county, most of whom live close to the town."

Edgar Cullis also rose, and said with less glibness, "Please do not upbraid me, Mr. Kenrick, but you should know that I regularly serve on the Committee of Privileges and Elections. After you have been elected, Mr. Tippet will return the writ with a note on the results to the House, naming you as the winner. Once the committee has examined the documents, they will report their findings to the House, which will then approve the election. I doubt that anyone could lodge a credible protest against you in this instance, but should one occur, you may rely on me to support your election wholeheartedly."

"Thank you, Mr. Cullis."

When he had seen them off in the yard of the great house, Hugh wandered back inside to his study, amused on one hand by the earnestness of the two men; and on the other, curious about why they thought him a credible candidate. He was certain that he had given them ample evidence that, first, he was not an advocate of "moderation," and, second, that "moderation" was not a practical policy to adopt in the circumstances. There was something wrong in their assessment of his value to them, something awry in the confidence they placed in him. But he could not identify it. "No matter," he thought to himself. "I will be what I will be, and say what I must say."

At his desk, he took from his letter box the report from Dogmael Jones, and reread the parts of it that concerned the political doings in London:

"If Mr. Grenville and the government were so confident in Parliament's legal right to impose internal taxes on the colonies — that is, taxes not approved by various of your legislatures there — they would not be coyly seeking advice and recommendations from so many quarters about the size or likely effect of our first minister's proposed stamp tax, but lay the impost on you people without the least doubt or hesitation. But the debt incurred by the Crown in the late war is so huge that it has shaken the confidence of even the spendthrifts, and they are casting about like a bevy of starving anglers for fish to catch, gut, and fry. There are, however, two bones of bother that have caused Mr. Grenville and his party to adopt the caution of pettifogging sneaksbies: the nagging fear that, regardless of the constitutionality or legality of such a tax, it would stir up protest in the colonies and move the more thoughtful politicians and leaders amongst you to call the beat to quarters; and doubts amongst many of the House's members here about the economic, practical, or moral efficacy of such a tax, doubts of which Mr. Grenville and his party are too well aware. And lest it be claimed that the merchant interests here predict disaster and forced idleness if a stamp tax is enacted, be advised that the fellow who has apparently pestered the Board of Trade for years on the advantages of such a tax is a Mr. Henry McCulloch, a prominent London merchant. My paid spies in the Board's offices tell me that, according to the musty correspondence they have been able to lay hands on, this gentleman has appended to this tax a Brobdingagish scheme that would yoke the colonies for generations, yet convince every one of them that it was for their own good and for the glory of English liberty. But, then, a man who beats his wife is also a paradox...."

But Hugh was not allowed to ponder the paradox of Reece Vishonn's and Edgar Cullis's determination to see him elected burgess, nor the paradox posed by Jones. Joseph Shearl, his master carpenter, came in to tell him that the first curved plank has been successfully fitted into the tarred and sealed bottom of the water tower. Hugh rushed out with him to inspect it, and was for the rest of that summer day occupied with a project perhaps more momentous to him than were the machinations of George Grenville, member for Buckingham borough, First Lord of the Treasury, Chancellor of the Exchequer, enemy of John Wilkes, brother-in-law of William Pitt, and bencher for the Inner Temple, and of whom, Horace Walpole, discreet diarist of the men who came and went in the House of Commons and Lords, wrote that while Grenville was "capable of out-talking the whole *Corps Diplomatique*," he had no "faculty for listening."

Grenville listened to and perused volumes of advice about his stamp tax, noted all the credible objections to it, but pushed it through Parliament anyway. Parliament was all-powerful, he was its pilot, and it would go anywhere he steered it.

Chapter 6: The Flames

"**Y**our sense of timing is impeccable," said Jack Frake with a smile. "In respect to what?" asked Hugh with a grin. "Arriving in time for supper? Putting up a water tower?"

"Deciding to run for burgess."

"Well, a good actor knows when to enter the stage on his cue so that it does not seem accidental or even premeditated, and conveys to an audience that it is just natural that he should be there." Hugh laughed. "I did not tell my visitors, but those two acts are what prompted me to decide in favor of their proposal. That is for them to infer."

Jack already knew about the Revenue and Currency Acts. Hugh had shared news of them with him and Thomas Reisdale and the contents of the letters from his father and Dogmael Jones.

Hugh rode to Morland after dusk the same day to inform his friend of his decision. He was a frequent and welcome guest in a house that had not had many visitors in years. Following the marriage of Jack and Etáin, Hugh often called on Morland to discuss politics and business with Jack, to bring new sheet music and magazines for Etáin and books for both of them. His manner toward the couple was gracious and cordial: toward Jack, he acted as though nothing had ever or could ever come between them; toward Etáin, he behaved like an affectionate brother. Because he could not repress the knowledge of his loss, he had allowed himself, at the beginning of these visits, to express on occasion an amused, implicit envy of Jack, and a respectful jealousy of Etáin, both expressions rendered benign by his gentlemanly distance from the subject. In time, even these references ceased.

In the supper room that evening, in the company of Etáin and John Proudlocks, Hugh asked his host, "Why have *you* never sought election, Jack?"

Etáin smiled and grinned at her husband from across the table. "The time is not right for a man of Jack's mettle to enter politics," she said. "Can you imagine him sitting on a bench in the Capitol, squirming with boredom as he listened to men quibble over small matters and points of procedure?"

"No, I cannot," conceded Hugh. "Nor can I imagine myself enduring much of that."

Jack glanced once with fondness at Etáin, then said, "Etáin is right. I could not be a party to the passage of half the laws that our own legislature is responsible for. But, then, I would never be elected. My views are too well known in this county, and frighten men." He added, with a chuckle, "And I could be arrested or censured if I spoke as I chose, or expelled from the Assembly. Remember that I am a former felon, too. Some meddling fool could contrive to have me sent back to England on charges of treason or for libeling the king, and called to the bar in Parliament to defend myself." He shook his head and his manner softened. "Then I might suffer the fate of your friends, the Pippins."

Hugh nodded in grave acknowledgment, and was at the same time astounded with how similar his friend's remarks were to Reece Vishonn's.

Jack said, "Etáin is right. Politics is not ready for me."

Etáin rose and poured the men more coffee from a silver pot. "Men must catch up with Jack," she said to the table at large. "They must either learn to, or settle for events to impel them in his direction." *You are the north,* she thought to herself as she bent to fill her husband's cup, glancing once at him to communicate her meaning. In Jack's eyes, she saw understanding. *In time, the needles of men's minds must ultimately point to you as the measure of what they ought to be and what they ought to do. They must reach a point where they are no longer frightened by you and what you are. As Hugh is not, and John there.*

Hugh laughed, and said, "They believe I am an exemplar of 'moderation,' and left still believing it after I gave them a taste of my oratory."

"What did you say?" asked Proudlocks.

Hugh gave a gist of his speech and his remarks that followed it.

After a moment, Jack said, "You are that, Hugh, after a certain point. You and I travel the same road, up to a fork in it. There we part: you on the road of reconciliation and enlightened empire, I, on the road that yet has no name; and the distance between those roads widens with every yard." He paused when Ruth Dakin, the servant from the kitchen, entered to clear the plates from the table. When she was gone, he remarked, "Even were all the laws of Parliament and the Board of Trade repealed tomorrow, I would expect the same conflict to arise again in a generation, for the same reasons, and with the same consequence."

Hugh shook his head and sat back. "I do not believe that would come about, once Parliament and the ministers and chancellors have been made to see reason."

Jack smiled again. It was not a happy smile. "What is going to compel them to see it? Who among all those men serves as an exemplar of unqualified reason? And, if he existed, why should they heed his example or advice, or care that he existed, if they have gotten this far by flouting reason?"

"What will compel them is the very real possibility of losing the colonies, our trade, and our friendship and natural affection."

This time Jack shook his head. "If they were *afraid* of losing any of that, Hugh, they would not continue to enclose us in the hedgerows of these new laws and the ones that are certain to follow." He sighed. "My friend, I would no more try to reason with London than I would attempt to persuade a highwayman of the unreasonableness of his robbing me, not even were he a courteous gallant who left me a shilling to get home on. And you forget one important aspect: To retain the colonies as Crown possessions, Parliament must assert its control. To assert that control, it must rule — whether in its own name or that of the king, it matters little. To rule, it must presume to order the lives and actions of those whom it rules. Which can mean nothing else but more revenue, currency, hat, and slave acts. And taxes. And laws skewed to the benefit of the merchants and any other parties that have the ear of a member of the Commons or an audience with a first lord or chancellor, such as Mr. McCulloh, who was mentioned by your friend Mr. Jones."

After a pause, Jack continued. "I believe I posed this question at Mr. Vishonn's ball, on the night we first met, Hugh: Why did the Crown fight so mightily for supremacy on this continent? I know that most colonials who fought with the regulars, fought for their liberty — such as it is, and such as they understand it — and to be free of the French threat. But, the Crown? Why would it bother with the expense, if power over this continent were not the motive, and if it did not expect to recoup that expense in the future? We colonists — even we former felons — are the ones who bestow any value on it, if I have correctly read Mr. Locke. Which means that you and I and Mr. Vishonn and John here and the humblest cobbler in Williamsburg and the most industrious freedman and mechanic in Boston are the ones from whom the Crown will expect to extract that value."

Hugh nodded. "I concede all that," he said. "But there must be some substance in a hope for reconciliation — or *rapprochement*, as the French would call it. If there is not, if you are right, and I am wrong, then all we can look forward to is chaos, and anarchy, and misery. Or, worse yet — democracy! Our only hope is an enlightened empire, in which reasonable men prevail over reasoned laws." He raised a hand and gestured to the world beyond the walls of the supper room. "Men here now are too contentious, too jealous of each other's advantage, too diverse in their interests....And, too suspicious of each other, and ready to resort to arms or fists to settle their disputes. Need I cite examples? There was that deplorable business between the Quakers and the Paxton gang and other western settlers over the Indians in Pennsylvania, and the trouble that is likely to occur between the western settlers in the Carolinas and their own governments. On the other hand, there are all those who rallied in support of Mr. Wilkes in London, and the number and eloquence of the radicals for liberty there." He paused. "I do not see such phenomena occurring here, my friend."

"Except for you, and Mr. Reisdale, and Jack," remarked Etáin. "And there are the gentlemen who attend your Attic Society meetings here. You have told me yourself about clubs and associations like it in Philadelphia, and Boston, and New York, and even in Williamsburg. How can you then say that Americans are indifferent to the form of their future, or are so mean-spirited that they would trade their liberty for a mess of pottage?"

"I did not say that they were that," replied Hugh with a frown, stung by the reproof, the first ever he had received from Etáin. "I meant merely that they are divisive, and are not united in a common politics, or even by a common idea of themselves, as are most Britons, even the unread and ill-mannered among them."

"Such as the ones who stoned you and your friends on the pillory at Charing Cross?" queried Jack with an unnatural, ominous tone in his words. "How many of them were schooled in the finer points of the Constitution? Presumably, very few of them, and those less so than were the judge and jury who sentenced *my* friends to hang in Falmouth."

Again, Hugh was stung, this time by the harsh bitterness of his friend's words, a bitterness directed not at him but at England. For a moment, he felt helpless, and was unable to reply. When he did, it seemed to him that his words floated to the air and were absorbed by the silence-heavy tension in it. "There are mobs and scoundrels in every society, even this one." It sounded more like a comment than an answer.

Until now, John Proudlocks said little, content, as usual, to audit the contravening wisdom of these two men. In the past, he had witnessed many debates of this kind between Jack and Mr. Kenrick. But never before had one reached the point of literal argument, never before had one ended in speechless stalemate. He wished to defuse the moment, for he did not like to see them quarrel. He glanced once at his mistress, Etáin, who looked worried and anxious. He said, "About the British Constitution, sirs: You know that I have read much of it, all of what Mr. Blackstone has written about it. In it, I see only the flames. But to understand this Constitution, to know truly whether it is friend or foe, it is necessary to seek and know what causes the flames."

They all glanced at him, knowing his reason for interjecting the not entirely irrelevant observation; and knowing also that, ironically, given the subject, there would be no further political discussion this evening.

Etáin flashed him a smile of gratitude. Jack and Hugh also smiled, but from a form of self-consciousness. Both at that moment also recollected something he had said to them once, over dinner here on a Sunday afternoon months ago.

Proudlocks had returned from attending one of Reverend Acland's services, one he held regularly for slaves and the poor of Caxton. It was curiosity, and not any desire to be converted, that allowed him to endure the two hours of immobility. He was aware of the animosity the minister had for his employer and friend. Jack had asked him how he found the service. Proudlocks said, "I cannot argue with everything Mr. Acland said about God and all the virtues and sins he attaches to the faith he preaches. But there is one thing I wanted to tell him, but did not. He was pleased to see me as I left the church with all the others, but I do not think he would have been pleased to hear what I wanted to tell him."

"What was that?" Hugh had asked.

Proudlocks had frowned and paused to choose his words. "There is much I wanted to question him about, for he said many opposing...no, contradictory things in his sermon. He said much about death and rewards and answering to God for one's actions in this life. I wanted to *tell* him that, in the end, when a man is on his death bed, or has fallen in battle, or is drowning in the sea, he will meet his first maker, the one he must answer to before he is judged by God for the character of his life, and be rewarded accordingly: himself." He had added as an afterthought, "He will smile in happiness, or be sad or sorry for things he has not done or said, or meet the devil of his soul and feel terror." After another pause, he remarked, "In my old life, before Captain Massie and my life here, I saw these ends many times in men's faces."

After desultory conversation about Hugh's water tower — "I shall fill it first from Hove Stream by means of buckets from the conduit" — the prospects for a good harvest, and the Williamsburg theater program that had appeared in last week's *Courier* for the beginning of the new Assembly session in October, Hugh and Proudlocks bid the Frakes goodnight.

Etáin asked her husband, as they prepared to retire, "What causes the flames in you and our friend? Why are you so much alike, yet so terribly different? Why am I afraid that you will someday become enemies?"

She stood in her nightgown at their bedroom window, looking out into the darkness. The only lights came from a ship's lanterns from a plantation pier far across the York River. Barely audible was the cacophonous chorus of tree frogs in the woods that surrounded Morland. Jack went over to her and held her in his arms. Etáin was his partner in innocence. He marveled at the fact that she was that without having to pay the price of so many tribulations, as he had. Perhaps the most wrenching thing she had ever experienced was having to say goodbye to her parents, Ian and Madeline McRae, when they closed their shop late in the spring and sailed for England on the *Nassau*.

"We won't become enemies, Etáin," he said into her hair. "We are too much alike for that to happen. We merely believe that each other is wrong."

"But, if one of you is right, then the other must own to it." Etáin paused. "Mr. Proudlocks sees it, too."

Jack did not believe that the severity of the events in his own life had forced him to become the man he was. Other men, he knew, had experienced the same kinds of events, or worse, and succumbed to them, because they chose to, either from fear of the consequences if they had not, or from fear of the requirements and responsibility of acting otherwise. Or from a helplessness rooted in a tenacious incomprehension. He did not believe that hardship was necessarily a parent of a man's character, or that it was something integral to its formation. There was Hugh, his friend, who had grown up and matured in comparatively comfortable circumstances, but these circumstances had not spoiled him or sapped his capacity for becoming the man he was. He knew that it would have been so much easier for Hugh to apologize to the Duke of Cumberland, so much easier to deny his association with the imprisoned Pippins, so much easier to simply regret the necessity of owning slaves and keep them in benevolent bondage. Wealth, Jack knew, could be as much a seducer as hardship, and spare one the care and obligation of becoming a man. As he stood in back of Etáin and pressed his face into her hair, he chuckled to himself in appreciation of John Proudlocks's subtlety. What causes the flames, indeed?

Etáin reached up and caressed the arms that encircled her. "What?" she asked.

"I was thinking about John, our resident peacemaker and lawyer."

"He is a better man than most," remarked Etáin. She marveled, too, at her husband's constancy, a constancy that never flinched in the face of a problem, never flickered between moods. He was always lucid, always in control of himself and of his mind, even when he was in doubt about something, or angry. Whatever was on his mind at any given moment received his fullest attention.

She blushed when she herself was the object of that attention, and then she would smile, in concert with him, in mutual self-awareness and self-assurance. She had stood before him on their wedding night, as Omphale should have stood before Hercules, as a penitent Circe might have stood before Ulysses, unafraid of his attention and desire for her, knowing that she was worthy of his attention and desire. And she let him know, that first night together with him, that he was worthy of her own.

Jack said into her hair just above her ear, "You know that Hugh honors a truth-teller as much as he honors a truth. Would you expect him to be so mean-spirited and petty — your words, my dear — as to resent me for being right?"

"I would not do him the disservice."

Later, as Etáin lay asleep in the circle of his arm, Jack pondered the paradox of his friendship with Hugh Kenrick. While he had won Etáin, he watched with grim certitude the succession of events in Virginia and England that would ultimately jeopardize his newfound happiness, events that must progress to an explosion. He was the only man in Caxton, and perhaps in all of Virginia, who knew that these events must end in a bloody clash between the colonies and the mother country. He also knew that he must be their passive observer. He was unhappy in that role, for he could neither accelerate nor arrest the progress of those events. Other men of like mind had not yet reached his state of certitude. He was grateful to Etáin that she understood that about him.

He knew that to recognize the nature of the coming clash, to know as well as he did that there was no fundamental *rapprochement* possible between the colonies and England, these men, many of them his close friends, would need to cast off the irrelevant sentiment of filial association, if they were ever to become men of their own making, instead of settling for being coincidental Englishmen, or Scotsmen, or Welshmen, or Irishmen. The elements of that new identity lay in each and every one of them; when the time came, each must become in his own mind and soul the person each of them must have had a glimpse of in himself before he surrendered to the pressures of society and circumstantial identity. When the time came, each must be convinced of the false security of his liberty, and of the absurdity of relying on a king to protect and ensure it. Kings, after all, even the best of them, must rule. And if they were mere figurehead kings, other men must rule in their stead.

Rational persuasion, Jack sadly knew, would not, this time and by itself, awaken in these men that latent capacity. Only a determined violence on their lives could ignite that crucial metamorphosis of self; only a traumatic crisis could wring from them the undiscovered honesty to recognize who they were and what was possible to them, and move them to shed the clinging, comfortable traces of their past lives. Only the glint of approaching bayonets, or the thunder of a volley, or the calculated toss of a torch into their homes would give them long enough pause to allow the truth about themselves and what they were witnessing to seize their beings and awaken in them the true nature of their peril. If Hugh Kenrick, the proudest, most honest, most virtuous, most complete, and most thoroughly rational man he had ever known, could not be persuaded of the logic of events, then how could he expect other men, men who were virtuous and honest and self-assertive, yet still unfinished, to be persuaded so soon of that logic?

On the other hand, he thought with a smile, there was John Proudlocks, wise beyond his years, a student of an alien society, whose wisdom seemed to come from his being an outsider. Somehow, Jack thought, John was a complete man, as complete as he himself was. Unfinished, yet still strangely complete.

Etáin stirred in her sleep. Jack disengaged himself from her, rose, dressed, and went downstairs. He lit a lantern and left the house for the path that led to Proudlocks's shack. He found him sitting in a chair, reading a dictionary by candlelight. There was a bed, and a table and two chairs, a fireplace, and a crude bookshelf made of planks and discarded bricks. Many of the books on the shelf were Proudlocks's own; many were borrowed from Jack's library. He put down his lantern and said, "We forgot to discuss tomorrow's business."

But he saw in Proudlocks's brief grin that he knew the real reason for the visit, that it was a form of thanks for having saved the evening. Proudlocks said, "I will suggest to Mr. Robins that we start the others in picking the corn. It is ripe. Their stalks should be left to stand, so that the beans on them can ripen. They are not ready yet." He lit a clay pipe and offered it to Jack, then lit another for himself. They sat and talked about what other plantation tasks needed to be done before the fall.

After a while, Jack rose to leave. Proudlocks said, "You will quarrel again. You are right, and he is wrong. But I will try to stop you from hurting each other." He pointed with the stem of his pipe to a picture he had nailed to a wall. It was an engraving of the Ramsay full-length portrait of George the Third, a page he had torn from one of his books. "Him? He will hurt himself."

"Why do you keep it?" asked Jack.

Proudlocks shrugged. "To remind me of this country," he answered. "When the things you say must happen, do happen, I will take it down. He will no longer worry us. But he is interesting to study. I do not think he is a happy man. He looks like a king, but I can see in his face that he does not believe he is one."

Jack nodded. "I am afraid he will try to be one."

"Yes. There is that to him."

Jack left Proudlocks and walked back to the house. He did not hate Englishmen, or Britons, or even kings. He was merely resolved not to be conquered by them. He did not hate Parliament; he merely feared its kingly powers. When he reached the porch of his house, he sat down and lit his own pipe, and let the quiet and darkness of the night coax from his mind another problem he had never been able to solve.

One thing he had been unable to put into words was why he thought of himself as complete, why, against all his instincts for privacy, and contrary to his notion of vanity, he still measured men in terms of his own completeness, why he was certain that he was right about it, and why he was certain that this aspect of him always had and always would come between him and the others. He was certain, too, that there were words that would explain the completeness. Perhaps he had read them somewhere, words whose author had struggled to say the same thing, but whose final, precise form had eluded him, too. The problem came to the forefront of his consciousness only at times like this one, when he was at peace with himself, when he was happy with the conduct and sum of his life, when he chose to rest for a moment and contemplate the pages and chapters of that life. The problem had perplexed him for as long as he could remember, clear back to his youth in Cornwall. It did not perplex him so much as remind him that it was there, waiting to be solved. He was in no hurry to solve it, though, for he knew that the words, once he found them, would simply confirm what he already knew, that everything he had ever done, had been right.

Sitting alone on the porch steps, under an evening sky brilliant with the dust of uncountable stars, Jack Frake thought of the distance he had traveled since Cornwall. He felt proud of that distance, and of the fact that the boy who had begun that journey would be pleased with the man he had become. The boy would look at him and say to himself, "This is the man I mean to be." He remembered that boy who, long ago, in a similar state of peace, sat alone before the fireplace of a seaport tavern, the boy who was not a stranger to him, and who still wondered what were the words for the unconquerable thing about himself that set him apart and permitted him a magnanimous certainty.

The boy who was now a man now wondered why he felt that his serene solitude was right for him, and right for all men, if they could learn to know it and be unafraid of it. Hugh Kenrick knew it; Jack was sure of it. So did John Proudlocks. As had Augustus Skelly and Redmagne. The words were missing, but would be found.

The light of the lantern at his side, a friendly, animate companion to his thoughts, glowed steadily on the calm lines of Jack's face as he looked with joyous solemnity and consecration upon his past, present, and future.

Chapter 7: The Burgesses

It was with a concentration of willpower, allied with a tenacious dedication to decorum, that Hugh Kenrick, burgess for Queen Anne County, was able to stifle his yawns throughout the days of the new session of the General Assembly in Williamsburg, a session that lasted from the 30th of October through the 21st of December, 1764. This was one of the more protracted sessions of the Assembly, which rarely sat for longer than a month. The last session, in January of the same year, lasted barely a week. A great deal of business had accumulated since that session, including cases that could only be heard in the General Court, which sat only when a General Assembly had convened.

Williamsburg was the seat of the Virginia empire, and the Capitol was its throne. Here laws were passed, bills debated, men and women tried for serious crimes, and balls held. The Capitol was modeled on the old Capitol building, which had burned down in 1747, in a figure *H*; the chambers and Hall of Burgesses were on the east side of the figure, connected by gallery and arcade with the west side of it, which housed the Governor's Council chambers and the General Court. Some arcane symbolism may have been intended in that arrangement, but not even Richard Bland, burgess for Prince George County since 1742, could say for certain what.

The west side of the *H* faced Duke of Gloucester Street; a mile down that boulevard sat the College of William & Mary. It was at the College that the Virginia Assembly sat while the present building was being completed. The new Capitol was more elaborately flounced than was the old Capitol. It featured a gabled neoclassical portico and balcony on the west side, made of white-painted oak, and wide, majestic steps. In front of these steps, leading from Duke of Gloucester Street, was a circular drive that encompassed a neatly cut lawn. It was a grand, imposing, and impressive façade, almost as grand and impressive as the Governor's Palace half a mile down the boulevard.

The Hall of the House of Burgesses was about half the size of the

House of Commons in London, so it was comparatively more spacious for its one hundred sixteen members than was the Commons for its nearly six hundred. The broad, rectangular windows, which had replaced the ovals of the old Capitol, could not be opened, so while they helped to keep out the cold, they also retained the heat of several score bodies and the smoke from the dozens of candles that were needed to light the chamber. This, and the enforced immobility of sitting on straight-backed benches, squeezed in between other burgesses, induced among the members either restrained irritability or a desire to nap. The constant drone of speech-making on mundane subjects also contributed to the mood of the burgesses. Many of them succumbed to the desire to nap, no matter how committed their attention to the matter before the House.

Hugh's boredom stemmed largely from lack of interest in the range of matters so far discussed and debated this session: private disputes between freeholders over the legitimacy or accuracy of land surveys; proposed bounties on crows and wolves in some of the Piedmont counties; the dissolution of some lapsed vestries, and the sale of glebe lands; the testimony of witnesses in the case of a fraudulent land transaction initiated by another member of the House; the need for more tobacco warehouses above the Falls and the selection of their locations; a request from Governor Fauquier for money to be voted as a reward for the apprehension of the men who murdered some Cherokees passing through the Shenandoah Valley; a prolonged debate on the need for a gallery above the present public space near the lobby, and how and when money could be raised for its intrusive construction.

Hugh waited patiently during those weeks for the House to take up again the matter of the proposed stamp taxes which Dogmael Jones wrote him were being prepared for passage in the Commons. On the 7th of November, Peyton Randolph, the colony's attorney general, read to the House the most recent correspondence from Edward Montague, an English lawyer and the House's agent in London, who discussed in detail the progress being made by the Grenville ministry in its pursuit of precedent and passage of a Stamp Act.

A special committee of the attorney general and seven of the House's most respected members had been appointed by Speaker John Robinson to compose an address to the king, a memorial to the House of Lords, and a remonstrance to the Commons protesting the tax now under discussion in London. The language and points in the documents had been discussed and debated by a Committee of the Whole House. Hugh had objected to the obsequious language of all the documents, believing that it was too humble and meek, and rose a number of times during the debate to raise that issue, but the Speaker had not deigned to recognize him. The documents were now in the hands of the Council of State for correction and amendment, and would come back to the House for a formal vote in a few days.

In the meantime, Hugh waited patiently for that day to arrive, and assuaged his boredom by observing the character and conduct of his fellow burgesses. There was John Robinson, burgess for King & Queen County, a huge, stout man who had entered the House in 1727, and had been both Speaker and Treasurer of it for twenty-six years. He sat in a raised, high-backed chair at the front of the Hall, much as did the Speaker of the Commons, and performed the same functions and held the same powers. There was George Washington, burgess for Fairfax, the tallest man in the House, who sat directly across from Hugh in the other battery of benches. He was a hero of the late war, a favorite friend of the Governor's, and occasionally appeared wearing his blue colonial officer's coat. Burgesses who sat next to him did not crowd him. There was Richard Bland, burgess for Prince George, prematurely aged in his forty-fifth year from constant study of ancient and modern law; he rose often in debate to enlighten or correct the House on seemingly abeyant points of jurisprudence. There was Edmund Pendleton, burgess for Caroline, a prim, fussy man who raised, in Hugh's estimate, too many objections during debates. There was Peyton Randolph, Attorney-General and burgess for Williamsburg, probably the most powerful man in the House after Robinson, chairman of the Committee of Privileges and Elections, and of the Committee of Propositions and Grievances. He was a handsome but stout man whose fastidious bearing and imperious manner approached the mien of a member of the House of Lords. As chairman of Propositions and Grievances, he and his fellow committee members controlled which bills would be introduced into the House for consideration, and which would be dismissed.

Except for his natural presence when the House was called into a Committee of the Whole, Hugh was not selected to sit on any of the standing or special committees, as some other new members were. He suspected that he was resented, or distrusted, or too much of a stranger to the ruling dynasties.

His election in September was hardly memorable. He was spared the effort of campaigning for the seat by Reece Vishonn, who even paid to entertain the voters with several pipes of ale and a round of suppers at the Gramatan Inn. Electors rode to Meum Hall all that month to meet him and discuss what was on their minds. Virginia law forbade him from actively soliciting a freeholder's vote, so he had to content himself with receiving an almost endless parade of men who solicited from him his positions on many matters. When presented with particular private interests, or matters men wanted drafted into private bills, he invariably referred these men to Edgar Cullis, his fellow burgess for the county. Cullis was more experienced in that aspect of Virginia political life, and certainly more interested and adept. His success in introducing and getting passed private bills over the years had ensured his continued reelection. This man also instructed Hugh on what to expect in the House, what were his duties, whom he should cultivate, and whom he should avoid, and he imparted these lessons even before the election was held one late September afternoon in Caxton's courthouse.

Hugh was the only candidate on that foggy day, and sat at a table with Sheriff Tippet on one side of him and Radulphus Spears, drafted as recording clerk from his duties at Meum Hall, on the other. One after another the planters and freeholders marched up to the table and said his name. There was a muted gasp of surprise among the witnesses and spectators in the courtroom when Jack Frake, who had voted infrequently ever since coming into possession of Morland, appeared at the end of the day, and pronounced Hugh's name. Hugh thanked each voter in turn, and saw in Jack's eyes that his friend took this moment very seriously and had given the matter much thought. When Sheriff Tippet confirmed the results of the election, Hugh joined the crowd of electors and spectators on the courthouse lawn. He could not remember what had been said by him or anyone else during the innumerable congratulations and speculations. Reece Vishonn hosted a victory supper at the Gramatan Inn that evening; Hugh could not remember what was said on that occasion, either.

He and Edgar Cullis rode together to Williamsburg in late October, and shared a room in the house of a distant cousin of Cullis's for the duration of the session. On the morning of the first day of the session, Hugh was escorted by Cullis to the Capitol and the second-floor chamber of the Governor's Council. There, in solemn, well-appointed surroundings, he and other new burgesses were administered the oath of loyalty to Virginia and the Crown by a clerk, witnessed by the eleven members of the Council, who were berobed as justices and sat collectively for this formality as the Council of State.

Later in the morning, Governor Fauquier arrived in his resplendent coach-and-six to the applause and cheers of the waiting burgesses and staff of the Capitol. Hugh stood at the small iron gate at the head of the circular drive, and got only a glimpse of the man's back as he ascended the stone steps. He was not invited to attend to the Governor upstairs when the latter summoned the Speaker and sixty other burgesses to the Council chambers to deliver his opening address and instructions and to formally open the session. Hugh joined the other burgesses outside to wait until a clerk came out and called them in. Later, Hugh noted the similarity in rituals, though, in the fact that all the burgesses stood while the Council members and the Governor sat, just as when a delegation of the Commons appeared before a gathering of the Lords the M.P.'s stood in deference to the sitting peers. He had a passing knowledge of the protocol of other colonial legislatures, and remarked to Cullis later that same day that the General Assembly, of all the colonial governments, most nearly resembled in form, ritual, and practice faraway Parliament. "That is not wholly a compliment," he added.

"Why not?" queried Cullis as they rode back down Duke of Gloucester that evening, after the first full day of the Assembly. They were returning to the house of his cousin, Mary Gandy, who was a seamstress and sewer of wigs for the capital's paramount peruke maker. There they would freshen up, have some cold luncheon, and ride back up the boulevard to join some other burgesses of Cullis's acquaintance at Marot's Coffeehouse near the Capitol.

"Neither Lords nor the Governor's Council is a true senate," explained Hugh. "Their memberships depend entirely on the largess and leave of the king, when in fact the composition of those bodies ought to rely exclusively on the electoral discretion of the lower Houses. Their first function should be to serve as protectors of English liberty against the whims and wishes of the *mobile vulgus*."

Edgar Cullis could not contest this assertion. His knowledge of practical politics lay in land patents and statutes. His mind was not friendly to hypotheses, although lately both Hugh and Parliamentary legislation had stirred his latent curiosity. He did not pursue the matter. When they reached his cousin's house near the College, he brought up another subject. He served as recording clerk for the Committee on Privileges and Elections, and reported that Hugh's election had been passed by that body and would receive approval by the House the next day.

"There was no dispute over the conduct of your election," he said in his cousin's kitchen over a plate of cold meats, "although Mr. Bland had a question about the status of your baronetcy, which he thought might prejudice your politics here. I assured him that you were not of that mind, that you were more consciously...how shall I say this?...*American* than many who were born here. He seemed satisfied with that answer."

"Thank you, sir."

"There were other doubters. Some members of the committee — chiefly Mr. Randolph and Mr. Carter — were concerned that you might somehow influence the Committee of Propositions and Grievances (which is half the House, of course) to introduce a bill proposing the manumission of the slaves. I assured them that you know that such a bill would not only be rejected outright by that body, but serve to give some members an excuse to contrive to have you expelled, or your election annulled." Cullis paused. "You must realize that the House will *not* entertain such an idea."

Hugh knew it, and shrugged. "I will work then to give slaves the same legal protection as the burgesses, or any other white citizen."

Cullis frowned, and shook his head. "That may seem to be a tamer project, sir, but I am afraid it may be twice as offensive. It is only half a glass, you see, when it could very well be filled to the brim. No, the House could not be tricked that way. If there is any injustice in the institution, the House will concede only that it is imposed on us by the Crown." The burgess studied Hugh for a moment. "I did not own this before, Mr. Kenrick, but your reputation precedes you. Many in the House are on their guard against you."

At the coffeehouse later that evening, Hugh was introduced to some of his colleague's friends, burgesses from a number of Tidewater counties. Cullis had not seen these men for nearly a year, and so the conversation over coffee and cocoa dwelt mostly on the fortunes and misfortunes of families, plantations, businesses, on marriages, births, and deaths.

Presently the talk turned to the impending business of the House. One of Cullis's friends boasted that Parliament would never impose an internal tax on the colonies. "It would be illegal, and unconstitutional," said the man. "And, besides, there are a number of prominent men there who are intimately acquainted with the colonies and our conditions — merchants, and bankers, and the consignment firms, and people of that sort. They'll convince Mr. Grenville and his party to think twice."

"It would be a violation of all our charters," remarked another burgess. "His Majesty would not tolerate such a tax. They are *his* charters, and such a tax would reduce his own revenues." He paused. "Such a tax could not help but reduce his income. Do you not see?"

Another burgess ventured, "I wish the House could hire the services of the Council's representative in London. Now, sirs, there's a fellow who's acquainted with the colonies and our conditions! Mr. James Abercromby, late of South Carolina! He was attorney general there for some fifteen years, I've heard, and a member of their legislature for nearly a score. He will speak for Virginia, for that is what the Council is paying him a stipend to do. He will *speak*, you see, for he is a member of Parliament himself!" The burgess paused to wrinkle his brow in hard recollection. "But, curse me, sirs, I can't remember whether he sits for county or borough!"

"Clackmannan and Kinross, in the north," said Hugh, who until now had been silent.

All heads turned to him. He said, "Mr. Abercromby's family are quite as numerous as are the Lees or Randolphs here, gentlemen, and their careers have been almost exclusively civil and military. And the Council, I must sadly inform you, unwisely enlisted the services of a man who allied himself with Lord Bute, and who just this summer past was granted a pension, undoubtedly through the intercession of Mr. Grenville." He shook his head. "No, sirs. He is not likely to argue Virginia's case with any enthusiasm. He is suborned. He is *bought*."

His table companions sat stunned, or incredulous, or in doubt of the news. "I do not believe it," said one burgess.

"That is an indirect slander on the Council, sir," said another. "What proof have you?"

"I was sent the *London Gazette* that contains the item," said Hugh. "You are all invited to call on me in Caxton to see it for yourselves."

"*I* have seen that item, sirs," said Cullis reluctantly, wishing that his colleague had not mentioned the matter. "It is true."

"Do the Council know this?" asked one of this friends.

Hugh shrugged his shoulders. "Perhaps. Perhaps not. But those gentlemen should not expect Mr. Abercromby to oppose Mr. Grenville in anything he concocts."

"Then, if it is true," posed another burgess, "the Council chose unwisely."

Another burgess agreed. "It would appear that they hired a man of their own mettle — a man who prefers satin chairs on which to rest his velvety principles."

"Caution, sir," said another. "Now you are close to directly slandering the Council. And bear in mind that a pension does not necessarily imply a purchase of principles."

Cullis said, "Well, at least the House chose wisely when it enlisted Mr. Montague. His reports from London have been regular and enlightening."

"Yes, he cannot speak in Parliament for us," said Hugh. "He can confer only with the Board of Trade and the Privy Council. If we have reason to resort to petitions in the future, he may not himself present them to either House in Parliament, nor even to the king. Only if he can persuade a member of either House to propose that a petition be admitted into debate or as evidence, can one be heard and entered into the record, but even that scenario is subject to a vote of the House sitting as a committee. I beg you, sirs, to keep in mind the rules of our own Assembly, for they are not dissimilar from those of Parliament's. That body may choose not to take cognizance of our remonstrances and memorials."

One of the burgesses sniffed. "It is a doleful perspective you offer us, sir."

Hugh said, "But a realistic one, given the circumstances. I will add further that while we may boast that Mr. Montague cannot be bought with a pension or place, we must remind ourselves that it is simply because he does not sit in Parliament. Please, do not conclude that I am aspersing his character or doubting his loyalty. I am saying merely that if he did sit in Parliament, he would be *approached*, just as, no doubt, was Mr. Abercromby." He paused for a moment, to let his listeners digest his remarks. "We should hope that Mr. Montague remains deserving of the House's confidence. After all, one could count the articulate friends of Virginia and the colonies in London on the fingers of one hand, and they are mostly outside of the government, and must beg for audiences with those who are in it."

"This is true," said one of the burgesses. "The friends of Virginia in London are as plentiful as Georgia silk!"

Most of the men around the table laughed. It was a standing joke about the founding of the thirteenth colony, Georgia, in 1733 with transported debtors and the poor from England's prisons and workhouses, first with private funds, and later sustained by Parliamentary grants. Its chief purpose was to produce silk and save Britain some £500,000 per annum in exchange and bullion in the purchase of foreign silk. But the silkworms died, the Georgia mulberry tree was the wrong tree, and the settlers became restive under the rigid discipline of their benefactors' rules of conduct. Georgia became a financial disaster, and reverted to the Crown in 1752.

Hugh merely grinned.

The burgess who had accused him of indirectly slandering the Governor's Council noted that Hugh had not joined in the laughter. He said, "Sir, you have a darksome view of Parliament's affairs. What are the grounds of your umbrage?"

"I am acquainted with some of its members, sir, though not in friendship. And I have correspondents in London who are friends, and who keep me regularly apprised of Parliament's affairs, perhaps more regularly does Mr. Montague keep the House." He paused. "My umbrage? Well, here are some Crown titbits you may chew on, and which should give you a taste of Parliamentary fare. General Isaac Barré, a member of Parliament, was dismissed from the army and his post of governor of Stirling Castle for having voted against Mr. Grenville's move to expel Mr. Wilkes. Lieutenant-General William Asshe-A'Court, another member, was removed from his regiment for the same reason. And, Lieutenant-General Francis Conway, another member, was shorn of his offices and removed from his regiment for voting against Mr. Wilkes's expulsion and against general warrants." He shook his head. "These are but a few of the instances that contribute to my umbrage, sir. One consequence of these actions has been to send those men into permanent opposition to sly encroachments on liberty."

A burgess chuckled. "It would seem that the government is determined to send all its generals to the other side!"

Again, the burgesses laughed. More jokes were made at the expense of the Grenville ministry. Finally, one of the men produced a pack of cards. "Enough of politicking, gentlemen! Who's up for a round or two of whist?"

Several of the men chimed in with agreement, including Edgar Cullis. Hugh excused himself from the game. "I have not the memory for card games, sirs," he explained to the company. "My younger sister has beaten me repeatedly at piquet and all-fours." Then he bid the men good evening.

* * *

After leaving the coffeehouse, Hugh mounted his horse and rode back to Mary Gandy's house in the night. There was some snow falling, but not enough of it to collect on the bare trees and ground. During the session, he frequently occupied himself with managing Meum Hall from afar. Tonight, after he had installed his mount in a barn belonging to a neighbor of his hostess, he settled in and opened his traveling desk. He wrote to William Settle asking him to report the progress being made on the construction of new rain gutters to be put up on the main house and connected to the water tower. "And remember that the cottonwoods and oaks near the house must be trimmed so that their leaves do not fall next year to clog up the channels...."

Next he wrote to Jack Frake, Thomas Reisdale, and Reece Vishonn about the business of the House. He dwelt on his annoyance with the style and content of the address to George the Third, the memorial to Lords, and the remonstrance to the Commons:

"When the House in a few days is handed back these documents with the Council's amendments, they will surely be revised in committee again, and returned to the Council for further discreet parsing. So many points and aspects of these official missives have been changed, struck out, and reinstated in squabblish debate in our own House, that the character and temper of the Council's deliberations beggar imagination. It is a torturously tiresome business. What has not changed is the language of craven submission, in which fully a quarter of the verbiage is couched in apologetic terms and conceded inferiority. Neither the Council nor the House will brazen a singular statement that denies Parliament's power or authority to tax us in violation of the original and standing charters — to which Parliament was no party, ever — and of the Constitution. That notion is disguised throughout in circumspect minuet around the subject, and is as busy and confounding to the eye as a folio of Playford's dancing steps. The neglect here cannot help but be noted by Mr. Grenville and his friends in that other house, and the end effect will not be so much a protest against his designs as an enfeebled complaint, or the peevish mewing of a misbehaved child on the verge of his expected punishment...."

Chapter 8: The Spectators

Hugh spent most of his evenings in Williamsburg alone, although he grew to enjoy the ambiance of Marot's Coffeehouse. The establishment reminded him of the Fruit Wench Tavern in London. Here he would take a supper, or sit near the fireplace reading newspapers with an ale or brandy. When the place became, in the evenings, too boisterous with gambling merchants, planters, and burgesses, he would leave. One evening, though, after a day in the House, he accepted an invitation to the Governor's Palace to attend a concert. Fauquier greeted him like an old friend, and at one point in the affair took him aside away from the other guests for a private chat.

"Well," broached the Governor, "how are you liking the business up the road, Mr. Kenrick?"

Hugh's grin was somber. "I endure it, your honor."

Fauquier nodded. "It is tedious but necessary business, I grant. But not nearly as tedious as my own daily routine. Why, if I imbibed, drop for drop, an equal measure of Madeira for every drop of ink I expend on signing papers and permits and the like, I could be brought up on the charge of public drunkenness."

Hugh merely smiled in sympathy.

Fauquier said, "But I did not think you would ever take an interest in politics, sir. The House's routine must be painfully dull for a man of your talents."

Hugh shrugged. "I adjudged an active interest necessary, your honor — in light of the Crown's intentions."

"Hmmm....Yes, I can understand that." The Governor paused to glance around, then said in a lower tone, "I know that you gentlemen are composing a set of impertinences. Have you lent your hand to the endeavor?"

"Not so much as a finger, your honor," said Hugh, shaking his head. "I was not invited to contribute to their composition."

"But, you do not deny they *are* impertinent?"

Hugh smiled. "Not as impertinent as I would wish."

"I see." Fauquier seemed lost in thought for a moment. "Well," he said at length, "it is not my place to caution the House at this point or to inter- fere in its business in any event, but forgive me if I say that little good will come from dunning the Crown for grievances it will not allow. In Mr. Grenville's eyes, the roles are properly reversed. It is Virginia that is the debtor, and the Crown the bearer of grievances. Mr. Grenville is merely seeking satisfaction."

"By usurping the Constitution, your honor?" asked Hugh, holding the Governor's glance.

The Governor looked away, and cocked his head, demurring. "*That* charge is open to interpretation, sir. It could be viewed as a reasonable accusation — or as a slander." He paused. "I advise you to be careful what you say in public, Mr. Kenrick, and especially to me. I count myself your friend, and a friend of Virginia. But neither you nor the House should expect me to remain silent when the Crown and its supreme agents are besmirched."

Hugh said simply, "You would be remiss in your duties, your honor, if you remained silent."

The Governor sighed. "Well, at least that is more of a compliment than I have ever had from the Board of Trade." He studied Hugh for a moment, then shook his head. "We will discuss politics no more here, sir. I can see that you are struggling with a clash between your decent tact and a desire to burst into oratory." He smiled in defeat by this young man's demeanor of frankness and studied reticence, and abruptly changed the subject. "I am thinking of holding another concert early in the spring, if my duties permit the time. I would be delighted to fit into it that young lady with the harp, the one I married to that young man April last."

Hugh relaxed visibly, but with a sigh, said, "Mrs. Frake? Yes. I believe she would be delighted to accept such an invitation, your honor."

"Excellent. I will have my secretary write a note to her, and you may convey it to her when this session is adjourned. Now, I understand that you journeyed to England recently. I miss England. Please, tell me about your stay. And allow me to introduce you to my wife and son...."

At the end of the brilliant evening, which acted as a tonic on his spirits, Hugh was accosted outside the Palace gates by one of the musicians who had performed with the Governor a transcription of a Telemann horn con- certo. The man tucked his violin case under his other arm and offered his hand. "Mr. Kenrick, I have not forgotten our first meeting, and your suggestion — or was it my own? — that we take in a play." He paused when he saw that Hugh, who was thinking of other things, did not recognize him. "Thomas Jefferson, of Albemarle."

"Oh, yes," replied Hugh, peering into the hazel eyes and recognizing the red hair by the flickering light of a cresset. "Mr. Jefferson! Forgive me my oversight." He took the young man's hand and shook it. "My compliments on your playing tonight."

"Thank you, sir." Jefferson glanced at the departing guests, some of whom were leaving on foot, while others ascended closed and open carriages. "Is one of these yours, sir?"

"No, I walked. I am boarding for the session in a house near the College. That is my destination now."

"Then may I join you as far as the end of the Green?" asked Jefferson. "There we must part, for I am boarding for the moment at Mr. Wythe's house" — he pointed to a residence they were passing — "and am reading law under that gentleman." George Wythe, a prominent Williamsburg attorney, was burgess for William & Mary College and a member of the House's two most important standing committees. "Even though his duties in the House consume much of his time, he this morning found enough time to assign me more portions of Coke to absorb, in addition to some Greek! I must attend to that now, for I spent most of the afternoon practicing for our entertainment at the Palace."

"It was time well spent," remarked Hugh as they strode together in the chilly night.

"There is a new acting troupe in town, directly from New York, Gascoyne and Pennycuff. Tomorrow night they put on *Richard the Third* and a short farce by Mr. Garrick, *The Lying Valet*. Are you game?"

Hugh smiled. "I cannot think of a better way to pass the evening."

"Wonderful!" exclaimed Jefferson. "I can meet you at the theater at six-thirty. I have heard that this troupe are very talented."

Hugh chuckled. "Well, even if they are not, Gascoyne and company are likely to offer more drama than does the House."

"Are you attending the debates?"

"I am now a burgess for my county."

"Oh...I see." Jefferson was silent as their shoes crunched over the cold, hardened ground. "Mr. Wythe tells me that the House and the Council are laboring over the protests to be sent to London over the proposed stamp taxes. He is composing the remonstrance, and Colonel Bland the address and memorial. How do you think the matter will end? Do you think the men in London will heed their words?"

Hugh shrugged. "I cannot say at this moment, sir. I am inclined to doubt that our advice will carry any weight. As the House despairs of convincing the Board of Trade and Parliament of the corrections of right reason, Parliament and the Board are habituated to their power over us." He paused when the carriage of John Blair, president of the Council, rattled by them. "I am quite certain that, in the future, we will have cause to pen numerous analogies that compare the differences between ancient Greek and Roman colonial policies."

* * *

Gascoyne and Pennycuff staged an abridged and mediocre *Richard the Third*, while *The Lying Valet* elicited a few chuckles from the audience. The theater was packed that evening. It was once a courthouse on the Palace Green, and had been moved to its present site not far from the House's side of the Capitol. Members of the audience marveled more at its conversion into a legitimate theater than they did about the main play. The place was empty most of the year, except when traveling musicians and magic shows came to town for a few nights.

Hugh and Mr. Jefferson hurried from the theater and made their way to the Blue Bell Tavern just up the street for a late supper. Over their meal they exchanged anecdotes from their lives. Jefferson asked Hugh if he had noticed a certain young lady in the audience, seated a few rows closer to the stage. "A few months ago I was gathering the courage to approach her on the subject of marriage, when I learned, quite to my dismay, and in contradiction to all the signs from her to me that the subject was not an unfriendly one, that she had gone and married a Yorktown merchant! I have only lately recovered from the blow, and sent her my wishes for her happiness."

"A wise course of action," remarked Hugh.

Later in their conversation, Jefferson revealed that before he attended the College, he spent two years attending a school in Fredericksville that was run by Reverend James Maury, the very same minister who had sued the collectors of that parish for back pay when the Two-Penny Act was disallowed by the Board of Trade. "He remains stung by memories of that day, sir," said Jefferson, "and by the charge that he was a 'rapacious harpy,' as that lawyer, Mr. Henry, suggested he was. Reverend Maury is a kind man and a superb teacher." He paused to smile. "Now, Mr. Wythe informed me some time ago, just after the Assembly convened, that this same lawyer represented a plaintiff before the Committee of Privileges and Elections, contending that Mr. Dandridge, his client, had lost his place in the House because the new burgess, Mr. Littlepage, had stooped to unfair practices in order to win election. The Committee dismissed the suit as 'frivolous and vexatious,' much as Mr. Wythe and the other members of the Committee believed was Mr. Henry's victory over Reverend Maury. I will confess that I was happy to hear it."

Hugh shook his head. "Perhaps Mr. Henry so styled him because he and the other clergy wished to profit from an arbitrary interference with Virginia's internal affairs, just as Parliament is prepared to do again." He held the eyes of his supper companion. "It would profit you, sir, to stand back from your intimacy with particular men and events to gain a broader vista of matters."

The younger man's face acquired a reddish hue nearly the color of his hair; his freckles quite disappeared in the flush. Hugh could not decide whether its cause was anger or embarrassment. He continued, "You are reading law now, Mr. Jefferson, and I presume that you intend to enter that career, once you have been certified by your mentors. Now, most lawyers based their careers on established law, and have little occasion — I will not say 'courage' — to question the propriety of the law they may practice. I have observed they rarely avail themselves of the opportunity to challenge the moral aspect of patently unjust statutes. It is a principal reason why the profession is not more honored, not even by those who find it lucrative. However, I believe that in the future, if the Crown presses its policies on us, that profession may have the chance to redeem itself. You will be a lawyer by then, and have both the occasion and the courage to participate in that redemption. That is my sincerest hope."

Jefferson said nothing for a while. The red faded from his face. He said, "You are an unsettling, presumptuous fellow, Mr. Kenrick, but, harsh as it may seem, the wisdom of your words is quite…correct." He nodded once. "I thank you for the confidence you place in me. I shall keep your words in mind." His throat was dry, and he took a sip of his ale. "Have you spoken in the House?"

Hugh shook his head. "Not as yet. The lawyers who govern the business of the House have not yet seen fit to hear me on any matter. After all, I am too fresh, and regarded as unschooled in the business, and as something of an interloper, as well."

Jefferson looked thoughtful for a moment. "I think I shall fit into my own schedule some time among the House's spectators."

Chapter 9: The Protests

By December 13th, the House had received from the Council corrected drafts of the address, memorial, and remonstrance. Only the address to "the King's Most Excellent Majesty" survived intact and as originally written, and would remain unchanged. The House in Committee again edited, emended, and rearranged the memorial and remonstrance, which were again approved by the Committee and returned to the Council for further review.

On December 18th, the House, now reduced in size by the departure of a number of burgesses who had gone home, made its last changes. Chairman Peyton Randolph moved that the House go out of Committee and into a formal session to hear last arguments for and against the documents, and to conduct individual votes on them. His motion was seconded by Colonel Richard Bland. After a short recess, the remaining burgesses, numbering about eighty, made their way through the crowd in the lobby and public space to their places on the benches. Hugh Kenrick and Edgar Cullis secured seats on the upper tier of the benches on the Speaker's left.

Young Thomas Jefferson managed to find a place on one of the front benches of the public space; there were few other benches provided for the convenience of spectators, most of whom were content to stand. Behind Jefferson sat a plainly dressed man of about thirty. This man had a high forehead, blue-gray eyes, and an aquiline, almost hawklike nose. His frock coat and breeches were dark, as was the ribbon of his tie-wig. In the course of this final reading of the protests, his neighbors seemed to think that he wanted to rise in protest of the protests. His narrow face would grow red with anger, and his wide mouth whispered inaudible maledictions. He watched the proceedings with an intensity that went beyond mere curiosity and idle interest. He behaved like a man who wished he had a say in the business.

Thomas Jefferson had noticed and recognized the stranger, whom he had met once during the Christmas holidays years ago, when he was en route to the College, but chose not to greet him other than with a nod of the head. And the man did not seem to recognize Jefferson. The law student was too engrossed by the spectacle of the House in session, and pushed aside memory of things he and another had said about the stranger not long ago.

The House reconvened in a formal session. An assistant clerk, William Ferguson, was directed by John Randolph, the clerk of the House, to rise and read each of the final drafts. Speaker John Robinson opened the floor after each reading to any member who wished to make remarks. No one rose to speak for or against the address to George the Third, which notified the king that "the Council and Burgesses of your ancient Colony and Dominion of Virginia...beg leave to assure your Majesty of our firm and inviolable Attachment to your sacred Person and Government," and asked that he "be graciously pleased to protect your People of this Colony in the Enjoyment of their ancient and inestimable Right of being governed by such Laws respecting their internal Polity and Taxation...with the Approbation of their Sovereign or his Substitute...." It was the shortest of the documents; Ferguson read it in five minutes.

John Randolph then conducted a vote, which Ferguson and another assistant recorded. The address was unanimously approved.

The memorial to the "Right Honorable the Lords Spiritual and Temporal in Parliament assembled" was next read to the House. It gently reminded these esteemed persons, in many more words than were addressed to the king, that since the colonies were not represented in Parliament, that body had no authority to tax them, and presumed that their "lordships will not think any Reason sufficient to support such a Power in the British Parliament...a Power never before constitutionally assumed, and which if they have a Right to exercise on any Occasion must necessarily establish this melancholy Truth, that the Inhabitants of the Colonies are the Slaves of Britons...." The memorial ended on a bright note, hoping that their Lordships would not construe the document as anything but the "purest Loyalty and Affection as they have always endeavored by their Conduct to demonstrate that they consider their Connexions with Great Britain, the Seat of Liberty, as their greatest Happiness...."

Speaker Robinson, when Ferguson had finished, glanced around the House. No one indicated a desire to speak. He nodded to John Randolph, who began to take a vote. As each burgess rose and said "Aye," the clerks recorded a stroke in their ledgers.

George Wythe, seated between Richard Bland and Peyton Randolph —

older brother of John and younger brother of Peter Randolph, Surveyor General and a member of the Council — glanced over the clerks' table that was situated on the floor between the benches, and noticed his protégé, Thomas Jefferson, sitting among the spectators in the public space. He was about to smile in approval when he noticed another face behind his student.

Peyton Randolph, also from his vantage point of a bench behind the Speaker's chair, noticed the face, too, and leaned closer to whisper to Edmund Pendleton, "Is that not the blustery scamp of the Dandridge suit last month? I thought we had sent him back to Hanover, chastised and mortified!"

"Who?" asked Pendleton.

"Mr. Henry," said Randolph with a surreptitious nod in the direction of the subject, "there, sitting behind Mr. Wythe's new student."

Pendleton squinted and identified the man. "Why, yes," he said, "it is he. What is he doing here?"

"I could not say, sir. But I will say now that we should regret having signed his license to practice law. I should have been happier endorsing his license to operate a tavern."

Pendleton snorted once. "I have heard that he failed in that enterprise, too."

The memorial was unanimously approved.

The remonstrance was twice as long as the memorial, and took William Ferguson twenty minutes to read to a restive assembly, for he paused before reading those sections of it that had been the subject of vigorous debate.

Hugh Kenrick voted "Aye" for the address and memorial, and intended to approve the remonstrance as well. But he fidgeted so much during the last reading that Edgar Cullis, seated next to him on the top tier of benches, and who had a vague notion of what bothered his colleague, glanced at him once with amused annoyance and sidled a little away from him.

The remonstrance to the "Honorable the Knights, Citizens, and Burgesses of Great Britain, in Parliament assembled," reminded the Commons that the "Council and burgesses...met in General Assembly...judge it their indispensable Duty, in a respectful manner, but with decent Firmness, to remonstrate against" the proposed stamp taxes for the colonies, and that they conceived it was "essential to British Liberty that Laws imposing Taxes on the People ought not to be made without the Consent of Representatives chosen by themselves." The document then reviewed in detail the logic behind that assertion, delicately raising the fact that since the colonies were self-governing by grace of *royal* charters, and not by Parliamentary leave or plan, it was unfair and "inconsistent with the fundamental Principles of the Constitution" to exercise a taxing power.

The remonstrance concluded with a litany of dire consequences for the colonies and Britain, even if the remonstrance conceded Parliament's power to levy internal taxes. The Council and Burgesses protested their "Reverence to the Mother Kingdom…in promoting her Glory and Felicity," and assured the gentlemen of the Commons that "British Patriots will never consent to the Exercise of anticonstitutional Power, which even in this remote Corner may be dangerous in its Example to the interior Parts of the British Empire, and will certainly be detrimental to its Commerce."

When Ferguson finished, a great sigh of relief rushed through the House. Everyone present knew that this was the high point of this session of the General Assembly. Speaker Robinson surveyed the chamber, tapped the silver knob of his cane with a finger, and waited for the noise of so much relief to subside. Then he asked, "What say anyone on this remonstrance?" It was a rhetorical query, half question, half warning to anyone who might have an objection or even a compliment. He wished to move on to the last business of the House, and in a few days go home.

To his surprise, a burgess rose from one of the upper benches to his left, one of the new burgesses, one whom he had deliberately ignored in the past, for the man had been pointed out to him over the last weeks. Unsavory things about this gentleman had been whispered in his ear. The Speaker therefore did not wish to encourage him to participate in the House's business. In this policy he had the tacit approval of his senior colleagues. But all the other burgesses, and all the spectators at the end of the chamber, saw the man rise, and they looked at him with inquisitive expectation. Speaker Robinson could not now ignore him without displaying flagrant discourtesy and bias. He wondered what this man could possibly have to say. He sighed, grimaced, and nodded.

Hugh Kenrick nodded in return with an icy smile, then glanced around the chamber at his listeners. Unlike a member of the Commons, he was not bound by the rule of addressing his remarks to the Speaker. He had faced crowds and mobs before, and was unafraid. To his left, Edgar Cullis, wanting to cringe, sat back on the bench, crossing his legs and folding his arms. He was afraid, for he had heard a sampling of his colleague's oratory months ago.

Hugh spoke. "I will say this only: that the language of the remonstrance wants keenness and vigor. This and its companion obsecrations correctly raise and stress all the intrinsical points that arouse our fears and concerns, but cloak them in coddling, pious terms so as not to disturb the confident composure of their intended correspondents. But this habit defeats the purpose of our communications and saps their force. And that composure, gentlemen, in all justice ought to be swiftly disturbed, to better awaken our colleagues in that greater House to the undeniable wrongness of their contemplated action, to warn them in no vague, fawning terms of the folly of their solution to their own extravagance, to advise them of the inherent belligerency of their means and ends. I feel compelled to remind this House that *humility* is not a practical, manly virtue in these circumstances. Humility has never met arrogance in the field and vanquished it. There are," said Hugh, his glance falling briefly on the attentive face of Colonel Washington across the chamber, "many soldiers here today who can attest to that truism. The supplicant who comes before his master with a bowed head, sirs, cannot see the sword raised above him. The ground and the shadow of his own disgrace on it may be the last things he will see before the sword whistles in the air and descends on his neck. I know that the Council and this House have discharged their tasks in the composition and final form of these missives, and believe their duties done. I will endorse these documents, but under this protest."

Hugh nodded again to Speaker Robinson, and resumed his seat.

Behind Thomas Jefferson, a man clapped his hands once, and said to himself, "Hear, hear!" This gesture seemed to trigger a burst of commotion among the spectators. Jefferson turned to face the stranger, who merely smiled in challenge and said no more. Jefferson turned again to study the man with whom he had shared his thoughts over a supper.

The spectators were in a state of excitement. A minister remarked with bitter anger, "That man is pagan! Humility never fails to vanquish arrogance — in the eyes of God!"

"Perhaps," answered a merchant next to him, "but only after one is dead, and what good would that do?"

"That fellow is capable of treason," observed a lawyer.

"But not Parliament?" retorted his companion, another lawyer. "Who has been the persistent intruder: We, or that 'greater House,' sir?"

"It is merely somber raillery," commented an instructor of the classics from the College to his wife. "You might have noticed that he insinuated the fate of Charles the First. That will cause him trouble!"

"He insinuated nothing," replied his wife. "I like his manner. When one is being assaulted with rocks, one should not respond by tossing pasties!"

A dozen burgesses shot up instantly amid the commotion on the benches. Speaker Robinson, sitting rigidly in his high-backed chair, did not know whom to recognize first. John Randolph, whose duty it was to gavel the House into order, was so stunned that he sat fixated on the empty space next to the gavel: a ritual had been overlooked in the haste to finish the business of the documents; the gold-plated mace of the House still rested under the clerks' table, when over an hour ago it should have been returned to its place on the black-cloth table to signify a formal session. He silently but angrily reproved one of his clerks, nodding to the empty space. The clerk rose and retrieved the mace, and laid it on the table. Only then did Randolph hear the desperate tapping of a cane, and with a blink looked at Speaker Robinson. He picked up the gavel and struck it several times on an oaken anvil, shouting, "Order in the House! Order in the House!"

Speaker Robinson stared resolutely into space, refusing to look at anyone, waiting for the burgesses to obey the gavel. Over a long minute, the noise abated; one by one the standing members resumed their seats. When he was satisfied that the House had regained its dignity, Robinson, with a quick scowl at Hugh Kenrick, said, "What say anyone to that...*reprimand*?"

Again, several burgesses rose, and the Speaker nodded to one. The others fell back into their seats. The recognized burgess said, "In reply to that member's remarks, I say that any correspondence with the stewards of the British Empire must conform to language commensurate with the occasion, and strive to reply in kind — not in the rude parlance of vagabonds and ruffians!"

"Hear, hear!" murmured several men on the benches. The burgess sat down with a smug, triumphant smile.

Colonel Bland was recognized. "In rebuttal to that member's contention, I say that bellicose words merely invite bellicose actions. One witnesses that phenomenon often enough outside the less congenial taverns and public places in this town and throughout the colony. *And,* I might note, in the histories of nations! We owe our *mother* country civility, and the respect due her."

Speaker Robinson acknowledged several more burgesses, all of whom he knew would speak against the rebellious member's remarks, and who did. Then the tall, commanding figure of Colonel Washington rose. Robinson knew that he could not deny this man his words and, out of respect, nodded to him.

Washington did not often speak in the House, and a special silence subdued the chamber as its occupants listened to the hero of the late war. "My attachment to civility and poise on all occasions is well known to this House, and frequently the subject of humor among certain of my colleagues. But, while I cannot fully agree with that member's sentiments on how best to protest the mischief at hand in London, I do believe that we may in time be civil to a fault and to our egregious disadvantage." Washington resumed his seat.

This surprising speech produced its own silence. Speaker Robinson pursed his mouth in regret. George Wythe sat staring at Washington, his eyes wide in shock. The burgesses who spoke against Hugh Kenrick sniffed in mortification. Thomas Jefferson regarded Washington with newfound awe. Edgar Cullis glanced in confusion at his colleague. Patrick Henry beamed.

And Hugh felt partly vindicated. He nodded in thanks to Washington across the space that separated them. Washington nodded imperceptively in acknowledgment.

Peyton Randolph, Edmund Pendleton, and Colonel Bland observed the silent communication, and made mental note of it.

Speaker Robinson took advantage of the hiatus. He tapped his cane once on the floor and announced, "The House is now closed to debate." He waved the cane at the clerks' table. "Mr. Randolph, please proceed with the vote."

The remonstrance was passed unanimously.

* * *

When he left the Capitol that evening and stepped out into the creeping dusk and chill, it was with a sense of accomplishment, even though the address, memorial, and remonstrance were repugnant to his principles. He was certain that they would prove to be futile, and perhaps even achieve the opposite of their purpose. Wythe's clerks were busy now and would work late into the night making copies of the documents for dispatch to several points: to the *Virginia Gazette* for publication; to interested parties in the lower houses of the Pennsylvania and Massachusetts legislatures; to London and the king, Parliament, the Board of Trade; to James Abercromby and Edward Montague. When he returned to Mary Gandy's house this evening, he would make his own copies of the documents; he had heard them read so many times over the last few weeks that their words were burned into his memory.

Outside the Capitol, Thomas Jefferson stopped to compliment Hugh on his speech. "That, sir, was *drama!*" he exclaimed. Other burgesses stopped to admit to him that they, too, were dissatisfied with the documents' wordings, and confessed that they lacked the presence of mind to raise their own objections.

Edgar Cullis, on his way to supper at the Raleigh Tavern with several of his friends, sent his company on so that he could speak for a moment in private with his colleague. "Well, sir, you won't be snubbed in the future! I will wager on it! What a maiden speech! What you tend to say often gives me the shivers, I don't mind admitting it, but you may be right. And, God! What a stir you made! Randolph, Pendleton, Robinson, Bland, Wythe — he wrote the remonstrance, you know, and Bland the others — well, they are all in a royal pet! You've made no friends in that company, sir, but Colonel Washington practically seconded you, and that will count for something among them." He paused. "Do you truly believe the style will make a difference?"

Hugh sighed. He was tired. He answered. "A proper, assertive style may have stayed Mr. Grenville's hand, or at least given him grave pause for thought. The adopted style, however, will either provoke or entice him and his party." Hugh patted his colleague's arm and hoped he did not sound condescending. "Surely, Mr. Cullis, you know that as bees are lured by the pollen of flowers, bullies are drawn by the funk of the timid!"

"Well put, sir," remarked Cullis. He laughed. "I am sure that if you had pronounced that maxim in the chamber, an even greater altercation would have occurred!" He paused. "Will you join me and my friends at the Raleigh?"

Hugh shook his head. "I am going directly to your cousin's. I have personal business to see to. And it has been a trying day. Thank you for the invitation."

After a brief exchange with Hugh on the House's remaining business, Cullis bid his colleague goodnight and rushed away down Duke of Gloucester Street. A cold wind rustled the trees nearby and caused the flames of the Capitol's cressets to whip nearly horizontally. Hugh buttoned up his long cloak, drew it closer around him, and turned to leave the Capitol grounds.

"A word with you, sir," said a voice behind him.

Hugh turned and saw a man he had noticed earlier among the spectators in the House, in idle conversation while he listened to the clerk read
the memorial to Lords. The man had a distinctive Roman character to his
face, like one he had admired in a book of engravings in his library. As he
came into the light of the cresset, Hugh saw that he wore a black cloak and
a hat with a round brim. "Yes...?" answered Hugh.

The man approached and held out his hand. "I am Patrick Henry, of
Hanover. I wish to commend you on your brave speech — and to thank you
for one other thing."

Hugh took the proffered hand and shook it. "Thank you, sir. And what
is it that you have to thank me for?"

"For helping me make up my mind."

"About what?"

Henry dug his hands into the pockets of his cloak. "I have for some
time entertained the ambition of standing for burgess for the next session.
You have helped me decide that I *must* follow that ambition."

"How so, sir?"

"I had some business here in the House last month, and went home
after it was done — though not to my satisfaction."

Hugh remembered what young Jefferson had told him. "Oh, yes. The
Dandridge and Littlepage matter."

"Yes," said Henry. "Well, that was more a favor for a friend than a
serious case. I half expected my client's suit to be dismissed, though not
with the airs I smelled in that committee. But, here is my main point. I
learned at that time that the House was proposing to act on information
received from the House's agent in London about the new taxes. I resolved
then to return here to see for myself what would be done. I would rather
have stayed in Hanover with my family and friends, but I journeyed here
and attended all the debates on the papers to be sent to London. And, until
you spoke, I thought I had wasted my time."

Hugh shook his head. "I spoke but a minute, sir."

Henry took a hand from his cloak and raised a finger. "But that one
minute, sir, and what it precipitated, revealed to me certain aspects and
habits of the House, and convinced me that certain things were possible. So
— and I will not take up much more of your time, Mr....?"

"Hugh Kenrick, of Queen Anne County and Meum Hall therein."

"...Mr. Kenrick — I shall enter politics here. I shall contrive to be
elected burgess, either of Hanover or some neighboring county. There are

vacancies expected. I shall realize my ambition because I agree with you that these encroachments on our liberties, such as a captive freeman's are, must be resisted. I agree that the encroachers must *know* they are observed and opposed. Forgive me for having overheard what you said to your friend a minute ago, about the bees and bullies, but if I had had the privilege of speaking to the House, that is what I would have said to it, at the risk of censure, expulsion, and even a program of duels with the offended!"

Hugh laughed for the first time in days. He took his hands from his own pockets and grasped the man's shoulders. "You, sir, are of my own mettle! I have endured censure, expulsion, and even fought a few duels, all in the same spirit!"

Henry smiled. "I wish the word had a positive connotation, sir, but you *flatter* me. Whether my efforts will result in a Thermoplyae or a Marathon, I cannot predict." He glanced once at the Capitol behind him. "There is a great weight of ballast to be moved in there."

Hugh's face expressed surprise at the classical references. But he said, "If you are successful in your election, Mr. Henry, I hope to work with you in the next session, and together we may move it."

Henry grunted in amusement. "Do you see, Mr. Kenrick? Even 'back-woodsmen' such as myself peruse the histories and wisdom of Rome and Greece. That material is not the exclusive preserve of these Tidewater grandees." He gestured contemptuously in the direction of the Capitol, then his brow furled in curiosity. "You are not a native of these parts, are you, Mr. Kenrick? Your manner and modulation of speech are distinctly...English."

Hugh said simply, "I removed here from Dorset and London, but count myself a Virginian."

"I see," said Henry. "Well, being English is not necessarily to your discredit, nor is your youth. When we have more time, you must relate to me your experiences with censors and expulsion. I am sure it is the stuff of epics."

Before Hugh could protest the compliment, Henry said, "But here is one more point I wish to make, and then I take my leave. I am sure that you made the same observation I did, that as the end of the session nears, attendance in the House diminishes."

"Yes," said Hugh. He had noted it. "But what importance do you attach to it?"

Henry cocked his head. "You would have thought that with such an important matter as a protest to the Crown in the making, the House would

have boasted full attendance. But the lazy and the thoughtless and the ignorant departed, resulting in less than half a House." Henry smiled mischie-
vously. "Keep that fact in mind, sir. I presume that the phenomenon is a
regular one and will recur next year. It may be used to advantage. The lazy
and the thoughtless and the ignorant can claim no say to the direction of
events they choose to absent themselves from."

"They are another kind of ballast," remarked Hugh.

"Precisely," said Henry. "You must know that at this time last year, I
wrung an extenuate defeat in the Maury suit in Hanover. That has brought
me some notoriety. You have scored a similarly curious defeat here today,
sir. Perhaps at the next session, we can pool our defeats and attain a genuine victory." He took Hugh's hand and shook it again. "Good night to you,
sir, good health, and thank you for your time and inspiration." With a
touch of his hat, Patrick Henry turned, shoved his hands into his pockets,
and strode in the direction of the Blue Bell Tavern.

Hugh watched him disappear into the darkness. Another gust of wind
blew against his back, whipping the yellow flames of the cresset behind him
and sending a shower of glowing sparks to dance in the wake of the man
with the Roman countenance.

The General Assembly adjourned on the 21st of December, and would
meet again on the first day of May the next year.

Chapter 10: The Purgatory Tavern

The tread wheel was fixed to a wall at a man's height, a few feet from the roaring oven-fireplace. It was a sturdy wooden and tin drum with bars in which was imprisoned the turnspit, a small mottled mongrel dog, which had little choice but to trot in the contraption. It could not stop to rest, for the sharp curve of the tread wheel did not lend itself to a dog's comfort. If by chance it did stop and lay down to rest, however uncomfortably, the serving boy attending the fireplace would jab it with a poker to get it moving again. The dog might yelp, or whine, or bark, or perhaps even growl in torment, but it would obey. It had no choice. The tread wheel was rigged to a series of pulleys that turned the iron bar of the spit, on which were impaled joints of beef, swan, and lamb. These were turned over the flames by the dog's exertions, assuring that all sides of the meat were evenly roasted. The tread wheel could be disengaged from the pulleys to allow removal of the cooked meat. These occasions were frequent enough when Parliament was in session and the number of hungry patrons tripled, so that the dog could enjoy a succession of brief respites from its duty.

Its home was the Purgatory Tavern, one of half a dozen such establishments in the Old Palace Yard, Westminster, to which members of Parliament, civil servants, and other functionaries repaired during recesses of the sessions. The Purgatory was also patronized by lawyers with business at the King's Bench and the Court of Common Pleas in nearby Westminster Hall, or in the Court of Requests, a kind of small claims court that adjudicated debts of five pounds or less, just behind the tavern. The Purgatory was conveniently connected to St. Stephen's Chapel, or the Commons, by a narrow passageway between the Court of Requests and the backs of other buildings. Up the Yard were the Caesar's Head Tavern, the Ship Tavern, Waghorn's Coffeehouse, and the Office of Ordnance. Adjoining the latter was what resembled a severely abbreviated Greek temple, which was the king's own entrance to the gabled lobby of the House of Lords. Across the Yard were various shops and merchants' offices, a constable's house and jail, a minor magistrate's house and office, solicitors' offices, and St. Margaret's Church, not much larger than a Nonconformist Chapel. Looming over it all on one side was the long sloped roof of Westminster Hall, and on the other, the ancient mass of Westminster Abbey, more commonly known then as St. Peter's Abbey or Collegiate Church.

A fresh February snow had fallen overnight and covered the roofs of all these edifices. It was already gray with the soot that also fell from the effluvium of London's countless chimneys, so that it was difficult to distinguish the rooflines from the winter sky. Before noontime, though, it had warmed up a little, and the broad cobblestoned ways of the Old Palace Yard and the New Palace Yard became lakes of slush. The thick, soaking mire hardly arrested the bustle of pedestrians as they hurried behind the stanchions that defined the "sidewalks"; the cold drove them on, as did the fear, too often realized, that they would be daggled with muddy slush from passing carriages, or splashed by the synchronized pumping feet of porters bearing sedan chairs.

Dogmael Jones, member for Swansditch, sat at his regular table not far from the fireplace. His leather boots were nearly dry from having this morning twice negotiated the chilly black puddles between the Purgatory, Waghorn's, and a disreputable tavern in one of Westminster's anonymous back alleys, a place frequented by hackney drivers, watermen, and apprentices, and which bore the grandiose name of the King's Table. At the latter, he had met a man named Trevors, a clerk to Thomas Whately, member for Ludgershall and George Grenville's private secretary at the Treasury. This man served as one of Jones's regular sources of information, for he had regular gambling debts, notwithstanding his salary and income derived from departmental fees, and so was appreciative of every little coin that came his way. Jones, generously endowed with money from his elector, Baron Garnet Kenrick, for just this kind of contingency, had exchanged five guineas for a packet of purloined correspondence, that is, letters and memoranda copied by Trevors from their originals. The furtive meeting lasted five minutes. After a quick glance at the documents, Jones had put them into his already bulging portfolio, bought the man a dram of gin, and departed. Trevors, who never ventured to audit the Commons from the gallery, for the business of the House did not interest him, did not know Jones's name, but only suspected that his terse benefactor was an agent for some eminence in Lords.

From the King's Table Jones picked his way to Waghorn's, where he met and conferred with his allies in the Commons about what to expect and what to say when the House met in a Committee of Ways and Means later that morning. These men included Colonel Isaac Barré and William Beckford, member for London and a past lord mayor of the City. The subject was the resolutions for the stamp tax bill that were to be introduced by Grenville that day. It was a brief meeting over coffee and hot toddies, held to reassure one another that they would speak against the resolutions in particular and against the bill in general when recognized by the chairman, Thomas Hunter. They did not agree on any fundamental principle for opposing the legislation; they agreed only that it must be vigorously opposed. For most of these men, passage of the bill into a Parliamentary act seemed fraught with dangers which they could associate only with a decline in trade, somehow connected with illegality. The bill was somewhat like a stiff, steady breeze that preceded a storm. A storm was certain, but of what severity and of what duration? The canvases on the creaking masts rumbled and complained from the contradictory winds, and the pennants rippled maddeningly, first east, then west, and then drooped ominously for no reason at all.

Dogmael Jones was the only man among them who denied Parliament's authority to tax the colonies in any manner for any reason. He rejected as irrelevant all the standard arguments for and against the bill. He was as dissatisfied with his allies' positions as his allies were unsettled by his own. It was an informal brotherhood for liberty that met at Waghorn's that morning, whose membership brandished a small forest of argumentative levers but could not decide on the proper fulcrum with which to dislodge Grenville's impending tax legislation. Like so many of their colonial counterparts, most of these men were sincere in their fear for British liberty at home and abroad, but were prisoners of their premises. They were vaguely aware of this weakness; Jones was acutely aware of it.

On several past occasions, before and during the new session, Jones had tried to persuade his fellows to abandon their scattered positions on the legislation and mount a broad, consistent assault based on a denial of Parliamentary authority over the colonies. And always, the retorts would be the same:

"I would never deny that authority."

"The authority is established. This is a matter of expediency."

"We would precipitate a constitutional crisis!"

"There would be a cessation of all legislation!"

"All the Empire would be in turmoil! Radicals and freethinkers and freetraders would clamor against all Parliamentary authority!"

"We oppose the present stamp tax being extended to the colonies, because it is of Mr. Grenville's initiative, not of His Majesty's."

"Mr. Grenville's bill *does* raise constitutional questions, it must be admitted. It would, however, be quite proper and correct if His Majesty lent his shoulder to the idea — indeed, if he had originated it himself — and then the propriety of it would be beyond constitutional question, and of no concern of ours."

"The colonies are no more exempt from Parliamentary imposts than are Birmingham and Bristol and so many of our manufacturing towns. But whether they are represented or no in the House, these towns rely heavily on colonial materials. So many merchants are worried that a tax would contribute to a reduction in the quantity of those materials and the frequency of their import."

"We must concede Mr. Grenville his desires, but work diligently to pare the number of items he may wish to tax and the rates he may wish to impose."

Jones had said, on all these occasions, "Then it is a *fait accompli*, sirs. Mr. Grenville has the power of precedent as an ally, which I needn't remind you is the precedent of power. You will neither disagree with him nor question his main point. We will lose."

Such disparate unanimity of the opposition, of which he was a member, confirmed in Jones's mind that defeat was inevitable. It was as though his party laid claim to a great gun that could blast the ministry's arguments in the Commons with a single shot, but all its parts lay unassembled on the ground. As the enemy advanced with beating drums and leveled bayonets, the crew argued over the best way to put the gun together.

He was doubly discouraged now. He had waited until he reached the familiar warmth and confinement of the Purgatory Tavern and his corner table there to read the documents he obtained from Trevors. Only one of them riveted his attention. He sat for a long while, as the busy tavern reverberated with the loud talk and laughter of its patrons, staring at the words that gave Grenville his confidence and momentum:

"...Though the question certainly does not want this, or any other authority, yet it will be a striking alteration to ignorant people, and an unanswerable argument ad homines; *and, therefore, I wish you would*

*employ somebody to look with this view into the origin of their power
to tax themselves and raise any money at all."*

The statement appeared in a letter dated the 24th of December of last
year, and was signed by Lord Chief Justice Mansfield of the King's Bench.
In the brief missive was a reference to Grenville's request for his opinion
on Parliament's constitutional power to tax and regulate the colonies. In
Jones's mind, this information was worth twice what he had paid Trevors
for the whole lot of confidential papers. He realized, of course, that he
could not use it in debate, neither as documented proof of Grenville's determination, nor in disinterested argumentation, not without betraying
Trevors and laying himself and that man open to criminal charges.

It was information, however, he was resolved to share with Garnet
Kenrick and his son in Virginia. Jones returned the documents to his portfolio and tied the leather strings. Then he sipped his ale, lit a pipe, and
called the serving girl over to order breakfast. He checked his watch; he had
an hour and a half to compose some remarks before the Committee of Ways
and Means reconvened in the House. Oblivious to the drone of voices and
the clatter and clink of dishes and glass around him, he sat thinking of what
he could say, and used the turning tread wheel as a focal point.

It was just after he had pushed his finished plate away and taken out a
notebook and pencil to jot down some thoughts that a large bulk abruptly
obstructed his view of the tread wheel. Jones glanced up and saw the wide,
well-fed frame of Sir Henoch Pannell, member for Canovan, a vocal and
nearly belligerent supporter of Grenville's stamp tax scheme.

Pannell regarded him with smug jollity. "Composing more injurious
eloquence, Sir Dogmael?" he asked.

Jones glowered up at him, not only because he disliked the man, but
because he had interrupted a thought. "Yes," he answered. "And, like
Demosthenes, I shall spit stones."

Pannell barked once in laughter. He and Jones had tangled this way
before. He enjoyed the encounters, and knew that Jones did not. They had
clashed frequently over John Wilkes and general warrants. "Bowler in the
House, sirs!" exclaimed Pannell with another laugh. "You are, sir — and I
admit this freely — the only decent bowler on the other team, if you catch
my cricketish drift. But, as you know too well, my team boasts an abun-
dance of superb batsmen. You've worried us something terrible, but not
once come close to the wicket!"

Jones did not close his notebook; his pencil remained poised over a page. "Yes, sir," he answered. "The comparison is quite plain to me. Now, if you would be so gracious as to state the purpose of this intrusion...?"

Pannell shook his head. "Purely a social one, I can assure you, sir." He gestured to the empty chair opposite Jones. "May I?"

Jones grimaced, sighed, and put his notebook aside. "For a moment only, sir." He was curious to hear the reason why the man had sought him out. Pannell removed his cloak and draped it over the back of the chair, which creaked when he sat in it. Jones thought he must weigh close to twenty stone. He remarked, "Surely, Sir Henoch, this place is too plebian for your society."

Pannell shook his head. "Oh, no," he laughed. "I am to be seen in all manner of places — gambling dens, cockpits, bagnios, the studies of great lords, and in the Commons." He turned and bellowed an order of ale to the passing serving girl. "I heard some fellows say that you frequented this place. I came to see what were your preferred societal associations — other than that of your patron."

Jones shrugged. "In past years, I have, at this very table, prepared numerous Crown frustrations, for delivery to the King's Bench."

"No doubt you believe you are preparing another, for the House."

"Perhaps. But I believe that Mr. Grenville is preparing the Crown for an even greater agony, and you are in his chorus." Before Pannell could reply, Jones said, "Now, sir: to your purpose."

Pannell smiled. "I came to offer sympathy."

"Sympathy?" scoffed Jones. "I do not know the dictionary that cites *gloating* as an associative of that sentiment. It is certainly not Dr. Johnson's."

Pannell frowned in mock concern. "Do I appear to gloat? I am sorry you have that impression. I must practice some sorrow. But sympathy I mean. You see, I have just come from Caesar's Head, where I usually partake of something before the House sits, and had a few friendly words with Mr. Abercromby and Mr. Beckford. In point of fact, most of *your* party were there. Mr. Abercromby is tepid on the whole business of Mr. Grenville's tax, while Mr. Beckford is, well, confused. Also, I overheard some talk between Colonel Barré and Sir George Savile there, on the same matter. I do not think they will pursue the constitutional question, for there is a rumor that Mr. Grenville has secured the assurances of an important person that there is no question at all. And I saw Mr. John Sargent of West

Looe and Mr. Richard Jackson of Weymouth — I know that you and your patron have been consorting with those gentlemen — speaking over a breakfast with that fellow from Pennsylvania, Mr. Franklin, who is a Quaker, to tell from his simple but refined garments, and nearly as large as me. They looked earnest, but not very confident."

Jones grimaced again. "And your conclusion, sir?"

Pannell chuckled. "Quite plainly, that Mr. Grenville shall triumph."

The serving girl at that moment returned with Pannell's ale. The man paid her and took a deep draught from the pewter mug. He wiped his mouth with a sleeve and beamed with haughty contentment at Jones.

Jones said, "Perhaps he shall, sir. Perhaps he will get all he seeks. I would even resign myself to his triumph, for I am certain that he will eventually smart from its Pyrrhic flames."

"Flames, sir?" inquired Pannell with a snort, but unsure of Jones's meaning. "Why so?"

Jones finished his own ale, then nodded to the tread wheel near the fireplace. "Humor me, sir, and direct your glance at the turnspit there."

Pannell turned in his chair and obliged. He grunted once, then asked, "What flummery must you lay on me now?"

Jones said, "You will observe how the beast contributes to its own predicament. The drum is turned by each stride it takes, and to keep pace with the rotation, the beast must stride again and again in near perpetuity, acting as both genesis and victim of a momentum which it itself creates. There is harnessed dumbness for you."

One of Pannell's eyebrows rose in question. "Fascinating observation, sir. But what is your point?"

"I am reminded by it of the colonies, and the great mercantile tread wheel they have been turning since the Rump Parliament of Cromwell's time."

"A fair comparison, sir," said Pannell, cocking his head in concession. "And one with which I confess an agreeable affinity." He paused. "Why do you communicate it to me?"

This time Jones smiled. "If you had not intruded upon my meditations, you would have been spared the comparison." He nodded again at the tread wheel. "Well, there, in the person of the turnspit, are the colonies, contributing mightily and without recourse to our country's health, diet, and ease within the machinery of our trade regulations." The turnspit happened to pause at that moment and attempted to scratch an itch. The boy attending the fireplace rose from his stool and rapped the bars of the wheel with his poker. With a pathetic whine, the animal began working again. "And, there you are, sir," said Jones, "in the person of that boy — though you are three times his stone weight, I should hazard — urging them on with laws and acts and taxes. Of course, the boy and the beast are earning their keep — forgive the alliteration, but it is a memorable one, is it not? — while you, sir, produce nothing at all. There's a conundrum to think on, a perfect caricature for some opposition magazine."

Pannell chuckled with uncertainty. "I would fain pretend not to know the scope of your humor, sir."

Jones frowned in agitation, then blurted with contemptuous astonishment, "Upon my word, sir! I cannot decide whether you are a Scapin or a Scaramouche!"

Pannell blinked once at this uncharacteristic outburst. "I do not know these arcane references," he replied airily. With feigned unconcern, he took another draught of his ale.

"*Arcane?* If you read plays, you would know them, and then you would take offense at the one, and pleasure at the other, and have wit enough to compose an appropriate reply." Jones looked thoughtful. "Perhaps you should engage a tutor, sir, an Italian gilly to accompany you on your conversational rounds and prompt you on your literary needs."

Pannell grunted again in disdain. "I have little use for literature, sir. I have done quite well for myself, having read perhaps three books from beginning to end in my entire life."

"Obviously, and quite true…if it is the whole truth," mused Jones. Then he searched his memory, and said with melancholy irony:

"And the same age saw learning fall, and Rome.
With tyranny, then superstition joined,
As that the body, this enslaved the mind;
Much was believed, but little understood,
And to be dull was construed to be good."

Jones noted the confused furl of Pannell's brow. "Mr. Alexander Pope," he explained, expecting some evidence of recognition. But the furl remained.

A glint of anger appeared in Pannell's eyes now. "Sir, you are skirting my censure. Please, do not ascribe motives of tyranny to *me*. I am as ardent a lover of British liberty as the next man."

"That man being Mr. Grenville?" inquired Jones. "Well, I overesti-
mated you, Sir Henoch. You are merely a Verges, helpmate to Constable
Dogberry."

Pannell pounded a fist once on the table. "Confound it, man! Will you
cease this elevated manner of speaking, and speak plainly?"

Jones laughed, and shook his head. "No, sir, I will not. You are a guest
at this table, and the table's rules require educated rumination and repartee.
If you cannot observe those rules, you are free to leave." He leaned closer
to Pannell's reddening face. "Come, sir. Own up! You boast of your dullness. Your like is to be found in both *The Dunciad* and *The Rosciad*!"

"I'll be hanged first before I abide by your rules, Sir Dogmael!" growled
Pannell. "I refuse to speak in acrostics! That manner may be balm for men
of your ilk, but plain, *dull* business demands plain, *dull* language, spoken
by plain, *dull* men like me!"

Jones shrugged and sat back in his chair. "To their everlasting loss.
Well, I can see by your visage that an active, well-stocked mind is but a useless toyshop to you — all baubles and trifles — in which nothing practical
may be purchased." As he reached for a bottle and refilled his glass, he
asked, "And what *is* your business here, sir?"

Pannell snorted once again and replied, "My business is done. You see,
I have some knowledge of the remonstrance that came to the House last
month, and also of the memorial sent to the Lords, from Virginia."

Jones hummed in speculation. "By courtesy of Mr. Abercromby and
Lord Danvers, without doubt."

"You may wish to think that. But both the memorial and remonstrance
are gravely upsetting. The foolish, ignorant people who authored them per-
sist in their attempts to blind Mr. Grenville and the whole House with the
mooncalves of representation and consent and the like. But Mr. Grenville
will have none of that. It is right out as a topic of debate. I came to warn
you, that is all."

Jones shook his head in amusement. "How thoughtful of you. But you
can be refreshingly brief and truthful, when sufficiently stirred," he
remarked. "However, you are neither Speaker nor Chairman, and I shall
speak as I please, no matter how many groans of disapproval fill the House.
Thank you, though, for your thoughtfulness."

Pannell took a last draught from his mug, then rose and put on his cloak.
"Suit yourself, sir." He took out a watch and consulted it. "It is nearly time.
And I believe I have taken up enough of your own," he added with a wicked

smile. With a curt nod, he turned and left.

Jones consulted his own watch, hastily opened his notebook, and scribbled some notes. Then he rose, collected his things, and donned his cloak. With one last glance at the tread wheel, he left the Purgatory Tavern for the House of Commons.

Of course, he knew exactly what the remonstrance from the House of Burgesses said; both he and Garnet Kenrick had received copies of it from Hugh Kenrick, who was now a member of that body. He had also sent transcriptions of the memorial to Lords and the address to the king. It pleased Jones that the young man had decided to enter politics; they shared the same passions and their correspondence had doubled. As Jones had sent Hugh Kenrick transcriptions of his own and other members' speeches, Hugh had reciprocated by sending one of his maiden speech, together with an insightful synopsis of the deliberations of the burgesses on the documents.

The remonstrance, Jones was certain, was not likely to be acknowledged by the Commons, nor even be allowed to be introduced by sympathetic members in Committee; the rules conveniently forbade it. Mr. Grenville had seen to that. Lords in all likelihood would emulate the Commons by the same rule and ignore the memorial. And His Majesty would not know what to think of the Virginians' address, not unless the Privy Council advised him what to think.

"What? What?" mused Jones out loud as he entered the House lobby, mimicking in derisive amusement the king's well-known habitual style of soliciting reassurance on a matter, whether it was tea-time, literature, or policy. Although he was deep in thought, he noticed the Serjeant-at-Arms scowling furiously at him as he pronounced the words, and guessed the reason for the man's offended expression. He paused long enough to grin, cup a hand over one ear, shake his head, and remark in passing, "Hearing impediment, sir! I was sure you'd said something!"

Chapter 11: The Committee of Ways and Means

George Grenville, First Lord of the Treasury, Chancellor of the Exchequer, and author-errant of the American Revolution, was the king's first minister because William Pitt was not. His tenure in that office was largely a consequence of the interminable tug-of-war between the king, Lord Bute, the Duke of Newcastle, and Pitt over who should rule the country with whose coterie in the cabinet. Because the differences between the contending parties were acrid and irreconcilable, and because the country needed a first minister, Grenville was a compromise choice. Appointed in April 1763, he enjoyed the king's confidence and support, until these steadily waned, for he attempted to exercise a determination and will in his legislative program that required the character of a Robert Walpole or a Pitt, which he lacked. Also, he forgot that he was a compromise choice, a relatively inoffensive occupant of the nation's highest office after the king. His political career, until now, had been a succession of lucrative, influence-secured appointments in the second echelon of government posts, only one of whose titles was preceded by "first," and dependent on the ambition and fortunes of men more energetic and imaginative than he. George Grenville filled a temporary vacuum of power and was not expected to last as long as he did, which was barely two years. If it had not been for George the Third's animosity for John Wilkes, he would have lasted barely one.

Early in the afternoon of that February 6th, 1765, the Commons resolved itself into a Committee of Ways and Means to hear and debate the particulars of Grenville's long-anticipated stamp tax bill. Formal introduction of the bill in Parliament the previous year had been postponed until now, ostensibly to allow its sponsor to collect information from the colonies on which documents could be taxed, and also to solicit alternatives to the tax from colonial legislatures.

Because no colonial legislature offered any alternative other than the conventional but unsatisfactory requisitions scheme, Grenville and his advisors presumed an implied acceptance of a stamp tax in lieu of a more effective method of defraying the costs of maintaining an army in the colonies, which was the proposed tax's stated purpose. Grenville perceived the requisitions scheme as unsatisfactory and inefficient because it gave those legislatures a measure of autonomy in the ways and means of raising revenue, an action which, too often in the past, they could not or would not perform to the Crown's satisfaction. The independence of these bodies, especially in fiscal matters, was regarded by many critics of the colonies, Grenville among them, as an intolerable abrogation of Parliamentary authority and prerogative. The first minister had followed Lord Mansfield's advice and investigated the language of the royal charters and proprietary grants of the colonies; he saw nothing in them that stipulated exemption from a stamp or any other kind of internal tax, nor anything that expressly insulated the colonies from Parliamentary authority. He had been amused when he heard that Benjamin Franklin had journeyed from Pennsylvania on a variety of errands, among them to protest the stamp tax bill and to petition the Crown to change Pennsylvania from a proprietary to a Crown colony.

The stamp tax bill, however, was not the main business of the Committee, nor even of the Parliamentary session of 1765. Grenville, who had instituted legal action against John Wilkes, and led the campaign to censure and expel him, was still struggling to persuade the House to approve the policy of general warrants, the instruments with which the government had attempted to silence and punish Wilkes. He also saw a crisis looming in the king's periodic spells of madness, and knew that he would become embroiled, as first minister, in the creation and passage of a regency bill that would settle the question of who would act as sovereign in the event the king died or was incapacitated by illness: the Duke of York, the king's younger brother, or his mother, the Princess Dowager, with whom was associated the detested and distrusted Lord Bute. Bute was out of power but still maintained a kind of paternal hold on the king, and still lurked behind the scenes and in the minds of Grenville's friends and enemies. Also pacing in the wings was William Augustus, the Duke of Cumberland and the king's uncle, who was now acting as an unobtrusive figurehead of the opposition. There was Charles Pratt, Lord Justice of the Common Pleas, who had ruled general warrants unconstitutional in direct contradiction to the opinion of Lord Mansfield of the King's Bench and in defiance of the government's need of them. And, of course, there was always Grenville's half-brother, Richard Temple Grenville, Viscount Cobham, the actual leader of the opposition, whose efforts to frustrate him were ceaseless and untiring.

Grenville, one of whose faults was his belief that an absence of tact was a sign of strength, knew that he was certain to incur the king's further displeasure over a regency bill, no matter how deftly he handled it. Also, he thought it unfair and unreasonable of the king to express annoyance with his justifiable complaints, discreetly voiced, that it was the king's favorites, and not his own, who were reaping the choicest places and preferments. These and other minor developments contributed to a growing mutual mistrust and a frosty relationship between king and first minister. Grenville saw a conspiracy to alienate and remove him from the king's sanction, or at least a desire to provoke him to remove himself and resign; George the Third, whose insular mind, public role, and inability to form his own judgment made him insecure and unpredictable, saw a conspiracy by Grenville and his party to control him.

Still, Grenville viewed his stamp tax bill as the vital centerpiece of his administration. He wished to be remembered, come what may, as the minister who saved the nation from insolvency by asserting Parliament's sovereignty over the colonies. To him, passage of his bill, an event of which he was inordinately confident, was not an issue of power versus British liberty. After all, he must have observed, Englishmen paid that same tax and many others in Britain, and still retained their liberties. Liberty and power were demonstrably compatible. So there was no moral, political, or even legal reason why the colonials should not submit to it, too.

* * *

Dogmael Jones took his seat on the benches that faced the Treasury benches across the aisle. Over there he saw Henoch Pannell and his friends sitting almost directly behind Grenville, his secretary Thomas Whately, and most of the bill party. He thought it ironic that he would eventually be called to address that phalanx of implacable, stubborn men; it was his own party that needed his persuasion. He glanced up at the gallery over the Treasury benches, and nodded to Baron Garnet Kenrick and his wife, Effney; they had come up to London at his urging, for he suspected that this first debate in committee would be the key debate. What was said here today would determine what was said in future debates until the bill was either abandoned or presented as a complete bill to be voted on in a regular

House session.

At the other end of the gallery he saw Benjamin Franklin sitting with several other colonial agents. He had met Franklin briefly early in January at John Sargent's house, and startled the famous Pennsylvanian, after they had been introduced, by saying, "I have read your treatise on electricity, esteemed sir. In the coming session, I intend to emulate you with my own daring experiments, by attempting to electrify a somnolent House over the perils to British liberty that threaten us all."

Franklin had smiled and replied, "Thank you, Sir Dogmael. But take care not to burn yourself in the effort. The government here can boast of an over-quantity of electrical fire. It propelled Mr. Wilkes clear across the Channel!"

When the nearly three hundred members had assembled, the House resolved itself into a Committee of the Whole. Speaker John Cust left his thronelike chair on a motion by a member that he do so, and retired to a bench as simply the member for Grantham. A clerk removed the mace from the table in front of the chair and put it underneath. The committee chairman, Thomas Hunter, member for Winchelsea and a member of the Treasury Board, took his seat at the head of that table. A low murmur, as usual, was to be heard in the chamber, together with the restless shifting of cramped bodies on the uncomfortable seats of the benches and the impatient tapping of canes and shoes on the floors.

As these rituals were being observed, Dogmael Jones felt a cold fear creep up in him, the same uneasiness he felt when he first appeared before Sir Bevill Grainger at the beginning of the Pippin trial years ago. He glanced around at his colleagues, many of whom were as determined as he to speak against the resolutions. He wondered, though, if the electrical fire that might burn him would instead come from these men.

When the House of Commons went into committee, the rules of a formal session, governed by the Speaker, were relaxed and governed by the committee chairman, not necessarily the same person. A member who rose to speak could address the whole House, and not just the Chair. He could speak more than once on the same subject, with relatively fewer limitations on his references, and engage others in genuine argument. He could take notes, and read from prepared texts and notes. Sometimes the gallery was cleared of "strangers" if a member objected to their presence, at other times not; in this instance, the galleries on both sides of the House and facing the Chair were nearly filled to capacity. In them were the usual ladies and gentlemen of leisure, but there was today a large contingent of merchants from around the country, many of whom had signed petitions to the House expressing concern for the consequences of a colonial stamp tax.

George Grenville, aged fifty-one and still in possession of the handsomeness of his youth, rose and in a clear voice introduced his preliminary resolutions in a speech that lasted nearly two hours. His address was largely an explication of the necessity of a stamp tax for the colonies and of Parliament's indisputable authority to impose one.

One after another, the first minister demolished every objection he had heard and read against his bill, speaking unhurriedly and without concern. He based Parliament's authority to impose the tax on the Constitution, and on the precedents of several past acts of Parliament, most notably the Revenue Act of the previous year; none of these had been challenged on constitutional grounds, and therefore were presumed by all to be just and proper. He reviewed the costs of the army and navy, and argued that since the increased costs of maintaining those forces were a direct result of policing and protecting the colonies, it was only logical that the colonies "contribute their proper share" of those costs. He assured the House that enforcement and collection of the tax would probably require fewer personnel than did enforcement and collection of the customs duties, chiefly because the tax would be intimately linked to the legality of any document that required a stamp, whether it was a contract, license, or university degree. He took time to address the subject of colonial distinctions between internal and external taxes, and denied that any existed, as far as Parliamentary authority was concerned. He asserted that a close examination of royal colonial charters revealed no clause or hint of colonial exemption from Parliamentary regulation and taxation.

In point of fact, he stressed — casting an insouciant glance up at the gallery and at Benjamin Franklin, whom he had met some days ago during a conference with colonial agents — the proprietary charter of Pennsylvania explicitly mentioned the right of Parliament to impose taxes on and within that particular "plantation." He asked the House what might happen in England if every county had leave to make distinctions and claims similar to those made by the colonies. He averred that non-representation was not a valid claim to exemption from Parliament's authority, and so neither was an absence of consent. The colonists, Grenville warned, "had in many instances encroached and claimed powers and privileges inconsistent with their situation as colonies. If they were not subject to this burden of tax, then America is at once a kingdom of itself, and they are not entitled to the privileges of Englishmen."

He ended his speech with the observation that the colonies had not proposed an alternative to the stamp tax, which in itself was an implicit admission of Parliamentary sovereignty, and that the "law is founded on that great maxim, that protection is due from the governor, and support and obedience on the part of the governed."

The first minister then bowed courteously to the Chair, and strode calmly back to his seat on the Treasury bench.

Dogmael Jones grimaced and muttered to himself, "And who, dear sir, will protect us from you, and what privileges might an Englishman's be?"

Thomas Hunter then opened the Committee to debate. Several members on Jones's side rose in unison for recognition. Jones tapped his pencil on a new blank page — his stenographic skills, honed by years as a barrister before the King's Bench, had allowed him to take down all of Grenville's speech — and forced himself to wait.

Hunter acknowledged William Beckford, member for London, who immediately inveighed against Grenville's arguments. "The North Americans," he said, "do not think an internal and external duty the same." He moved that Hunter leave the Chair, so that more information could be had from the colonials on which to base a proper decision, and also because he wanted to delay a vote on the resolutions. Colonel Isaac Barré, member for Chipping Wycombe, seconded the motion, warning the House that "the tax intended is odious to all your colonies and they tremble at it." Thomas Townshend, member for Whitchurch, and one of three Townshend family members in the House (a fourth had recently entered Lords as viscount), spoke against the stamp tax resolutions, as did Sir William Meredith, member for Liverpool, who pointed out that passage of such a bill would obviate all the colonial assemblies and in effect abolish them.

"There's a fly fellow," remarked Grenville in a low voice to Whately. "I had not expected anyone to think that far ahead of the matter."

Whately nodded and shrugged. "I am afraid, sir, that we shall hear much brilliant novelty today."

Frederick "Lord" North, member for Banbury and Lord of the Treasury, rose to emphasize that no colony had entered a specific objection to the proposed tax, while Robert Nugent, member for Bristol, said that no one, neither colonial nor member of the House, had contested the principle behind the tax. Charles Garth, member for Devizes and agent for South

Carolina and Georgia, secured a promise from Grenville that colonial petitions against the tax could be submitted after passage of the act, as petitions against any proposed tax in the Commons were not permitted. Charles Townshend, member for Harwich and current president of the Board of Trade, rose to endorse without reservation both the tax and Grenville's reasoning for it, and referred with mock bitterness to the colonies as "planted with so much tenderness, governed with so much affection, and established with so much care and attention, nourished up by our indulgence, and protected by our arms. And now they begrudge us the pittance we ask from them to help relieve us of a heavy burden! Well, sirs, I am certain that every parent has experienced the same dearth of gratitude!"

Much of the House chuckled at this deprecatory delivery. Dogmael Jones winced in contempt at the laughter. George Grenville smiled blandly. Thomas Townshend, nephew of that speaker, pursed his lips in hard thought for a reply. But even before the president of the Board of Trade could resume his seat, the towering, massive figure of Colonel Barré shot up in anger and began speaking before Chairman Hunter could recognize him. Hunter's first instinct was to motion him down, but the wild look in the man's eyes, the fierceness of his words, and the musket ball that was still lodged in one of his cheeks, both frightened and fascinated him.

"They planted by *your* care?" bellowed the man who was at General Wolfe's side when he died at Quebec. "No! Your oppressions planted them in America! They fled from *your* tyranny to a then uncultivated and inhospitable country....They nourished by *your* indulgence? They grew up by your neglect of them! And as soon as you began to care about them, that care was exercised in sending persons to rule over them, sent to spy out their liberty, to misrepresent their actions and to prey upon them, men whose behavior on many occasions has caused the blood of those sons of liberty to recoil within them!....They protected by *your* arms? They have nobly taken up arms in your defense, have exerted a valor amidst their constant and laborious industry for the defense of a country whose frontier and interior parts have yielded all its little savings to your emolument....Remember I this day told you so, that spirit of freedom which actuated these people at first will accompany them still....However superior to me in general knowledge and experience the reputable body of this House may be, yet I claim to know more of America than most of you, having seen and been conversant in that country. The people I believe are as truly loyal as any subjects the king has, but a people jealous of their liberties and who will vindicate them if ever they should be violated...."

When Barré sat down again, the House was quiet for a long moment, so quiet that the ticking of the clock above the Speaker's empty chair could be heard in the chamber's farthest corner. For some members, it was the quiet of shame; for others, the quiet of petulance when a truth could not be denied or hidden; for many, the quiet of dumb astonishment or admiring awe. Colonel Barré sat and stared into space with the quiet dignity of a man who had spoken his piece. Charles Townshend sat speechless and mortified. Other members on the Treasury bench cast sly glances at the first minister. George Grenville merely crossed his legs in an attitude of waiting, and observed the tip of his shoe as it tapped patiently in the air.

Dogmael Jones, member for Swansditch, put aside his prepared remarks and rose in this silence. Chairman Hunter frowned, eyed him warily, and nodded. He was of the pro-bill party, was keenly aware of Jones's power of oratory, and did not savor what was likely to be said by the man.

Jones first looked at Colonel Barré and tipped his hat. "I commend my valued colleague, the member for Chipping Wycombe, for his brave and heartfelt words. They will be remembered, when my own and others' are not." He paused and swept the opposing benches with his eyes. "The maxim with which the honorable minister concluded his address may have been appropriate and enough for our ancestors, in a distant time when kings were true kings, barons true barons, commoners the dross and drudge of the realm, and when all were ignorant of a larger canvas of things. In point of fact, that maxim applied exclusively to kings and barons; commoners were never a party to its formulation, limited as they were by law and custom to merely support and obedience, a lesson harshly taught them on numerous occasions.

"But much progress has been made since those ancient and brutal times, and things seen but dimly then are clearly perceived in these. It is neither appropriate nor enough for us to pursue a policy or pass an act founded on that maxim; to attempt it would be a call for a return to dullness and ignorance. After all, the man whose genius ended our dependency on that maxim was Mr. John Locke, and I very much doubt that any of us here today could credibly dispute him in the most carefully prepared disquisition. And while this nation may have so corrupted and compromised his clarity on the issue of rights versus power — or perhaps even repudiated it — we all here today should be mindful that the colonials — those 'sons of liberty,' as they were just now so trenchantly knighted by my esteemed colleague — take Mr. Locke very seriously. The conflict which the honorable minister labored at the beginning to deny exists, is not so much a political one as a philosophic one, and I feel it my duty to inform the honorable minister and his party that *Nature* is, and will continue to be, on the side of the Americans." Then he paraphrased something he had heard in the Turk's Inn during Hugh Kenrick's visit. "Nature will rise up and either overturn a corrupt system or abandon it in a vindication of natural right.

"I had planned, on the opportunity to speak, to review the honorable minister's record as evidence of his hostility to British liberty, by citing, among so many instances, his purchase of the Isle of Man in order to extinguish the smuggling trade there — a trade born and sustained under the aegis of taxation — his efforts to more efficiently collect land and salt taxes, his frustrated attempts to conquer Jersey and Guernsey, and most especially his campaign against publishers and printers in this very metropolis who evade the same stamp tax.

"But his address was evidence enough of that hostility. The purpose of his proposed tax, he says, is to help defray the costs of maintaining an army in North America and a navy in its waters. Consequently, that part of the Crown budget would be reserved for its usual outlays. The budget, of course, rests on revenues, and those are derived from taxes. And for what purpose are all those taxes laid and collected in an ever-mounting debt? Why, to sustain an overbearing, conceited stratum of placeholders, receivers of pensions, and beneficiaries of perpetual gratuities. It is for their sake that these laws and taxes are enacted and enforced — and subsequently flouted and evaded. So much money is diverted to sustain so much *nothing*, when it could go to increasing the tangible prosperity of this nation under the shield of genuine liberty, which I hasten to stress is not to be confused with the shallow, corrupted, mockish husk of it that we boast of now. We should blush in contrition when we are complimented by men abroad, and even compliment ourselves, for that vaunted liberty. The establishment of the sustained and the entitled do not object to prosperity, and they have a mean, grudging regard for liberty, so long as the prosperity guarantees their causeless incomes, so long as liberty does not impinge upon or threaten to deprive them of their lucre. I ask this question, not queried by the honorable minister: Can we expect the colonials to grow in prosperity under the insidious burden he proposes to lay upon them, and can the obdurate stratum of the idle expect to profit from their certain poverty?"

George Grenville sat looking at his shoe, which had grown still. Thomas Whately watched Jones from under his brow, and picked his teeth with the top of a quill. And a low murmur, almost a growl, was heard in the House.

Jones was aware of these things, and spoke on in a raised voice. "I ask this House — or that half of it who deign to attend today — not to rush to oblige the honorable minister until they have devoted some hard thought to this tax. I invite the proponents of these resolutions to set aside some time to ponder the contradictions inherent in their policies, actions, and desires. I likewise invite my colleagues in opposition to consider the folly of their concessions to the honorable minister's principal arguments. If his administration derives any strength at all on this matter, it comes not from his party, but from the fatal confusion of the well-meaning of *our* party, one not dissimilar from that of a thirsty, shipwrecked man who, out of desperation, drinks sea water for want of a purer, uncontaminated elixir."

The men who sat near Jones looked at him with uncomprehending surprise.

"I end here with my own warning, sirs. I do not expect the Americans — for let us refer to the colonials as Americans, and not mistake them, as the honorable minister will not, for Englishmen — I do not expect them to submit to this tax except at the prodding of a bayonet or legislative extortion, and, perhaps, not even then. If you contrive to humble them, you should not expect that they shall long remain in the thralldom of humility, for perhaps we are all mistaken, and they are not Englishmen at all, but the inhabitants of another kingdom." Jones paused long enough to smile pointedly at Grenville, who could not decide whether Jones's expression was one of gratitude or animosity. "Colonel Barré is correct when he warns that the Americans will not surrender their birthright — and I refer to that expounded by Mr. Locke — for a mess of pottage, no matter how much you dulcify the bowl with bounties, rate reductions, and similar bribes for them to remain on their knees. I am confident they will tire of the business and assert their full freedom."

Jones happened to have glanced down at Grenville again at that point, and saw in the man's pinched face an expression of undisguised hate. He had intended to end his speech here, but now added, "In conclusion, I am grateful that a man of subtler persuasion is not at the helm of this matter, for that man may at least depend on the esteem in which the Americans hold him, and thus be able to persuade them to concede and capitulate. But we all know that he would possess the wisdom not to pursue the folly." With a nod to Chairman Hunter, Jones braced his shoulders and sat down.

Chapter 12: The Member for Canovan

The House exploded in a furor of anger. Several members above the Treasury benches rose to reply and were clamoring for recognition by Hunter. Jones looked over at Colonel Barré, whom he found studying him with a smile that seemed to wish it could be happy.

Thomas Whately pleaded with Grenville. "Sir, you *must* reply to that...insult! It is outrageous! Move that his words be taken down!"

Grenville shook his head once. "No, Mr. Whately. I should have to make a motion to censure Barré, too. It was *he* who imputed tyranny, not *that* rascal." He paused for a moment. He could not take his eyes off Jones. "Does Sir Dogmael occupy a place somewhere in the government?"

Whately sighed. "Not to my knowledge, sir," he said. "He was, I believe, offered a vice-lordship in the Admiralty, a year ago, I think, but he spurned the appointment because he said he knew little more about ships than that they either floated or sank, and that this did not qualify him for the post of powder monkey. That is what Sir Fletcher Norton related to me, at least."

"What impertinence!" growled Grenville. "So...he cannot be punished. But perhaps he can be...rewarded. He has a style of speaking....There is a place on the Board of the Green Cloth that has remained vacant...."

"Pitt put him up to that!" exclaimed George Sackville, member for Hythe, to his older brother, Charles, member for East Grimstead and soon to leave the Commons for Lords as the third Duke of Dorset. "Damn his gall!"

"I don't know that they have ever met," remarked Charles. "He has a fine baritone quality, don't you think? He ought to be paired with the bass of that Barré chap on stage at my theater. They should need to learn a little Italian, of course."

"Oh, you and your blasted opera!" fumed George Sackville. "Where's your head, man? There's a fight brewing here!"

Charles Sackville sniffed. "When Father dies, and I go to Lords, you shan't be able to speak to me like that in future...*sir*."

Thomas Whately shook his head at the pandemonium in the House.

Grenville put a hand on his arm. "Sir, it is not my place to speak. I have nothing to defend. But you may answer that fellow. Signal Mr. Hunter. No, wait. He has recognized one of our party." The first minister and his secretary turned their heads and saw members behind them retake their seats, leaving Sir Henoch Pannell, member for Canovan, standing.

Pannell waited until the House had regained its composure, then surveyed the benches on both sides of the aisle, his sight pausing briefly on the attentive face of Dogmael Jones. "I had not planned to speak today, sirs," he began, "but late, offensive words make it my duty to. I commend the honorable minister on so clear a presentation of his bill. I will say at the beginning that I may be relied upon to support his resolutions now before this committee to be discussed, and any amendments to them in future, for such are surely to occur in this contentious House. And I oppose Sir William's motion to postpone a vote on the resolutions. They are a simple, uncomplex matter to be simply disposed of.

"I will say further that the honorable minister's scheme is an ingenious one that will relieve this nation of some of the expense of victory, by obliging our colonies to contribute their equitable — and, may I say, *tardy* — share of that expense, for, as the honorable minister so aptly pointed out, the greatest part of that expense went to the preservation of those colonies, and of their liberties. In brief, I concur with every reason and sentiment offered by the honorable minister that this should be so — but for one or two trifling ones."

Grenville, Whately, and many members on the Treasury side frowned in surprise at this last remark. Pannell was known by them to be almost rabid on the subject of the colonies. Even Dogmael Jones, busy transcribing the speech, paused in his labors at this point.

"The honorable minister contends that if the colonials were not subject to this proposed tax, 'they are not entitled to the privileges of Englishmen.' With all modesty, and with the greatest deference to his experience, and only seeming to agree with the member for Swansditch, may I point out to the House an error in cogitation here? *I* say that the colonials have *never* been Englishmen, for they have *never* been burdened by the proposed tax, which, it is a matter of common knowledge, is simply an extension of the one we pay here, and have paid since the time of Charles the Second. That fact constitutes an onerous kind of *privilege*. And, on that point, I will carry the honorable minister's assertion one step further, and contend that if they wish to be Englishmen, let the colonials submit to this and other taxes, and praise this body and His Majesty for the opportunity. It is *they* who have been negligently privileged" — Pannell threw a smug glance at Colonel Barré here — "all these decades. It is time for them to earn the glorious appellation of Englishmen."

Pannell paused to survey again the expectant faces of his audience. "Allow me, patient sirs, to point out not so much as another error in the honorable minister's assumptions, as an oversight. As I do not regard the colonials — and I mean those on the continent, I do not include our West Indian colleagues here today — as I do not regard those persons as true Englishmen, I say that the colonies ought *not* to be represented in this House, and for two reasons.

"The first is that historians of my acquaintance record that the colonies of ancient Greece and Rome were not represented in the legislatures of their capitals." Pannell's words became more forceful. "They were *administered*, not represented! At times wisely, at other times, not so. That is beside the point. I do not believe that any colonial has been so foolish as to request representation, nor do I believe that the honorable minister has seriously contemplated the notion even in the abstract. Still, the question to ask is: Why should we make precedent and depart from that policy?

"The second reason I must broach at the risk of confounding my first. I wish to offer my shoulder with others in the sad but necessary duty of pallbearer in the funeral of the colonial complaint of taxation without representation in this House. The colonies *are* represented — as the honorable minister explained — even though their populations are not even counted among the one-tenth or one-twentieth of the enfranchised populace of this nation who are directly represented. That is the way the Constitution and custom have arranged matters, and that is that. Now, we hear no similar complaints of non-representation from those towns and regions of this isle that do not send members here. That is because those people *know* they are represented, in spirit, in the abstract, in kind — *virtually*, as that oft-heard word describes their situation. And, they submit with happiness to Parliament's authority. The colonies, however, exist by grace of the Crown and His Majesty and for the benefit of this nation, and I have always questioned the folly of allowing them the leave to determine expenditures and their own methods of allocation and collection. The colonies have of late been especially hard-mouthed over the reins of supervision from this House and the Board of Trade." Pannell paused again to smile in fond memory. "They have not been properly *lunged*, sirs, and they will never be ridden unless a commanding hand takes them under training."

Grenville leaned closer to Whately and whispered into that man's ear, "Zounds! That fellow could blow enough glass to repane all the windows of St. James's Palace — but I do wish I had made some of his points."

Whately replied, "I concede that, too, sir. But thank him for his wind. Economy of oratory is not to be desired on our side. Such storms of words leave less time for rebuttal, and this may be a long sitting."

Grenville nodded in agreement.

"I believe I made a speech," continued Pannell, "on this vexatious colonial matter some time ago — why, at the beginning of the late war! I believe I warned this House, then sitting in a Committee of Supply, that this colonial pestering and posturing over the twin mooncalves of taxation and representation would not abate, would not cease until Parliament scolded its children and banished all discussion of the matter. My remarks were dismissed then, not without good cause, for I had, in the heat of my concerns, digressed from the business then before the committee. I will not belabor the points I made then, but only repeat that if these colonials wish to be represented, let them come *here* and take up residence, so that they may be properly represented! Some of them have done so. There is Mr. Huske," said Pannell, pointing to that member, "born and reared in New Hampshire. And there is Mr. Abercromby, who, although born here, spent so much time in the southern plantations that he acquired a unique but not unpleasant pattern of speech. Now, they are not only represented — they represent!"

Pannell paused to clear his throat. "Have patience with my support, sirs. I come to a close here. Having been curious about the origins of the word that has given us so much pother, I availed myself of the wisdom of some notable wordsmiths — etymologists, I believe they are called — and my consultations allowed me to discover that two possible meanings may be had from the word *colony*. Friends of the resolutions may adopt either meaning with no prejudice to their good sense and regard for truth. The first meaning is indeed ancient, for our word *colony*, coming down to us from the Romans and Greeks without loss of implication, means to *coloniate* with husbandmen and tenants on a property. And, indeed, what are our own colonists, or colonials, but husbandmen and tenants of His Majesty's estates? They must be that, or why do we impose quitrents on them? Keep that fact in mind, sirs, when you think upon the justice of the honorable minister's proposed tax.

"The other meaning can be taken to suggest — and the House will please forgive the indelicate but necessary reference, for there is no other way to talk of it — the route of egress of the *bile* and *waste* of the kingdom, with which these same estates have been notoriously populated and *manured* for so many years. Of course, sirs, I appropriate the first meaning in strictest decorum, while I leave the second to be caricatured in private conversation for deserved levity."

Many members of the House clucked their tongues in disapproval of this last remark, while others chuckled or snickered. Grenville murmured to himself, "Oh! You great billowy hulk, no more of that, if you please! You have done me a service, and I beg of you — end it there!"

Dogmael Jones also muttered to himself. "You, sir, have wrung from me an ounce of pity for Mr. Grenville, for having you as an ally."

"Well, sirs," continued Pannell, "that is the gist of my thoughts. Mr. Townshend there made relevant reference to the ingratitude of distempered children and the grief they bring to their parents. *Our* colonial children are wayward and profligate, and it is time that they were bled so that they may be cured of their outlandish distemper. The honorable minister's tax can but only cure them of it, and then this kingdom and its colonies will again be a happy family." With a nod to Chairman Hunter, the member for Canovan took his seat again.

A sigh of relief on the benches was partly camouflaged by a general murmur of agreement and the restlessness of men who had sat immobile for too long. Crispin Hillier, member for Onyxcombe, was seated next to Pannell. He remarked, "Fine ranting, Sir Henoch, and I am sure that Mr. Grenville is appreciative. But did you need to verge on Billingsgate humor?"

Pannell assumed a look of hurt dignity. "Not all the gentlemen here have heads suited for high-mindedness, Hillier," he replied. "They require something *familiar* to assist them in their occasional ruminations."

After a short recess, several more speeches for and against the resolutions were made that day and into the evening. At eight o'clock, Chairman Hunter conducted a vote on William Beckford's motion to postpone a vote; it was rejected by an overwhelming majority. The fifty-one resolutions, carefully drafted by Thomas Whately, were then each read, voted on, and passed, the last one at ten o'clock.

"Three books, from beginning to end, in your entire life, Sir Henoch?" remarked Dogmael Jones to the member for Canovan as that man passed him in the lobby of the House on his way out.

Pannell was in the company of Mr. Kemp, member for Harbin and a constant card game partner, and Crispin Hillier. They looked as tired and drained as most of the other members who were hurrying out into the night. Pannell paused to face Jones, trying to remember the cause of his question. Jones added, "I cannot imagine why you should want to mislead me on the subject of your reading habits."

"I did not mislead you, sir," replied Pannell with a broad grin. "I have *not* read more than three books from beginning to end in my entire life. That's a fact. I merely neglected to mention that I have *peeked* into many dozens."

"There is much that you neglect to mention."

Pannell shrugged with a chuckle. "Well, that is the art of oratory, is it not? You bandy truths before the House, and I bandy neglect and omission. And tonight we saw whose style of oratory is preferred and effective. Goodnight, sir."

Chapter 13: The Stamp Act

Early in the following evening, Sir Dogmael Jones presented himself at the door of the residence of Charles Lennox, third Duke of Richmond, and asked to see Baron Garnet Kenrick. The Duke's spacious, terraced house overlooked the Thames, not far from Westminster Hall and the House of Commons. The Baron, his wife, and daughter were guests of the Duke's while Parliament was in session. The Kenricks no longer stayed at Windridge Court, a close neighbor of the Duke's residence, for the Baron's brother, the Earl of Danvers, was in residence for the same reason. As Jones threaded his way through a multitude of carriages parked outside and inside the Duke's courtyard, he remembered that his sponsor had mentioned something about a concert being held here this evening. The Baron had come alone to the Commons, but departed before the day was half finished.

Jones was conducted by a servant to the antechamber of a larger room, from which came the sounds of a clavichord. He wrote a note on a slip of paper, and handed it and a copper coin to the servant. The servant went inside the larger room, and closed the door behind him. While he waited, Jones paced back and forth in the richly appointed room almost in time with the music being played. Its soaring, urgent quality seemed to match his mood. Jones did not like the clavichord, but was struck by the melody. He thought it would be glorious if performed by an orchestra.

Minutes later the door was opened by the servant and Garnet Kenrick came in. The servant closed the door on them. The Baron looked expectantly at Jones.

Jones said, "It is done, milord."

The Baron sat down in an armchair. "I see."

Jones remained standing. He was too wrought up to sit. "Mr. Whately reported the resolutions to the House, and the committee have appointed nine persons to draw up a bill. All the Lords of the Treasury, the Secretaries, and the Attorney-General and Solicitor-General — all friendly to the tax. It will receive its first reading in a full House a week from now."

"Well," sighed Garnet Kenrick. "It is done, then."

"Some of the colonial agents plan to compose petitions opposing the bill — Fuller for Jamaica, Montague for Virginia, Jackson for Connecticut, Garth for South Carolina — but they seem to be at a loss over how to compose a protest without offending the House." Jones scoffed. "It cannot be done. In any event, I am sure that Mr. Grenville will dismiss any attempt to introduce petitions into the proceedings. He has that privilege. It is a House rule."

The Baron grimaced. "Rules! Even Admiral Byng was undone by rules! And even *he* was allowed to speak his own eulogy before he was executed! But the colonies may not!"

"I managed to speak with Mr. Franklin today. He is also resigned to passage, and says that he intends to order stamps for his firm in Philadelphia, and recommend to Mr. Grenville a friend there for the post of distributor."

"I did not expect that of him."

"Nor I, milord. But, resignation can, at times, compel a man to do strange, desperate things. He believes that the Americans will grow accustomed to the tax."

Garnet Kenrick studied the barrister for a moment. He said, "My son is an American now, as you well know. He will not grow accustomed to it." He paused. "*I* spoke with his grace earlier this evening, before the concert, and on this very point."

"The Duke?"

"Yes. He ventured the opinion that if the Americans submit to this kind of blacklegging, there would be no end to what they will tolerate in future, which would simply provoke more abuse. He hopes they will do something. He also opined that if there is any chance for a change in conditions and practices here, it must first be exampled by the Americans."

Jones smiled. "I cannot disagree with that opinion, milord."

"Nor can I," chuckled the Baron. "His grace is more radical, or liberal, than you or my son. I own that I cannot disagree with much of what he says."

"I must some time make his acquaintance," mused Jones. The music now was reaching a crescendo. "What is that being played, milord?"

"That? A toccata fugue by the late Mr. Bach. One of his sons is here this evening, and requested that it be performed by the little genius."

"The little genius?"

"That Austrian prodigy, Mr. Jones. Wolfgang Mozart. Only nine years old, yet he performs as though he has played for ninety. Do you know that he can play with a blindfold, and with a keyboard draped, virtually any composition handed him, after only a glance at the notes, and improvise on it? His older sister, Marianna, is here, also, and they sat together and gave us some variations on Mr. Handel. The whole family is here, on tour. They may even come up to Chelsea, close to us, for the father's health, until they return to the Continent."

Jones sighed. "I think I envy the little genius and his family, milord," he remarked. "They must be serenely oblivious to what concerns us."

"I am sure they are," said the Baron. "To hear the Duke tell it, music is the only world they know." The Baron studied his friend again with sympathy. "You probably have not been told this, not even by your colleagues in the House, but I appreciated your speech today, in which you compared the stamp tax to the practice of ransom by the Barbary pirates. In the colonies, one's legal existence and protection may, by this tax, be held hostage by the Crown unless one pays the ransom of submission to it. You called it an insidious, Faustian scheme to purchase one's soul. Very eloquent, sir, and very effective!"

Jones lay his hat, cane, and portfolio on a table, and took an armchair near the Baron. "Thank you, milord. Eloquent? Perhaps. That is for you to judge. Effective? I think not. At times I feel like a musician playing one of those clavichords in the next room for the mob at Tyburn Tree. The crowd is so fat-witted and noisy that I cannot be heard." He shook his head. "Eloquence has not worked here, milord, except to more tightly seal the minds that do not wish to hear the subject of that eloquence. Some form of action may be necessary. Perhaps a simple refusal to pay the tax."

The Baron hummed in doubt. "That, my friend, may invite a call for the bayonet," he remarked. Then he glanced around, and asked in a hushed voice, "Sir Dogmael, are we not discussing *treason* here?"

Jones nodded, unconcerned. "By law, yes. By our principles, no. It is Mr. Grenville and his party who intend treason, under the guise of patriotism and national interest. However, if I made that bare charge in the House, I should be escorted out of the House by the serjeant-at-arms and suffer the fate of Mr. Wilkes." He paused. "I did not tell you this earlier, but an envoy from the Lord High Steward approached me in the Purgatory Tavern this morning, and communicated to me an offer of a place on the Board of the Green Cloth, provided I withdraw my remarks about Mr.

Grenville and the bill, cross the floor, and join his party — or, at least, remain silent. I nearly slapped the fellow for his brazenness, but instead shook my cane at him and routed him from the place."

"Well," said Garnet Kenrick with an ironic smile, "you might have agreed to the offer and profited from it. It would have given you a chance to prepare cases against peers being investigated for capital indiscretions."

Jones shook his head. "It is a number of commoners who deserve that attention, milord. Those men have shut the door to persuasion. They are a whole gang of Mr. Hogarth's idle apprentices, dissolute, arrogant, insensible to reason and practicality —" Abruptly, Jones's expression changed.

The Baron noticed it. "What is it?" he asked.

"I have an idea," said Jones. He rose and began pacing again. "It will not stop passage of the bill, but it will capture the proposed act in all its salient aspects."

"What?"

"A caricature, milord."

The Baron made a disgusted face. "Must we stoop to that?"

Jones shrugged. "It is the last weapon handy, milord. Perhaps it will help men to understand why they should protest, petition, and speak against the bill. Now, Mr. Franklin knows many printers and engravers here, and could recommend someone discreet to do it. It could appear in the *London Weekly Journal*, a magazine friendly to our cause, or, at least, to British liberty. It could be sent to the colonies for edification there."

"What is the caricature?"

Jones, his face now animated with hope and mischief, stopped to describe his idea.

Garnet Kenrick burst out laughing and clapped his hands once. "You may rely on me, Mr. Jones," he said, "to defray the expenses of this venture!" He laughed again. "Mr. Grenville and Sir Henoch have earned the ribaldry. I cannot wait to tell Effney about this!" He paused when they heard the sound of applause come from the concert room. The Baron rose and put a hand on Jones's shoulder. "Well, enough of that kind of genius for the day! Join me in the concert here and listen to another kind! I will introduce you to the Duke and Duchess. Effney and Alice will be delighted to see you again." Then he asked, "But when should this devilment appear?"

Jones looked thoughtful. "Provided it can be done to our satisfaction, soon after the House has passed the bill, but before it goes to Lords. It is a money act, you know, and naturally will carry a *noli me tangere*, which the lords will not contest, of course."

Garnet Kenrick frowned. "Of course not. And no doubt my brother there will think it too lenient."

* * *

George Grenville laid the bill before the House on February 13 for its first formal reading. On the 15th, the opposition rose again to protest it on technical points. One member asked to present a petition from Jamaica, which lamely declared that the subjects of that colony would be unable to pay the stamp tax. As Jones and other members expected him to, Grenville cited the House rule against receiving petitions against proposed taxes. He also corrected Sir William Meredith and said flatly that the bill had been postponed from the last session "to give time for information, not for opposition" from the colonies, as the member for Liverpool had claimed. Other petitions from North America were introduced and similarly rebuffed.

Jones attended every sitting, and spoke when he was recognized, which was fewer and fewer times. He watched with disgust as Grenville and his party slyly led the opposition down the futile path of squabbling over particulars of the bill, thus belaying any further argument over general principles. The pro-bill party won every argument, he knew, because it was consistent and loyal to its own set of principles; it won because the opposition conceded Parliament's sovereignty over and right to tax the colonies. He gave a short speech that criticized the opposition's stance and tactics, calling his colleagues "unprincipled," without meaning to asperse their characters. But many in the opposition were offended by the remark, and refused to consult with him. His attempts to explain his remarks were met with cold silence.

He was ostracized by government and opposition alike, even in the Speaker's Room, where members often retired to talk strategy, to absent themselves from a vote, or simply to rest from the business of the House. Once, Henoch Pannell found him standing alone in the crowded room, and said with loud bluster, "Well, Sir Dogmael, I suppose you regret having left the cloisters of the Inns of Court for politics. Quite a brutal field of conflict, in there on the floor, littered as it is with the casualties of so many worthy causes."

"I have not left the Inns of Court, sir. I am a Templar for liberty, while you are a Tartuffe for tyranny." He saw that Pannell knew he should be offended by the remark, but did not know how much. He added with an icy smile, "That is a reference to deception and hypocrisy, sir. Pray, *peek* you into a book of French plays."

Pannell snorted at the slight. "More table talk rules, sir? Well, I *shall* investigate the reference," he replied. "But pray *you* remember that His Majesty frowns upon dueling!"

"Then you would do well to save us both from his displeasure, and not address me again with such *dullness*."

"As you wish, sir." Pannell turned and walked away to join his friends.

As the member for Canovan had predicted in his past speech, the Stamp Bill was altered in some respects from its original form. The opposition fought for, and was satisfied with winning, the few concessionary crumbs tossed in their direction. These, however, concerned government documents: bounty warrants, proclamations, and Indian land purchase instruments, which were exempted from having to bear the stamps. Grenville also generously agreed to allow Halifax, Nova Scotia, be replaced in the bill by Charleston, Philadelphia, and Boston as sites for the new jury-less vice-admiralty courts.

On February 27, the amended bill received its third and final reading before the House. Members of the pro-bill party and the opposition traded some last-minute exchanges over the vice-admiralty courts and Grenville's "undue haste" in introducing and piloting the bill through the House. Thomas Townshend rose to attack, not the bill, but a recent pamphlet, published by Soame Jenyns, member for Cambridge borough and a member of the Board of Trade. Townshend complained that the pamphlet, titled *The Objections to Taxation of Our American Colonies Considered*, treated the Americans with "levity and insult."

Jones quickly rose after him and was recognized. "Some years ago," he said, "this Mr. Jenyns published a book on the nature and origin of evil. I wonder, though, if he knows the bottom of his special subject, for he has not risen once to question the *moral* foundation of this bill." Jones heard gasps and groans in the House, but went on. "He may claim, together with the honorable minister and his party, that the revenue raised by this tax will remain in the colonies. I say that the distinction is fribblous and without merit. Peter and Paul are, in those colonies, inopportuned host and unwelcome guest respectively, but Peter must be robbed to pay Paul, who is there to ensure that Peter pays. I should like to know the gentleman's thoughts on *that* peculiar ethic."

Soame Jenyns pursed his lips to stop himself from stammering, but did not rise to reply.

Grenville did. He ignored Jones and replied to Thomas Townshend, chastising him for having failed to mention the many published libels and insinuations on the government. After a last reassertion of Parliament's right to tax the colonies, the first minister resumed his seat.

A moment passed, and no one else rose to be recognized by the Chair. The debate was over. Speaker John Cust knew that the House was in near unanimity on the bill; he now had the discretion to forgo a vote and declare the bill passed.

He noticed the first minister and his secretary watching him expectantly. Those men, he knew, held a low opinion of him as a Speaker. Likewise, his younger brother, Peregrine Cust, member for Bishop's Castle and a prosperous government linen contractor, often chided him for not maintaining as strong a rein on the House as had his predecessor, Arthur Onslow. He sensed his brother's contemptuous eyes on him from above the Treasury bench. Cust did not blame any of these men for the low esteem in which they held him.

He was guilty, on many occasions, of having let order in the House lapse into "all the riot and tumult of a Southwark greyhound race, or a cockfight in the bowels of London" (as he had overheard Horace Walpole describe one such occasion). He knew, also, that the first minister wished him to exercise his discretion on the bill so that it would seem a complete victory. But the Speaker felt a little spurt of defiance well up within him, and he resolved, for order's sake, to be fair.

Sir John Cust asked the House if there were any members who intended to vote against the bill, "for if there are not, the House will be spared the commotion of a division, and the tedium of a vote, if all are in accord."

No one rose to answer him. No sound was heard but the ticking of the clock above the Speaker's head. George Grenville happened to glance up at Dogmael Jones across the floor, a smile primed on his lips, ready to greet that man's defeat. But even as he looked, Jones rose with his glance. Whately remarked, "That chap does not know humility!"

Jones addressed the Chair. "The House is *not* in accord, Mr. Speaker. The member for Swansditch will vote *No*." He sat down in the silence. No one looked at him, not even his allies.

The Speaker felt vindicated, almost grateful for the moment, and dryly instructed the clerk of the House journal to record the lone dissent. Then he said, with some relief that this acrimonious matter was finished, "The bill is passed. The chief clerk will prepare copies for the Lords. This House will recess until four of the clock." Cust then left the Chair and retired to the Speaker's Room. He did not agree with that lone dissenter, but this was Parliament, and he had had his say. It was what Arthur Onslow would have done.

As the House rose to file out or congregate on the benches and on the floor to discuss the bill, a furtive, urgent conference took place between George Grenville and Thomas Whately. The secretary abruptly stood up and approached the clerk's table. The chief clerk had left his seat to follow the Speaker on some matter, while the second clerk, his back turned to the table, seemed to be distracted by the presence in the gallery of some pretty ladies above the opposition benches. Whately deftly stepped onto the dais and leaned over the shoulder of the recording clerk, whose quill was poised to enter the dissent.

"Certain influential interests would be pleased if the journal reflected passage of the bill *without* a dissent, my good man," he said in a low voice, almost a whisper, "*and*, there is a vacant clerkship of two hundred pounds per annum, excluding fees, in the office of the Paymaster of the Forces."

The clerk looked across the table into space, and gulped once. He sat frozen, afraid to turn and face the presence hovering near his ear. The voice said, "Stay your pen, sir, and that less fatiguing place is yours." The presence then withdrew, and the clerk heard him step down from the dais.

He watched Whately return to the first minister, who was busy receiving congratulations from pro-bill members. In the course of answering a question, Grenville managed to stare briefly but pointedly over someone's shoulder at the clerk. The clerk blinked in quick thought: What did it matter to him? It was a single vote against how many hundreds, and may as well be a zero. The bill was passed, and no one would look into the journal again. And if anyone did, he could always claim that it had been expunged on some technicality. He had a family of six to support, and debts to pay, and things he coveted. And no one was watching. He bobbed his head once in surreptitious answer, and turned the page of the journal. With shaking hands, he consulted the agenda at his elbow, moistened the nub of his quill on his tongue, and wrote at the top of a blank page the heading for the next business of the House.

Henoch Pannell, awaiting with Crispin Hillier an opportunity to express his pleasure to the first minister on passage of the bill, observed, without himself being observed, this dexterous exercise in malservation, and chuckled quietly in unsurprised wisdom. Hillier looked inquiringly at him. He said to that equally experienced man, with calm but undisguised triumph, "The record will show that he approved the tax."

"Who?" asked Hillier.

"The Templar for liberty," replied Pannell, but he would not elaborate.

Dogmael Jones did not stay long enough to witness the misdemeanor. By the time the clerk had finished inscribing the new heading, he was in the New Palace Yard, stepping into a hackney with Baron Garnet Kenrick.

Chapter 14: The Caricature

It was a quiet, placid morning on March 1 in the breakfast room of Bucklad House, home of Sir Henoch Pannell and Lady Chloe Pumphrett-Pannell, a short walk from Windridge Court, to which place the couple had been invited for a celebration that evening of passage of the stamp bill. Lady Chloe picked a copy of the *London Weekly Journal* from the top of a pile of newspapers and periodicals a servant had just deposited on the table, while Sir Henoch reached for a copy of the *London Gazette*, the government's official register of the news.

Lady Chloe was searching for gossip worthy of her attention; Sir Henoch, for court and foreign news worthy of his. There were going to be many other guests at Windridge Court tonight, and both felt that they must have something else to talk about other than Grenville's victory in the House. Basil Kenrick, the Earl of Danvers, had assured Sir Henoch and his party that passage of the bill in the House of Lords was a certainty; it had been read once in that august chamber, and a committee of lords appointed to examine some of its clauses. The Earl did not think they would alter a comma. The bill was docketed for a vote on March 7 in Lords.

Lady Chloe's glance was drawn almost immediately to a caricature — or a political cartoon — on page three of the *Journal*. She gasped, glanced at her husband across the table, then burst out laughing, startling her mate enough to cause him to spill some of the tea he was about to sip. When he put down the cup and stared unbelievingly at his wife, he saw that she was laughing hysterically, pointing at him with a mocking finger that shook with the rest of her body. "Chloe!" he shouted, "get hold of yourself! What's wrong?" But she did not hear him. Could not hear him.

The Baronet of Marsden, Essex; Surveyor-General of Harwich, Suffolk; Inspector-General of the Custom-Houses of the Cinque Ports; Gentleman of the King's Bedchamber; and, since last year, Teller-General and Cofferer of the King's Closet, a very informative and delicate position — none of which posts required his presence, knowledge, or active interest, but all of which came with handsome salaries, some of which he was obliged to deduct to pay the men who actually performed those duties — was not accustomed to this behavior in his wife, and snatched the *Journal* from her hand as her peals of laughter rang in his ears. As Lady Chloe rocked uncontrollably in her chair, almost losing her wig, Sir Henoch turned to page three, and spotted just as quickly the cause of her hilarity. It was an unsigned caricature, titled at the top, "The Old Britain Tavern; or, the Colonies Tamed."

He saw a representation of himself — although he could not swear it *was* one of *him* — as the center of a busy tableau of figures, sitting almost slumped in a chair, his back to a tavern table, stocky legs thrust out so that the bottom of his shoes were visible. The head of this portly figure lolled to one side, eyes closed in sleep, mouth open, and wig askew. One arm hung over the arm of the chair, and dangling from the fat hand was a half-eaten goose leg. The hand of the other arm held a tipped-over mug whose contents had spilled onto the figure's breeches and the floor. The waistcoat was stained with drink and gravy. Across the full belly of this figure was the label "Preferments."

The table behind this figure was laden with a riot of bottles, dishes, and platters of food. Two other figures, equally portly, whose tricorns were labeled "Pensioners" and "Sinecures," were seated at the table, eating ravenously and none too neatly from their plates. Two small dogs, labeled "Placemen," fought beneath the table over a scrap of meat from a dish that had fallen from the table and broken. The figure of a serving boy, resembling George Grenville, approached the table with another heaping platter of food.

In the background was a fireplace, its mantel inscribed "St. Stephen's Hasty Oven." On the spit were joints of beef, lamb, and swan, labeled "Industry," "Thrift," and "Property." In the fire beneath the meat could be seen the spines of many books, some of which read "John Locke," "Constitution," "Algernon Sidney," and "The North Briton."

To the right of the fireplace was a large tread wheel, whose spokes were conspicuously marked "Stamp Act," "Currency Act," "Navigation Acts," "Hat Act," "Molasses Act," and "Board of Trade." In the tread wheel was a scrawny, almost emaciated man, trotting on his hands and knees to turn the wheel. This figure's torso was labeled "The Colonies."

Beneath the tread wheel sat a last figure on a low stool; the stool was labeled "Treasury," and the face of the figure vaguely resembled that of

Thomas Whately. In one hand it held a poker, ready to discipline the turn-spit; in the other, another book, whose spine read "British Liberty," which it was about to pitch into the fireplace.

The caricature emulated the economy, detail, and force of a Hogarth satire, and anticipated the style and scope of Gillray and Rowlandson, niceties lost on Sir Henoch in his present state of mind

The Baronet of Marsden rose and tossed the *Journal* to the floor, exclaiming, "Damn his eyes!" He knew who was responsible for the cari-cature. "I'll bring suit against him for libel!" He sucked in his belly and straightened his shoulders — the caricature made him self-conscious of his appearance now — and glared at his wife. "Silence, you gormless woman!" he ordered.

Lady Chloe waved her hands in a gesture of helplessness, attempted to control her laughter, produced only a hiccup, but could not stop. She rose and left the room. Her laughter could be heard beyond the door she closed behind her.

Pannell remained standing, a prisoner of conflicting hurt and anger. He felt hurt because, until now, he had not known the depth of contempt in which his wife held him, one that allowed her to indulge in levity at the expense of his hard-won dignity. He was angry because he knew that many of his friends in the Commons and in his social circle would recognize him, or claim to recognize him, in the caricature, and cast subtle looks at him tonight with unexplained chuckles, or make witty, discreet references to his napkin and table habits. Some of these people he could threaten with a scowl; others would be above his reproof — the Earl could be cruelly mer-ciless in his humorless humor — and he would have to endure their jests without the satisfaction of reply.

Most of all, he was angry because the practical in him knew that he was powerless to avenge himself. He knew that the best action was no action at all. The thing was done. Not even Grenville could afford to prosecute the *Journal*'s publisher without drawing attention to himself and to the issue. The man was still smarting from his actions against Wilkes and *The North Briton*.

He was angry, too, because what he most wanted to do was not sue Sir Dogmael Jones, but corner him and beat him to within an inch of his life.

Pannell stooped to retrieve the *Journal*, glanced again at the caricature, and let the newspaper drop from his hand. He wandered about the room in deep thought, and eventually convinced himself that the harm it might

cause would be repaired and forgotten in the press of other ministerial matters, especially the likelihood of a Regency bill.

* * *

"Do you think it will have much effect?" asked Garnet Kenrick the
next day. He and Jones sat over a serving of port at a table in the main
coffee room of the Shakespeare's Head Tavern in Covent Garden. A copy
of the *Journal*, opened to the caricature, lay between them. Outside, the day
was dreary and overcast, but their spirits were light.

"None that we shall see immediately, milord," replied Jones, puffing on
his pipe. He removed it from his mouth and gestured to the room at large.
"In honor of our ancient host: 'How far that little candle throws his beams,
so shines a good deed in a naughty world.'" He saw the Baron frown in the
effort to recollect the line, and added, "Portia, to her lady-in-waiting, Ner-
issa, in *The Merchant of Venice*." He paused to smile. "I passed through the
Royal Exchange this morning, and saw some merchants and traders gathered around one of the cards I had put up there. They were arguing with
some heat about it. That is an effect."

"Well, let us hope that Grenville and his party do not try to snuff out
that candle. It must light up this nation and half a continent."

Jones shrugged. "Even were they successful in the attempt, it is too
late. Yesterday I posted copies of the *Journal* and a hundred copies of the
caricature to your son. He should receive those and transcriptions of all the
principal speeches on the act before this session adjourns."

Jones remained ignorant of the malicious expunction of his dissent
from the House journal. For all the disdain he heaped upon the Commons,
he did not doubt that it abided by its own inviolate rules. His dissent, he
presumed, was a matter of permanent record, and was, in fact, a quantum
of solace for him.

Through Benjamin Franklin, he found an artist working for an
engraver. The caricature went through several renditions until Jones was
satisfied with what was said by it. One thing he dropped from the tableau
was the imputation that Sir Henoch Pannell was among the many members
of the Commons whose vote for approval of Lord Bute's treaty was literally
purchased by Henry Fox, then a member for Dulwich, now Baron Holland
in Lords. It was common knowledge in the House that Pannell and the
others had been bought, but there was no proof. Provided he would con-

vince a judge that the one figure in the caricature was meant to be him, Pannell could have sued Jones and the publisher for libeling his character. Against his wishes, but in obedience to his better judgment, the goose leg dangling from the figure's hand replaced the bulging purse of coin that had been marked "The Treaty of Paris."

"Do you think Sir Henoch could bring action against us for the figure itself?" asked the Baron, leaning over to study the sleeping figure in the picture. "It *is* a remarkable capturing of him."

Jones shook his head. "I am prepared for that. Two score members of the House answer that resemblance, as well as many dozens of gentlemen throughout this metropolis. A magistrate would dismiss Sir Henoch's action in the blink of an eye." He picked up his glass of port and raised it in a toast. "Long live Lady Liberty, milord."

The Baron chuckled and raised his own glass. "Well, I thought you would never ask me to join you in that, sir," he said. He touched Jones's glass, and replied, "Long live Lady Liberty."

* * *

The caricature appeared in a scattering of newspapers and periodicals across the isle, including the *Bristol Post-Boy* and the *Lincoln Ledger*. It may have been seen in the latter by a recently widowed exciseman in the port town of Alford, Lincolnshire, by the name of Thomas Paine, who at that time was struggling with a conflict between his tax-collecting duties and a growing revulsion for his career and the corruption and humility required to pursue it. He was a young man in search of an enlightened ethics, and had dabbled in Methodism and, when he could find the time and money, attended lectures in science and politics. He was not yet ready to disown his native land for a new one. Jones's small "candle," however, may have helped light another in the restless, inquisitive mind of this luckless Englishman, who would, in time and in desperation, forsake his country for a land that was about to become another kingdom.

Chapter 15: The Spy

In the company of others, he addressed his father as "your lordship"; in private, "sir." The latter address was the sole concession to intimacy his father would grant him. His father, in turn, rarely addressed his son by anything but "sir"; he had never deigned to call him "son," had never called him by his Christian name. He had never embraced him, never so much as put a reassuring hand on his shoulder. Nor would he ever. These rules had been imposed on the son and strictly enforced for five years, after he was abruptly brought from the port town of Lyme Regis, Dorset, where he was born and raised, and introduced to his father. He was now thirty years old, finely dressed, exhibited the comportment of a dandy, and passed for a gentleman.

When Baron Garnet Kenrick and Sir Dogmael Jones at length rose and left the Shakespeare's Head Tavern, this gentleman, who sat alone at a table across from them, after a moment also rose and departed. He made no effort to follow the pair, for by their conversation he knew where each was going; the Baron to his bank in the City on business, Sir Dogmael to the Commons. Instead, the gentleman made his way through a light drizzle in the direction of Charing Cross. He spotted an idle hackney on another boulevard, and engaged it to take him to Windridge Court. His day, he knew, was nearly done. He had followed them to Covent Garden after having loitered this morning outside Sir Dogmael's lodgings near the Middle Temple. Jones had taken a hackney to the residence of the Duke of Richmond, where he was joined by the Baron, and together they were driven to the tavern.

At Windridge Court, he informed Alden Curle, the *major domo*, of his business. Curle informed him, somewhat tentatively, that the Earl was preparing to leave for Lords. "He will want to see me," said the visitor. This was more a command than an informative statement, as both men well knew. Curle led the gentleman to the Earl's bedchamber. Basil Kenrick was being dressed by his valet, Claybourne. This man and Curle were subsequently dismissed.

"Well?" asked the Earl. Except for his frock coat, he was nearly dressed. He tightened the belt of his silk lounge robe with a single jerk, and went to a sideboard and poured himself some tea. There was an extra china cup and saucer in the service, but he did not invite his damp caller to avail himself of the warming beverage, nor did he offer to serve it. He sat in an armchair, took a sip of the tea, and glanced expectantly up at the man.

The gentleman removed his hat and tucked it under his arm. He repeated, as near as he could remember, the conversation he had overheard in the Shakespeare's Head Tavern, ending with, "I believe they are responsible for the satire, sir. At least, I believe Sir Dogmael was the one who had it made up and placed in the newspaper and posted about the city. He had been somewhat difficult to observe over the last week, not being in his usual places of custom. Your brother, the Baron, expressed concern about a suit by Sir Henoch over the likeness. Sir Dogmael replied that there are numerous members of the House and citizens of the town who resemble Sir Henoch, and that a magistrate would dismiss a suit. They spoke of the satire as being a candle that must illumine England and North America. Shortly before they left, they made a toast — not to the king. They both said, 'Long live Lady Liberty.'" The gentleman paused. "A noteworthy negligence, sir."

The Earl nodded. "Sir Dogmael said he had sent the satire to my nephew?"

"Yes, sir. I concluded that copies were already enroute to Virginia."

The Earl sipped the last of his tea and put down the cup and saucer on a side table. "I see," he said after a moment of thought. "Well, I have persuaded Sir Henoch to not pursue the matter. He knows that he would simply cause more ridicule than he has already suffered. Mr. Grenville is of the same mind, Mr. Hillier reports. And a suit would cause other consequences, ones far more serious than Sir Henoch's humiliation." The Earl stared into space with his own thoughts for a moment, then glanced at his visitor. "That is all, sir. Thank you for the information. There is some correspondence to be copied into the letter book in the study, and then the day is yours. Send Claybourne back in, if you would."

The gentleman prepared to bow. "Beastly weather, sir," he volunteered. "Is there anything else to be done?"

"Just the letters, Mr. Hunt," replied the Earl.

"Good day to you, sir, and thank you." The gentleman bowed, turned, and left the room, hoping that he had not looked too startled when his father pronounced the pseudonym by which he was known in the house. It happened rarely enough; the gentleman sensed it was his father's way of expressing gratitude and satisfaction. He found and instructed Claybourne, then threaded his way through the mansion to his room, a spacious, richly appointed domicile that was once part of the Baron's quarters. Here he removed his coat, hat and wig, poured himself a glass of Madeira from his own sideboard, and lay down on his bed to rest. He propped the glass atop his chest, put a hand behind his head on the pillow, and pondered, not without some regret mixed with contentment, his past and present.

* * *

His name was Jared Turley. Only he, his father the Earl, and Crispin Hillier knew this, and that he was the illegitimate son of the Earl and Felise Turley, a maidservant in the Danvers household long ago. She had been the object of his father's and grandfather's amorous attentions. Not an infrequent situation among the high- and low-born, he reflected. The grandfather, Guy Kenrick, the 14th Earl of Danvers, had expired in the room of a Weymouth inn in the course of expressing those attentions. Some time following his funeral, the son had expressed his own. She must have been a comely wench, thought Jared Turley, to have aroused the passions of both father and son. Felise Turley, unmarried, continued on in the household until her pregnancy could no longer be concealed. She was subsequently dismissed by the Earl, although his brother, the Baron, persuaded him to confer on her a small income; whether that was motivated by sympathy, or by a desire to purchase conditional silence, Turley could not say. She left Danvers to live with her own brother, a saddler in Lyme Regis.

Jared Turley sometimes regretted not being able to remember what his mother looked like. Two years after his birth, she died of a fever. He was raised by his aunt and uncle, and none too gently. They were garrulous, religious, and often brutal disciplinarians. They continued to receive his mother's "pension" — though they knew not from whom — and used some of it, fortunately for Jared, an unwelcome charge, to send him to a local grammar school. The uncle also felt it his right to apprentice Jared to his trade. When he was seventeen, the aunt died, and when he was twenty, so had the uncle, of exposure during a drinking binge in the middle of a terrible winter storm. Jared found himself in possession of a shop and a trade, neither of which he was particularly fond of. But the saddler's trade was all he knew. He just barely managed to keep the shop afloat. He dabbled in smuggling, and inherited from his uncle a profitable alliance with the local revenue rider for the receipt of American leather; bribing that man cost him less than did the duties. Then, five years after he took over his uncle's shop, Crispin Hillier appeared, swore him to secrecy, divulged his relationship with the Earl, arranged for the sale of his shop and cottage, and took him to Danvers.

He was seduced and put off-guard the moment he stepped inside the great house of the ancient family of the Earls of Danvers. It was only later that he realized that, his shop and home in Lyme Regis having been disposed of, he had no alternative but to agree to the proposition put to him that first day in another, magnificent universe, other than being turned out and reduced to beggary. His father, the Earl, a cold, formal man, that first day in the great house described what was expected of him and the rigors of what he must learn and of what he must become. Then Mr. Hillier bedazzled him with a mental box of rewards for submitting to the Earl's demands: the freedom of the household, and, when in London, of the city; an allowance of £100 per year, exclusive of bonuses, many times more than what was paid the most senior servant in the household; his own quarters in the household; connections and introductions to influential persons; in the future, possibly his own house, free and clear; possibly a seat in the Commons; a sinecure and place in the government. Hillier described a life far better than that of a tradesman, an existence immeasurably superior to the grimy, smelly, sweaty daily labor of beating, cutting, and treating leather for saddles.

Hillier had made the then-cryptic comment, which Jared Turley later knew was a warning: "You have left Lyme Regis for what I hope will not be your Sedgemoor."

Turley heard a fuss somewhere in the house, and presumed that it was the Earl leaving for Lords. That was just as well, he thought, for his father was in the habit of stopping in the study to make certain that things were in order. Turley had his own small desk in a corner of that room, inherited from the Earl's late secretary, and if he had been at it, bent over the task of filling in the letter book, his father would have frowned. His father, he knew, preferred to have things done; he did not like to see them being done.

With all those precious, impossible baubles whirling in his mind, he, the humble and nominally literate saddler, agreed to submit to the Earl's expectations. He was even obliged to sign a contract to that effect. For the next two years, he endured a rigorous, often frustrating regimen of tutors in history, grammar, ciphering, dress, manners, and deportment. He was even taught the art of stenography and the science of bookkeeping. He was trained to be his father's secretary and amanuensis, and later, his retainer, messenger, and legate. In short, his extraordinary factotum. He became his father's human appendage.

There were conditions. From that first day onward, he was to be known, and to refer to himself, as Jared Hunt. Or, simply, "Mr. Hunt." His actual surname was never again to be pronounced by anyone. His relationship to the Earl was to remain secret, even to the Earl's staff. Jared Turley did not mind this condition; he learned early on that his mysterious presence and close association with the Earl and his friends carried more power and commanded more respect and deference among the staff than if they had known his true identity. He was never to communicate with his new uncle, the Baron, or with his family, never to identify himself to them, never to let them know that his father had reclaimed him. There was more secrecy in this arrangement than shame, reflected Jared Turley.

And he accepted the fact that he was reclaimed not from any motive of paternal love or atonement for past indiscretions. He had been brought to Danvers and incorporated into the Earl's routines, he learned later, shortly after the Baron and his family had completed their move to Milgram House near the town. He supposed that the Earl presumed it was wiser to trust "blood" for the position than a complete stranger. It was odd, he thought, to think of the Baron as his uncle; the man was a complete stranger to him, other than what he had learned from his father and by his own observations.

The Earl remained a stranger to him, too, keeping him at arm's length in all their meetings. Turley reciprocated. They had never supped together, never shared tea or a glass of wine, except when another commoner happened to be present, such as Crispin Hillier, or Sir Henoch Pannell, whom, he knew, the Earl regarded as a commoner notwithstanding his title and appointments. Turley did not mind this situation either; for he did not like his father, and he was certain that his father harbored no affection for him. He had, over the years, grown to see the mutual advantage in the distance they maintained between themselves. Turley had no scruples that would prevent him from performing some of the tasks assigned him by his father, and his father had no scruples in assigning him those tasks. A modicum of affection for each other, or even on the part of one of them, would have spoiled the arrangement, and led to its eventual dissolution. This, neither father nor son desired. They remained intimate strangers.

Another condition of Turley's employment was that he was never to commit an action for which he could be arrested. The Earl was firm on this point, having, on that first day in Danvers, lectured him with almost maddened zeal that in the event of arrest, regardless of the offense, his son could expect no assistance from him, and no recognition. He would deny any knowledge or connection with "Mr. Hunt." Turley believed him, and kept his gambling and carousing to a self-conscious, disciplined minimum. He had a weakness for card games, wine, and women. In Lyme Regis, he had built a reputation for those diversions, one in which he reveled — and one which was also known to the Earl. He knew that he himself was the father of at least two bastards in that town.

His initial elation at the great fortune of being in his father's secure employ, however, had dwindled to fear; the butterfly of his astonishment reverted into a crawling caterpillar of caution, and finally into a larva of anxiety. Every day, especially here in London, he observed on the streets the repellent state of men and women of meager means — the near-paupers in their ragged clothes, their practiced desperation, their hollow-eyed, unnatural ages, their perilous, grasping lives — and knew that he could be quickly reduced to their state and consigned to their company for just a single infraction of his father's rule. Later, he tremulously, discreetly enquired of Crispin Hillier the reason why the Earl was adamant on that point. The gentleman had replied, "His lordship had the humiliating occasion to bail out his nephew — your cousin now, I suppose — from the Tower. You will, in time, learn more about your cousin. My advice to you is that you adopt his lordship's view of him. His lordship absolutely refuses to endure again the immolation of his family's standing."

Partner to Jared Turley's fear of being returned to the state from which he had been delivered, was his own repressed humiliation. That, together with the fear, gnawed with little, hardly felt bites at his consciousness. He was moved by them almost as much as by the pleasure he derived from being the Earl's many-talented servant. In that role he was often an anonymous force that called on men in their homes with instructions or news. These men always heeded a visit by "Mr. Hunt," and paid him close attention and courtesy. The humiliation, though, often nagged him more than did the fear. It was the humiliation of a son who understood his value to his father, but who knew also that, apart from his utilitarian value to that man, he did not exist.

A man who is unsure of his own worth, or who, at least, is sure that his worth is greater than what others choose to see in him, rankles at the sight of those who are sure of their own worth, and who are indifferent to his existence. Such a man may develop a bitterly acquired facility for memory — of the indifference, of the many intended and unintended affronts, of the rare, accidental compliments. Turley possessed such a memory.

Turley, being as unscrupulous as the Earl, was willing to perform any service his father required of him. He had no principles, no ethics, no convictions — that is, no convictions other than the one, absorbed by him over his lifetime, and demonstrated repeatedly by those with whom he usually associated, that all life was a vale of corruption, and that one must endeavor to find a profitable, comfortable place in it.

But even corruption needs an ethics, a two-headed creature by which the good for the corrupt can be measured with a commensurate, practical gain; and against its eternal companion, the incorruptible good. Jared Turley did not think of his corruption in these terms, but they were his premises. His remarkable memory and stenographic skills, for example, had allowed him to sit in the gallery of the Commons as a spy, and record, for the Earl's edification and peace of mind, the principal speeches on the pending Stamp Act of all the main speakers.

Once he had finished that task, and transcribed his notes, the Earl read them. The Earl then dictated to his son letters of thanks to Sir Henoch, Mr. Hillier, and others whose seats were in the bloc he controlled. About Sir Dogmael's speeches, the Earl remarked only: "Some day, Mr. Hunt, some *thing* should be done about my brother's lackey. He is too sharp by a guinea. He is almost dangerous."

Turley was sensitive to the ominous suggestion in his father's appraisal of Sir Dogmael Jones. His corruption allowed him merely to note the hint and brace himself for the service of doing "some *thing*" about the man, some day.

Turley was corrupted, not only by fear for his secure employment and station, but by an unexpressed contempt for his social superiors. The contempt was likewise partnered with an envy for their station, privileges, and power. Over the years the force that drove his unfailing and unquestioning service had also been reduced from obedient gratitude to a species of obedient malice. It was like a thick, lush vine that had grown over a marble column, and whose roots ate away the strength and purity of the stone. When he sat in the gallery that overlooked the august space of the Commons, he did not think: "If only my mates in Lyme Regis could see me now!" He did not think of them; they were forgotten. They were below him now, because he lived and moved on a higher plane. He knew that if he were to return to Lyme Regis, he would revel in the envious attention of his former friends, but be offended if one of them slapped him on the back and called him a hale fellow.

So he would never return to Lyme Regis. His former friends there conspired for shillings and pence; he was the envoy of a man who conspired with others for governments and nations. Ergo, he was superior to those ill-clothed, ill-spoken, and ill-bred men. He had been one of them, but that Jared Turley had died, and gone to a temporal heaven. The thought occurred to him that contempt was contagious, and bred its own hierarchy of swaggering disdain. The master despised the servant, the servant his master and the tradesman, the tradesman the pauper, the pauper everyone. It was the natural order of things, he supposed, and he did not reprove himself for having succumbed to the phenomenon.

On that thought, Jared Turley finished his Madeira, put the glass aside, closed his eyes, and took a nap. An hour later he awoke, rose, and pulled the bell-rope near his bed to signal the kitchen for his dinner. While he waited for it to be brought up, he read some newspapers. The Earl required him to have knowledge of affairs in the court, in the city, in the country, in the world. When he had finished his dinner, he went to the Earl's study, sat at his desk, and completed his chore with the letter books.

One letter amused and reassured him, because it was so in character with his superior existence. In a note to Sir Henoch Pannell, the Earl discussed various strategies his bloc in the Commons could employ to defeat the opposition, including a closer cooperation and selective alliance with the king's own bloc, which was considerably larger. Near the end, the Earl remarked:

> "It is hoped that Mr. Pitt's arrant and scathful behavior will keep him out of favor and out of government, should Mr. Grenville injure himself with His Majesty and be compelled to return the seals of office. The minister is certain to offend the king with his justifiable reluctance to clearly name the Princess as Regent; and it is rumored that His Majesty is anxious for a pretext to replace him, and this would serve his purpose. Cumberland, Newcastle, and Rockingham are the likely candidates to follow Mr. Grenville. Mr.

Pitt, though, waits in ambuscade, and if he cannot be prevented from coming out, perhaps he can be lured out with poison. He exerts an influence in your House, even in his absence from it. Many in your House would abandon him, should he don the scarlet and ermine. He may believe he is being rewarded, or even bribed by the king, but the total effect of such an action would be to injure Mr. Pitt and reduce his following. We should hope that, if this event comes about, Mr. Pitt's mind will be too clouded to perceive the danger, or too arrogant and swollen with his own demands to believe that accepting a peerage would make a difference. We should all work amongst our sets to accomplish this end: I shall hint to my colleagues that Mr. Pitt ought to be rewarded; you should persuade Mr. Pitt's loyalists that his acceptance of a peerage would be a disgrace and a betrayal. These insinuations cannot but help to reach, in time, the attention of His Majesty, and perhaps affect the course of his own cautious, terrible deliberations...."

Jared Turley was amused — almost entertained — by the Earl's sly scheme, and reassured because such doings comprised the natural order of things. It gave him a sense of efficacy to play a role in it all. Before he was reclaimed and transformed by the Earl, he had had no political convictions. He still had none, but had since imbibed the Earl's, and became a staunch believer in the status quo.

Done with the letter book, he closed the letters and sealed them with his father's seal. He searched for and found Alden Curle on the terrace that overlooked the Thames. Curle was supervising some servants in the removal of the slush that had accumulated. With him was Horace Dolman, the Earl's steward. He informed Curle that he was taking some letters to the post-office, then going to the Pantheon, and would return some time in the evening, should the Earl ask after him.

Turley and Curle had much in common in their characters, but neither man was eager to cultivate the other's friendship. They remained strangers, too, for both had secrets they did not think it wise to share. Curle was a little afraid of Turley, for Turley was a mystery, a contradiction, and still a stranger to him. Turley was not afraid of Curle, whom he regarded as a sniveling, fawning toady with his own score of scandals to hide.

When Jared Turley left, Curle clucked his tongue and said to Dolman, "There goes a *wicked* man, Mr. Dolman. Overflowing with himself is Mr.

Hunt, I should say. I swear, I don't know what his lordship sees in him."

"Perhaps, himself," mused the steward, who quickly added, once he realized what he had said, "which is not to say that his lordship is himself wicked."

But it was too late. Curle narrowed his eyes and stared at Dolman. "Of course not," he said with mocking reassurance. "You could not have meant *that*."

*　*　*

Jared Turley, alias "Mr. Hunt," caught Sir Henoch Pannell mounting a hackney at the gate of Bucklad House, and handed that man there a letter from the Earl. Pannell was on his way to the Commons, presumed that "Mr. Hunt" had waited for him to emerge, and eyed him suspiciously. "Mr. Hunt" tipped his hat, Sir Henoch nodded in acknowledgement, and the two went their separate ways. Turley engaged a sedan chair at Charing Cross, and was conveyed to the post-office, where he deposited and paid for the rest of the letters. From there he was conveyed to the Turk's Head Tavern in Soho. He smiled in happy contentment that he had not let on to Sir Henoch that he, too, had seen the caricature in the *London Weekly Journal*, and chuckled in instant amusement. That he had managed to conceal his contempt for and envy of the man convinced Turley that he had some power over that corpulent member for Canovan. His success in this ruse reaffirmed his conviction that he was among the right people and a part of the natural order of things.

At the Turk's Head, he ordered port and cold meats, read some other newspapers, and planned the rest of his evening. He felt the need of female companionship, and knew that he would need to seek and perhaps satisfy it beyond the realm of Windridge Court; the Earl was likewise adamant that his son should not entertain himself within the walls of that realm. Although the staff of Windridge Court was at his beck and call, Turley did not trust them enough to honor a conspiracy of silence, should he have ever brought a willing lady back to his quarters. Well, there were plenty of taverns and inns that reserved rooms for just that purpose, and numerous idle ladies who could be persuaded to enter them for the price of a few glasses of brandy.

While he was plotting the course of his evening, Jared Turley heard a man exclaim, on the other side of the partition, that the British government "approached nearest to perfection than anything that experience has ever shown us, or history has related!"

Jared Turley smiled again, and wrung up the impudent courage to stand on his chair and peek over the partition. There he saw a huge, ungainly man holding court over a table of other men. He saw the other men nod or exclaim in agreement. He sat down again, and silently toasted the stranger with his glass of port.

Jared Turley, factotum and servant-without-livery, did not know that the speaker was Samuel Johnson, and that the company was the regular Monday evening meeting of the Literary Club. Indeed, he did not know that such a group of men existed, and that it was a part of the country's intellectual and literary establishment. Had he been aware of such an establishment, he would have assumed that it had little more influence over the course of history than did cricket or boxing, and that it was the diversion of men who talked and wrote. He would have scoffed at the assertion that power such as was practiced by the Earl and by men like Sir Henoch Pannell derived from or was sanctioned by men like Johnson and a host of thinkers who Turley would never discover.

Turley was one of those men who received, without reservation and without judgment, the few scraps of ideas, tossed from the tables of such lights, as happened to come his way. He saw no conflict between the stranger's pronouncement and the tone and content of the Earl's letter to Sir Henoch. He did not think it was possible to draw any conclusion from these phenomena but that, laying the one thing next to the other, this was the natural order of things. The pronouncement, heard and endorsed by a younger man in that company, Edmund Burke, an intellectual who was about to become the private secretary of the man who would succeed George Grenville, was to Turley but a pouncet-box that sat atop a keg of gun powder.

And because he did not think it necessary to project a wider grasp of men, ideas, and their roots than this, Jared Turley could not imagine that such a closure could possibly be the death of him. He could never know that Samuel Johnson would have held him in contempt, should he have contrived to engage that man in conversation, for while the "Great Cham" did not often tolerate disagreement with his pronouncements, neither did he admire servile agreement.

PART II

Chapter 1: The Flambeaux

On March 8th, the House of Lords passed the Stamp Act without amendment or dissent. On the 22nd, George the Third, indisposed with illness, assented by commission the Act, which was to go into effect the following November. Two more acts, passed in May, also received his assent: the American Mutiny or Quartering Act, which required colonial legislatures to provide the army, without charge, with barracks, housing, and necessities; and the American Trade Act, which added more enumerated items to the Revenue Act of 1764, but granted the colonials leave to send iron and lumber as ballast and product to Ireland without duty. George had protested, and pressured George Grenville to revise, a stipulation in the original Quartering Act that soldiers and offices could be billeted in private homes; inns, ordinaries, taverns, and outbuildings such as barns were substituted instead, even though these, too, were private property. George sensed that such a requirement would surely rile his subjects and lead to unpleasantness. But a man who merely senses potential difficulties without further probing the cause of his uneasiness remains essentially blind to their fundamental causes. In this respect, George the Third was no more enlightened than was George Grenville.

The unpleasantness was to be caused by another thing altogether. News of the two additional acts did not reach the colonies until long after that of the Stamp Act. Beginning in April, candles of awareness sprang up in fits and starts in every North American colony, lit by men who acted as *flambeaux*: moral men, thoughtful men, well-read men, selfish men, men anxious about what loomed on the horizons of their lives; men who, like Thomas Paine, were also in search of a reasonable ethic. The *flambeaux* of any liberal society are its thinkers, its intellectuals, men who concern themselves with the causes and character of their civilization. They can transmit the received wisdom of their age, or refine it, or become independent of it and found new schools of thought. They can sustain their society, or call for its prudent alteration, or lead it to tyranny. They can revolt against incipient tyranny, or rebel against it, or acquiesce.

To rebel and to revolt are not synonymous actions. To rebel is to protest a power, campaign to exact certain concessions from it, fail or succeed in the effort, but in the end leave the power intact with greater or reduced legitimacy. To revolt is to throw off that power and replace it with one compatible with one's ends.

The *flambeaux* of the colonies were rebels. They did not wish to overthrow Parliament or abolish the monarchy; they could not conceive of a better polity than the one that existed. When they examined the politics of Spain, France, Germany, and even the Netherlands, they counted themselves fortunate. They merely wished to be left alone to live and prosper under the shield of Britannia. But they were not willing to become slaves. They and the candles they lit were men who were, as Colonel Barré warned insensate and indifferent minds in the Commons, "jealous of their liberties" under that shield, "ready to vindicate them if ever they were violated." Those minds chose not to believe him. But across an ocean the *flambeaux* and the candles joined together to create a conflagration. The brightest and most fiery *flambeau* burned in the Virginia House of Burgesses, spread to the other colonies, and imparted a new color to the flames that roared up in those venues of the empire. The ferocity of the conflagration took both England and its loyalists in the colonies by surprise. Parliament counted on familiar docility in the colonials; the colonials counted on a recognition of injustice and an admission of their appeals to reason. Neither was forthcoming. The result was a test of wills.

George Grenville was dismissed from office in July, long before the Crown felt the heat of the first flames of that conflagration. He fumbled the Regency Bill by contradicting George the Third, whose bloc in the Commons altered the legislation to his own satisfaction and got it passed, much as Grenville had pushed through his Stamp Act. Even before Grenville was dismissed, wrangling had begun over who would be the next first minister. By the time Charles Watson-Wentworth, the second Marquess of Rockingham, was accepted as First Lord of the Treasury to replace Grenville — who went into opposition as the member for Buckingham borough — the Board of Trade, the Privy Council, members of Parliament, merchants, colonial agents, and correspondents were receiving the first reports of trouble in the colonies from colonial governors, Crown officers, colonial merchants, and worried friends. While Rockingham struggled to put together a ministry friendly to all parties, including the king, and to lure

William Pitt out of seclusion and into a place in the government, half a year would pass before Parliament and the government acknowledged that they faced an open and possibly disastrous rebellion.

* * *

"Do you think it will mean war?"

Jack Frake glanced up at Etáin with a bemused, startled smile, wondering what had prompted her question. Then he realized that she had been studying him as he re-read the documents before him on his desk, documents loaned to him by Hugh Kenrick. In the pile were transcripts of speeches made in the Commons, together with notes and observations made by Hugh's friend Dogmael Jones. With the documents were a copy of the Stamp Act in the form of it sent to the House of Lords, and a copy of the caricature.

It was late April. The *Tacitus* had called on Caxton the day before, bringing with it a thick parcel of correspondence for Hugh. He had come this morning to Morland and showed his friend everything in it. Jack and Hugh had talked for hours. Etáin was present for most of Hugh's visit, but did not join in. Hugh left in mid-afternoon, and the day had passed. Jack repaired to his study to complete some plantation business. When he did not come to her for their evening stroll around the house and to the York River's edge — a habit they had established when the evenings were pleasant — she fixed some tea and took it to the study. She recognized the documents on his desk, and, after pouring him a cup from the pot, paused to note the pensive, faraway look on her husband's face.

Jack asked, "Why would you think it could mean war, Etáin?"

"It is the way you looked, just a moment ago."

Jack shook his head. "No, it will not mean war. Heads may be bloodied, and men threatened, and property destroyed." He paused, and he tried to sound reassuring. "War will come, but not for some time. Not for years."

Etáin sat down in a chair opposite the desk. "When other men catch up with you," she said. It was not a question.

Jack smiled. "If you wish to put it that way."

"Then they will look as you just did."

"How did I look?"

"Sad," said Etáin after a moment. "Resigned. Determined."

"Yes," replied Jack. "Then, there will be war."

Etáin pointed to the documents resting between her husband's elbows. "I know what is in those papers, Jack. And I do not understand why it must take so long for other men to see what they mean. You can see it. And Hugh, and Mr. Reisdale, once he reads them. Even Mr. Proudlocks. You have convinced me that it can only end one way. In war."

Jack cocked his head in thought. "The idea has occurred to many of those others, Etáin. However, they do not believe it will be necessary. I *hope* it will not be necessary. Hugh's friend in the Commons, Mr. Jones," he said, tapping one of the pages before him with a finger, "made reference to it. Nature will, in time, persuade them of the necessity. It is a larger conflict than mere politics. Mr. Jones, I believe, understands this. Other men, such as this Colonel Barré, almost understand it."

"Hugh does not think war will be necessary. I heard him tell you so."

"That is because he knows men in England who reason as we do. He believes they can make a difference, that they can persuade Mr. Grenville and his party to recognize a folly, or a contradiction. But, to put it as you do, those same men must also 'catch up.'" Jack smiled, almost happily, and leaned forward to read from another page. "It is a tempting belief. Listen to what Mr. Jones said to them in the Commons, Etáin. It's wonderful. 'For perhaps they are not Englishmen after all, but the inhabitants of another kingdom.'" He shook his head in appreciation. "*That* is something I would like to have been there to hear."

Etáin smiled in return, pleased with the sentiment, pleased that something in the ominous pile of papers could cause her husband to smile. "Mr. Jones, it would seem, has less distance to travel than most."

Jack nodded. "Yes. But that short distance may be the hardest ground for him to travel. And for Hugh. I do not envy them."

"You do not believe, though, that he can make a difference."

"No. Not he alone, nor a regiment of men like him. If he could, then Parliament would not have passed the act at all. This *is* another kingdom," he said. He paused to grin in memory, and to look up at the framed sketches that Hugh had drawn for him, and then down to a pair of volumes on a bookshelf beneath the pictures. "This is *Hyperborea*, Etáin. What was the world of my friend Redmagne's imagination was becoming a reality even while he lived. I wish he and Skelly could be here to witness its birth."

In the candlelight, Etáin saw the wistful, regretful look on her husband's face. It was the first time she had heard him wish for anything. She said, "They *are* here, Jack. *You* are here." She rose and went around the desk. She stood behind him, wrapped her arms around his neck, and rested her cheek on his hair. "They gave me you."

Jack raised a hand and clasped it over one of Etáin's. "I loved those men," he said quietly.

"As you should have," said Etáin. "As you still do, my *north*. They did not die in vain. You are here. You brought their spirit with you, here. It was transported as much as you were. There is no distance to be traveled between you and them." She paused. "Nor between us."

He remembered the day when the *Sparrowhawk* sailed from Falmouth, and he wore an iron collar around his neck, and he stood on the deck, watching England drift away. He gripped Etáin's hand in gratitude and acknowledgment.

They remained like that for a while.

Etáin asked, after a moment, "What are you thinking?"

Jack said, "When I was with Colonel Massie and General Braddock in Pennsylvania, there was a British officer who rode back into that carnage after the army had fled across the river. He was brave, and rode back for a very strange reason. It was not to rescue any of his fellows; that was beyond hope, for they were all dead or dying, or the wounded among them were being dispatched by the Indians by then. He rode back among the looting, scalping, screaming savages, over all the mounds of redcoats, through all the abandoned baggage wagons and artillery, to retrieve a single thing."

"What?"

"His regiment's day book. That was all. And he came back with it, without a scratch."

"That was a brave act. What made you think of that?"

Jack shook his head slightly. "It's a measure of the determination of what may be our future enemies. Of what we may need to face, now, and in the future. And they will want to salvage an empire." He paused, and changed the subject. "Hugh will speak in the House next month. He will give Barret at the *Courier* a copy of the act to publish in the next issue." He picked up the caricature and studied it. "That, and this. Also, he met a man during the last session who plans to run for burgess. He's planning something with that person. He would not tell me what. You heard him. He will not even confide with Mr. Cullis."

"He will speak against the act?"

Jack chuckled. "Most assuredly, he will speak against it. He asked that we be there to hear him and to witness what they have planned together."

"Who is this other man?"

"I know only that he is from Hanover, or Louisa County. Hugh mentioned his name: Patrick Henry. I think he was the one who was mixed up in that parson's suit some years ago." Jack turned, put his hands on Etáin's waist, and sat her on his lap. "In the meantime, I will send for Mr. Reisdale, and Mr. Vishonn, and the others, and make my own speeches. Explain to them in my own words what this act means, and what they must think of doing."

"What must they think of doing?"

"As a beginning, teach our 'mother country' that she needs us more than we need her." Jack paused, then added, "If that lesson is accomplished, the next one will be to enlighten our friends here, to move them to examine more closely those needs, and to spurn them."

Etáin ran a lingering hand over her husband's face. Gone from his eyes now were the sadness and resignation; only the determination remained. She thought that she would like Hugh to make a sketch of Jack's face as it looked now.

Jack was almost oblivious to his wife's loving scrutiny. He said, more to himself than to her, "Even should we successfully defy this act, we would remain captives of the Crown." He reached over again for the caricature and waved it once in the air. "You were right about Mr. Jones, Etáin. He has less distance to travel. He captured our predicament precisely. He *knows*."

Etáin took the caricature from his hand and studied it. "Yes, he did. But who is the sleeping man here?" she asked. "I heard you and Hugh laughing about him."

"He is a mutual enemy of our mutual acquaintance," replied Jack. "That is Henoch Pannell, the man who sent my friends to the gallows. Mr. Jones copied his speech in the Commons, and made some observations about him. He is in service to Hugh's uncle." He chuckled with irony. "It would seem that I am still his captive, too."

"When will you make your own speeches?"

"When Hugh returns. He has gone to Hanover to see his friend there." Jack patted his wife's back. "Well, enough talk about this, Etáin. Let us take our walk to the river."

*　*　*

It had taken him two days to ride to Hanover County, and another half day of following planters' and farmers' direction to find Piney Slash in the lower part of the county. It was pouring rain when he spotted the modest, clapboard cottage that stood among some trees near a muddy road. Smoke rose lazily from the wooden chimney. There were lights shining in the wax windows, and he notice two horses locked into an adjoining stable. A battered but serviceable wagon stood next to it. He must be here, thought Hugh, and not abroad elsewhere in the county. He rode up to the front door, dismounted, and tethered his mount to a post. He removed a pair of saddlebags and a traveling valise, walked up to the door, and knocked on it. The rain clouds had turned the afternoon into an artificial dusk. He was tired and sopping wet. Whether or not this was the home of Patrick Henry, he resolved to pay the occupant for some hospitality, if only to rest and dry himself out in it.

The door opened, and it was Henry who opened it. The man looked startled at first, then recognized him and smiled. "Well, sir, we meet sooner than I had expected." He stood aside and waved an arm. "Welcome, Mr. Kenrick. To what do we owe your call?"

"The Stamp Act," replied Hugh, stepping inside.

* * *

With Dogmael Jones's parcel of documents had come a crate of things from Hugh's father by way of Benjamin Worley. In it were books, new clothes, some household necessities, and three tea chests that contained, not tea, but British money in payment for Meum Hall's tobacco consignments. The money caused Hugh to smile; the documents did not.

He had had no time to sit and savor the books, only enough time to glance longingly through them as he unpacked the crate. Here were volumes on law by Puffendorf, Grotius, and Vattel, recommended by Dogmael Jones; Sir William Pultney's treatise against excise taxes; two volumes of *The Gentleman's Magazine*; Burgess's volumes on modern painters; sixteen volumes by Dossie and Barrow on the arts; eight bound volumes of Addison and Steele's *Spectator*. There was also a set of Richard Steele's *The Ladies' Library*, and new sheet music, which he intended to present to Etáin as anniversary gifts; and an Italian spyglass and books on agriculture, which he intended to present to Jack, for the same occasion.

He tore himself away from these things to reread Jones's correspondence and the Stamp Act. Twin bolts of anger and inspiration shot up his spine and ignited a mind that worked furiously. He drafted Mr. Beecroft, his business agent, and Mr. Spears, his valet and servant, to help him make copies of the act. Together they worked well into the night, and before dawn had produced six copies. One would be sent to Otis Talbot in Philadelphia, accompanied by Jones's caricature. Another would be taken by Spears to Wendel Barret at the Caxton *Courier*. He made a copy of the act for Edgar Cullis, his fellow burgess for the county, and another for Reece Vishonn. Then, without thought of sleep, he assembled all the original documents and took them to Morland Hall and Jack Frake.

When he returned to Meum Hall later that day, he inspected the seed beds of the next tobacco crop, and decided that the shoots would need another week of growth before they were ready to be moved to the fields. He instructed Mr. Settle to begin sowing the corn and oats. Repairs needed to be made to sections of the conduit, the whole of which was stored in a specially built shed; he gave orders to Bristol and Pompey to mend the sections and to reassemble them over the field. He checked on the progress of the brickyard in producing the bricks that had been ordered by a merchant in Richmond, who was planning to build a new warehouse on the James River. He would be away for a month in Williamsburg for the new session and there were many details that needed his supervision and authorization.

"I shall return in three or four days, Spears," he told his valet, who watched his employer hurry about his room, collecting and packing things into his valise.

"The session will have opened by then," said Spears. "I believe that Mr. Cullis is preparing to leave for it."

"Yes, I know. Send a man with a note to him, informing him that I will join him in Williamsburg in a week, and asking him to have his cousin make the same arrangements for my stay there."

"Yes, sir." Spears discreetly noted that his employer still looked strange. There had been something of a look of madness in him yesterday morning, when Mr. Kenrick had dragooned him and Mr. Beecroft into the arduous task of making copies of the Stamp Act. Some of the madness remained, but Spears could not be sure that it was simply exhaustion and lack of sleep. He ventured, "Where are you going, sir?"

"To Hanover, Spears. I shall leave in half an hour. Have a mount ready for me, will you? The bay. She's sturdy."

"Yes, sir." Spears left the room for the stable to see to the saddling of the horse.

Back in his library, Hugh put a copy of the Stamp Act and some of his notes in a tarred, weatherproof pouch. He paused for a moment; he had the odd feeling that he was being watched. He glanced up at his renderings of the Society of the Pippin, and smiled in salute, and with confidence that they would have approved of what he was about to do. His sight rested on the image of Glorious Swain. For some reason, he felt that the journey he was about to embark on was part fulfillment of a promise he had made to that man in a London garret, long ago. It had been a promise to live, and to find certain words that made living possible: *"...You do not know who you are....The name for you has not yet been devised. The answer lies in you, and only you can put it into the right words....You are the future, my friend! And I forbid you to die until you have lived it...."*

He thought: I *have* lived. He remembered everything he had done since that fatal day on the Charing Cross pillory, and everything before it. He felt transported into the cathedral of his own life then, and felt the rapturous pride of a man who knows his own glory. I *have* lived, he addressed the memory, but I have not yet found the words. Words I will speak in the coming Assembly, and perhaps they will bring me closer to the ones your wisdom was certain I should find.

Hugh thought of Jack Frake, and knew that something about the man had prompted the memory of him, too. He thought: Perhaps we have the same task, and have made the same promise. But which of us is the true future?

Chapter 2: The Alliance

Aform of this sense returned to him when he was in the presence of Patrick Henry. After his mount had been stabled and a supper prepared for him by Sarah, Henry's wife, they had talked for a while about mundane things: the dim prospects for a bigger tobacco crop this year; his host's recent sale of the cottage, a ramshackle collection of rooms that had been built over the ashes of the original place, a wedding gift from Henry's father-in-law, and Henry's plans to move his family to Louisa County; about muskets and the best way to bring down game; the poll in Louisa County and Henry's virtually guaranteed election as burgess; Henry's suspicions, shared by Hugh, about the purpose of a loan office proposed by Speaker John Robinson, which they were both certain was intended to be a ruse to disguise some malfeasance and skullduggery; about mutual friends and acquaintances in the region and in Williamsburg.

Hugh mentioned Governor Fauquier and his frequent guest at the Palace and fellow musician, Thomas Jefferson.

"I do not know the Governor," said Henry, "though I am sure that he will come to know me, but not as a friend."

"Mr. Jefferson is not your friend, either," remarked Hugh.

"I am acquainted with Mr. Jefferson. I hope he does not hold an unjustified animus toward me." Henry smiled tentatively. "We met one Christmas holiday, years ago, when he stayed at Captain Dandridge's place on his way to the College. A convivial young man, as I recollect, a gay and promising fellow. But I sat near him on the occasion of your speech, and he did not recognize me. Perhaps the Governor's society has spoiled his memory and manners."

Hugh shrugged. "He felt that you had hurt Reverend Maury, his early teacher, whom he esteems, over the Two-Penny award."

"I see." Henry shrugged in return. "I will not apologize for having injured his or Mr. Maury's feelings. Well, if Mr. Jefferson is honest, he may change his mind, in time. So may the good reverend."

Later, Henry and his guest retired to talk about Hugh's purpose for the visit. In area, the cottage was smaller than Hugh's library. They sat together at a table surrounded by books in Henry's office-study, a small, cramped addition to the place. Hugh could not decide whether the brimming, roughly hewn shelves and the stacks of tomes that rose precariously from the wood floor held up the room or threatened to bring it down. He sat nearest to the fireplace, with a cup of warm port and a dog-eared copy of Trenchard and Gordon's *Cato's Letters*, which he picked from a shelf to read while Henry read the copy of the Stamp Act. As the rain pounded on the shingled roof not far above their heads, his host turned the pages of the document in silence.

Finally, Henry spoke. "To go into effect the first day of November. All Saints' Day." Hugh looked up at his host, and saw that the man's face had taken on a tinge of red. "But saints did not contrive this act, and only dogs would submit to it!"

"That is my estimate," said Hugh.

Henry grunted once, and turned the pages to one in particular. "Young man, I note here in the act that even papers necessary in ecclesiastical courts must be stamped to have any legal force." He leaned forward with narrowed eyes, which seemed to drill his guest in some kind of test. "However, there are no ecclesiastical courts in this or any other colony on these shores. What means that, sir?"

"That the Crown may be contemplating creating an episcopate here. I have heard there is a clamor for it in the northern colonies. And a colonial episcopate would be consistent with the general character of the act."

Henry nodded in agreement and in satisfaction with his guest's answer. He sat back and said, "Which would mean that, aside from imposing the Test Act here and the whole paraphernalia of religious conformity — an event that would not be celebrated by half the good people in these contiguous counties, who are not of the Anglican faith — it would mean that we would also be taxed to support bishops hostile to nonconformists." He pointed an accusing finger at the pile of papers in front of him. "There is more evil in this act than the filching of mere pounds and pence, sir! One must think ahead of the particulars in it to see what is truly intended by it and what it seeks to accomplish."

Hugh closed *Cato's Letters* and pushed it aside. He said eagerly, "Precisely, Mr. Henry. That is why I came. To give you a copy of the act, so that you would have time to think about it, and about what you may say about it in the House." He paused when he saw an inquiring look on his host's face. "You are respected, sir, among the general populace, and even by some members of the House. And you are feared by older members there. What you may have to say about the act will count for something."

"And not what you may say, Mr. Kenrick?"

Hugh shook his head. "No. But I have thought this through. A division of labor is required here. I will speak against the particulars of the act — I and whoever else wishes to ally himself in opposition against it. I can present the facts of this legislation. You may smelt the slag of the particulars into a sword of reason. You have a style I have not."

Henry smiled. "You acquit yourself of vanity, sir, but, all the same, you should not discredit the power of your own words. They played no little role in my own motivation." He paused. "And you have not heard me speak in court. What could you know about my style?"

"You have spoken to me," said Hugh with a grin. "Mr. Addison, falling back on Mr. Locke, wrote a pretty essay in *The Spectator* on the distinction between wit and judgment. It is a rare man who can wed the two virtues, especially in oratory. I size you to be such a man."

Henry chuckled. "Again, I wish there was a good meaning to flattery, and I thank you. But why not you alone? You seem able to wed wit and judgment."

"In the Commons, when members go into opposition, and speak against Crown folly or a minister's policies, they are opposed more to the man than to his policies, and argue for liberty from happenstance, not on settled principle, from convenience, not from conviction. I know some men in that body who are exceptions to that rule, but this is true of most of the members. Here, I am a young man, perhaps the youngest in the Assembly. The same rule is in effect. I would be opposed, or ignored, on that point alone, as I was in the last session, regardless of what I said."

The lawyer shook his head. "Opposed you were, sir, but not ignored. Nor will you be ignored in this next session." He paused. "A 'sword of reason,' you say? Your plan is a good one. But the kind of sword I prefer to wield may frighten men off, men we would want to support what you called a keen and vigorous protest. Swords mean conflict, sir, and having the bottom to use them in a fight."

"In my experience," said Hugh, "even a sword half-drawn from its sheath may frighten off an enemy, and embolden one's nascent allies."

Henry sighed. "This is also true. Allies we will have, Mr. Kenrick. They are not numerous, certainly not as numerous as the ballast in the Assembly, and in this our country of Virginia, and in the other colonies, but you and I and they may make a difference."

"I hope we shall," said Hugh. He nodded to the Stamp Act. "You doubtless have noted the presence of one item in this act, and the absence of some others. The Governor can be fined a thousand pounds, should he not actively enforce the provisions. I am not certain that Governor Fauquier will have either the inclination or the power to perform his prescribed duty."

Henry shrugged. "That will be his choice, risk, and misfortune," he replied.

"And marriage licenses, commissions for justices of the peace, and notes-in-hand were made exempt from having to bear stamps. At least, I did not see them enumerated. I cannot decide whether that was an oversight or intended. Every other legal document and commercial instrument, however, must carry one."

"I noted the omissions, too," said Henry, his broad mouth twisting in irony, "which I would not ascribe to oversight or even generosity. Doubtless *they* were exempted in order to encourage an increase in the number of His Majesty's subjects who can pay the tax, the number of impoverished households that can be dunned for not being able to honor promises to pay their stamped debts, and the number of justices who can marry couples and subsequently oversee the seizure of their property."

The rain had not abated, and the artificial dusk beyond the room's single window grew into a genuine one. Hugh and Henry talked late into the evening, and were interrupted twice: once by a slave who came to report that a waterlogged pine had fallen across a section of worm fencing that divided some of Henry's three hundred acres from his neighbor's land, and once by Sarah Henry, who came in to announce that she and their two young boys were about to retire. When Henry returned from instructing the slave and bidding his wife and sons goodnight, Hugh remarked, "I did not know you owned slaves, sir."

Henry sat down and sipped his glass of port. "I had six, but sold three a while ago, to pay some debts." He scoffed. "I can only wonder why the harpies who prepared this act did not think to devise a special stamp to affix to the persons of every slave and indenture here."

He paused when he saw the inquisitive look on his guest's face. "Ah! I see what you are getting at, sir! Well, the king derives an income from the traffic in these people, and his trade laws oblige us to engage in their commerce." He shrugged. "When we are rid of those laws, then something may be done about ridding ourselves of the institution and our dependency on it. Esteem me as much as you may, young man, but I have not an answer for what may be done, and so in turn acquit myself of the vanity of omniscience. One must first have secured one's own liberty to know how to secure that of another who may be in a worse fettle. For the moment, that is beyond the pale of my abilities."

Hugh conceded the truth of Henry's statements, and told him about his arrangement with Novus Easley, the Quaker merchant in Philadelphia.

Henry thought about it for a moment, then said, "Truly an ingenious ploy, sir. I commend you for it and for your devotion. But are there so many Quakers who could be persuaded to emulate your friend? I do not begrudge those people, but I have observed that their principles oft-times are only as deep as their purses. And if there were so many of them who were amenable to the ploy, I fear it would cause more commotion in these parts than this Stamp Act is likely to." He shook his head. "No, sir. First things first."

Close to midnight, when the only drops falling on the roof above were those driven by wind from rain-soaked trees, Henry yawned and stretched. "*Vae victis!*" he exclaimed. "Down with the defeated! You, sir, look as tired as I feel! If you intend to leave so early on the morrow, you must sleep. I have no better amenity to offer than my hunter's roll. You may sleep here by the fire. Sarah will fix us some breakfast."

Hugh slept soundly on the floor that night. His last conscious thought was that he was right to have journeyed here. The last thing he saw, before his eyes closed, was the flickering light from the fireplace dancing on the spines of hundreds of books, from which his host had drawn so much wisdom.

Hugh awoke the next morning refreshed and invigorated. Over a breakfast of bacon, eggs, and coffee, Henry and he traded anecdotes from their lives. Henry also assured Hugh that he would find other burgesses who would endorse a protest against the Stamp Act.

Outside, the morning was sunny and the air was filled with the sounds of chirping birds, and from the rear of Henry's cottage came the sounds of chickens and other livestock. Hugh stood next to his resaddled mount, preparing to say farewell until he and Henry met again in Williamsburg. "Thank you for your hospitality, Mr. Henry," he said. "I did not doubt the reception I found here. Still, I feel compelled to quote Mr. Sidney. 'It is not necessary to light a candle in the sun.'"

Henry laughed in acknowledgment of the compliment, but then a sober look altered his expression. He said, "Speaking of Algernon Sidney....Well, I must confess that what must be done in some measure affrights me. What must be said — and I *will* find the words, after some digging, sir, to smelt your facts into a sword of reason — what must be said could very well lead to our choice to example that brave man, when Cromwell forcibly usurped the Commons, and Sidney refused to leave it and was obliged to be escorted from that chamber by military men. Can that be the fate of our own Assembly, sir? Will the king's men some day put hands on our own shoulders?"

Hugh studied the worried look on his host's face. He said, "Only after they have knocked the sword from my hand, sir." He turned, gripped the pommel of his saddle, put a boot into the stirrup, and thrust himself up onto his mount.

"Fine words, sir, and I know they are not mere bravado. Well, even Cromwell may have his use in this matter." Henry smiled up at Hugh and offered his hand. "God speed, Mr. Kenrick. I thank you for the intelligence." Their hands shook, but Henry did not let go of Hugh's. "And I quote Mr. Sidney here, too: 'This hand, unfriendly to tyrants, seeks with the sword placid repose under liberty.'" Only then did he release Hugh from his grip.

Hugh doffed his hat, waved once to Sarah Henry and the two boys who stood at the door watching, and said, "*Adieu*, Mr. Henry." He reined the horse around in the direction of the many roads back to Caxton.

Chapter 3: The Caucus

"It little matters to me, gentlemen, as it should matter little to you, whether this act is a consequence of premeditated policy, or of divers coincidences. It is driven by a logic of expediency and presumption, and the result will be the same — the beginning of our enslavement by the Crown. Should we submit to this act without protest, we would eventually be reduced to the state and condition of most Englishmen. We would witness the gradual re-creation here of the corrupt and corrupting circumstances from which our forbearers fled, the same circumstances that sent me here."

John Proudlocks was oblivious to the disapproving looks of many of the other men in the library of Reece Vishonn at Enderly. At the moment, most of those men were oblivious to his presence. He had accompanied Jack Frake, his employer and friend, at the latter's invitation, when he and Hugh Kenrick, just returned from a mysterious journey to Hanover, rode to Enderly to meet with Caxton's leading planters and merchants.

Reece Vishonn had called the meeting, at Jack Frake's suggestion. Ralph Cullis and his son, Edgar, who had delayed his departure for Williamsburg at Vishonn's request, were here, as were Ira Granby, Henry Otway and his son, Morris, Sheriff Cabal Tippet, Wendel Barret of the *Courier*, Thomas Reisdale, Lucas Rittles, Vishonn's son, James, and many of the farmers, smaller planters, and tradesmen from in and around the town. These men had been notified by Vishonn that an important meeting was to be held to discuss the meaning and effect of a law presumed to have been passed by Parliament. When Jack arrived, he asked his host what he planned to say.

The planter countered, "Me, sir? I am *speechless*! Each time I read the document Mr. Kenrick was kind enough to send me, I sputter and babble like a newborn babe! I cannot fathom its carelessness! But you have apparently given the matter much cool thought. Say what you believe must be said."

Jack nodded, and glanced inside Vishonn's library, which was noisy with the talk of two dozen men. He saw two persons he did not think should be there: Arthur Stannard, the British tobacco agent, and Reverend Albert Acland. He asked his host why they were present.

Vishonn shook his head. "They came with some of the other guests, Mr. Frake, and I could not gracefully turn them away. I do business with Mr. Stannard, and Reverend Acland is my pastor."

"No matter," remarked Jack.

They stood in the vestibule directly outside the library. Vishonn glanced at Hugh. "Mr. Kenrick, I know that you sent Mr. Barret a copy of the act as it was passed by the Commons, with the intention that he should print it in the next *Courier*. In the name of caution, I have requested that he refrain from printing it, except for an item written by him on the act's likely, but only rumored passage by both Houses. And then, it cannot become law until His Majesty signs it, and God knows how long that may take him."

Proudlocks said, "The king will put his mark on this law, Mr. Vishonn, as the King-in-Parliament." He stood behind Jack with Hugh.

Vishonn seemed to notice Proudlocks for the first time. He frowned, and his first impulse was to ask this Indian, "What would *you* know about such things?" But he had heard that this tenant of Jack Frake's read books from both his employer's and Hugh Kenrick's collections. The bronze-hued man contradicted everything he knew about Indians and gentlemen. Proudlocks stood there, in his frock coat, breeches, stockings, and moccasins, hat in hand, waiting politely for a polite answer. "Why are you so certain of that...sir?"

Proudlocks spoke with an assurance that was not to be challenged. "How can he be a king without obedient subjects? He expects them to obey, good law or bad law. If his subjects do not obey, or obey only laws they think are just, then they are not his subjects, and he is not their king, unless he must make himself their king by doing violence."

Vishonn merely blinked at this answer, and glanced inquiringly at Jack Frake. The latter repressed a grin and said, "John's reasoning would be mine, sir." He nodded to the library. "May we go in?"

Vishonn waved a hand, and Jack and Proudlocks went inside. Hugh Kenrick did grin, and as he passed his host, patted him on the shoulder and quipped, "Blink, blink! It's such a chore to think!"

"Excuse me, sir?"

"That is the Bilbury Lament, sir," replied Hugh. "Some day I shall complete the full verse, and Mr. Barret will print it, but not before His Majesty gives his assent to the law."

Hugh followed his friends into the library, leaving the host standing with an even more perplexed look. Vishonn sighed, gathered up his dignity, and followed.

It was Jack Frake who had spoken at length on the consequences of servile, passive submission to the Stamp Act, after Reece Vishonn had introduced him and Hugh Kenrick to his guests as men who had advance news of the act. "I am persuaded," said Vishonn, "after having read the particulars of this act, that our prerogatives as a self-governing colony are being abridged. Mr. Cullis there," he added, indicating the burgess who stood with his father, "agrees with me that this is the case, for he has read a copy of the act, which I hasten to add is not yet official news."

Wendel Barret said to the gathering, "The act may not reach Virginia until long after the next session has adjourned. The Governor will have the full act published in the *Gazette* in Williamsburg, which may not be until the middle of the summer. I will, however, pen a digest of the law as we know it here."

But when Jack Frake spoke, Proudlocks, standing at the side of the stately room, observed changes in the mien of the men who were here. Some of the planters looked uncomfortable; the farmers and tradesmen assumed the look of men who were hearing their characters called into question; Arthur Stannard and Reverend Acland seemed to become rigid with resentment. Jack Frake said, "Mr. Kenrick will speak in protest of this stamp law, as will some other burgesses. He will now read some of the charges you may expect to pay, come November."

Hugh rose from his chair and took out a sheet of paper and read from it. "Gentlemen, here will be some of the costs to us for the privilege of living our lives. Various legal documents, such as declarations, petitions to the court, deeds — three pence. Copies of wills, of libels, of surveyors' warrants, documents needed in any court exercising ecclesiastical jurisdiction — six pence. Original grants, deeds or conveyances of land of more than one hundred acres — two shillings; if of more than two hundred acres — five shillings. Licenses for retailing wine — three pounds, or four, depending on the circumstances of the innkeeper or publican. A university degree — two pounds. Bills of lading, cockets, and clearances — three pence. Playing cards — one shilling. Dice — ten shillings. Attorneys' licenses to practice in our own courts — ten pounds. Well, some of you gentlemen are already in the practice, but what is to say that the Crown will not require you to regularly renew your licenses at the cost of eight, or perhaps of twelve?"

Thomas Reisdale exclaimed, "I would rather allow my license to lapse than pay that extortion!"

"What about bills of exchange?" asked Lucas Rittles.

"And tobacco notes?" asked one of the smaller planters.

"They are not mentioned in the act," said Hugh, "but we may be sure that some busy person will remind the authors of this law of their oversight." He referred to the paper again. "Here are the taxes on our knowledge, gentlemen: On newspapers, stamp taxes of one-half pence, one pence, and two pence. On almanacs, taxes of two, four, and eight pence. These rates are exclusive of the extra costs which printers must pay for the special paper that carries the stamp itself."

A farmer inquired with sarcasm, "Will we be stamped for rising in the morning, or standing in the sun?"

Hugh grinned in irony. "Presumably not, sir, if you can prove a *legal* reason for rising and standing." He brandished the paper over his head. "Depend on it, sirs, there are not many actions you could take under His Majesty's sun without having to purchase stamps. I have read to you only a fraction of the enumerated items cited in the act as it was passed by the Commons."

Some of the men in the room grumbled; others stood in frank astonishment. One small planter asked, "But, sir, where are we to get the money to pay for these stamps?"

Hugh shrugged. "Parliament and His Majesty will count on your diligence, honesty, sense of duty, and hard work to answer that question, sir."

The planter replied with an angry scoffing. Others murmured obscenities.

Arthur Stannard glanced around at the other men, and then spoke. "You make too much of the burden, Mr. Kenrick," he said, and, briefly glancing at Jack Frake, added, "and exaggerate the effects of this act, Mr. Frake. The Crown asks for no more than what is borne by Englishmen at home."

Hugh shook his head. "In many instances, Mr. Stannard, the rates are much higher than those imposed in England. And we are not at home."

Jack rose from his chair. "We have enjoyed more liberty here than Englishmen have known at home, sir," he said to the agent with a hint of anger in his words. "We will not relinquish it. It is a liberty which our English cousins have yet to discover."

"Pish, sir!" snorted Stannard. "That is a nice sentiment, but it hovers near the coast of rebellion, and insults our countrymen in the bargain."

"I can come closer to shore, if you wish, sir."

Reece Vishonn, alarmed at this exchange, rose and spoke. "But the late war, Mr. Frake: Should we not contribute to its cost? It seems only fair."

"If we wish to, and if the General Assembly can find a means of raising the money without burdening us," said Jack, "but not by command to us or to our Assembly."

Ira Granby said, "But, sir, the army is in the west, checking Pontiac and his allies. From what accounts I have read, the war there has been most severe, and the casualties of our troops very high."

"We have paid for the expense of that army many times over, Mr. Granby, and General Gage did not invite us to help combat the menace."

Henry Otway remarked, "But the army will also protect us from French and Spanish designs. That seems to me a legitimate purpose." Some of the other planters nodded in agreement.

Jack shook his head. "The army's first allegiance is to protect Crown claims and interests on this continent, Mr. Otway. And *we* every one of us constitute a part of those claims and interests, for *we* give this continent any value, and the day has come when we ourselves are seen as a threat to Crown interests and claims here as much as may be the French or Spanish."

Hugh remarked. "*Quis custodiet ipso custodies*?" He added, "Who will guard the guardians? Our militia? Should the Crown abrogate the power of our legislature to call up the militia, what force will protect us from Indians, the French, *or* the army? The Constitution? But *that* law, Mr. Otway, has been nullified by *this* one." Again he brandished the paper he had read from.

Reverend Acland looked from Hugh to Jack and back to Hugh. "I smell treasonous resistance to authority being alluded to here, sirs, and wild fears and terror being manufactured over this simple and just act! Mind your tongues, sirs!"

Jack Frake would not speak to the minister, and sat down. Hugh studied Acland thoughtfully for a moment, while all the other men waited for him to reply. Then he exclaimed, "Ah! *Terror*!" He turned to survey the books in the shelves behind him, located one, and pulled it out. He opened it and flipped through its pages. "A sprinkling of wisdom is to be found even in this gentleman's harsh observations, Mr. Acland, and his hostility to liberty is well known." He paused to scan a page. "Ah! Here it is!"

He raised a finger and addressed the gathering. "'If a man by the terror of present death be compelled to do a fact against the law, he is totally

excused, because no law can oblige a man to abandon his own preserva-
tion.'" Hugh snapped the book shut and spoke to Acland. "On that point,
Mr. Hobbes is in agreement with Mr. Locke, who says the same thing in his
Second Treatise, though in many more sympathetic words."

"What work is that?" inquired Acland with a doubting frown.

"*Leviathan,*" replied Hugh, returning the book to its place on the shelf.
"If you wish to express your own hostility to liberty in subtler terms, sir,
then I recommend that you become acquainted with Mr. Hobbes and
versed in his language. But pray get you a copy of his work before you must
pay a stamp on it."

Acland scoffed at the insinuation. "I shall write the Bishop of London
about what is being said and contemplated here!" he said. "*And* their lordships on the Board of Trade!"

Hugh smiled. "You are still free to do so, Reverend, and to write whatever you wish to whomever you please, on *untaxed* parchment."

Jack said, addressing Hugh but throwing a challenging glance at
Acland, "Perhaps you are wrong, Mr. Kenrick. The reverend here is an official of the church, *and* a state functionary, and may in time be exempted
from having to pay *any* stamps at all."

All the other men in the room turned to stare at the minister, and
waited for his reply. Acland's face shot red in anger, and his mouth pursed
to form words he dared not speak, for he was a minister who preached
against profanity. He glanced around at all the expectant faces, then rolled
his shoulders in defiance. "I have heard enough, gentlemen. Good day to
you." He strode out of the room and slammed the library door behind him.

After a moment, Edgar Cullis quipped, "There goes a rancid fellow!"

With a half-chuckle, Reece Vishonn said to Jack, "That man does not
like you, sir."

"Nor I him," answered Jack with unconcern.

Thomas Reisdale shook his head. "I'll wager that he *will* write to the
Bishop of London, and to the Board of Trade, and try to persuade them to
bring a charge of *scandalum magnatum* against the both of you through the
General Court here." He looked from Jack to Hugh. "Perhaps even to try
you both in England."

"*Scandalum what*, Mr. Reisdale?" asked Vishonn.

"Uttering a malicious statement against the Crown or against any
officer or agent of the realm," explained the attorney. "And, in the steelyard
of Crown law, permit me to add, such a charge, argued by a sharp prose-

cutor, could conceivably be weighed into a more serious offense, and be construed as seditious libel."

"He had the insolence to correct our minds and speech, Mr. Reisdale," said Hugh, "and to presume to be our unsolicited shepherd. We shall await the warrant that names the charges against Mr. Frake and me, and solicit your services for our defense against it."

Arthur Stannard volunteered, but with less force than before, "Englishmen know their duties as well as their liberties." But no one replied to his statement.

Henry Otway said, "The king is obliged to protect us from such laws as this one! *He* will see the folly and ruinous effects of the act!"

"Yes," said Ira Granby. "I cannot but agree with that sentiment. The colonies are answerable to His Majesty, not to Parliament! *He* will waive our duty, and encourage our content."

Reece Vishonn rose from his chair. "Now here's talk that makes sense! Enough of Mr. Hobbes and Mr. Locke! I have tried to read those fellows, Mr. Kenrick, but found them a task. What we want, sir, is a politics that will spare us the tiresome, pothering complexities of philosophers!"

Hugh shook his head. "That, sir, is neither possible nor advisable. Not possible, for we are, for better or worse, heirs to their work. Not advisable, for then the encroachments of stamps and bayonets will always seem a mystery to us."

"Perhaps, Mr. Kenrick," said Vishonn. "But Mr. Granby has something there. This act is so careless, I cannot even imagine that the House of Lords will pass it. Surely, *that* House is populated by wiser men."

"That House will not contest the act," countered Hugh, "and those wiser men will not risk contradicting the Commons and instigating a crisis."

"This is true," said Reisdale. "Long ago the Commons wrested the national purse from the Lords, and is as jealous of it as any king."

"What is an ecclesiastical court?" asked one of the smaller planters.

"What would replace our vestrymen," answered Reisdale, "in all matters of faith, good will, and charity."

The debate went on for another few hours, broken at one point by refreshments. Edgar Cullis took the opportunity to stand with Hugh, Jack, and Proudlocks on the spacious, colonnaded porch outside. "I have read the act," he said, "and am aroused by it as much as you, sir. But, what is to be done?"

"Speak against it," said Hugh. "In the House."

Cullis shook his head. "How can that be done?"

"Forcefully." Hugh paused, and added, "Remember what I said about bees and bullies."

"I remember it well. But speaking against this act will only create enemies in the House. The men who composed our protests last December will think those enough, and will want to wait for replies from London."

Jack remarked, "Our enemies are across the ocean, Mr. Cullis."

The burgess turned sharply to face Jack, and stabbed the air with his finger. "Now, there! *That* is the kind of speech that could put us all in trouble, Mr. Frake, with the House *and* with the Crown! Reckless and irresponsible speech!"

"So be it," said Jack calmly.

Hugh said, "Do not count on replies to our protests from London, Mr. Cullis. Our remonstrance to the Commons was not admitted into debate — nor was any other colonial petition, and there were three or four — the memorial to Lords is very likely gathering dust in some velvet-lined drawer, and our address to the king was probably never read by him or to him, some eminences on the Privy Council doubtless judging that it was not worthy of his attention."

"Perhaps not," said Cullis. "And if what you say is true, then it may be taken as a measure of the futility of further protests!"

"The king will put his mark on the law," interjected Proudlocks, "as King-in-Parliament. He will protect himself before he thinks of protecting his colonies or subjects from Parliament. His purse, too, is in the hands of other men."

Cullis looked at Proudlocks with incredulity and disdain. "That is a villainous thing to say about His Majesty!" he exclaimed. He might have said more, and more offensive things, but he knew that the man was Jack's friend, and forced himself to dismiss the subject. "See here, Mr. Kenrick," he said, turning back to Hugh. "Just as Mr. Vishonn cannot imagine Lords obstructing the Commons, *I* cannot imagine our House, even together with the Council, obstructing the will of Parliament." He spread his hands in helplessness. "The Randolphs, Bland, Wythe, Robinson, all the others — they are a power in the House, sir, and loyal to the Crown, whatever its shortcomings and whatever their misgivings about it." He paused. "They would sooner see you hanged, or sent to England in irons for uttering malicious statements — you heard Mr. Reisdale comment on that — than risk crossing blades with Parliament. They know we would lose, forfeit the good will and beneficence of the Crown, and incur punitive actions!"

Jack laughed out loud with bitterness and contempt. "Has *that* not already happened, Mr. Cullis?"

Cullis and Hugh both stared with astonishment at him: Hugh, because he had never before heard his friend laugh that way before; Cullis, because he had never before seen Jack so much as smile, and the laugh that had answered him made him now both fearful and somehow ashamed. Proudlocks, who stood beyond Jack, was also studying his employer with amused curiosity.

Cullis faced Hugh again. "I am not urging you to remain silent, Mr. Kenrick. Egads! Something must be said against this act. *I* might even speak, should the matter arise. What I *am* urging is that, well, you speak in a more…moderate manner, in a less hostile manner." He shook his head in exasperation as he searched for better words. "Chuck them under the chin, if you will, rather than smack them with a boxer's blow."

Hugh laughed. "A wet match never lit a fire, Mr. Cullis. And you worry over-much. When the time comes, I shall merely recite the facts behind and ahead of the act."

Cullis looked uncertain about this reassurance. "Very well, then." He started to turn to go back inside, but stopped. "I have wanted to ask you: Why did you go to Hanover?"

"To deliver a copy of the act to Mr. Henry."

"Oh…But he is not in the House."

"He will be, before session's end," said Hugh.

"And…he plans to speak against the act?"

Hugh smiled. "With thunderbolts, Mr. Cullis."

Cullis scoffed. "Well, then let it be on his own head. I have heard him speak before the committee. There will be consequences." The burgess let curiosity get the best of him. "What will he say?"

"What needs to be said," replied Hugh. "In what words or form, I cannot predict." He paused. "When he arrives, you shall meet him again. I am asking you now to support us."

Cullis merely nodded with reluctance, turned, and strode back inside the mansion.

Chapter 4: The Virginians

Reece Vishonn ended the meeting an hour later, and gave a speech to his guests. "Now that we know something about this Stamp Act, and how each of us feels about it and stands to be hurt by it, I recommend that we wait to see what transpires in this session of the Assembly. By session's end, we should know whether or not this act has indeed become law. Then we may know what to say, or do, depending, of course, on what action the House chooses to take."

Most of the men who came to Enderly alarmed or curious, left late that afternoon subdued, resigned, and despondent. Vishonn shook the hand of each one at the front door, and saw in each man's eyes and bearing both anger and a sense of doom. This was not what he had hoped to achieve by the meeting. He himself was not certain what he sought by gathering these men together, except, perhaps, commiseration. His and their minds seemed to stop at a certain point, unable to imagine what else could be done.

"If the House does nothing," said Henry Otway near the end of the meeting, "then we can do nothing but obey the law as best we can."

There had been no change in Jack Frake's mien. Vishonn said to him as he went out, "Thank you for suggesting that we air our concerns, Mr. Frake. And," he added with humor, "take care riding home. Reverend Acland may be waiting for you in ambush!"

"In that unlikely event," replied Jack with a serious smile, "you and your fellow vestrymen may need to begin searching for a new pastor."

To Hugh Kenrick and Edgar Cullis, Vishonn said, "I would like to be present when this matter comes before the House, sirs. When do you think that might be?"

Cullis sighed. "If at all, toward the end of the session. They will want to put it off until the very end." He chuckled in irony. "Of course, by that time, most of our colleagues may have already left, so that there may not be enough of us left to form a quorum. Then the matter will not be raised at all. I will send you a note."

Hugh said, "Mr. Cullis and I will endeavor to persuade enough members to stay through to the end to ensure a quorum, sir. He advises me, however, that if Mr. Montague has not forwarded the House a copy of the passed act, or if one arrives too late, Mr. Robinson could very well use that as an excuse to prohibit debate on the act, nor even allow it to be proposed as House business."

"And," added Cullis, "Mr. Robinson and some of his friends may be up to other deviltry. There is some truth in the rumor that he and others may attempt to burden this colony with debts of their own, through a loan office."

"I've heard that rumor," said Vishonn. "God's furies, sirs!" he exclaimed. "We are assailed by caitiffs and coiners wherever we turn!"

* * *

Jack, Hugh, and Proudlocks rode back to their homes together. Jack said, shortly after they left Enderly, "Mr. Kenrick, I almost envy you for being a burgess. I almost regret not being able to sit in the House among so many heaps of defeat and despairing decorum."

"Why?" asked Hugh.

"You will have a chance to speak. And when that chance comes, I know you will speak with more force than I heard from you today." He turned in his saddle with a grin for his friend. "By then, you will have stoked a greater fire in your oratory."

Hugh shook his head. "Thank you, sir, but I shall merely lay the firewood, and arrange the kindling, and leave it to a better speaker to light a match to it."

"Your friend, Mr. Henry?"

"Yes," said Hugh. After a moment, he added, "You and he are much alike. I believe he will speak as you perhaps would speak, and so he will speak for you." He paused. "You must meet him when you and Etáin come to Williamsburg."

"I look forward to it."

The two men talked of other things, as a kind of rest from their concerns about the Stamp Act. Jack thanked Hugh again for the anniversary gifts. "I have you to credit for Etáin's inattention. She has been busy transcribing the Italian music you gave her for her harp. I shouldn't complain, though, for I have been buried in the books you gave me. I found in them some interesting ideas on how to reduce the salt I put into the field every time I water them from the river."

Hugh spoke of things reported to him by his father and mother in a letter that had come with the crate of books and clothes. "The Duke of Richmond, now a friend of my father's, may go to Paris as ambassador....A Dutch physician is in London, and published an article on something called variolation, a treatment by which one is given smallpox with a needle, in order to stave off a worse case of it....My father subscribed to Mr. Johnson's edition of Shakespeare's plays, and applauds his preface, in which he credits and defends Shakespeare for having exploded the unities of time and place. Those rules *do* cripple our drama. I must write him for my own copy....An Austrian boy by the name of Mozart seems to have enchanted London. He moved with his family to Chelsea, not a few houses away from my parents and sister. There he composed two symphonies. He is only nine, or ten, my mother writes. My family heard him perform under the Ranelagh rotunda. Quite remarkable...."

Hugh was silent for a while. Jack glanced over and saw that his friend's eyes were closed. He reached over and shook his friend's arm. When Hugh opened his eyes and looked at him, Jack asked, "When was the last time you slept?"

Hugh shook his head once to rid his mind of the drowsiness. "I stopped at an ordinary somewhere between Williamsburg and Richmond, but elected to sleep in its hayloft, where there seemed to be fewer vermin than in the accommodations. They were fewer, but bigger. Not since then. I have not had the time."

"That was two days ago, Hugh," said Jack.

"I suppose."

"When we reach Meum Hall, I shall order Mr. Spears to put you to bed and not disturb you for twenty-four hours. Don't instruct him otherwise, or he will have to answer to me."

"But Jack," Hugh laughed, "you will only confuse the man."

Proudlocks, riding behind them, also laughed. Jack and Hugh turned in their saddles to face him.

"The men at the meeting," said Proudlocks, "they are divided, not among themselves, but...within...themselves. They each have a little man inside, who tells him what is right and what is wrong. The bigger man, the one we see, does not always agree with what his little man tells him. But no matter how much the bigger man ignores him, the little man will be heard."

Hugh and Jack exchanged perplexed glances. Jack waved his tenant forward. "Please, explain that to us, John," he said, "and how it concerns Mr. Kenrick's condition."

Proudlocks urged his mount forward and rode between the two planters. "It is Mr. Adam Smith's idea," he said.

Hugh studied the Indian with surprise and admiration. "You have read Mr. Smith's *Theory of Moral Sentiments*, have you not?" He seemed to recover from his drowsiness, and was fully awake now.

"Your own book, sir," said Proudlocks. "I borrowed it from your library, with Mr. Spears's permission, when you were in Williamsburg at the Assembly last year."

"I see. What did you think of it?"

"It is a difficult book to read. Mr. Smith is a confused man, and he confused me." Proudlocks paused. "You see, when you spoke of confusing Mr. Spears, I thought of the book, and how Mr. Smith would describe the men at the meeting. I have been trying to understand them."

"Well," said Hugh, "there are many instances of wisdom in Mr. Smith's book, but I do not place much confidence in those particular allegations of his. Frankly, I find them preposterous. They are a recasting of the Catholic notion of conscience, and of other such dichotomous doctrines. No such thing exists as an 'inner man' who acts as an 'impartial spectator,' not in any man. Each man is of a piece, he is whole, and he makes himself."

Jack asked, "Are you saying that Mr. Smith fished for trout, but landed an ill-fed croaker?"

"Yes," said Hugh. "I judge his theory to be very little meat dressed on brittle bone."

Proudlocks said, "I did not say I believed what Mr. Smith said in his book. I said that the men at the meeting acted as if they had little men who troubled them. They know what is right, and true, but are…reluctant to heed their own caution."

Hugh sighed. "Such as my colleague, Mr. Cullis," he remarked.

Proudlocks nodded. "Yes. And Mr. Vishonn, and many of the others." He looked at Hugh and Jack. "You and Mr. Kenrick are not so troubled. This I know: Each of you is woven whole, like the finest basket in Mr. Rittles's stores." He paused. "You are not governed by little men. You move yourselves." Proudlocks considered this observation, then added, "I move myself." He chuckled. "It is, as you say, Mr. Kenrick, a…preposterous idea."

Hugh studied the Indian again. "Mr. Proudlocks," he said, looking ahead over his mount's bobbing mane, "should you some day decide to write a book of your own, you will allow me the privilege of subscribing to half of your cost."

Jack said, "And I will cover the other half."

"Perhaps you will decide to pen an answer to Mr. Smith, and incidentally to Mr. Hume, and Mr. Hobbes, and even Plato," speculated Hugh. "Make visible Mr. Smith's 'invisible hand.' Confound Mr. Hume's notion of regular happenstance. Dispose of Mr. Hobbes's fettered, uncouth beasts."

The trio rode west together into the spring dusk, three men from mutually radical backgrounds, but united in friendship by their esteem for themselves and for each other. The earth was good, and it was their own.

* * *

The next morning was a Sunday, and in Stepney Parish Church, Reverend Albert Acland delivered a caustic sermon to his congregation.

"...It is a hard matter for men, who do all think highly of their own wits, when they have acquired the learning of a university, to be persuaded that they lack any ability requisite for the government of a commonwealth, or even of *this* dominion, especially having read the histories of those ancient but pagan popular governments of the Greeks and Romans, among whom government passed in the name of liberty."

Reverend Acland was indeed versed in Thomas Hobbes, though he had not in years thought that the philosopher was a proper source of material for his sermons. When he returned home from the meeting at Enderly, he rummaged through his small library for his own copy of *Leviathan*, found it, and spent the evening discovering that it was a wellspring of material. Today, he borrowed liberally from it without informing his congregation that he was paraphrasing and, at times, plagiarizing the philosopher. The objects of his sermon this morning were Jack Frake and Hugh Kenrick, though most of his congregation did not know this. They noted only that their pastor's words contained a peculiar vehemence, which they assumed was directed toward libertines, unbelievers, and other sinners.

"Before the enjoyment of liberty," he spoke, "must come the acknowledgment and *habit* of *duty*. For duty is an unalienable companion of liberty. Without the restraining hand of duty, liberty descends of its own nature and accord into the frightening, licentious chaos of anarchy!"

Reece Vishonn, sitting with his family in one of the front pews, merely blinked his eyes and wrinkled his mouth in distaste for the homily. Henry Otway, Ralph Cullis, and Ira Granby stared up at Reverend Acland with blank, unquestioning expressions. Arthur Stannard, sitting in a pew with his family near the back of the church, muttered to himself, "Amen."

Chapter 5: The Overture

As John Proudlocks directed the transplanting of thousands of young tobacco plants from their seed beds to Morland's hills, and contemplated a better way of describing his employer's character than as a tightly woven basket; as Hugh Kenrick rode with Edgar Cullis to Williamsburg and the new session of the General Assembly; and as Etáin Frake enchanted her husband in the evenings on her harp with transcriptions of Corelli sonatas, a hand invisible to them, but visible nonetheless to anyone discerning enough to notice it, was busy in Europe.

Adam Smith was, at this time, on a grand tour of the Continent as tutor and companion to young Henry Scott, third Duke of Buccleuch and the stepson of Charles Townshend, president of the Board of Trade and recently the mortified object of Colonel Barré's oratory in the Commons. Smith, who owed his present employment to Townshend's admiration for *The Theory of Moral Sentiments* — for his employer regarded himself as something of an economist and moralist — was fresh from a meeting in Geneva with exiled Voltaire, and in the midst of note-taking for a book on economics that would become, eleven years later, an *Inquiry into the Nature and Causes of the Wealth of Nations*.

Now in Paris, he was being introduced to the cream of the French Enlightenment in the capital's intellectual and literary salons by his lifelong friend David Hume, secretary and chargé d'affaires for the British embassy, himself lately the lion of French *haute esprits* and busy arranging new editions of his *History of England* and *Essays and Treatises*. That pioneer of formal skepticism may have had at hand then a recently published and circulated treatise by Immanuel Kant, a professor of philosophy at the University of Königsberg, Prussia, *Observations on the Feeling of the Beautiful and the Sublime*, perhaps shared it with Smith, discussed its merits and logic, and speculated on the rumor that Herr Kant was, like themselves, the son of a Scotsman. Smith, however, would be more influenced by his conversations with François Quesnay, the leading physiocrat economist, author of the *Tableau Économique* and contributor to the *Encyclopédie*. Outlawed John Wilkes was also in Paris, living comfortably on his supporters' donated money, watching events in London, and waiting for the inevitable change in ministry that might allow him to return.

Jean-Jacques Rousseau — whose profile graced a wall of Kant's study — author of the controversial *Émile* and *The Social Contract* and now at odds with the knowledge-celebrating *Encyclopédie,* and still on the run from civil and ecclesiastical authorities, was brooding in Bern, Switzerland, from which he would also be expelled. David Hume, who knew of his plight, would later that year invite him to settle under his protection on his estate in Derbyshire, England. Young Antoine Lavoisier, physicist and chemist, was performing astonishing work that would gain him admission to the French Academy of Sciences at the age of twenty-one. Pierre Augustin Caron de Beaumarchais, future author of *The Barber of Seville* and *The Marriage of Figaro*, was then a struggling watchmaker tinkering with comedy-writing. Carl Bellman, a Swedish poet and songwriter, and a protégé of Prince Gustavus, future benevolent despot of Sweden, published his *Eighty-two Epistles*, a compendium of ballads and drinking songs.

In England, churchman Thomas Percy published his *Reliques of Ancient English Poetry*, a collection of English and Scottish ballads. In Bristol, very young Thomas Chatterton began to fabricate the poetry of Thomas Rowley, a fictive fifteenth-century monk, in a style so epic and convincingly "ancient" that for twelve years, no one suspected that the verses were a fraud. Thomas Reid, a philosopher, like Hume and Smith a product of the Scottish Enlightenment, and an exponent of the "common sense" school, published his *Inquiry into the Human Mind*, which disputed both Hume and Locke. Reclusive chemist Henry Cavendish, also a Scot, was on the verge of discovering hydrogen, while Joseph Priestly, theologian and scientist, was on the verge of discovering oxygen, though it would remain for Lavoisier to name those elements later in the century. The first Lunar Society was founded in this year by "mechanics" to discuss philosophy and politics; its later members would be Priestly and James Watt, who was then an instrument-maker at the University of Glasgow and a student of steam engines.

In London, women were boldly partaking of the Enlightenment, for the most popular intellectual and literary salons were being hosted by a trio of Elizabeths: Montagu, Vesey, and Carter. Drinking and card-playing were banned from their gatherings. Hume, Smith, Locke, and other thinkers were the subjects of their lively but genteel conversations, as well as the works of the French *philosophes*. Many of the attendees could read Italian, and so were able to argue the pros and cons of the then-published *Essay on Crime and Justice*, by Italian economist and jurist Cesare Beccaria.

Elizabeth Robinson Montagu held her liquorless levees on Berkeley Square, attracting the cream of English intelligentsia, and in this year was herself taking notes for what would become a lengthy and patriotic reply to Voltaire's verdict that Shakespeare was a "drunken savage." In it, she would incidentally second her grudging admirer Samuel Johnson's critique of the Bard and likewise defend the latter's flouting of classicist formulæ and the sacrosanct unities of time and place in the drama. Catherine Sawbridge Macaulay, in the meantime, was preparing her second volume of *The History of England from the Accession of James I*. Among her own numerous and frequent guests was Benjamin Franklin; she would later champion the American cause through all its intransigent phases.

And William Blackstone, member for Hinden in the Commons and Vinerian Professor of Law at Oxford, in that year argued, in the first volume of his *Commentaries on the Laws of England*, for not only Parliamentary supremacy over all that Parliament surveyed — which included the colonies — but endorsed the notions of literal as well as "virtual" representation in that body.

While Europe percolated, the American colonies were about to smolder, and later burst into flames. Except to a very few discerning observers among them, the hand that lit the flames was as invisible to the English and the Continentals as was the modest colonial capital from which they rose.

The hand had a name: Patrick Henry.

* * *

The red, white, and blue of the Great Union fluttered lazily on a staff above the bell tower of the Capitol building in Williamsburg, Virginia, presiding over a wide boulevard that was carpeted with the traffic, commerce, and gaiety of the spring Public Time. For a mile that emanated from the imposing steps of the colonial legislature, the straight, sandy Duke of Gloucester Street was noisy with rumbling, shouts, and commotion as stately carriages and nimble riding chairs vied for space with horsemen, produce-laden wagons, and darting pedestrians. On both sides of Duke of

Gloucester, old, established shops competed for business with ramshackle stalls erected by traders and farmers from nearby counties and villages. A town of tents had sprung up around the county courthouse on Market Square. Merchants, planters, and ships' captains did business in the open-air space of the Exchange between the Capitol and the theater. Gentlemen and ladies in their European finery promenaded along the sidewalks and traded discreet appraisals with farming couples in their rough homespuns, while both sets glanced with amazed distaste at scruffy, bearded mountain men in their hunting shirts as they rode into town leading packhorses loaded with mounds of deer and beaver pelts.

The air was also filled with the sounds of the hammering of carpenters repairing damaged English and French furniture brought to town by their owners, of the clinking of blacksmiths shoeing horses or repairing carriage wheels, of the laughter of children watching puppet shows, magicians, and jugglers, of the songs and melodies of traveling minstrels and musicians.

On the fringes of the town on any day during that May, two more somber events took place: a slave auction, and an indenture auction. The slaves were displayed on the bed of a wagon that had brought them here, and examined by prospective buyers, and their virtues and histories narrated by the auctioneer, who was either the owner or the broker. Men, women, and children were sold to the highest bidders, either separately, in parcels, or in families. In the crowd of spectators and buyers were planters great and small, farmers, mistresses of small households, sailors, and black freedmen. In a field across the side street seven-year indentures were sold by the men who owned their time and who were called soul-drivers. These unfortunates — poor men, women, and children from England and the Continent whose passage had been paid for by others — considered the stop in Williamsburg a rest, for their masters walked them from town to town throughout the colony, chained together, until the last person had been sold.

East of the Capitol, and beyond the racetrack where so many sleek Virginia horses proved their superiority over all other colonial stock, was a gallows. Six slaves were hanged there for having robbed their owners, and three white men for "coining" — or counterfeiting — and murdering the under-sheriff who had come to arrest them. All had been tried in the General Court.

But even back among the gaiety and bustle on Duke of Gloucester Street, a somber undercurrent governed the actions and dispositions of the people. Nearly everyone glanced now and then up at the Capitol and the Great Union that floated above it, except children, slaves, and indentures as they hurried through their play, chores, and errands, even though they may have heard their parents, owners, or masters talk among themselves about the Stamp Act. Anyone now in Williamsburg who had any reason to worry about a stamp tax learned of its proposed passage during the Public Time last fall.

This month, residents and visitors alike found nailed to the walls and posts of many shops, taverns, and coffeehouses, and over the clutter of announcements and advertisements on wooden billboards, copies of a finely drawn caricature. The picture elicited a mixture of responses, from anger to humor to bewilderment to despair, among the curious who chose to examine it. In a few instances, it was ripped down by gentlemen who declared it offensive to the Crown or to good taste, or to both, and torn by them to pieces, often to the cheering of a crowd. On one occasion, the gentleman who performed that public service got into a heated argument with the innkeeper who had given the caricature a prominent place on his billboard, and he was banned from entering the establishment.

Hugh Kenrick was responsible for the caricature's appearance in Williamsburg. On the morning after their arrival in the capital, he and Edgar Cullis traversed the length of Duke of Gloucester and put it up wherever a proprietor permitted, using the supply of copies sent by Dogmael Jones. Hugh had also wanted to post and distribute printed copies of the Commons text of the Stamp Act, but Wendel Barret of the *Courier* would not undertake the task. His special printer's license, granted by a private act in the House and signed by a past governor, prohibited him from broadcasting laws and actions of any nature unless reprinted from the *Virginia Gazette* or a British periodical. His license could be revoked, his presses seized, and he fined for violating the stricture. He was not allowed to compete with the *Gazette* in Williamsburg, the colony's official newspaper, which was controlled by the governor. He agreed, however, to compose a short piece on the Act and print it in the next issue of the *Courier* as an item he could claim was copied from a London newspaper.

In the upstairs committee room of the House, two days after his arrival with Cullis, Hugh had approached Peyton Randolph, the Attorney-General and a member of the committee that was in correspondence with Edward Montague, the House's agent in London, and showed him a copy of the Commons text of the Stamp Act. He proposed that the Act be made an early matter of business and opened to discussion and debate, or at least firmly scheduled on the House calendar. Randolph agreed to examine the document, and, after consulting with his colleagues on the committee, Speaker John Robinson and Thomas Nelson, Secretary of State, as well as with George Wythe, Richard Bland, and Edmund Pendleton, the next day, in the same room, handed Hugh back the sheaf of papers. He said, without apology or concern, "We cannot with decency pursue this matter, sir, nor speak to any effect about it at this time, not until this House receives an official copy of the passed act that bears His Majesty's seal and signature."

"But," countered Hugh, "if one arrives after this session has adjourned, the House will not have a chance to discuss it." He paused. "Mr. Montague may not have procured a copy in time to send us. However, a friend of mine in the Commons is certain to have posted one to me, once he has been assured that His Majesty has signed it. That copy may come before the end of this month. You may admit it as evidence of enactment, and allow it to be discussed."

The Attorney-General, who did not like being told what could be done in the House, had shrugged, and Hugh thought that he saw a hint of satisfaction in Randolph's eyes. "Thank you for the offer, sir, and the opportunity to review these documents," said the man, "but I very much doubt that your friend's mail packet will be speedier than Mr. Montague's." He shook his head. "If a copy does not arrive here in time, then the matter must wait until the next session, in November. That is all there is to say to that."

Edmund Pendleton sat next to Randolph at the committee room table. On the other side of the Attorney-General sat George Wythe and Richard Bland. The four men studied Hugh with veiled hostility. Pendleton spoke. "We will not introduce the precedent of discussing rumor or hearsay, young sir. It would be improper, not to say illegal, to treat the mere draft of a law as an enacted one."

Bland volunteered, "And you must know, Mr. Kenrick, that petitions and protests against proposed taxes are not permitted by the Commons. Even though Parliament's *rumored* precedent on this matter may seem to require an exception to that rule — a *quid pro quo* in protest, so to speak — it would seem wiser to wait until we are certain that the act has actually been made law."

"We would not want to embarrass the ministry and the Commons by seeming to be wiser than they, sir," remarked Wythe. "Such an embarrassment could provoke more evil."

Hugh ignored the other men, and studied the round, disinterested face of the Attorney-General and the severe, closed features of Pendleton, and remembered that these two men were among the six who composed the last session's protests in a special committee. It had taken them a month to complete those protests. Cullis had told him that they pared down the "intemperate" and "rash" language of Richard Lee's original drafts. Lee, a burgess for Westmoreland, had been the youngest member of that committee, and was resented by the older members for his vitality and family connections. The Lees were also political rivals of the Robinsons and Randolphs.

Hugh decided that further entreaty would be useless. He tucked the sheaf of papers under his arm, and bowed slightly. "Thank you for your advices, gentlemen," he remarked, "and for the time you devoted to my proposal." Then he stood straight and added, "This House is but a cameo of the Commons."

The contempt on his face must have been evident to all four men around the table. Randolph said, with some confusion, "Surely, sir, that was meant as a compliment."

Hugh's expression was too innocent. "As you please, sir." Then he turned and left the committee room.

Randolph grimaced as he watched the retreating figure. "There goes a thoroughbred that wants breaking, gentlemen."

Bland queried, to no one in particular, "What is to say that, if he could be broken, he would not still wish to throw us?"

Although the Stamp Act was on the minds of most of the one hundred burgesses who had journeyed to Williamsburg, few of them showed any desire to speak of it, either in private or within the walls of the Capitol. Most of these men were resigned to conceding submission to a painful fact. An unwritten rule was in effect during this session, observed Hugh: Since an official copy of the Act was not at hand, it could not be treated as a fact. The Speaker prohibited discussion of it; the Attorney-General would not allow it. They preferred to wait for official notification, or for replies to the address, memorial, and remonstrance of last fall. But Edgar Cullis had informed Hugh that these men knew that no replies would be forthcoming, that the House's protests had not been accorded serious attention in London. Cullis had been told by George Wythe that Edward Montague and James Abercromby, the Council's agent, had written as much to Speaker Robinson and Council President John Blair.

In the meantime, the House occupied itself with safe, routine business.

Hugh derived some consolation from a writ for a new election in Louisa County that was passed from the House to Lieutenant-Governor Fauquier for his signature; Patrick Henry was certain to arrive later in the session. The House also passed a number of private acts that concerned land, entails, surveyors's reports, and road improvements. It approved of an address to Fauquier for a reward for the "detection" and arrest of the men who murdered some Cherokees in the Shenandoah Valley. And, a trial of sorts was held in the House: Thomas Prosser, a burgess for Cumberland, was charged with fraud, forgery, and suborning a county jury for the purpose of legalizing his theft of another's land. The evidence against him, unlike a copy of the Stamp Act, was at hand and overwhelming; the House voted to expel him from that body and bar him from ever sitting in it again. He was not subsequently remanded to the custody of the General Court, however. Hugh thought it ironic that it was one of a burgess's privileges that, while he was a burgess in attendance at a session, he could not be charged in a civil court for any crime but murder. The House of Burgesses was indeed a cameo of the Commons.

Hugh was not alone in his frustration over the "gentleman's agreement" on the Stamp Act. After each sitting, he met with other members of the House at Marot's Coffeehouse near the Capitol to discuss strategy and their concerns. There were John Fleming of Cumberland, whose fellow burgess had just been expelled, and George Johnston of Fairfax, both of them lawyers. They were joined by Colonel Robert Munford of Mecklenburg. "They are willing to let our liberties slip away and be forgotten," said Hugh one evening to these men the day he was rebuffed by Randolph and the committee. He added, with bitterness, "They do not wish there to be a problem. There is no *evidence* of a problem at hand. Ergo, there is no problem."

"Well," said Fleming, "don't be so harsh on them. They are in a bad patch of policy here. They know that if they protest what may well be a law, they could be charged with a crime much worse than merely not liking that law or the way it was passed."

"Also," remarked Johnston, "consider Mr. Lee's dilemma. They had the satisfaction of knocking him down to size over the protests last session." He paused when he saw the quizzical look on Hugh's face. "Why do you think Mr. Lee is not attending *this* session?"

Hugh shook his head. He had not met Richard Henry Lee, but knew that he was an enemy of the men who controlled the business of the House.

"I had heard that he was ill."

Johnston glanced at the other older men in silent question, and they nodded. Johnston said, "Not as ill as he might be, had he come to prod Mr. Robinson and the House to protest the Act. You see, shortly after Mr. Robinson informed the House last session — on the first day of November, as I recollect, and you were there — that the Massachusetts Assembly had informed him of Parliament's intention to pass a Stamp Act, and before the House received information from Mr. Montague in London of the futility of protesting that intention...well...Mr. Lee dispatched a letter to his brother in London asking him to request Mr. Grenville's naming him for the post of stamp distributor of this colony."

Hugh fell back in his chair in genuine shock. "That could not be true!"

"You may take it to be," said Fleming. "Why else would he choose to miss an opportunity to confound and scatter his family's rivals in the House? Those gentlemen have kept as many Lees out of our politics as they could for almost a generation. Ask yourself, this, young sir: How could he argue with any credibility against this Stamp Act, when Mr. Robinson could rise and query him about his application to be named a stamp distributor? What injury would that do to our cause?" Fleming waved a hand. "Mr. Lee is in as bad a money straits as any of us. But, as a stamp distributor, he could claim a certain percentage of the stamp revenues as his entitled salary. That is stipulated in your text of the act, and is certain to be retained in the official text. The number of stamps he would sell, together with a strenuous enforcement of the law, would put him on a pretty perch."

Munford puffed on his pipe, and added with a note of sarcasm, "His growing solvency would be in direct proportion to our plunging insolvency, sir, and that's a fact."

George Johnston leaned forward and said softly, "This information must not be repeated beyond this table, Mr. Kenrick, though it is certain that our Speaker has shared it with Mr. Randolph and the others."

Fleming said, in the same hushed tone, "Mr. Lee knows that he has compromised himself, and so has chosen to absent himself from this session so that our cause will not be compromised." Then his face brightened. "Mr. Henry, on the other hand, cannot be compromised. He has made no careless statements in company that could be reported to Mr. Robinson, as Mr. Lee had. Mr. Henry has no recriminations to fear, no scandal to stay his tongue, no feud to regret. He expressed an interest in coming here, and we heartily endorsed it. He has a talent for confounding and scattering chaste complacency."

Munford added, "We are fortunate that he can substitute for Mr. Lee, whose own powers of persuasion needn't defer to Mr. Henry's." He sighed. "It would have been interesting, though, to see them both in action, and to observe Mr. Robinson's party tremble in fear."

Hugh spent other evenings either alone in his room at Mary Gandy's place, composing special instructions for Meum Hall, which were picked up every other day by Bristol, or working on the points he would make in the House, or attending suppers or balls at the Palace. At one of the latter, he found himself in the company of most of the Council members and their wives, together with Peyton Randolph, George Wythe, and John Robinson. The Lieutenant-Governor took him aside at one point and, after some idle chat about the drought in the Northern Neck and what Fauquier called the "sullen mood of the people," asked Hugh what he planned to say in the House, if the Stamp Act was taken under consideration. "I have heard that you are eager to worry the subject," said Fauquier, "and that you even have a draft of it." Fauquier grunted in self-effacing irony. "Doubtless, *I* will not see my copy of it for perhaps half a year. Nearly that time passed before I was ever presented with a copy of the Proclamation. The Secretary of State can be so neglectful."

Hugh smiled. Across the ballroom he noticed Peter Randolph, who was on the Council, and his brother, Peyton, glancing at him. He said, "I would gladly furnish you with a copy of the act, your honor, so that you may know what executive duties are expected of you — onerous as I may expect those to be." He paused, and added, "As for what I plan to say in the House about the act, I am disappointed that you should ask, and will answer only that I will say what others appear not to care to hear."

Fauquier frowned in apology. "I regret having offended your sensibilities, Mr. Kenrick, and withdraw the question. And I have no doubt that what you will say in the House will not surprise me. Anguish me, perhaps, but not surprise me."

Hugh shook his head. "If you are anguished, your honor, do not grieve over-much. What I will say will be in the name and spirit of British liberty, which, unless I am very much off the mark, you esteem as much as I do. So I am glad that you will not be so surprised."

Fauquier gave his companion a wistful look, then glanced across the ballroom. "Ah! There's Mr. Washington," he exclaimed. "He is staying here, you know. And I see that young Mr. Jefferson has arrived as well.

Now we can proceed with the music."

On the evening of May 16th, hours after the Prosser expulsion had been concluded, Hugh was sitting on Mary Gandy's porch with Edgar Cullis, discussing the day's session and enjoying the pleasant evening air, when Bristol rode up, leaped from his horse, and rushed up to Hugh with a large, flat parcel. "The *Sparrowhawk*, she came this afternoon, sir!" he said as he thrust the parcel into Hugh's hands. "And Mr. Ramshaw came up special to give this to Mr. Spears, and Mr. Spears said you wanted this quick if it came, and here it is!"

Hugh nodded. "Thank you, Bristol. Tether your mount, and go inside and ask Miss Gandy for some cider and a bite to eat."

Bristol bobbed his head once and went inside the cottage. Hugh opened the parcel and removed a thick sheaf of papers. Pinned to the top sheet was a note from Dogmael Jones, dated the first of April:

"My Fellow Burgess:
Lucrece has been outraged by Sextus Tarquinius. Perhaps you can persuade her not to forsake this mortal coil; there is no protest in that final quietude. The pile of infamous misery to which I append this note is by courtesy of Mr. Thomas Whately, though he does not know it (his clerk is richer by ten pounds). You will see that it has been sealed and engrossed by His Majesty. I hope that the caricature has been a sensation. Please report, in your next missive, that Mr. Grenville and Sir Henoch have been hanged in effigy. Your family does well, and writes separately.

Your most obedient servant and ripening Pippin,
D. Jones, Esq."

Hugh laughed in joy, in relief, in vindication, and turned to Edgar Cullis. "Now, sir, they will have something to talk about!" he exclaimed, waving the sheaf in the air. "Now, they *must* accept it as an enacted fact!"

It was an official copy of the Stamp Act.

Chapter 6: The Hand

On the evening of May 19th, Patrick Henry rode unrecognized into Williamsburg, found himself a billet in one of the lesser taverns, and the next morning strode to the Capitol and presented himself and his sheriff's election certification to a clerk in the Council chambers. The clerk, by proxy, administered to him the oath of loyalty to Virginia and the Crown, and after some other minor formalities, freed the new burgess for Louisa County to make his way to the House and find himself a place on the benches.

Instead, Henry stood with the spectators in the public space and listened to a debate among the burgesses over whether or not to vote money for the construction of a public gallery. When the House recessed in midafternoon for dinner, he approached the Speaker and Attorney-General and formally introduced himself. Those two gentlemen welcomed him with icy courtesy, while George Wythe, Richard Bland, and Edmund Pendleton warily appraised the newcomer from a distance. Henry's dark, somber apparel contrasted sharply with the shimmering colors of the frock coats of those burgesses. They noted, however, that Henry's suit was new, and that he wore a plain but new tricorn over his own tied-back hair. This lured them into the hope that perhaps he did not portend trouble and that he was open to concession.

When Henry left the Capitol after a brief conversation with Robinson, Colonel Munford, George Johnston, John Fleming, and Hugh Kenrick were waiting for him outside.

"Let us repair to the Blue Bell for our supper," suggested Fleming to the group. "I would prefer Mrs. Campbell's fare, but the *great ones* in the House will be there and their ears would be too...hungry."

The four other nodded in agreement. The Blue Bell Tavern was not much frequented by members of the House. Henry said, "I have been put on the Committee for Courts of Justice. There is some work to do there, but not enough to divert me from my purpose here."

Johnston chuckled. "I can only imagine that your instant employment is Mr. Randolph's manner of *embracing* you, Mr. Henry."

"And that, sir," replied Henry with a laugh, "would indeed be a *suffocating* friendship!" The group laughed in turn and began walking away from the Capitol. "They are more concerned about Mr. Robinson's loan office scheme, gentlemen, than they are about the Stamp Act, and are saving consideration of it for later in the session. That was Mr. Robinson's assurance. But I did not assure him that I had an opinion of it."

Colonel Munford snorted. "When half the House will have gone home, and many of those who remain will have a special interest in the scheme."

"It must be defeated," said Henry. "They are as secretive about its details as a table of sharpers playing whist. But I do believe it is a form of this Stamp Act. The people of this colony will be expected to subsidize this ostentatious oligarchy, through special taxes to keep a fund available for those expensive paupers...."

Hugh followed the four men and listened to them discuss other House matters. When they arrived at the Blue Bell, they were able to secure a table in a corner of the busy establishment. Henry was a favorite patron of the proprietor's, for he often stayed here when he came to Williamsburg on law business.

After some cordial talk about their families and properties, Henry steered the conversation to what was most on all their minds. "Mr. Kenrick," he said, "I must thank you again for the copy of the act you left with me. It helped me to form some thoughts on what must be said and done." He paused to open his portfolio, and took out a sheet of paper. It looked like the blank leaf of a book. "It is my hope that this company unanimously agrees that what are needed are not more remonstrances or memorials, but plain, unhumble *resolves*." He handed the page to John Fleming. "There are five there, dictated by me to my dear Sarah. I was too impatient to pen them myself."

Fleming read the five resolutions on the page. When he had finished, he said, "These, sir, comprise the proper language of protest." He passed the page on to Munford. Johnston moved closer to the colonel to read them, too.

Henry reached again into his portfolio, and produced another page. "I have two more," he said to Fleming, "which I composed when I stopped at an ordinary in New Kent. These are logical companions of those five." He handed Fleming the paper.

The burgess nearly gasped when he read them. He cocked his head in appreciation, and said, "Well put, sir. These *are* logical companions, but I fear that they have little chance of success in the House." He ran a hand worriedly but thoughtfully over his face. "The first five will be difficult enough, even though they are more vital assertions of the last session's protests. There is nothing in them that Mr. Bland and his friends could object to, for they have already said the same things, though in meeker language. But, these two are nearly...revolutionary!"

"But true," replied Henry.

"Yes," said Fleming with a nod. "They are that."

Hugh read the first five resolves after Munford passed them over to him. He grinned in exultation when he finished, and said to Henry, "These are in a proper language, and I will support them."

Johnston pushed the second paper across to Hugh. "And these, sir?"

Hugh read the sixth and seventh resolutions. After a moment, he said, "Yes, and these." He glanced at Henry. "Taken together, sir, these seven resolves comprise the sword we spoke about." He paused. "Mr. Fleming is correct, though, in his certainty that these last two will be too violent for the House. Nevertheless, I am willing to argue for their adoption, as well."

Fleming, Johnston, and Munford all nodded in agreement and in support. Fleming drew the two pages toward him and reread the resolves. When he was done, he said, "They want a preamble, Mr. Henry. An overture."

"You may compose one, if you think one necessary," said Henry.

Hugh reached into his own portfolio and drew out his copy of the enacted Stamp Act. He passed it across the table to Henry. "For your perusal, sir. The gentlemen here and I have discussed the best time to present it to Mr. Robinson and Mr. Randolph. We agree that it should be some time before the loan office matter has been disposed of. Of course, Mr. Montague's copy may arrive before that."

Fleming chuckled and shook his head. "Forgive me my wisdom, sir, but if we must rely on those gentlemen to report the arrival of that document, we may never know it." He reached over and patted the sheaf of Stamp Act pages with a loving hand. "Our friends in the House are playing an interesting game of faro, gentlemen, and believe themselves supreme dealers. But here is a king of hearts they are wrongly betting will never emerge from the shoe."

Colonel Munford laughed and raised his glass of port. "Gentlemen, a toast to our country — to Virginia!"

The other four men joined him, raised their glasses, and clinked them together over the center of the table. "To Virginia!" they said in chorus.

Hugh added, to the surprise of his companions, because they had never heard it before, "And, long live Lady Liberty!"

Chapter 7: The Gamblers

"There are but two important topics remaining for the House to consider, sir: Mr. Robinson's loan office, and the late act of Parliament."

"You may count on my signature under the loan office, Mr. Wythe, provided, of course, the Council approves it." Lieutenant-Governor Francis Fauquier paused to clear his throat. "As to the late act, well, I believe that will give us all a stretch of bother, and you may *not* count on my signature, if whatever answer to it your fellows contrive I judge to be indecent and offensive."

George Wythe, burgess for Elizabeth City near Norfolk, was not with his fellow "great ones" at Mrs. Campbell's Tavern that same evening, but had supped with the governor and George Washington at the Palace. Washington often stayed at the Palace when he came to Williamsburg. At the moment, their supper behind them, they sat together around a table in a small room near the Lieutenant-Governor's quarters, playing a brisk game of five-card loo. At their elbows were piles of wooden chips and glasses of French brandy. A window was open to the pleasant May evening air, which stirred the curtains and the candlelight. A stack of chips sat in the middle of the green baize cloth that covered the table.

"It is hoped that nothing is contrived," remarked Wythe. "What needed to be said was said by us last session. But the act may be debated in the coming week, provided, of course, there is something to debate. Mr. Robinson and Mr. Randolph would lief wait until a copy makes an appearance."

Washington said to Fauquier, "I have a suspicion, sir, that what the House may contrive will not require your signature."

The Lieutenant-Governor hummed in thought at this remark. "It is a prudent thing that Mr. Robinson will not permit debate on the act until an official copy of it is at hand," he said. "Is one, my friend?" he asked Wythe.

Wythe shrugged. "I have no knowledge of it, sir, if one has indeed arrived." He shook his head. "And if one does arrive, it is too serious a matter to consider calmly in so short a time. I will then recommend that discussion of it be deferred to the next session."

Fauquier nodded in satisfaction. "You may convey that sentiment as my own to the House, Mr. Wythe." He turned to Washington. "Of course, if what the House contrives is of a rash and defiant nature, I will have no choice but to dissolve the Assembly."

"That would be your privilege and duty, sir," replied Washington with a restrained deference that seemed to cloak an inexplicable hostility, one which the Lieutenant-Governor had never known before in the man.

Wythe nodded in agreement. He acted as the Lieutenant-Governor's unofficial spokesman in the House. "Loo!" he exclaimed suddenly, after the governor had dealt him a replacement card. With practiced grace, he fanned his card hand over the green baize; they were all of the same suit, which beat the hands held by Washington and the governor. He reached over and added the stack of chips to his own pile.

It was Washington's turn to deal. As he collected the cards and shuffled them, Wythe asked him, "What are your thoughts on the loan office, sir?"

Washington frowned and said over the whisper of the cards moving in his fingers, "What little has been said about it, sir, I dislike. True, a loan to us by British merchants would bring us some true sterling here. God knows, we need such money in these parts. But I must ask this: For how long would that sterling stay in our purses, before it was whisked away in duties and taxes and the debts we already owe those gentlemen?" He shook his head. "I am not in favor of increasing our debt to them. My children and grandchildren would needs spend their whole lives paying it off, living on their own property as mere tenants of absentee landlords in London, for that would be the only end consequence." He smiled gravely at Wythe, to let him know that he had other thoughts on the subject, but would not voice them here. He dealt the cards.

"I see," said Wythe. He picked up the cards Washington had dealt him. "And...on the Stamp Act?"

Again, Washington shook his head, but glanced first at Fauquier as he replied to his fellow burgess. "With all due respect to our host and the Crown, I believe it is as villainous a piece of legislation as can be imagined. It is the logical successor of the Proclamation of '63. It must be protested again, if not in this session, then in the next. That is when I expect words to be exchanged over it, and many of those may be my own. I do not think the people of this colony will long tolerate it, and will press their representatives to contest the act. Now, I have a wheat harvest to oversee, and that will not wait. I shall depart after the loan office matter has been voted on. But, come next November, I *will* have something to say about that act." Relaxing his scowl, the colonel turned again to study the hand of cards he had dealt himself.

Wythe blushed in embarrassment; his cards dropped from his hand, and he stared first at Washington, then at Fauquier. The Lieutenant-Governor blinked in astonishment. He could hardly believe his ears. This man, he thought, so reserved and cool, had not expressed a word of anger on any matter, except once, during a game last November, when he had a winning hand but failed to trump in time.

Fauquier felt compelled to answer his description of the Stamp Act as "villainous," but did not know how to answer without provoking an argument. He feared any confrontation with Washington. This man, he also knew, could swear worse than any army sergeant, and his liberal use of profanity had probably saved Braddock's routed army from complete annihilation many years ago. The Lieutenant-Governor studied his cards without seeing them. "Villainous, you say?" he remarked. "Well, it is your privilege as a burgess to call it what you wish, my friend." As he spoke, he could only imagine the ludicrousness of his small frame standing toe to toe in opposition to the towering figure of Colonel Washington.

Some anger flared in Washington's eyes, then annoyance. "It is my privilege as a burgess, sir, and my liberty as a British subject. I make no distinction."

"Yes," replied Fauquier with some humility, "of course not."

Wythe ran a hand through his hair, and nodded to his exposed cards. "I have blown my hand, sirs, and spoiled this round. Shall we begin over?"

His partners agreed, and Washington collected the cards again. As he reshuffled them, Fauquier said to the colonel, "I shall miss your company, sir, when you leave for home. And, perhaps you shall miss mine. I am thinking of writing the Board for permission to return to England for a year or so. I miss England, of course, and there are family matters that require my attention, and physicians to consult on a complaint. Perhaps I shall spend some time at Bath."

Wythe had recovered enough to smile at the Lieutenant-Governor. "Should you be granted a leave, sir, I pledge to exert myself to the fullest to help maintain the peace here, so that you may return to a serene and dutiful colony. Mr. Blair, who would act in your place, I am sure will give you the same pledge."

Fauquier sighed. "That, Mr. Wythe, is all I ever wished this colony to be — serene and dutiful." He glanced at his new hand. "Ah! Shall we put wagers on a trick, gentlemen?"

But although Wythe and the Lieutenant-Governor tried to recapture the exuberance of the game and their own sense of craftiness, they were so preoccupied in their minds with the uncharacteristic surly mood of their giant partner that Washington looed them in three consecutive hands, and ended the evening thirty pounds richer.

* * *

The Lieutenant-Governor, George Wythe, and Wythe's fellow conservatives in the House were subsequently trumped by more serious events. After Washington had retired to his room for the night, Fauquier expressed concern about the other burgesses.

Wythe assured him that the only talk he had heard among the burgesses about the Stamp Act was a proposal to abolish the Tobacco Act of 1730, which established inspectors and warehouses throughout the colony to control the export of "trash" leaf. All tobacco exports required inspectors' notes, which were often used in lieu of money, but which also could now require stamps. "Their talk is subdued and weary, sir," said Wythe, "and hardly intemperate. The idea is not likely to be debated at any length, nor even likely to be admitted as House business. However, we may see petitions on the matter presented next fall."

Fauquier's features widened in incredulity. "But even should the Tobacco Act be abolished, Mr. Wythe, there is a likelihood that the Board and Parliament would reply with a disallowance of the repeal itself. Their eminences know that the inspectors' notes change hands often enough that they would insist they carry stamps, as well. Imagine the mountains of pence that would accrue from all that business!"

"Mr. Robinson, Mr. Randolph, and Mr. Pendleton and I have discussed that aspect, sir. It is not a promising business for the House."

"And Mr. Robinson's loan office?" asked Fauquier. He wagged a finger. "Be warned, my friend: I will not sign another bill without it having a suspending clause. And Mr. Robinson and his friends should not breathe easier if the bill is passed. The Board of Trade must approve it, and then the merchants, who must then have introduced in the Commons a companion bill and secure its passage. It may be two or more years before any borrowed sterling reaches these shores."

"Mr. Robinson and his friends are aware of those contingencies, sir," said Wythe.

On May 23rd, after some minor private bills were voted on, Hugh Kenrick rose before John Randolph could gavel the House into a dinner recess, and was recognized by Speaker Robinson. He said, "I move that the House accept into its hands a copy of the Parliamentary law known as the Stamp Act. An official copy of it has recently arrived, and may now be scheduled for consideration by the House."

John Fleming rose. "I second the motion."

Startled, Robinson glanced briefly at an equally startled Peyton Randolph, then said with some impatience, "The House will not consider discussion of a *rumor* of a law, sirs." He turned and addressed the House. "The gentleman has but a *draft* of the said act, but we all know the fate of so many mere drafts," he said with some humor, "both here and in the Commons." He paused. "Mr. Randolph and the committee of correspondence have informed me that an *official* draft is not at hand."

"Begging your pardon, sir," said Hugh to the berobed figure, "but an official copy of that act, signed by commission by the Lord Privy Seal for His Majesty, was forwarded to me by *my* correspondent, who, unlike Mr. Montague, is a member of the Commons, and apparently availed himself of a speedier mail packet." He grinned briefly at the Attorney-General in emphasis, then held out a hand. Edgar Cullis put into it a thick mass of bound papers. Hugh held it up, so that all could see the elegantly printed first page. He lifted the sheaf to expose the last page that bore the seal and commissioned signature of King George the Third.

A murmur of curiosity stirred in the House.

Robinson had no choice. He asked to see the document. Hugh descended from the benches, approached the Speaker, bowed courteously to him, and handed the papers to him. Robinson inspected the first page, then hastily turned to the last. There he saw the sealed endorsements of the Houses of Commons and Lords, and the Great Seal of the king and the signature of George Spencer, fourth Duke of Marlborough. Robinson nodded to Hugh in dismissal. Hugh threw a secret grin at Patrick Henry as he walked back to his seat next to Cullis.

Robinson, with ill-concealed consternation and disgust, said to the House, "This is a true copy of the said act." He gestured to the Clerk of the House, John Randolph. "It is committed to the Committee on Propositions and Grievances." A clerk rose, took the document, and handed it to John Randolph.

As many burgesses filed out of the chambers, others gathered around the Clerk's table to look at the document. Hugh was asked several questions by other members, and joined them at the table. Peyton Randolph studied this young man for a moment, and interrupted another burgess's question to ask, with cold formality, "How is it, Mr. Kenrick, when neither this House nor the Council, nor even his honor the Governor himself, has been graced with a copy of this law, that your correspondent could so easily lay hands on one?"

Edgar Cullis looked worriedly at his fellow burgess. Hugh shrugged his shoulders once, and answered, "He is an intimate friend of the Duke of Richmond, sir." It was folderol, and a truth, thought Hugh, but he was not going to betray Dogmael Jones or his methods. He knew how much Randolph and many of the other older members regarded the nobility with reverential awe, and perhaps even envy. He also knew how reluctant they were to begin serious debate on the Stamp Act.

Randolph's eyebrows went up in surprise. He replied, with as much dignity as he could muster, "I see." There were no further questions.

Patrick Henry remarked to Hugh, as they walked to the Blue Bell Tavern for dinner, "They will still call it a copy, though its seals seem to have fixed in their minds the reality of the malignity."

On Friday, May 24th, the loan office proposal was introduced and debated. Edmund Pendleton rose to explain the intricacies of the scheme. Other planters spoke in its favor and advocated that it be assigned to a committee to be worked into a bill. Speaker Robinson, its originator, was unusually quiet during this debate, neither advocating its adoption nor questioning its baffling complexity. Although he noted the pensive and confused looks on the faces of many of the burgesses, he did not require Pendleton to clarify the proposal's more abstruse points.

In answer to one burgess's question about the benefit of a loan office to Virginia, Pendleton answered that "the depressing circumstances of this colony — the present low price of tobacco, the recent ban on our ability to issue money, the nullification of so many patents on land west of the Blue Ridge — all these factors, and others, have obliged so many persons here of substantial property to enter into great debts, which, if their payments were severely demanded, would ruin those men and their families and all who depend on them, and their ruin would with certainty harbinge the ruin of men of lesser and other circumstances throughout this colony. A loan office, supervised by men of the strictest virtue, would enable those more substantial persons to pay their necessary debts with greater ease, and help to put this colony on a firmer and unassailable economical footing."

Hugh observed that Pendleton's answer was more a plea than an answer. He wondered if Pendleton was one of those men of "substantial property." The man was a key member of the Loyal Land Company and had title to thousands of acres of land in the now-forbidden Ohio Valley and beyond. Many other burgesses in the chamber were also speculators. There were no looks of confusion on their faces, he noted, only a common one composed of hope, patience, and made-up minds.

Then Patrick Henry rose, was recognized by Robinson, and stunned the House. He excoriated the complexity of the proposal — "only a Newton could conceive of such a Gordian labyrinth...or should we say a charlatan?" — and pointed out that not only did British merchants already control the price of the colony's exported tobacco, but that the scheme would "allow them to pick our pockets afresh with the proposed ten shillings per hogshead levy, for ten long years, in order to pay back the loan." He ended his speech with the question, boldly addressed alternately to Speaker Robinson and Pendleton: "What, sirs? Is it proposed then to reclaim the spendthrift from his dissipation and extravagance by filling his pockets with money?" He waited a moment for a response, and when none came, the burgess for Louisa sat down. No one in the House rose to reply to him.

Pendleton and Randolph exchanged questioning, almost sly glances. The burgess for Caroline and the Attorney-General were not quite certain which was the object of Henry's rhetorical query: the colonial government itself, which had a debt of £250,000; or the colony's largest planters, who owed nearly a million pounds to British merchants and the Crown; or particular planters who would be the beneficiaries of a loan office.

Edgar Cullis leaned closer to Hugh and whispered into his colleague's ear, "Mr. Robinson is looking oddly contrite." Hugh glanced at the Speaker, who seemed to cringe in his chair. He also saw that Pendleton's face, while it had grown rigidly closed and almost monkish, was just a twitch short of the sneering expression of a man who was protecting a lie.

Pendleton rose and read the loan office resolutions to the House, and a

vote was conducted on each. Hugh, Cullis, Henry, and many of the newer
burgesses voted "Nay." It reassured Hugh that even Washington, who was
associated with the Ohio Company, a rival of the Loyal Land Company,
voted against the office.

The scheme, however, passed by a comfortable margin, and was
ordered prepared for submission to the Council. The plan's advocates suggested that a special committee be appointed to present it to that body. This
was done, and the day was over.

"They are worried, even in victory," said Cullis to Hugh, "lest those
twelve wise men see through the 'labyrinth' and shake their heads." They
walked leisurely down Duke of Gloucester Street back to Mary Gandy's
cottage. They had not decided whether to have supper there or in a tavern.
When Hugh did not answer, Cullis looked at his colleague and asked,
"What are you thinking, sir?"

Hugh tipped his hat in greeting as they passed a pair of ladies he had
met at the Governor's Palace the week before. Then he asked in turn, "All
those paper notes that were issued during the war and which were supposed to have been retired and burned — is there any evidence that they
were destroyed?"

Cullis searched his memory for a moment, then emitted a slow gasp.
"Why...well, I don't know...Mr. Robinson is the Treasurer....But, now
that you mention it, well, I don't recall that he ever reported to the House
that it was done...." He looked at Hugh with shock and amazement. "I see
what you are suggesting. And now I know why Mr. Henry was so coy in
his accusations today....It puzzled me, why he was not more forward in his
opposition to the scheme...."

Hugh sighed. "It cannot be proven, not unless the Treasurer's books
are very closely examined," he said. "Mr. Henry is eager to press for an
investigation, but not until the next session. But you see how simple a task
of legerdemain it would be for Mr. Robinson to substitute the expected sterling notes for those paper monies, at least in the account books. If there
have been secret loans of those condemned notes, their amounts and dates
could be altered to conform to the sterling. And then, the paper notes could
truly be destroyed — and with them, any evidence of malfeasance. And it
is Mr. Robinson who grants leave for an examination of the books. His own
private account books would need to be examined as well, for that is where
the truth would be found." Hugh shook his head. "He got away with it last
time, as you related to me, by blaming the deficit on delinquent tax collec-

tion by the sheriffs. But I do not believe he could fox another inquiry of that kind. Why propose only a two hundred and fifty thousand sterling loan, and not some other amount?"

"It was Mr. Richard Lee who pressed the matter, and sat on the examining committee," said Cullis.

"And he sat on the committee that composed the protests last fall," said Hugh. "You said that the language he proposed was not prudent enough for the others. It is little wonder that he has absented himself from this session." He chuckled. "Well, Mr. Henry has given them a warning."

The sun was beginning to set over the main building of the College of William and Mary in the distance, casting it into a long shadow. They heard the rattle of a carriage and the thud of hooves on the sandy boulevard behind them, and turned to see who was coming. It was the open landau of John Blair, president of the Council and Auditor-General. With him were Thomas and William Nelson of York County, and Peter Randolph, members of the Council. Hugh and Cullis doffed their hats in courtesy as the landau passed them, and the passengers nodded in answer. Behind Blair's came two more carriages, occupied by the rest of the Council. The carriages turned right on Palace Green and drove toward the Palace.

Before the last one was out of sight, Hugh stopped abruptly, his face twisted in sudden disgust and frustration. He tore off his hat and angrily flung it into the air. "Oh, what a conniving club of uncles, cousins, brothers-in-law, and nephews!" he exclaimed. He faced a startled Cullis and waved a finger at the Capitol far down Duke of Gloucester Street. "It is too much that we are dunned without by petty thieves in London, *and* snivelled within by that...*that* rookery of rogues!"

Cullis blinked in helpless silence at the outburst. He looked around, found his colleague's hat, picked it up, and handed it back to Hugh. All he could think to say was, "I am certain that the Council will reject the loan office, sir."

Hugh took his hat and slapped it once against his leg to shake off the dust. He nodded once in thanks to Cullis, replaced his hat, then asked, "Why are you so certain?"

Cullis said, "The Nelsons...they are a merchant family, not planters. They will see the guff in the scheme, and persuade the others to vote against it."

"I hope you are right, sir," said Hugh. He smiled then, and touched his colleague's shoulder. "Never think that I disvalue your advice and greater experience in this place," he said. He nodded to a tavern across the boulevard. "Come. I will treat you to a bumper of spirits to raise our own."

* * *

"Look, sirs," remarked Patrick Henry to his companions, "they begin to retreat even before the enemy comes into sight."

He sat on a bench outside the Raleigh Tavern with John Fleming, George Johnston, and Colonel Munford. The Saturday morning sun shone down on a boulevard that now was busy with the beginning of an exodus. Duke of Gloucester was alive with the passing of carriages, riding chairs, wagons, and horsemen as burgesses, traders, and farmers departed the capital for their distant homes and plantations. The General Court had discharged most of its cases, and the General Assembly was nearing the end of its session, which was actually a continuation of the session from last fall.

John Fleming lit a pipe, and, tossing away his match, said, "They are certain that the loan office will be approved by the Council and governor, that is all." He was one of the seven men appointed to present the proposal to the Council. He believed in its practicality, and did not ascribe ulterior motives to its purpose, as did his friend Henry.

"That is the only reason they attended," said Johnston, "to ensure passage of that proposal." Like Henry, he suspected there was more behind the idea than a means to salvage the colony's finances.

"Who is their enemy?" asked Colonel Munford, leaning over to address Henry, who was separated from him by Fleming and Johnston.

"Their immortal souls," said Henry. "Well, good riddance to them. Their departure almost guarantees adoption of at least one of our resolutions. If they were to stay, not one of them would pass, for these fellows are mere ballast, and would have voted against every one of our resolutions without Mr. Randolph or Mr. Robinson having to use his partisan to keep them in line — those two gentlemen being the sergeants of these feckless troops."

Munford said, "This is true, sir. But still, we face obstacles. The sergeants remain, who are supported by their best marksmen. Mr. Pendleton, for one."

Johnston said, "A few more members are sure to depart tomorrow after the service at Bruton, and more on Monday and Tuesday, when the Council returns our bills and proposals with their decisions."

Fleming posited, "By then, there may be just enough of the House left to form a quorum, and then we will be almost evenly matched."

"Or divided," remarked Munford. Then the colonel frowned in sudden, astonished realization. He leaned over again and saw a broad grin on Patrick Henry's face. "You foresaw this, didn't you, sir?"

Patrick Henry laughed quietly to himself. "Foresaw it, sir? Say, rather, I depended on it!" He nodded to the passing carriage of one of the wealthier burgesses. "The flight of these gentlemen is the greatest service they could perform for their country. They will not stand up to the Crown. They are making way for men who will." He glanced down the row of men on the bench. His smile vanished, and he rose to face them. Doffing his hat, he said gravely, "I salute you, sirs, for choosing to remain with me on this perilously empty field of honor and liberty."

Chapter 8: The Kindling

The exodus continued the next day and throughout the week as the House of Burgesses was steadily deserted by departing members. Washington, disappointed that the loan office proposal had passed, and certain that it would be approved by the Council, left on Sunday, May 26, after attending services at Bruton Parish Church with Lieutenant-Governor Fauquier. Other burgesses left that same day, confident that a loan office and financial rescue were in their future.

On Monday, the 27th, the loan office committee conferred with the Council.

On Tuesday, the House resumed its business, and the Council returned to it several bills that it had passed and received the Governor's signature, and one that had not—the loan office proposal, which was unanimously rejected.

During that day's afternoon recess, in the arcade that connected the House and Council chambers, an inconsolable Edmund Pendleton met with some of the "old guard" of the House and announced his own imminent departure. "This very evening," he said. "My work is finished here, and was fruitless. The Council, acting on bad and perhaps slanderous advice, has seen fit to ignore our pleas and scuttle the only accomplishment this session could have boasted."

He could not be persuaded to stay even to join them for dinner, although it occurred to none of his colleagues to urge him to stay and help defeat whatever mischief was afoot among the new burgesses concerning the Stamp Act, which was scheduled to be considered in the House the next day. Nor did it occur to Pendleton that perhaps he would be needed in this task. They were all certain that some resolutions would be proposed; and they were all certain that these would be deemed redundant and subsequently voted down. Peyton Randolph, George Wythe, and Richard Bland all felt equal to the task. It was not an issue of whether or not it could be done, but rather one of how quickly it could be done, so that the House could finish its business and adjourn the session.

After a round of handshakes, farewells, and Godspeeds, Pendleton left the arcade for his inn to begin packing for the long carriage ride home to Caroline County.

It was a caretaker House that reconvened at the ten o'clock bell on May 29. Of the one hundred and sixteen burgesses who held seats in the House, perhaps only eighty attended that May session. By this morning, just thirty-nine took their places on the benches in the chamber, only eleven more than were needed for a quorum. They were outnumbered by the crowd of spectators in the public space near the lobby door.

Hugh Kenrick sat with Edgar Cullis on one of the upper benches, above Patrick Henry, John Fleming, George Johnston, and Colonel Munford. He glanced around the sparsely occupied chamber with a sense that history was about to be made in it. This sense was buoyed by his recollection of something Henry had remarked to him last fall, after his maiden speech on the original protests. He had come to know most of the absent burgesses well enough that he was certain that he had a right to think this about them: The lazy did not care to think about the Stamp Act, let alone debate it, feeling that the subject was beyond their presumption of approval or disapproval; the thoughtless were indifferent to both the importance of the Act and to anyone's objection to it, believing with the lazy that the Act was not so bad that they could not in time adapt themselves to it; and the ignorant were oblivious to anything of importance.

Hugh suspected that most of these men wished that history and great men and great events would pass them by and leave them alone. Great events meant trouble and the upsetting of routines of thought and action. Being asked to think and act outside the familiar, safe confines of mundane concerns was, to them, an infuriating invasion of their perceived right to exist in careless, guaranteed, undisturbed anonymity.

The spectators were composed largely of merchants and tradesmen, observed Hugh, with a sprinkling of Council members. Thomas Jefferson had come too late to find a seat on the benches, and stood near the lobby door with the House usher. Seated on a front bench behind the railing that separated the public space from the floor were Jack Frake, Etáin, John Proudlocks, and John Ramshaw, who was staying at Morland. Hugh had sent Jack a note on Monday, alerting him to the impending discussion of the Stamp Act. Jack and his party arrived in Williamsburg this morning, and were staying at the house of an acquaintance.

Behind them also sat Wendel Barret of the *Courier*. After discussing the idea with Henry and his allies, Hugh sent Barret a separate note in which he proposed that the publisher print in secret all of Henry's resolves and post them to other colonial newspapers, regardless of what the House did about them. Both he and Barret doubted that Joseph Royle, editor of the official *Gazette*, would print them even should they receive unanimous endorsements.

"Where are all your patriots?" Ramshaw had asked earlier that day, when the remaining burgesses were gathered in the yard outside the House, waiting to go in, and Hugh stood with his visitors. The captain waved a pipe around the yard, and incredulous doubt was in his face. He had attended on occasion, in the past, sessions of the Commons, and was accustomed to seeing hundreds of men and hearing the babble of as many voices. Jack Frake was also surprised; he had expected to encounter near-full attendance on such an important occasion. He stood next to Ramshaw with a lit seegar, studying the burgess in dark clothing who dominated a conversation across the yard. Hugh had introduced this man, Patrick Henry, to his visitors, and after a brief exchange of cordialities, the intense burgess excused himself when he was approached by his allies for an impromptu, private conference.

Hugh had smiled and nodded to that group. "They are there, Mr. Ramshaw. We shall be seated on the right side of the House, on the Speaker's left, with the arcing sun behind us."

The morning and early afternoon passed quietly as the House approved of the Treasurer's accounts — "That won't come so easily next session," predicted Edgar Cullis — heard readings of other bills, and voted on the allocation of fifty pounds to repair the organ at Bruton Church. Hugh voted against the latter, while Cullis voted for it. "Why, sir?" he asked Hugh in whispered surprise. Hugh had replied, "If the parishioners there wish to hear an organ, let them be more generous in the collection plate."

Hugh noticed that Robinson, Wythe, Randolph, and Bland and other members of the "old guard" threw surreptitious glances at Patrick Henry and many of the new burgesses from the western counties, unsure of what to expect of them today. They seemed to be bracing themselves for an assault on their hegemony in the House. They were right to be anxious. The "new guard," cleaved from the "old" not only by a generation, but by a combination of its own alliances, sympathies, wealth, and ambition, was determined to either force the "old guard" to more forthrightly address the

issue of growing Crown power, or replace it in leadership. The muted anxiety and nonchalant confidence of the two groups created a premonitory
tension in the chamber as routine business matters, one by one, were taken
care of.

During a brief hiatus in that business, while John Randolph and his
clerks were busy shuffling papers, and the House was loud with the
shifting restlessness of burgesses and spectators, and Peyton Randolph was
conferring with Richard Bland on some matter, George Johnston rose and
was recognized, almost as an afterthought, by Speaker Robinson.

Johnston spoke, and the hubbub ceased instantly. "I move that this
House resolve itself into a Committee of the Whole House to immediately
consider the steps necessary to be taken by us as a consequence of the resolutions of the House of Commons, that have now passed into law, relative
to the charging of certain stamp duties in the American colonies."

As soon as Johnston sat down, Patrick Henry rose. He spoke calmly, so
as not to frighten the men he knew were afraid of him. "I second the
motion." He sat down and began sifting through some papers he took from
his portfolio.

Speaker Robinson could do little else but acknowledge the motion. The
day's scheduled business was completed, except for discussion of the Stamp
Act. A refusal to debate a "rumor" was out of the question now; too many
burgesses had seen the official copy yesterday, and had read much of it at
the Clerk's table. And news of its arrival had spread around town, many of
whose inhabitants were present as spectators. And two hours remained
before the House could recess for dinner. Robinson and Peyton Randolph
exchanged looks of insouciant resignation. Perhaps the matter could be
concluded, once and for all, before dinner, they told each other in that
silent exchange. With swift, meaningful looks at Richard Bland and George
Wythe, Robinson tapped his cane once on the floor and said to the House,
"This House has elected to go into a Committee of the Whole to discuss the
late statute known as the Stamp Act. The clerk will remove the mace."

As the Speaker rose and walked to a bench to sit as the burgess for King
and Queen County, Peyton Randolph rose and stood by the Speaker's chair.
In one hand he held a rolled-up sheaf of papers, the bound copy of the
Stamp Act presented to the House the day before. William Ferguson, who
had read the address, memorial, and remonstrance to the House in
December, on a cue from John Randolph, the chief clerk, came around the
table and with both hands picked up the gold-plated mace. At that moment,

through one of the tall, rectangular windows above the benches occupied mostly by the "new guard," a ray of sunlight glinted on the object in a single brilliant flash, then was gone as Ferguson gently put the mace on a shelf beneath the draped cloth of the table. Peyton Randolph then stepped up to the table and laid the Stamp Act in the mace's place. The same ray of sunlight shone now on the white first page, and after a moment, was gone.

Peyton Randolph turned, walked back to the Speaker's chair, and sat down in it. The Attorney-General leaned back, crossed his ample legs, and announced, "The floor is open, gentlemen. What say you?"

George Wythe rose and was recognized by Randolph. He spoke as though he were repeating for his colleagues's sake the simple rules of arithmetic. "Any discussion of the act by this House now would be premature, not to say discourteous, for we have not yet received replies to our protests of December last, at the beginning of this session. Such action by this House now would appear to be hasty, unwarranted, and precipitant. The particulars of this statute deserve discussion, and hearty discussion at that, but it would be unfair to ourselves and to the authors of those particulars if this House passed formal judgment on them without having given our cousins in London an opportunity to reply to our misgivings." Wythe sat down.

John Fleming rose from across the floor and was recognized. He said, with a restrained mockery whose object was unclear, "I must remind you, sir, and this House, that if our protests were going to be answered, we should have had those answers long before a copy of the act came into this House. I say that we have waited in vain for pigs to fly." This remark drew some laughter from both sides of the House, and among the spectators. "And," continued the burgess from Fairfax in a more serious tone, "it is my understanding that Mr. Montague and Mr. Abercromby have already informed their correspondents here that neither the Commons nor Lords have deigned to recognize our protests." He smiled pointedly at Wythe. "May I remind you, sir, and the House, that a spurned, unread letter cannot be replied to or answered?"

Colonel Richard Bland, the House "constitutionalist," rose, was quickly recognized by Randolph, and rescued the chairman of those committees of correspondence from the necessity of explaining to the House why they had not informed it of those reports. "That those bodies have not recognized our protests, sir, does not imply that we should not any day now receive replies to them, nor does the tardiness of those replies imply any right of ours to rush to judgment. It is the privileged discretion of Parliament to recognize protests and to answer them, or not." He paused to clear his throat. "Further, the intricacies of our excellent Constitution preclude rash assertions about whether our Parliament has remained within its bounden precincts, or has overstepped them. Neither is *this* a subject to be discussed in haste." Bland sat down.

John Ramshaw leaned closer to Jack Frake and scoffed, "Gadso, my friend! These fellows find themselves in a sinking ship in mid-ocean, yet they quibble that water is wet and may soil their shoes, so they will not help man the pumps!"

John Proudlocks, who overheard Ramshaw's remark, murmured to himself, "They are afraid of their little men."

Jack said to Etáin, "They are trying to salvage their own day books." Etáin nodded in understanding. Her husband had been sent a copy of Henry's resolves by Hugh. She understood him again when he added, "But another book is about to be written here today."

Etáin smiled. "I am glad that Hugh will have a hand in writing it."

Colonel Robert Munford rose and replied directly to his fellow militia officer. "The firelock has been rammed with double steel ball, sir, the priming pan packed with the driest powder, and the cock pulled back!" He turned to address the House. "*Must* we now wait for the muzzle to be pressed against our heads before we are *absolutely certain* that our elective brothers across the sea mean us harm? I know of no rule of civility that commands a man to behave like an addled half-wit in the face of a menace!" He gestured to the Stamp Act on the Clerk's table. "There is the weapon, sirs! It will be leveled at us on November first! Let us disarm it, or move ourselves beyond its range!"

"Hear! Hear!" exclaimed many burgesses on the right side of the chamber.

The House was then treated to a novelty: John Robinson rose to speak. None of the burgesses, not even those among the "old guard," could remember the last time he had anything to say in this forum on any matter, though his voting habits were well known. He said slowly, almost shyly, "I shall only paraphrase something which the esteemed Mr. Bland remarked here in December, gentlemen, that warlike speech may provoke warlike...consequences. I fear that the belligerent mood of many in this House today, if it is allowed in *any form* to be communicated to our brethren across the sea — and to His Majesty — may justifiably provoke an unfortunate and irreparable hostility. If we must discuss this statute, let us calmly discuss the facts of it, and refrain from seeing devils and demons in it. Let us spare ourselves the dangerous similes and absurd writhings of mis-careered thespians. This House is not a theater, and we are not a troupe of players." Robinson smiled, nodded once to Peyton Randolph, and sat down. He looked across the floor at Colonel Munford, and reserved for him a smile that was both smug and daring.

While most of the House chuckled at the Speaker's remarks, and some voices exclaimed, "Hear! Hear!" Patrick Henry glanced briefly up at Hugh Kenrick. Hugh girded himself to rise, but was beaten to recognition by Richard Bland.

"I am obliged to my colleague," said Bland with a bow to the Speaker, "for complimenting me with his remembrance. And I will support his sentiment by adding only that this matter ought not to be made a vehicle for Phocensian despair." He bowed again before he resumed his seat, this time to Randolph for the opportunity to speak again so soon.

Edgar Cullis's face wrinkled in confusion. "What did he say?" he wondered out loud to Hugh.

But Hugh did not hear his colleague's query. He was standing before Cullis had uttered the first word.

Peyton Randolph saw that the burgess for Queen Anne had risen even as others were still rising. He did not quite disguise a grimace, but nodded in recognition. He committed precedent, though, and allowed himself a sardonic comment. "Ah, Mr. Kenrick. Doubtless you are about to correct our learned colleague's antiquitish lore."

The House laughed. Even Cullis permitted himself a chuckle.

Hugh replied, "No, sir. I would not presume to offend Colonel Bland's wisdom with correction, but merely annotate his remark to say that when the men of Phocis ploughed the field of Delphi, it was neither Apollo nor his oracles who declared war on them, but their superstitious neighbors. The men of Phocis despaired of defending themselves against the invaders," he said for the House's edification, "and rather than be conquered and punished by them, built a funeral pyre for themselves and their families. But, before it could be lit, and as the invaders approached, those same men, because they wished to live, instead marched out in desperation and defeated their enemies."

Hugh turned and addressed Bland. "It may be presumed that an oracle of reason told them to plough the field, and also to fight one last time for their liberty. You may correct *me*, sir, but did not that incident occur during one of the Sacred Wars?"

This was not the reply that anyone in the House expected to hear. The Attorney-General gaped with an open mouth, which soon snapped shut, while Colonel Bland blinked in surprise. That man rose, nodded in reluctant concession, then resumed his seat. Patrick Henry turned his head to smile up at Hugh in his own admiring astonishment.

Hugh continued, "But this particular foray into antiquity was not how I wished to open my remarks, although I will say that I hope that, given the subject of our discussion, we will not find ourselves some day in a state of Phocensian despair. My purpose is to comply with Mr. Robinson's caution, and present for this House's consideration some *facts* about the Stamp Act."

He stood tall and straight, with his head held high. He spoke without notes, without fear, without care. He had promised Henry that he would present the slag of particulars to the House, and he proceeded to seduce that body with them, even those in it who did not wish to hear them.

"Gentlemen," he said, "we are faced with a conundrum over the veracity of our colleagues in faraway Westminster. What label shall we append to their words, actions, and designs: Attic faith, or Punic faith? How shall we unravel the riddle, and what will it reveal to us when we construe the puzzle it contains? And, having done that, what should we do about it?

"Sirs, a man's powers of persuasion rest not solely in his eloquence, but in how successful his style orders the facts he presents. I ask you, therefore, not to judge my eloquence, but the facts.

"Let us proceed to those facts, and scan some simple arithmetic. It is claimed by the authors and proponents of the Stamp Act, a copy of which is now in the custody of this House, that from these colonies, the levies enumerated in that act will raise some one hundred thousand pounds per annum. It is not denied by these gentlemen that the tax is an internal one, nor that it has been one long in contemplation. They make no distinction between that tax, taxes on our exports and imports, and any passed by this or any other colonial assembly. Nor should we, but that is another matter to be taken up, in future. We are assured by these gentlemen, the authors of this act, that the revenue raised by this new tax — a tax that may be paid in sterling *only*, let me stress that aspect, neither in kind nor in our own notes, but in rare sterling — that the revenue will remain in the colonies to defray the cost of the army here.

"Well, sirs, here is an instance of Punic faith! Britain may rightly abhor a standing army. Britain, so close to her regular enemies France, Spain, and the Netherlands, can exist in security and confidence without the burden and imposition of a standing army! We colonies, however, are spared that abhorrence, even though our close enemies to the west are less a threat to us than a single French privateer! Why are we to be relieved of that just fear? Well, you have all read the Proclamation of two years past. Allow me to read to you the reasons behind that qualification, that ominous exception, written by eminences in London who lay claim to being *friends* of these colonies."

Hugh paused to take from his coat pocket a sheet of paper. "Here is what a person in the train of Lord Shelburne wrote in his recommendations of policy: 'The provinces now being surrounded by an army, a navy, and by hostile tribes of Indians, it may be time, not to oppress or injure them, but to exact a *due deference* to the just and equitable demands of a British Parliament.'" Hugh paused to read another page. "And here is what an agent for Georgia wrote in recommendation: 'Troops and fortifications will be very necessary for Great Britain to keep up in her colonies, if she intends to settle their dependency on her.'"

Hugh paused to return the papers to his pocket. "It is such recommendations that influenced the wording and intent of the Proclamation, sirs. I trust I needn't repeat the encircling particulars of that document. The records of the Board of Trade, of the Privy Council, of the Secretary of State are rife with such recommendations, written, for the most part, by subministers and undersecretaries."

Peyton Randolph, not a little astounded by this information, raised a hand and remarked, "You are something of a magician, sir. How did you come by those damning citations? And who were the authors?"

"I cannot divulge that information, sir, without compromising their source. But you may take those citations to be authentic. You have my word on that."

"Doubtless, your purloining friend in the Commons," said Randolph.

Hugh smiled in wicked challenge. "One who is a member, and one who is not. You will recall that my colleagues in London are close to the Duke of Richmond and other worthies." He was not concerned about Randolph's suspicions. There were nearly five hundred and sixty members in the Commons, and innumerable officials and functionaries. "May I continue?"

Randolph conceded defeat and waved a hand.

"What," continued Hugh, "is the estimated cost of our standing army? Mr. Grenville asserts four hundred thousand pounds per annum. Where will the balance of that estimate come from, other than from the projected one hundred thousand raised by this stamp? In the best conjecture, from here, from there, but mostly from *us*, by way of all the duties we pay on manufactures and necessities brought into these colonies. Parliamentary trade estimates show that these colonies provide the Crown with a revenue of two millions per annum. That number represents not only our purchases, but all duties, indirect excises, and other charges and levies paid by us. What assurances have we that neither the army nor its subsidy here will not grow?" Hugh paused, and said, after the chamber was quiet, "*None.*"

Hugh reached into another pocket and took out another sheet of paper. "More arithmetic, sirs. Not all of you have had the opportunity to peruse the tome of taxation now resting on the Clerk's table. I now read to you some of the new costs to you and your fellow Virginians, when this statute becomes active law — when the trigger is pressed on November first." He read off many of the stamp duties he had read in Reece Vishonn's study weeks ago. When he was finished, he folded the paper and returned it to his pocket.

"Paltry sums, to be sure, you may be thinking — paltry to His Majesty, who thinks nothing of spending one hundred thousand pounds to guarantee his party's election to the Commons, or to purchase a party there after an election." Some hisses came from across the chamber, together with some muttering among the "old guard." Hugh said, "Paltry sums, sirs, but are *we* so prosperous and solvent that we can pay them? If the Crown will not accept our notes, even after discounting, or Spanish or French silver, with what can we pay these duties? With our credit? We have all but exhausted our credit with the mother country and the merchants there. If new credit is to be granted us, on what terms?"

Patrick Henry smiled to himself. Peyton Randolph looked fascinated, in spite of his dislike for the speaker. George Wythe looked thoughtful.

Hugh went on. "So much for the arithmetic, gentlemen," he said, knowing that he had a captive audience. "On to the *budget* of our liberty, and to what lies ahead for us if we submit *humbly* to the authority of this statute.

"Firstly, we will have conceded to Parliament the right and power to levy this tax, a tax contrived and imposed in careless violation of precedent, legality, and our liberties. This tax, sirs, if admitted and tolerated by us, will surely serve as an overture to other taxes and other powers. And, having granted Parliament that power *in absentia* — a power to raise a revenue from us, which was never the object of any of the navigation and commercial laws, burdensome and arbitrary in themselves — we will also have invited Parliament to render *this* body, and all colonial legislatures, redundant and superfluous! What would be the consequence of that negligence? That we would have representation neither here nor in Parliament! The very purpose and function of this assembly will have been obviated! This chamber, though occupied by men, would become a shell, a mockery! Think ahead, gentlemen. What would then prevent Parliament or the Board of Trade or the Privy Council from concluding that a costly assembly of voiceless and powerless burgesses should be forever dissolved? What would prevent the sages of Westminster from replacing a governor with a *lord-lieutenant?*"

Hugh paused again to plant clenched fists on his hips. "Ah, sirs! Here is more arrogance in the offing! A lord-lieutenant, he says. What impudence! Impossible! Our charters grant us the right to governors, dependent on our assemblies for their pay! Well, sirs, there is talk in the dank closets of Westminster of revising the charters of all the colonies, in order to exact a 'due deference' from them! A lord-lieutenant, may I remind you gentlemen, has neither an assembly to address, nor one to answer to. Such a false 'governor' would not be dependent on the benefices of an elected assembly, but would be paid directly by the Crown from our stamped pockets and purses, to ensure enforcement of Crown law! And, here is another — Sir! I am not finished!" exclaimed Hugh, pointing a finger at George Wythe, who had risen in an obviously agitated state.

Peyton Randolph glanced at Wythe, whose face was flushed red and whose hands shook in rage. Randolph shook his head once at the man. Wythe, glaring at Hugh, slowly sank back on the bench.

Hugh nodded thanks to Randolph, and continued. "And here is another ominous provision of this Stamp Act, sirs. In any case concerning violation of it, a prosecutor may choose between the venues of a jury court, and a juryless admiralty court in which to try a defendant. I leave to your imaginations, sirs, to think of which court would regularly find defendants so charged at fault, and promote the careers of interested informants and Crown officers.

"What would we be left with, sirs? Nothing that we had ever prided

ourselves in. We would become captives of the Crown, paying, toiling captives in a vast Bridewell prison! The one thing will follow the other, as
surely as innocuous streams feed great rivers. Mr. Grenville is first minister
now. Who will follow him? Another minister with his own notion of 'due
deference'? I shall paraphrase something I heard uttered not long ago," said
Hugh, turning to glance at Jack Frake among the spectators. "It should
matter little to us whether this law and the Proclamation are a consequence
of premeditated policy, or of divers coincidences, when the same logical end
is our *slavery*."

The chamber was quiet enough that Hugh heard a burgess across the
floor mutter a word.

"'*Traitor*,' did you say, sir?" he asked, addressing the man whose half-
closed, contemptuous eyes he noted. He took another sheet of paper from
his coat. "Allow me to read to you the words of another 'traitor,'" he said
with anger, "words on which I had planned to end my remarks, but which
ought to shame you for having pronounced your one." He brought up the
paper and read from it. "'The people who are the descendents of those, who
were forced to submit to the yoke of a government by constraint, have
always the right to shake it off, and free themselves from the usurpation, or
tyranny, which the sword hath brought in upon them, till their rulers put
them under such a frame of government, as they willingly, and of choice
consent to.'" Hugh glowered at the man. "That, sir, was Mr. John Locke, to
whom we all owe a debt of thanks, and you, sir, an apology." Then he
turned from the burgess and addressed the House. "I do not perceive in this
Stamp Act, sirs, either our will, our choice, or our consent!"

Hugh paused to take a breath, and continued. "The time to say 'No,'
gentlemen, is *now*, and to give ambitious, careless men notice that we will
not be ruled and bled to feebleness. If we succeed in a new, more vigorous
protest, then the stage will be set for us to correct other imbalances, other
injustices, other impositions. Better men than those who authored and
passed this act are in Parliament now. They spoke for us. They were over-
whelmed by the inertia of ignorance and the arrogance of avarice. But if we
stand our ground now, more like them will take heart and come to the fore,
men who see in this encroachment jeopardy of liberty in England itself,
men who recognize the possibility of a partnership between England and
this ad hoc confederation of colonies. We are Britons, sirs, and will not be
slaves! We are Virginians, sirs, and should be wise and proud enough to
find this tax repugnant to the cores of our souls!" He paused before con-

cluding, "Let us be known for our *Attic* faith!" Then he sat down.

George Wythe could not be contained. He shot up and began speaking before Randolph had a chance to recognize him. "What you are proposing, young sir," he shouted across the floor, waving an accusing finger at Hugh, "is lawlessness and rebellion!"

Hugh rose again and replied, "Lawlessness you shall have, sir, should this law become a permanent feature of our lives and its costliness banish so many men from the rule of law! You are an attorney, and ought to see ahead of things. As for proposing rebellion, I propose no more than what Mr. Locke prescribes, that we remind our presumptuous rulers of the proper forms of government for liberty!"

"There are constitutional methods of reminding them of that, sir!" said Richard Bland, who now stood with Wythe.

Hugh pointed a rigid finger at the Stamp Act. "Is *that* constitutional, sir?

"If a high court deems it such, yes, it may well be!"

"Then you are qualified to be Caesar's attorney, sir!"

By now, burgesses on both sides of the chamber were on their feet, clamoring for recognition or shouting accusations and retorts across the floor at one another. Only the spectators were quiet. Jack Frake and Etáin held hands in solemn excitement. John Proudlocks gazed up at Hugh in admiration. Captain Ramshaw was grinning broadly, while Wendel Barret behind him cackled with delight.

By the lobby door, Thomas Jefferson glanced over the heads of other spectators crowded around him, undecided whether to laugh in celebration or frown in sympathy for Wythe. He mused to the usher who stood next to him, "My mentor has been thoroughly lathered and shaved." And the usher could not decide whether the young man was expressing joy or grief.

Peyton Randolph's eyes were wide with fright. The pandemonium was worse than what which occurred last December and beyond his experience. He nodded urgently to his brother John to gavel the House back into order. That equally alarmed man seized the gavel and hammered it repeatedly, shouting above the shouts, "Order in this House! Order in this House! This committee will come to order!" He took the trouble to rise and remain standing, demurely hefting the gavel in his hand, until he saw that the last member had again taken his seat. The burgesses, in what seemed an eternity to him, reluctantly obeyed, muttering half-heard last words in answer to grumbled imprecations from across the floor.

The sole burgess who did not join in the verbal fracas was Patrick

Henry. He had remained seated while his allies and enemies traded blows, serenely observing, listening, and thinking. When Colonel Munford was again at his side, Henry leaned closer to him and said softly, "Each side has now expended its venom, and so minds will be clearer for the next business." He turned to glance up at Hugh, and nodded once in acknowledgment and appreciation.

John Randolph, satisfied that the House was in order, turned and sat down at his table. His brother Peyton looked warily around the chamber, and spoke only when he was certain he had regained his own composure. "Now that we all seem to have had our say on Mr. Kenrick's remarks, gentlemen, we may put away our grappling hooks and muskets, and be pleased to move on. Has anyone something of better substance to say on this subject?"

The burgesses were not certain of the object of the Attorney-General's veiled rebuke: themselves, or Hugh Kenrick.

Patrick Henry rose, and a special hush blanketed the House, as though every person in it had stopped breathing. He stood holding what looked like a page torn from a book. Many of the spectators edged closer to the railing to hear what he had to say. Peyton Randolph, suddenly alert and it beginning to dawn on him that perhaps he was not in full control of the proceedings, stared at this new nemesis for a moment before deciding to recognize the burgess from Louisa County.

Henry nodded, and said, "I wish to introduce a number of resolutions to the committee for its sagacious consideration."

Chapter 9: The Resolves

The floor, the audience, and the moment were Henry's. He spoke, and as he spoke, his eyes swept the House and graciously included his known enemies as men worthy of his address. He was bareheaded, having given Colonel Munford his hat to hold. The chamber was still enough now so that its occupants frowned occasionally in annoyance at the intrusive sounds of the distant rattling of a wagon as it passed the Capitol, of the muted tread of someone pacing in the Council chambers, of the chirping of birds in nearby trees beyond the closed windows.

"Sirs," said Henry in a clear voice, "this House's original entreaties to Parliament and His Majesty in protest of the then contemplated Stamp Act — entreaties written in astonishing deference, but doubtless from a sense of reason and justice — stand as of this day without the reciprocate courtesy of reply, except in the enactment of this act. We therefore find ourselves in a predicament which will not correct itself, not unless we take corrective actions. Many members of this House are in agreement that stronger and clearer positions must be transmitted to those parties, in order to elicit from them a concern for this matter commensurate with our own, lest Parliament and His Majesty construe our silence for passive concession and submission.

"We propose that this House adopt and forward to those parties, not genuflective beseechments or adulatory objurgations, but pungent *resolves* of our understanding of the origins and practice of British and American liberty, resolves which will frankly alert them to both the error of their presumptions and our determination to preserve that liberty. These resolves, in order to have some consequence and value, ought not to be expressed by us in the role of effusive mendicants applying for the restitution of what has been wrested from them, but with the cogently blunt mettle of men who refuse to be robbed."

After a pause to take the measure of his listeners, Henry continued. "And what is it we are being robbed of? The recognized and eviternal right to govern ourselves without Parliamentary interference, meddling, supervision, or usurpation! As another member here has so well explained, the Stamp Act represents not merely the levying of taxes on our goods, but on our *actions* to preserve our property and livelihoods. This law, he explained, will serve to remove from the realm of most of the freemen in this colony, and in our sister colonies, all moral recourse to justice and liberty.

"Surely, some here will counter: *That* is not the intent of this law and those duties. But, nevertheless, wisdom prescribes *that consequence*. And, in the abstract, even should every man in this colony have the miraculous means to pay these duties, the question would remain: Ought they? For if submission is an imperative, then they ought to submit as well to laws that would assign them their diets, arrange their marriages, and regulate their amusements and diversions." Henry smiled in contemptuous humor. "I am certain that in the vast woodwork of British government, there lurks an army of interlopers and harpies whose notions of 'due deference' and an ordered, dutiful, captive society fancy that direction in the matter of governing these colonies, an army that, until now, has been kept in check by its fear of ridicule and by the regular, bracing tonic of reason. The Stamp Act alone will not prompt that army to forget its proper inhibitions. But our submission to it will, and invite it to emerge from that worm-eaten woodwork like locusts to further infest our lives by leave of a Parliamentary prerogative that we failed to challenge."

Henry held up the page in his hand and shook it as he spoke. "Challenges, sirs, not remonstrances, are in order today! Resolutions, not memorials!" Then he dropped his hand, and gazed up at the ceiling and the cream-colored walls of the chamber. "Look around you, gentlemen. This is *our* forum, *our* legislature. It is a living, honorable thing, this hall, because we may meet in it to conduct our own business." Then he lowered his head, and looked around him with stern eyes. "But," he said in a warning, almost menacing voice, "neglect to challenge this law, and I foresee the day when this hall of liberty will become a mausoleum, redolent with the fading echoes of a distant, glorious freedom which from shame you may be reluctant to remember, and of which your children will have no notion, because we failed. Posterity will not look kindly upon us, should we fail. What might happen to this chamber? Well, in one of the many inglorious chapters that comprise the downfall of ancient Rome, it is noted that the Hall of Liberty was made to serve as a barracks for the mercenaries of an emperor. But perhaps events will be merciful, and this place will be burned and leveled by our wardens to prevent us from ever again presuming to conduct our own business without fear of offense or penalty."

All in the chamber listened in many varieties of quietude. Some men wished that they had said these things — and also that they had never heard them, for they knew that no answering oration could persuade men to forget what they were hearing. Others were rapt in thought and imagination, and listened to this man with a reverent attention they had never paid a minister, and never would, for Henry spoke, not of heaven, or of God's grace, or of afterlife damnation or reward, but of the requirements for the salvation and nobility of their souls here on earth.

Among the men who wished they had never heard his words were George Wythe, Richard Bland, and Peyton Randolph, and the word that convinced them that Henry must be opposed and answered was *emperor*. That word made them tremble with fear, lest the Governor hear that it had been spoken, and naturally conclude, just as they did, that it was an allusive reference to His Majesty. Henry had so far said nothing they could disagree with. They believed, however, that Parliament could be reproved without scolding it, and that the king could be advised and corrected without rebuking or offending him. They believed it was possible to revolt without reprimand, risk, or revolution. Besides, they felt offended by Henry's characterization of their past efforts as "genuflective beseechments" and "adulatory objurgations," and of themselves as "effusive mendicants." These slights weighed as much with them as did their practical fears.

Henry held up the page in his hand. "Here are some resolves." He began pacing before the first tier of benches, sometimes reading from the page, sometimes reciting its contents from memory.

"Whereas, the honorable House of Commons in England have of late drawn into question how far the General Assembly of this colony hath the power to enact laws for laying of taxes and imposing duties payable by the people of this, His Majesty's most ancient colony; for setting and ascertaining the same to all future times, the House of Burgesses of this present General Assembly have come to the following resolves."

Henry stopped to gesture once with his other hand in acknowledgement of an obvious fact. "Resolved, that the first adventurers and settlers of this His Majesty's colony and dominion of Virginia brought with them, and transmitted to their posterity, and all other of His Majesty's subjects since inhabiting in this His Majesty's said colony, all the privileges and immunities that have at any time been held, enjoyed, and possessed by the people of Great Britain." He paused to allow a protest or contradiction to be voiced by someone on the other side of the chamber. No one rose to speak. He read on.

"Resolved, that by two royal charters, granted by King James the First, the colonists aforesaid are declared entitled to all the privileges, liberties, and immunities of denizens and natural-born subjects, to all intents and purposes, as if they had been abiding and born within the realm of England."

Again, Henry paused to glance around. No one rose to protest, comment, or contradict him. He exchanged looks with the chief opponents on the other side of the House — Wythe, Bland, Robinson, and Randolph — and saw in their set expressions and frozen eyes that they wished they could protest, but could not.

He went on. "Resolved, that the taxation of the people by themselves, or by persons chosen by themselves to represent them, who can only know what taxes the people are able to bear, and the easiest mode of raising them, and who must themselves be equally affected by such taxes — an arrangement," interjected Henry, "which is the surest security against burdensome taxation by our own representatives —" then continued to read from the page, "is the distinguishing characteristic of British freedom, and without which the ancient Constitution cannot subsist."

Henry paused again, and Peyton Randolph, who was nearest him, imagined he saw a devilish smile fleet over the man's face. "Resolve the fourth, gentlemen: That His Majesty's liege people of this his most ancient and loyal colony of Virginia, have without interruption enjoyed the precious right of being thus governed *by their own Assembly* in the article of their taxes and internal police, and that the same hath *never* been forfeited or in any other way given up or surrendered, but hath been constantly recognized by the kings and people of Great Britain."

Henry stopped and glanced around the chamber. "Those, sirs, are the premises of a uniquely extended syllogism. Here is its conclusion." He snapped up the page and read from it in a precise, impavid voice. "Resolved, that the General Assembly of this colony have the *only* and *sole* exclusive right and power to lay taxes and impositions upon the inhabitants of this colony, and that every attempt to vest such power in any person or persons whatsoever, other than the General Assembly of this colony, has a manifest tendency to destroy British as well as American freedom!"

Henry read the fifth resolve in the manner of an ultimatum, of a royal decree, of a commandment. It was delivered with the authority of an absolute, unquestioned, and unquestionable moral certainty.

Some burgesses groaned in fear. Others scoffed in anger. Richard Bland muttered to himself, "But only three parts make a syllogism!" Peyton Randolph, who faced the spectators, saw in that crowd too many faces that regarded Henry with an admiration that meant more than mere agreement with him.

Henry's hand dropped to his side, the lethal page fluttering in the air. He addressed Randolph. "There are two more resolves to be read, sir, but these five are their foundation, and must be adopted before the sixth and seventh can have any meaning or force." He nodded in courtesy to the chairman. "You may open the floor to contest." He returned to his seat and sat down. Colonel Munford handed him his hat. Henry put it back on his head with a gesture of finality.

Randolph looked to his allies for some indication from them that they were immediately prepared to argue the resolves back onto that fluttering page and out of men's minds, to confound Henry's oratory with eloquence of their own. But all he saw in their expressions was angry, closed-mouth dumbness. He, too, was in a state of speechlessness. Randolph silently cursed Edmund Pendleton, their best speaker, for having gone home.

Not a single truth in the resolves could be denied, thought Randolph. He was even willing to concede the truth contained in the fifth. But it was a dangerous truth, a truth which, if uttered to the Governor, or written in a formal protest, would directly challenge Parliamentary authority. It was a truth that could be extended and applied to *all* Crown authority. It was a truth that contradicted the entire apparatus of the Empire. It was a truth that could bring war, if it were allowed to emerge from the House as a conviction.

Randolph had been Attorney-General for twenty-one years. He remembered that he had served well both Virginia and the king all these years. He remembered now, with some bitterness, his journey to England over ten years ago to represent the colony and this House in the conflict over Governor Dinwiddie's pistole fee and the legal authority of a royal governor imposing his own land tax. A compromise had been reached, even though then, too, the House's resolves were rejected by Parliament and the king. Randolph well remembered the contemptuous harangue of the King's Counsel and Attorney-General, William Murray, now Baron Mansfield and Chief Justice of the King's Bench, against "this little assembly — this puny

House of Burgesses," for having "boldly dared to do what the House of Commons never presume to attempt," that is, to question the king's right to dispose of his lands as he pleased. The counsel for the House had argued that the burgesses were objecting, not to their sovereign's actions, but to those of his viceroy. The result of that conflict was that Dinwiddie's wrist was slapped by the Board of Trade, and the matter was dropped. But Murray upheld the Crown's right to govern the colonies, whether in the name of the king or of Parliament.

And here was a man who denied that right, who flouted and contradicted centuries-old wisdom! Randolph thought: *I*, who trained for the law at the Middle Temple, was not permitted to argue this colony's case, and had to hire a councilor! Yet *this* man, this…country boy who may as well have appeared here in a hunting shirt, who had only just recently discovered law books, and had no legal training whatsoever, *this* man presumes to match himself in the Cockpit of the Privy Council against Baron Mansfield, Chief Justice? Why, the prospect was absurd, it did violence to the mind! Those two at bare fists over the king's pleasure and the Constitution? Murder would be done by one or the other! And, no matter who remained standing, Virginia, and any man here who approved of the fifth resolve, would pay a penalty too terrible to contemplate! No, thought Randolph, resolves we might have — but not *those* resolves!

Some words came to his mind then, words that inadequately described what he had just heard: *keenness* and *vigor*. Then he remembered who had spoken them, and when, and why. He glanced up at Hugh Kenrick, who sat above Henry. Both men — indeed, most of the members on that side of the House — were studying him with a daring air of patient expectation. What an unholy alliance! wondered Randolph.

He sighed and spoke. "The gentleman will please read again *his* resolutions to the committee, so that they may be discussed and voted on by the House, in accordance with proper form." He composed himself as best he could, bracing himself for the violence he was certain would erupt.

Henry rose and read the resolves. After each was read and seconded by George Johnston and others in Henry's party, a lively debate ensued, and Randolph, torn between a desire to seem fair and impartial, and an instinct for judging the time right to end debate and call for a vote he hoped would defeat each resolve, became visibly agitated at the acrimony and course of events.

"I object to these resolutions for two reasons," proclaimed Wythe.

"They are redundant, for they merely reiterate our protests of last fall! And those protests have now been cast in imprudent and, one may say, *insolent* language!"

George Johnston replied, "The gentleman complains that the Roman geese are too noisy, and disturb his sleep!"

"The language of these resolves is abhorrent and bellicose!" insisted Bland.

Henry replied, "I saw no purpose in the sham piety of this House's former protests — and I see no consequence!"

"*Sham piety*?" retorted Landon Carter, burgess for Richmond. "Do you doubt our loyalty to His Majesty? That is more likely a description of your own dearth of respect for the Crown!"

"My respect for the Crown is not a whit less than that which I have for British liberty and the Constitution, sir!" roared Henry.

"Sham piety may amuse us in a farce," said Colonel Munford, "where it is held to ridicule and produces laughter! But that mawkish behavior has never protected a man's property or person from a highwayman, and it will not serve that purpose now!"

"If our past protests were written in sham piety, sir, *I* have not heard the timbers of this House crack or shake from the rollicking gaiety of its members!"

"These resolves are riddled with ungenerous insinuations that cannot but be noticed and marked by their lordships and our brothers in the Commons."

"These resolves are near treasonous!"

"And not this act?"

"His Majesty will protect this colony, and all his dominions, once he perceives the folly of this act!" said another burgess. "But were he to read the language of these resolves, he may think the devil may take us, and who would blame him?"

"Who is to instruct him in that folly, sir? That phalanx of philosophers on the Privy Council? That synod of sages on the Board of Trade? Lord Bute? That man seems to have instructed his pupil well in the role of king."

"You go too far, sir!"

"May I remind the gentleman that His Majesty commissioned the Privy Seal, Lord Marlborough, to endorse this act, and in so doing confessed his approval of it as a mode of 'protecting' his dominions, as surely as if it bore his own signature!"

"And may I *also* remind that gentleman that his late Proclamation erected the walls of a prison here, and that this act represents the first of *many* fees we are likely to be charged for inhabiting this prison? The analogy of that young gentleman to Bridewell Prison is quite appropriate!"

"You asperse the character of the king, sir!"

"Then I asperse what is not there, sir! Hardly an offense!"

"We are represented in Parliament, gentlemen, by the Constitution and the king! If we were not, would Parliament have dared pass this act?"

"We are *not* represented, sir, and this act is extralegal in that context!"

"Why all this fuss and noise over a few pence and shillings?"

"Our liberty is worth at least a few pence and shillings, sir! Ought we to wait until it is worth a few pounds or guineas to make a fuss? A sack of Spanish dollars? Perhaps, our very lives?"

"You gentlemen and these resolves build a bonfire to roast a pigeon! That is all I am saying."

"You may depend on it — *I* will not surrender my liberty for a farthing, never mind a penny! No stamps will ever blot my life!"

"Brave words, sir, but they sound like bluster! Wait until you are caught between idealism and inconvenience!"

"I am a veteran of the late war, sir, and if I could do it, I would call as witnesses to my 'bluster' the score of Frenchmen and Indians I killed in personal combat! Decorum forbids me from showing the House the scars of battle that map my body!"

The House forgot to recess for dinner that afternoon, so engrossed were the members by the necessity or danger of the resolves. At one point, when Peyton Randolph was discouraged by the bitter exchanges and the ominous course of the voting, he pulled out his watch and saw with a gasp that it was nearly six o'clock. He conceded defeat, ignored a number of members who had risen on both sides of the House, and abruptly called for a vote on the fifth resolve. John Randolph, William Ferguson, and Clough Anderson, who had recorded the resolves and the first four votes, prepared themselves for the last.

The first four resolves were passed by the Committee of the Whole House by twenty-two to seventeen. The fifth passed by a single vote. Peyton Randolph announced, "The Committee has seen fit to adopt Mr. Henry's resolutions, which will be reported to the House on the morrow. The hour being so late, the House will recess until the bell at ten o'clock."

It was a stream of angry, sour-faced older burgesses that first filed out past the spectators from the chamber, leaving first by courtesy of the younger members out of deference to age and wisdom. Henry and his party lingered behind on the benches, in a manner of having won and held the field of battle.

Hugh Kenrick stepped down from his seat and held out his hand to Patrick Henry, who took it. They shook with a feeling of triumph. "My congratulations, sir," said Hugh. "You wield an effective sword. I have much to learn from you."

Henry laughed. "No, sir, you do not. But I tolerate sham modesty more than I do sham piety!" He paused when Johnston, Munford, Fleming, and the others who had voted for the resolves and who had gathered around him all laughed. Then he said, "Sirs, I fear that we may still have a fight to face, especially over the fifth resolve. Be prepared. Those other gentlemen are moved by fear, and that can be just as powerful a force as certitude. I beg you to recall Mr. Kenrick's remarks on Phocensian despair. Our work will be completed when the House adopts all five resolves, and God willing, the sixth and seventh."

* * *

As the remaining burgesses left the chamber with a boisterous crowd of spectators, Hugh was met at the railing by his friends. His mind was still spinning from the victory and his role in it. He was only dimly aware of what his friends were saying.

"You acquitted yourself magnificently, Hugh," said Etáin, who leaned up to buss him on the cheek.

"Well done, son!" laughed Wendel Barret. "I don't care if the Governor revokes my license for it, but I shall print those resolves and send them to every newspaper in these colonies! They ought to light more fireworks like we saw here!"

"By God, Jack," exclaimed John Ramshaw as he slapped and gripped Hugh's shoulder, "this lad and Mr. Henry blew the heads of those nay-sayers as surely as you ended Paul Robichaux's career! They are dead in the water!"

Hugh shook his head. "You over-credit me, sir. I was merely the lin-stock. Mr. Henry was the gun."

John Proudlocks shook Hugh's hand and said, "That Mr. Henry, sir, he is the sachem of a band of warriors new to me...warriors of the mind. You are all...brave! I am glad I witnessed this day. Thank you."

Jack Frake could do little else but beam proudly at Hugh. He was lost in a wonder he had not felt in years, not since he found himself in the caves of Marvel in Cornwall, and met a crew of heroes called the Skelly Gang. The words, emotions, and spirit he had experienced here in this chamber somehow matched the words and spirit he had known in the caves. He was thinking of the night, long ago, when he sat on a beach with other men, waiting for a galley to land contraband goods, and he had turned over in his mind the cruel irony of being a free man only in the night, and in the caves. *We must move in darkness, and exile ourselves to the shadows.* And here were men who were stepping boldly from the caves, from the darkness, and from the shadows! What a moment! he thought. What a leap, from the caves to the sunshine of this chamber!

Etáin glanced at her husband, and noticed a special, almost wistful kind of happiness in his face, and was happy for him.

Jack offered his hand to Hugh. "Well done, my friend."

Hugh felt, besides his own pride, an odd, almost incongruous vindication. He, too, saw the happiness in Jack's eyes, and in his entire manner, and as he reached out to grasp his friend's hand, sensed that he was reaching across all their years to congratulate the boy he had never known but whose story he knew. For a long moment, which was only a half-second, he was confused by the phenomenon of congratulating Jack, when it was Jack who was congratulating him. Then it became clear to him: He was congratulating himself for the story of his own youth, whose victories now included this day. In that timeless moment, he was the boy Hugh Kenrick meeting the boy Jack Frake; they recognized and saluted each other, then parted to live their lives and become what each was now, up to and including this moment. He saw in Jack's eyes that he felt this meeting, too.

Their hands clasped, and they shook twice. "Thank you, Jack," said Hugh.

As the sergeant-at-arms and usher herded spectators out of the chamber, Thomas Jefferson shyly approached Hugh. "Mr. Kenrick," he said, "I am in your debt, and Mr. Henry's. What heroic oration! I could not help but think, as I listened to you and him," he added haltingly, "that if Mr. Henry is a Jason of some new Argonauts in search of the golden fleece of liberty, then you are his Lynceus, who can see so many leagues ahead over the prow of the *Argos*! What an adventure lies in the future for us now!" He shook Hugh's hand, almost as if it were a presumption to touch him. "I shall come tomorrow, to witness a further episode of this adventure!" He bowed to Hugh and his party, then turned and rushed out.

Outside, in the Capitol courtyard, stood a number of planters and merchants, among them Reece Vishonn. Vishonn accosted Hugh and offered his compliments, which he qualified with fearful concern. "I don't know if the Governor will stand for such talk, Mr. Kenrick," he remarked. "He may postpone the next session until heads have cooled."

Hugh shrugged. "These are our protests, sir, not his own. All he can do is dissolve the Assembly for our having made them."

The party made its way down Duke of Gloucester Street into the evening sun. Etáin, walking between Jack and Hugh, linked her arms through theirs.

Edgar Cullis trailed behind them, convinced of the correctness of his votes, but wondering now what the consequences would be. He was afraid.

Chapter 10: The Treason

The bluntness of the resolves was not the only thing that moved the conservative leadership and membership of the House to oppose Henry and his party. It was also the twin fears of the abrupt challenge to their hegemony by the younger members, most of whom represented counties west of the fall line, and of reprisal by the powers in London. Even though they begrudgingly agreed with the resolves and the reasoning behind them, it was imperative that they work to defeat them. In that goal, however, lay a vexing conundrum: to support the resolves, in a public forum, would be to concede leadership to those who originated and advocated them; to oppose them would elicit the certain contempt and censure of the electorate, which would express that disapproval in the next elections.

Further, they knew that the king, on the advice of his Privy Council, as punishment for the resolves, could just as soon revoke the charter that allowed them to meet in political assembly, as allow the powers of the legislature to be whittled away over time by the Stamp Act and similar acts in the future. Hugh Kenrick's prediction on this point was not lost on those who disagreed with him.

And so the older burgesses and their leaders cursed their predicament, and while cursing it fumed with each other and with themselves over the stark reality of that predicament and the best way to insulate themselves from it. Determined to maintain their hegemony, they chose to argue for civility, loyalty, tradition, and the preservation of the General Assembly against two potent enemies: those who wished to assert their rights and liberties, and those unseen men who could destroy them.

The next morning the lobby and public space were crowded with more spectators than had come the day before. Word had spread in the town that an unusually lively and rancorous debate took place over the Stamp Act, and people came to hear and see for themselves what the burgesses were saying and proposed to do. Peyton Randolph, John Robinson, and other older burgesses looked askance at the larger mob that milled beyond the railing, and knew why its size had almost doubled: No mere political controversy could have or ever had attracted such interest; secretly, they knew that it was a moral issue, and that they were caught between the uncomfortably close poles of a moral dilemma.

In a mood of spite for Henry, his party, and the spectators, Robinson drew out the business of minor bills as long as he could, for hours, until there was nothing left to do but ask Peyton Randolph to report the committee's resolves from the day before. The crowd, Robinson furtively noted, had not dwindled, but seemed to have grown.

Jack and Etáin Frake, John Ramshaw, John Proudlocks, and Wendel Barret had come early enough again to find seats on the same bench. Reece Vishonn and Ralph Cullis stood in the crowd behind them. Thomas Jefferson again found himself standing at the lobby door.

Well into the reading and voting on the resolves, more spectators arrived, among them a middle-aged Frenchman, the Chevalier d'Annemours, who entered Williamsburg at noon from Yorktown in a riding chair, and who went immediately to the Capitol because he had been told by an innkeeper that important things were happening there. Under the alias of Alphonse Croisset, commercial agent, the nobleman had been touring the colonies, and had spent the last month in Maryland and Virginia, on behalf of the French government, reappraising the colonies' legal and illegal trade potential. Standing just outside in the House lobby with other spectators, he had to crane his neck and strain his ears to appreciate what was transpiring inside.

Hugh Kenrick and Edgar Cullis this time sat on the first tier of benches, several places down from Patrick Henry. Hugh was tired. He had sat up half the night before, after having supper with his friends, assuring his colleague from Queen Anne that all the resolves were worth voting for, and that he should not change his vote on any one of them. "If the House adopts these five, then the sixth and seventh stand a chance, too. The five alone will give Parliament pause for thought. The sixth and seventh will cause Mr. Grenville and his party to choke on their brandy. Remember what I said about bullies."

"I remember," said Cullis. "But these bullies have a navy, and an army not a week's march from here! We...we could be hanged!"

Hugh had shrugged. "You are only conceding my argument, Mr. Cullis."

Today, many older burgesses glared at Hugh from across the floor. He could not decide whether it was from pure malice, or resentment for having raised truths they had rather not have heard. He found himself imagining what Dogmael Jones must have endured in the Commons, a single man among hundreds, defying a political process manipulated by shrewder and less scrupulous men than any who practiced here.

Reluctantly, Peyton Randolph rose and read each of the resolves to the House as though he were reading obscene literature. Some desultory debate occurred between members on both sides of the chamber. The first three resolves passed by the same margin: twenty-two to seventeen. When Randolph finished reading the fourth, George Wythe rose again to protest. "I maintain that proper deference must be shown to Parliament, and I remind the gentlemen across the floor that, should these resolutions pass, they will be read by their lordships in the upper House, by His Majesty, *and* by eminences throughout the kingdom too numerous to name here. We will seem to be upstart renegades, not only by England, but also by our fellow colonials here. I cannot imagine a more distasteful consequence!"

Patrick Henry rose and was recognized by Robinson. He asked, "If *this* House elects to wait on Parliament, sir, may I ask in what capacity? Ought we to wait idle in the foyer of those eminences' concerns, in the mental livery of a menial, while they complete the latest business of oppressing the good people of England, not daring to whisper the persecution of their own brethren, lest it somehow insinuate our own?" He turned sharply away from Wythe, whose eyes were wide with anger, and addressed the House. "Some men in this chamber may prefer to approach the bar of Parliament, hats in hand, on raw knees, as humble supplicants, in search of redress and restitution. *I*, sirs, prefer to wait for Parliament to call on me, to beg *my* forgiveness for that body's attempt to dupe and enslave me *and* this my country!"

He was answered, not by anyone from the other side, but by an assenting murmur among the spectators. Henry did not seem to take notice of the sound, and sat down. Robinson, Bland, Wythe, and their party, however, all glanced in the direction of the spectators in a range of expressions from disgust to trepidation to indifference. The Speaker ordered the clerks to conduct a vote. William Ferguson rose and read the fourth resolve for a last time. His colleague, Clough Anderson, marked down the Ayes and Nays as each burgess rose and spoke. The fourth resolve passed and was adopted by the House by the same margin as the day before, twenty-two to seventeen.

Peyton Randolph rose and read the fifth resolve. The Speaker could not contain his emotion as he heard again the words of that resolve; he gripped the cane in his hand and the arm of his chair, eyes closed in agony, as though a physician were lancing a boil. Spectators who had not heard the resolve read yesterday gasped or groaned in surprise. Patrick Henry, Colonel Munford, and others in that party sat calmly as Randolph read from the document that had been prepared from Henry's law book page. Edgar Cullis, next to Hugh, fidgeted nervously in his seat.

Immediately Randolph finished, almost all the older burgesses rose to be recognized. But Randolph had not taken his seat after his chore was finished, and Speaker Robinson nodded to him. Acting now not as Attorney-General or committee chairman but as burgess for the City of Williamsburg, Randolph said, in a somber, almost petulant tone, "The gentleman who authored this resolve and those that have already passed this House, together with the gentlemen who endorse them, accuse the steadier members of this body of wishing merely to suggest, not to affirm, of choosing to insinuate, not to state, the alleged means and ends of the act in question. I now most emphatically protest that view, because it denigrates not only the Crown, Parliament, and His Majesty, but the characters and motives of those here who have argued for the just independence of this body for perhaps many more years than certain of those gentlemen have trod the earth. I insist here that we are neither oblivious nor indifferent to the dangers to our liberty contained in this act. We are rendered a disservice by those who say we are, and our honor is consequently besmirched."

Randolph exercised his privilege as the second most powerful man in the House to step away from his seat and stand near the Speaker's chair. "However," he continued, "I, for one, in a gesture of Christian virtue, am willing to forgive and forget those charges and that impetuous slander. I maintain, in agreement with another offended gentleman here, that this particular resolution, more than any of the others that have passed this House — resolutions whose adoption by us can only disgrace us — is nothing less than an invitation to tragedy! It imputes Parliament *and* His Majesty no honor, no room for doubt, no capacity for error, no quantum of dignity. It grants them no sphere for honorable concession or conciliation. There is no charity in any of these resolutions, no tolerance for human frailty, no allowance for misguided intention."

Randolph strode to the middle of the floor and pointed a finger at each of the burgesses on the opposite side. "You gentlemen," he said with embittered warning, "who rear your heads in anger and toy with the hilts of your swords, you, sirs, who by endorsing these resolutions confess an ignorance of the difference between foolishness and wisdom, mark my words: You will rue this day *and* your enthusiasm if this particular resolution is transmitted to London! You forget the virtue of moderation, you think only of yourselves, of your pride, of some book-bound, airy abstraction of liberty! In doing so, you also forget those who will surely suffer the same penalties as you will bring upon yourselves! And penalties there will be!"

He walked back in the direction of the Speaker, and paused across from Henry. He gestured to that burgess. "This particular resolution is presumed to rest on a rock foundation, when the gentleman here who authored it asserts himself that its substance depends on the Crown's benevolent favor! This House has, in the past, met the Crown in the bountiful pasture of conciliation, and come away from it with the successful preservation of our independence here. But enter that field clad in the false armor of righteous certitude, and you will find ranged against you the lawful guns that will check your advance to folly and anarchy! I ask you gentlemen to remember what happened here not a century ago, when Nathaniel Bacon presumed to challenge the lawful authority of the Crown!" Randolph scoffed once, and glanced down at Henry with a withering look. "This, too, is *my* country, and I will do everything in my power to prevent a repetition of that chaos, misery, death, and destruction!"

Randolph returned to his place near the Speaker's chair. "That curious colony to the north, Massachusetts, has a number of times in the past drunk the heady wine of revolt, but, in the end, settled for the calming beverage of accommodation, and has grown and prospered from the lesson. Are we to be less wise than that province?" He paused. "Accommodation, gentlemen! Only accommodation with the Crown as a partner in empire has brought about the liberty we enjoy today, and fruits of liberty. If, however, we presume to elevate ourselves above the Crown and its lofty ends, we can only guarantee our own ruin, and that of the Empire! The Empire may recover from that misadventure, but I can assure this House that our place in it will be its meanest and most pitiable element — and justly so. When once Virginia was great and prosperous, it will be poor and despised. Gentlemen, our future is in your hands." The Attorney-General bowed slightly to both sides of the House, then strode purposefully to his seat.

Hugh Kenrick rose before any other burgesses could. Robinson was obliged to recognize him. Hugh said, "We who endorse these resolves are

neither ignorant of the difference between foolishness and wisdom, nor
oblivious to the virtues of those who have trod the earth before many of us
came into it. Virtue, said Socrates, springs not from possessions — and I
mean here not merely our tangible wealth, but our liberties as well — not
from possessions, but from virtue springs those possessions, and all other
human blessings, whether for the individual or society. In these circumstances, the virtue which that gentleman accuses us of lacking has become
a vice. Call it moderation, or charity, it will not serve us now. We exercise
the virtue of righteous certitude, for it alone has the efficacy that conciliation and accommodation have not. That virtue is expressed — and I believe
that the honorable Colonel Bland there will concur with me on this point —
that virtue is expressed in one of the original charters of this colony, and in
the first charter of Massachusetts, and has merely been reiterated in these
resolves, but in clearer language. Moral certitude is a virtue itself, and in this
instance is a glorious one, because it asserts and affirms, in all those charters and resolves, our natural liberty and the blessings it bestows upon us!"

Hugh's mouth bent in a devilish grin, and he wagged a finger at the
members on the other side. "Let us not imbibe the hemlock of humility,
duty, or deference, sirs! Socrates did not have a choice in that regard. *We*
have. Should we choose to rest on the virtue boasted of and advocated by
that more experienced gentleman, that will be a more certain path to the
despair, defeat, and regret he fears, and we will have nothing left that we
can call our own!" Hugh glanced around once more, then took his seat.

"Damn that *boy*!" muttered Peyton Randolph to himself.

"Bravo!" whispered Etáin Frake.

"That was shot straight through their gunport!" chuckled John
Ramshaw.

"My friend," Jack Frake addressed the figure on the bench, "you are
glorious in your own right."

"What a sublime contest!" exclaimed Thomas Jefferson. Like most of
the spectators who stood with him, he was completely enthralled by the
drama taking place in the chamber. And like them, he did not seem to
notice that he was pressed by bodies front, back, and on his sides. He was
tall, though, and could see over the heads of the crowd before him. A few
more spectators arrived at this moment, nudging Jefferson and others
around him further into the public space.

"*Pardon, s'il vous plaît*! I cannot see!" complained one of the newcomers.
Jefferson, surprised, turned briefly to see a short, wiry Frenchman standing

on tiptoe to peer over the heads and shoulders that blocked his view.

The older burgesses, in the meanwhile, sat stunned and mute. The contradictory prospects of ruin by adoption and ruin by accommodation caused their many minds to spin fruitlessly in search of rebuttals. Both arguments were convincing. Given the time to compose their thoughts over Madeira, soothed by an evening breeze, they may have devised a riposte. But there was no time. Many of them, too, realized that there was nothing to say.

Patrick Henry, however, had more to say. His colleagues nearest him noticed that his face had grown red, and that his blue-gray eyes were set in a murderous fury whose object they did not envy. Henry rose, and those eyes fastened on Speaker Robinson. That man otherwise would have fallen back on the rationale that since Henry had already spoken, he could be denied recognition. But he knew by the ferocious set of Henry's features that this man would not be silenced. In the hiatus, no one else had risen, and he was bound to allow this man to speak.

Henry had removed his hat and handed it again to Colonel Munford. He took a step away from his seat. "The honorable gentleman there," he said, pointing boldly to Peyton Randolph, "spoke now, not of the rightness or wrongness of the resolve in question, but of ominous consequences should this House adopt it. I own that I am perplexed by his attention to what the Crown can and may do, and by his neglect to speak to the propriety of the resolve and the impropriety of this Stamp Act. Should he have examined for us the basis of his fears? Yes. But he did not. Perhaps he concluded that they were too terrible to articulate. So *I* shall examine them, for I believe that he and I share one well-founded fear: The power of the Crown to punish us, to scatter us, to despoil us, for the temerity of asserting in no ambiguous terms *our* liberty! *I* fear that power no less than he. But I say that such a fear, of such a power, can move a man to one of two courses. He can make a compact with that power, one of mutual *accommodation*, so that he may live the balance of his years in the shadow of that power, ever-trembling in soul-dulling funk lest that power rob him once again.

"Or — he can rise up, and to that power say '*No!*,' to that power proclaim: 'Liberty cannot, and will not, ever accommodate tyranny! I am wise to that Faustian bargain, and will not barter piecemeal or in whole *my* liberty!'"

Henry folded his arms and surveyed the rows of stony-faced members across the floor. "Why are you gentlemen so fearful of that word?" he demanded. "Why have not one of you dared pronounce it? Is it because you

believe that if it is not spoken, or its fact or action in any form not acknowledged, it will not be what it is? Well, *I* will speak it for you and for all this
colony to hear!" His arms dropped, but the left rose again, and he shouted,
stabbing the air with a fist, *"Tyranny! Tyranny! Tyranny!"* The arm
dropped again. "There! The horror is named!" He suddenly strode to the
clerk's table, seized the bound pages of the Stamp Act that lay next to the
golden mace, and violently thrust it back down, causing John Randolph and
his clerks to wince, and loose papers to blow to the floor. *"Tyranny!* There
is its guise, sirs! What a Janus-faced object it is, smirking at you on one side
of its mask, shedding tears for you on the other! What a contemptible set
of men who authored it, but whom you wish to *accommodate*! What a dis-
graceful proposition! And what a travesty you ask us to condone! 'Tis a
mere pound of flesh we propose to remove from you, they tell you in gentle,
proper language, and we promise that you will not bleed. *Hah!"* barked
Henry with scorn. "You will recall how the Bard proved the folly and fal-
lacy of that kind of compact! Are not accommodation and compromise
another but greater form of it? He proved it in a comedy, sirs! You propose
to prove it in a tragedy, and if you succeed in penning *finis* to your opus,
you may rue the day you put your names on its title page!"

Henry wandered back in the direction of his seat, though his contemptuous glance did not leave the men on the opposition benches. "You gentlemen, you have amassed vast, stately libraries from which you seem to be
reluctant to cull or retain much wisdom. Know that I, too, have books, and
that they are loose and dog-eared from my having read them, and I have
profited from that habit." His voice now rose to a pitch that seemed to
shatter the air. "History is rife with instances of ambitious, grasping
tyranny! Like many of you, I, too, have read that in the past, the tyrants
Tarquin and Julius Caesar each had his Brutus, Catline had his Cicero and
Cato, and, closer to our time, Charles had his Cromwell! George the Third
may —"

The opposition benches exploded in outrage. Burgesses shot up at the
sound of the king's name, released now from their dumb silence, and found
their argument. They cried to the Speaker, "Treason!" "Treason!"
"Enough! He speaks treason!" "Expel that man!" "Silence that traitor!"
"Stay his tongue!" "Treason!"

Speaker Robinson was also on his feet, shaking his cane at Henry.
"Treason, sir! Treason! I warn you, sir! Treason!"

Henry, determined to finish his sentence, shouted about the tumult,

"— may George the Third profit by their example!"

"Treason!" insisted more of the older members. "Sedition!" "Treason!" "Speaker, silence that man!"

Henry stood defiantly, facing his gesturing accusers, then raised a hand and whipped it through the air in a diagonal swath that seemed to sweep them all way. "If this be treason, then make the most of it!" he shouted. He stood for a moment more, then turned and strode back to his seat. But, he did not sit, for he was not finished.

John Randolph was shouting now, "Order in the House! Order in the House!" He hammered his gavel repeatedly until its wood handle stung his hand. His clerks bent to retrieve the papers blown to the floor. The Chief Clerk, angry that his position had not allowed him to join in the hue and cry of treason, shook the gavel at the excited throng behind the railing. "You people, there! Be quiet, or the House will order this chamber cleared of strangers!" He struck the gavel twice more.

Jack Frake had risen from his seat in silent, uncontrollable agreement with Henry. Etáin's eyes were moist with approval. John Ramshaw stared at Henry with joyous wonder, and John Proudlocks with happy amazement. Reece Vishonn and Ralph Cullis exchanged looks of worried bafflement, undecided about whether their sense of danger came from Henry or from the men who talked and expostulated around them.

Thomas Jefferson rubbed the sides of his face with his hands, his eyes aglow with exaltation. "Oh, what eloquence! What heights men can climb!" he said to himself. "He speaks as Homer spoke!"

In a collective excitement, the standing crowd had pressed forward even closer so as not to miss a single word or action in this drama. Alphonse Croisset had taken out a little notebook and pencil, and, amid the jostling and hubbub, managed to scribble down in halting English the words and events he was witnessing through the shifting cracks of the noisy wall of bodies that imprisoned him.

When the House was quiet again, Speaker Robinson rose gravely from his chair and pointed his cane at Henry. "This man has spoken treason, sirs," he declared with regret and spent anger, "and I am sorry to observe that no one here was loyal enough to His Majesty to stop him before he had gone so far."

Hugh remarked to Edgar Cullis, "They are not afraid to pronounce *that* word!"

Cullis, though, stared back at him with wide, frightened eyes; he was shaken by the violence of the event.

As the Speaker slowly settled back into his chair, Hugh said to his colleague, "I will defend him." He rose and waited for the Speaker to recognize him.

Robinson glanced up from some horrible reverie of his own, and
nodded to the waiting figure without recognition or care.

Hugh spoke. His words did not come easily now, for he exerted an
effort that was alien to him, and with difficulty said each word as though
he were renouncing his life and his right to it. "If the last speaker has
affronted the Speaker or this House, I am certain he is ready to ask pardon.
I have no doubt that he would prove his loyalty to His Majesty at the
expense of the last drop of his blood. What he said now must be attributed
to the interest of his country's dying liberty, which is foremost in his heart,
and in the heat of passion may have led him to say more than he intended.
If he has said anything wrong, I am sure he would beg the pardon of the
House and the Speaker."

"Who speaks now, s'il vous plait?" queried Croisset, who could not see
into the chamber. No one answered him, for no one heard his question. But
the voice he heard reciting an apology sounded like the one that had pro-
voked the protests. Croisset wrote rapidly in his notebook.

Hugh observed the mollified looks on the faces of the older burgesses,
and sat down again.

"Sham piety!" muttered George Wythe.

John Robinson turned to look at Henry, who had not resumed his seat.
Henry returned the glance with narrowed, waiting, unrepentant eyes. The
Speaker averted those eyes, and stared at the floor before him. He was
afraid of this man. He felt the expectant eyes of Peyton Randolph, Richard
Bland, and all the older members on his person and position. He was now
afraid of them. He could not force himself to require Henry to beg his
pardon. There was something about the man that caused him to be both
afraid of it, and afraid to betray it. And this man's opposition to the
defeated loan office proposal seemed somehow connected with the necessity of forgiving him. Robinson thought: Who am I to cast a stone at this
man? With an imperceptible shake of his head, he said, in a curious
manner of atonement, "The apology is accepted, and the matter is to be
dropped." He glanced again at Henry, to whom he felt transparent. Henry
nodded once, and with a slight bow of his head, turned and resumed his
seat. Robinson looked up and said to the Chief Clerk, "Mr. Randolph, you

will read this last resolution and conduct a vote."

William Ferguson was instructed to read the fifth resolve for the last time. He adjusted his spectacles and obliged. As he read, Peyton Randolph's mouth pursed in grim bitterness. Wythe and Bland, daggers in their eyes, both regarded the Speaker with a disappointment that verged on disdain; it would have been a small triumph to hear Henry himself stammer an apology. Robinson would not look in their direction. Their assessment of him did not change even when he was called on to voice his vote, and he said "Nay."

Hopes for the defeat of the resolve were crushed when four older members shocked the "conservatives" and voted "Aye," then were raised when four younger members voted "Nay." Among the latter was Edgar Cullis, whose mind still reeled wildly from Randolph's dire warning and Henry's fiery vehemence.

* * *

The fifth resolve was adopted by the House by a margin of one vote, twenty to nineteen. Patrick Henry leaned back in his seat, his eyes closed in relief. Peyton Randolph's features twisted in anger. Members on both sides of the House realized now whose vote could have caused a tie, whose vote would have been against not only the fifth resolve but all its companions: Edmund Pendleton's.

That man had left Williamsburg in high dudgeon over the defeat of the loan office scheme. With his vote on the transcendent fifth resolve, Robinson could have exercised his capacity and privilege as Speaker and voted again to break the tie.

Pendleton's conspicuous absence yesterday and today festered in the minds of the House's leaders, particularly Peyton Randolph's. Pendleton could have made a difference these last two days, he thought. His clear, orderly mind and calm but effective manner of speaking could have persuaded some of the younger members to oppose all the resolutions, and not just the fifth. And then this session could have ended on a far more amicable and satisfactory note.

Randolph glanced at Robinson. The Speaker looked beaten, ashamed, and troubled. The Attorney-General thought: My old friend has not long to occupy that chair; he is losing his hold on the House, and this day has cost him.

Robinson ordered an adjournment until the next morning. Again, the older members led the way out of the chamber, brushing hurriedly through the knot of spectators to reach the lobby doors. Peyton Randolph was one of the last of them to leave, following Wythe and Robinson. He was still incensed over the outcome. His world seemed to be falling apart, too; the resolves could have been negatived, but for the stubborn, spleenish obstinacy of one man — Pendleton! And then, he was defeated by a man half his age, a man whose license to practice law he should have opposed. Moreover, he was bested and confounded by that too-learned English youth from one of the most insignificant counties. All in all, a thoroughly humiliating day.

A tall, familiar figure stepped out of his way as he approached the lobby doors. It was a distant cousin, Thomas Jefferson, who regarded him with an odd species of sympathy that contrasted with the flushed contentment on his face. Here was another know-it-all boy, thought Randolph, his head filled with bookish learning and airy ideals. No doubt he enjoyed seeing a kinsman pelted with classical allusions and grand oratory. Pent-up anger got the best of Randolph, and he blurted into that young man's face, wanting to erase the innocence from it, "By God, I would have given five hundred guineas for a single vote!"

But Jefferson merely blinked in astonishment and took a step back. The Attorney-General snorted once, then shouldered his way past the equally astonished Alphonse Croisset, his huge frame almost knocking the Frenchman over, and stepping on the shoe of John Tyler, a friend of Henry's from Hanover.

Chapter 11: The Wound

"Thank you, sir...for the gesture. I was not prepared to make it myself, not even at the price of expulsion." Patrick Henry paused. "Forgive me the policy, but I never beg pardon for speaking what is on my mind."

Hugh Kenrick shook his head. "It was a necessary gesture, sir, to save the resolves."

They stood with Colonel Munford, George Johnston, and John Fleming in the courtyard of the Capitol. Another burgess, Paul Carrington of Charlotte, had joined them. He was one of the older members who had voted for the first four resolves, opposed the fifth, but changed his vote on the last reading.

Henry studied Hugh, and in his scrutiny was sincere admiration. "You have my profoundest gratitude, sir," he said. "I know that you are not by nature an obsequious man. You have my apology for causing you to speak in my defense. But had I apologized in there — had I the strength to screw up the mortifying courage to mouth those words —" he added, nodding to the Capitol behind them, "it might have cost the resolves more votes. Whether my apology was genuine or an exercise in sham piety, more of our party might have seen some value in humility...and deference, and voted governed by their weaknesses."

Hugh turned this over in his mind for a moment, then replied, "That may be true, sir. But, to be frank, I did what I did, also because I did not wish to hear you speak an untruth. Nor did I wish to see you punished for refusing to speak one. And I wished to save the resolves."

Carrington spoke up. "Had there not been an apology, sirs," he said to the group, "I truly believe that Mr. Robinson would have been persuaded by that devil Randolph to chuck the resolves and begin expulsion proceedings, in preparation for a trial in an extraordinary session of the General Court." He turned to Henry with a frown. "Then you *and* the resolves would have been lost."

Colonel Munford patted Hugh's shoulder. "Then Virginia and every liberty-loving soul in it owe this man their thanks, sirs! He has mine!" All the other men acknowledged the truth of this statement, and doffed their hats to Hugh.

Hugh gravely inclined his head in acknowledgment.

The group was one of many that had collected in the courtyard. Some were composed of younger burgesses talking excitedly about the resolves and their role in their adoption. Older members huddled together to express their disgust and fears. The largest, though, was made up of lingering spectators; it was obvious that the focus of their distant fascination was Henry.

Hugh glanced around the courtyard, hoping to spot Edgar Cullis. His colleague had left the chamber without a word, rushing to follow the older members in their exit. Hugh saw his friends from Caxton standing apart from the other groups near the Capitol gate, waiting for him.

Henry was saying now, "...My wife is not in her best health, sirs, and my property needs attention. I have been away for too long. I will take my leave for Hanover tonight."

His friends were stunned. "But we need you to present the sixth and seventh resolves," protested Fleming. He added with half-hearted amusement, "None of *us* has the 'old guard' showing their tails!"

Henry shook his head. "My mind is made up. And think of this: If I stayed to argue those resolves, Mr. Randolph and the others might take it into their heads to retract the whole lot. You know how vengeful and dangerous a wounded bear or mountain cat can be. The five resolves will stand. You and our friends here may present the last two. Your advocacy will not jeopardize what we have accomplished. So I shall emulate Mr. Lee, and remove my offending presence. But beware of skullduggery." He turned to Hugh. "You were right, Mr. Kenrick. Our Assembly is a miniature of the Commons, with all the same virtues and faults. I know now from experience how such men can oppose a principle by opposing the man who proposes it, in an unattractive union of fear and spite."

"And, of *accommodation,*" Hugh reminded Henry with a pained smile.

"The watchword of compromise and cowardice!" scoffed Colonel Munford.

Henry said to Hugh, "You can assure us that your printer friend, Mr. Barret, will run off the resolves and post them? Now that five of them have been adopted, I feel better about that scheme."

Hugh grinned. "He is eager to return to Caxton and take up his compositor's stick."

* * *

Later that afternoon, with Colonel Munford and the others, Hugh saw Patrick Henry off on his journey back to Hanover, and shook his hand once more. This time it was Henry who reached down from his saddle to grasp Hugh's hand. "We work well together, Mr. Kenrick," he said as he clasped and shook. "You have obliged me to reassess somewhat my estimate of England. You are a late product of it. I did not believe that it could still produce men of such courage, dedication, and vitality."

"Thank you, sir," replied Hugh after some hesitation, for he could not imagine what instance of courage he had exhibited for Henry to observe. "I look forward to working with you again, next session."

After bidding last goodbyes to his friends, Henry urged his lean mount on and rode back down Duke of Gloucester Street and into the late afternoon sun. As he passed Bruton Church, he broke into a canter.

The group stood watching his dwindling figure. George Johnston remarked, "Gentlemen, there goes a weave of the best of us."

* * *

A celebration by the victorious burgesses was held in one of the taverns that night, with fiddlers, country dancing, and an open table of food and punch. A ball at the Governor's Palace marked the closing of the session. Hugh was invited to both occasions, but attended neither, instead having a supper with his friends in another inn. Here he was regaled by John Ramshaw and Wendel Barret, and granted respectful deference by Jack Frake, Etáin, and Proudlocks. For a reason he could not understand, but for which he chided himself, he was glad, for once, when the time came for them to part, to leave their company.

When he returned to Mary Gandy's house near the College late that night, he encountered Edgar Cullis, and wondered about the fickle power of oratory. His colleague meekly announced that he was returning to Caxton in the morning with his father.

Hugh felt a pang of insult — he was certain that Cullis was afraid of him now — and said, before he could check himself, "I had not intended to reproach you, Mr. Cullis. Not this afternoon, and not now."

"You have no right to rebuke me, sir!" snapped Cullis, his eyes flashing angrily. "I voted with my conscience, and that is my business!"

"Of course," said Hugh. "But there are two more resolves to introduce."
He paused. "And I heard some talk outside the Capitol about a motion to
reconsider the fifth. We are counting on your presence."

Cullis shook his head. "I cannot endorse it or the last resolves." He
looked away from Hugh. "Neither will I oppose them."

"Very well," said Hugh. "We will not discuss the matter further."

The same speech that could convince some men of a truth and to act
on it, he thought, could dissuade others. With the latter, it was not an issue
of denying the truth of a thing, but of rebelling against or fearing the conditions necessary to pursue and uphold it, that could cause a man to oppose
what he knew was right. He studied Cullis for a moment. The older man sat
at the kitchen table, reading a pocket Bible by candlelight. He turned and left
him alone, went to his own room, lit some candles, and took out his writing
instruments for the task of transcribing Henry's and his own words in the
House today, as well as others spoken in that modern coliseum.

In the midst of copying what he could remember of Peyton Randolph's
speech, Hugh paused. The truth of one thing would not leave his mind; it
had not left it all day. It was his apology to Robinson. It had more than
dampened his elation over the victory; it nearly drowned it. He agreed with
Henry that an apology by him would have somehow diluted the importance
of the resolves, that an apology by Henry himself would likely have given
Randolph and the others an excuse to insist on a tempering of the resolves's
language. Hugh did not hold Henry responsible for the necessity of an
apology, and would not score him on his inability or refusal to make one.
The man had authored the resolves and chosen to risk making himself an
object of enmity to accomplish their adoption.

Hugh understood now why he had been uncomfortable when Henry
had ascribed courage to him, why he had been glad to leave the company of
his friends this evening. Jack, Etáin, Ramshaw, Proudlocks, and Barret had
all looked at him over supper and conversation with more than admiration,
with a new esteem he was unable to identify. He resented the granting of
that esteem, for what he felt was shame. The nature of the apology troubled
him to the core. It had required words, words employed in an expression of
dishonesty to protect the honest words of the resolves. It was a lie, he
thought, uttered to foster and advance a truth.

Courage? he scoffed, throwing down his pencil, for an answer to his
uneasiness was beginning to dawn on him. He pondered the many forms of
courage that that virtue could take. He thought of his friend Roger Tall-

madge, picking up the King's Colors at Minden, and in so doing attracting the enemy's fire. He thought of Glorious Swain, rushing to protect him on the Charing Cross pillory. Of Jack Frake, on the *Sparrowhawk*, fighting a French privateer, of grappling with Indians at the Braddock disaster. He thought of Henry today, hurling defiance back at his accusers. He thought of so many instances of courage, but could not convince himself that his own action deserved a place in that family of distinction.

In time, he remembered the day he refused to apologize to the Duke of Cumberland.

He fell back in his chair with a cry of pain, struck by the justice of the memory. He sobbed once in protest. Who am *I* to be called courageous? he thought. Who am *I* to cite Socrates on virtue, to lecture anyone on words and moral certitude? Who am *I* to despise cringers and cowards? In one thoughtless moment, I rushed to speak a lie! There was no sincerity in my words, and everyone knew it, everyone knew the purpose of my lie, and I committed a fraud in my own mind and in the minds of those who heard those words! I hated every word I spoke then, and every effort to speak them, yet some maddened, desperate impulse drove me on! Was that courage? What else could Henry have meant by my courage, except that lie? And he and the others saluted me for it!

He tried to reconcile courage, honor, and his soul, and could not. The blatant fraud of the lie would not let him. I have abased myself, he concluded. Dishonored myself, besmirched my own worth, betrayed that which I once was! I have begun my own corruption, allowed its incubus to begin its work! What I did was a willful choice to bow, to submit, to offer my neck to an unseen sword! If courage was often an unpremeditated act of bravery, how can my life conform to that description?

Hugh's mind whirled and tossed in shifting concentric circles of logic and self-reproach that would merge, then fly apart, and duel each other for supremacy over and over again. The resolves were saved, but at what price? He could not think clearly about the apology and a guilt he had never before experienced.

He stopped pacing when he heard a knock on his door, and was astonished to see that he was on his feet, and had been pacing. He frowned, went to the door, and opened it, expecting to see Cullis. Instead, standing in the diminished candlelight, he saw Jack Frake.

Jack looked at him with an odd, almost compassionate expression. Hugh heard him say, "Mr. Cullis heard you moving about, and sent me up."

Then Hugh found himself sitting on his bed, and Jack seated opposite him, watching him with intimate concern. Hugh felt a burning sensation on his cheeks, and realized that it was tears, and that his chin and neck were moist with them. The room seemed brighter now; Jack had relit or replaced the candles that had gone out.

Hugh asked, "Why are you here?"

"I was...worried about you," said Jack. "So was Etáin."

"Why?"

"I suspected what it must have cost you, to make that apology to Robinson and the House. I could see it as you spoke today. So could Etáin."

"How...could you know...before I knew...?"

"It was the way you spoke, Hugh. It was not your usual manner." Jack paused to search for words. "You spoke with a difficulty which you disguised in a...slow, measured pace. You had spoken just before Mr. Henry. It was easy to note the difference, and to guess the cause." Jack shrugged. "Well, they got their damned apology, but I believe that, in the end, it will be worth less to them than an unsigned tobacco note. But we both presumed that you know you were trying to save the resolves — which I believe you did — and that your apology for Henry was worth even less to you." Jack smiled briefly. "And then, I remembered something. Your reticence tonight with us — or what Etáin calls a 'tell-tale shyness' — it told us that you were not happy with what you thought necessary to do. We had expected to see your wonderfully arrogant self tonight. Instead, we found ourselves toasting a man of reluctant modesty. Only we knew that it was not modesty that could explain why you were so...quiet." He shook his head. "We knew that you were troubled, and were certain why."

"What did you...remember?" asked Hugh.

"What you told me about you and the Duke of Cumberland."

Hugh leaned forward, and each word he spoke was enunciated as though he wished it was a rod that whipped him. "I committed a crime worse than the treason they accused Mr. Henry of!" he exclaimed. He closed his eyes in agony. "The great thing that was accomplished today — it depended on a lie! And I spoke it! I cannot forgive myself...."

"You gave them what they wanted, pitiful thing that it was," remarked Jack. "And I am not convinced that this great thing — and it *is* a great thing, Hugh, the first of many great things, I think — I am not convinced that it needed a lie." Jack seemed to smile again. "I am not certain that Randolph and the others were prepared to hold the resolves hostage until an apology was paid." He reached over and put a reassuring hand on Hugh's shoulder. "Here is the most important thing, my dear friend, and it concerns you and you alone: When you spoke then, you were risking, not your life to save those resolves, but your soul. I had not seen that kind of courage before, not that kind of honor, not that kind of devotion. That...makes you a kind of brother to me, you see. When you spoke the apology, I also envied you the chance to speak it. I envied you the chance, but not the pain." Jack gripped Hugh's shoulder and shook it. "The pain, Hugh. I suppose it is a natural thing to feel. But Randolph and Robinson and the others, they could not wound you. You wound yourself. You should not belittle or chastise or punish yourself over the matter." He paused. "You will collect yourself again, Hugh. If brave men survive their risks, that is all they can do. We honor their memory, if they perish, for we are the heirs of their bravery. And we honor them if they do not, for then we are their beneficiaries, and we can enjoy their company."

Hugh asked, "How can you know I will collect myself?"

Jack smiled sadly, let go of Hugh's shoulder, and looked away. "I did...after I hanged my friends at Falmouth....I collected myself before I did that. Before we were separated...before I was taken from the jail and put into that orphanage with bars, Skelly and Redmagne remarked that if they were going to be hanged — and they were certain they would be — they agreed to request that they be hanged together. That was how I knew what I must do...and I was not certain then that I had the courage to do it...." Jack seemed to be gazing at a time and place of long ago.

"Oh, Jack!" whispered Hugh. He stared at his friend, and sat in amazed wonder for the man who could be what he was, a man who some would claim was an accomplice in the murder of Augustus Skelly and Redmagne. Yet here he was, a man with the cleanest soul he had ever known. "Can you forgive me for having forgotten that...?"

Jack shook his head. "There's nothing to forgive, Hugh. That was my crisis. This is yours." He smiled again, then reached inside his coat and took out a folded slip of paper. He handed it to Hugh. "Etáin wanted you to have this. She made me wait while she copied it out. Thinking she would be bored with the House's business, she brought along one of the books you brought her from London. The works of Thomas Browne. She does not think much of what he writes, but she did find that." He patted Hugh's shoulder once more, then rose. "I was right to come here. I bid you goodnight. Your friends look forward to seeing you in the House tomorrow."

Hugh smiled weakly. "Yes….Mr. Henry has gone home."

"That should not make a difference, even should Randolph and the others manage to gut his resolves."

"Gut them they will try," mused Hugh. He rose and saw Jack to the door, and shook his hand. "Thank you for coming…Jack," he said. "It *has* made a difference…."

He waited until Jack's footsteps faded away, then returned to the table and opened Etáin's message. He smiled in gratitude as he read an excerpt from Browne's essay, "The Heroic Mind":

"…Where true fortitude dwells, loyalty, bounty, friendship, and fidelity may be found…. Small and creeping things are the product of petty souls…. Pitiful things are only to be found in the cottages of such breasts. But bright thoughts, clear deeds, constancy, fidelity, bounty, and generous honesty are the gems of noble minds…."

This was followed by Etáin's signature. That was all.

Chapter 12: The Old Guard

That same cloudy, rain-threatening evening, several older House members, and a trio of Council members, met in joyous desperation outside the gate of the Governor's Palace before they presented themselves and their wives at the ball.

"Henry has left!"

"Thank God!"

"How careless of him!"

"What hubris!"

"Support for those resolutions must now collapse!"

"Well, not quite collapse, as be reduced in strength."

"We must persuade those who are left to change their votes. Especially on the fifth resolution. And to agree to a modification of the language of the first four."

"Yes....But I understand that they have two more to introduce."

"Let them be read, and even debated! If the House reverses itself on the fifth, those last two, which must be as seditious as the fifth, will fall with it!"

"Is there a precedent for the House changing its mind on resolutions it has already adopted? I cannot recollect."

"On resolutions, I think not. But I am sure that something of the sort was done on a minor matter. We must conform to established practice. We must scour the journals for a precedent."

"And if no precedent is to be found...?"

"Then we must make one, damn it all! We cannot allow those resolutions to go to Parliament and the Board of Trade as they stand!"

"Why the hugger-mugger over a hotchpotch of articles, sirs? I don't see that their style can make a difference. Very likely, the Commons committee that receives them will consign them to unread oblivion, or use them to wrap engraved plate to present to His Majesty as a token of mutual comity."

"Need I point out, sir, that these resolutions, in their present form, are just a rung or two short of...a declaration of independence from the Crown?"

"This is true, sir. We want to communicate a statement of legitimate grievance *and* natural kinship, not a…petition for divorce!"

"A *declaration of independence*, did you say? How rude a notion! We don't want anyone to believe that *that* is what we are up to. God save us from the very idea! It is a notion to be discouraged at all costs. Why, recall what happened to the Netherlands when those provinces revolted against Spain and cocked their noses at Philip the Second! Their complaints were likewise legitimate, and the petition of redress the nobles presented was likewise ignored, and many of its signers executed. There are some lessons from history to be heeded here, sirs!"

"I do recall, sir. But the Netherlands won their independence."

"After eighty years of misery and war and strife between brother and brother and the Spaniards, too. We should not mount our own hubris and presume that we would be exempt from such a phenomenon."

"Well put, sir. But enough talk about what we all agree is a treasonous absurdity! Here is what must be done. Two or three of our party have also left for their homes, and three or four of Henry's, as well. Before the bell tomorrow morning, we must invite a few of these remaining hot-heads to the committee room and sponge their brows with some cool advice…."

It was only when a strategy had been agreed on, and tasks assigned, that the group's members breathed easier and allowed themselves to rejoin their wives and the company inside the Palace.

* * *

The Chevalier d'Annemours arrived early the next morning to ensure that he found a better place from which to observe the remarkable proceedings than he had had yesterday. He noticed a tall, red-headed youth pacing in the arcade that linked the two halves of the Capitol, and recalled him from the day before as the person who was subjected to the unprovoked outburst by the very substantial Attorney-General, Monsieur Randolph, who had also nearly bowled him off his feet and stepped on the toes of other gentlemen on his way out. The Chevalier approached the young man and introduced himself as Alphonse Croisset, commercial agent. The Frenchman had been very careful to maintain that deception throughout his sojourn in the colonies, for one slip of the tongue could get him into trouble with the English government, which, if it ever got wind of his true mission here, could have him locked up as a spy. And rightly so.

Croisset tried to strike up a friendly conversation with the youth about the House and the drama they had both witnessed the day before, but there was a faraway look in the lad's eyes, and his replies were distracted and his queries merely courteous. He was helpful, though, and accompanied the inquisitive visitor into the chamber to explain some of the features and functions of the place. They found another person in there, however, sitting at the Clerk's table. "Excuse me, sir," said the youth, who then left the side of his companion, passed the railing, and walked up to the lone, richly dressed person.

This large, florid-faced person was Peter Randolph, Surveyor-General of the southern colonies and a member of the Council, and also a distant cousin of Thomas Jefferson. He was rapidly turning the pages of a bound, oversized tome that was one of the House journals. Jefferson greeted him, and inquired about his purpose.

Peter Randolph sighed. "Searching for a time when this House negatived its own determination, or at least changed its mind on some matter."

"To what end, sir?"

Randolph shook his head. "To put a stop to some very disturbing business, Master Thomas."

Jefferson frowned. "The resolves?"

Randolph nodded. "Only one. Perhaps others. We shall see."

Jefferson did not reply. He stood looking over his cousin's shoulder as the man pored though one tome, then another. The Surveyor-General did not stop his perusal until he noticed, with some embarrassment, that the public space was filling up with spectators, and that John Randolph and his clerks had arrived and were waiting to prepare the table for the day's sitting. He put the last tome in its place beneath the table and, without a word to Jefferson or anyone else, rose and left the chamber.

With some chagrin, Jefferson saw that all the public benches were now occupied. He resigned himself to standing again at the lobby doors. As he passed the railing, he nodded once to the inquisitive Frenchman, whose name by now he had forgotten. The little man looked happy; he had a front-row seat.

William Ferguson retrieved his brass bell and went out to the courtyard, rang the bell, and returned with most of the burgesses in tow. There were now only thirty-four members left. When John Robinson took his seat in the Speaker's chair, he rang it again to mark the beginning of the day.

Hugh Kenrick, seated above Henry's other allies, Johnston, Fleming, and Munford, had greeted Jack Frake and his party in the courtyard before leading them inside to procure seats. Nothing in Jack's or Etáin's manner reminded him of the terrible night before. After he had greeted them, he glanced around and asked, "Where is Mr. Barret?"

"He left for Caxton early this morning to begin setting his press to print the resolves," said Jack.

"He believes he can get broadsides of them onto some vessels riding now at Caxton and Yorktown," said John Ramshaw, "and into the hands of newspapers up and down the coast. I have asked him to set aside a few for me. The *Sparrowhawk* will be stopping at New York and Newport on our way back to England. We'll weigh anchor in two days. And I know some men in the papers back home."

"Mr. Barret is very proud of his country," remarked Etáin.

John Proudlocks remained silent. He noticed the dark rings around Hugh's eyes, and wondered what ordeal his friend had endured between their supper last night and this morning.

In the chamber now, Hugh observed with alarm the reduced number of members. After a brief conference with Munford, Johnston, and Fleming, he learned that three of their party had gone home, or were preparing to. He in turn advised the older men that when he came into the Capitol lobby with his friends, he saw several members of their party descending the stairs from the committee room above, their faces pale and closed. "They did not return my greeting, and went out to await the bell."

"'Beware of skullduggery,' indeed," sighed Johnston. "I believe the enemy has rallied and reformed to our disadvantage."

"We shall fight on," said Colonel Munford.

From his own seat on the second tier, Hugh sensed a new tension in the House. Among the spectators, it was caused by the absence of the man they had come to see and hear. The older members across the floor seemed imbued with a confidence that verged on smugness, while most of the members on Hugh's side seemed less bold and less certain.

Speaker Robinson said, "It was stated yesterday that there are two more resolutions to be introduced and possibly added to the five adopted yesterday by this House. Let the House resolve itself into a Committee of the Whole, so that they may be introduced."

Colonel Munford seconded the motion. As the golden mace was removed from atop the Clerk's table, Robinson and Peyton Randolph switched seats. Fleming rose and was recognized by the Attorney-General.

The burgess for Cumberland addressed the House. "Sirs, my colleagues and I view these last resolves as logical and ineluctable extensions of the first five, and propose that they be adopted by this committee and by the House in the same spirit."

"Proceed," said Peyton Randolph, who stared with patient boredom into the space before him. His one word was spoken in an ominously dismissive tone, thought Hugh, as though he already knew the fate of the last two resolves. That one word convinced him that, no matter what was said here today, the last two resolves were doomed to rejection.

"Resolved," said Fleming, "that His Majesty's liege people, the inhabitants of this colony, are not bound to yield obedience to any law or ordinance whatever, designed to impose any taxation whatever upon them, other than the laws or ordinances of the General Assembly aforesaid."

George Wythe narrowed his eyes in hostility. Richard Bland looked perplexed. John Robinson looked bored. The Attorney-General raised one eyebrow, and seemed to smile.

"Resolve the seventh," said Fleming, "that any person who shall, by speaking or writing, assert or maintain that any person or persons, other than the General Assembly of this colony, have any right or power to impose or lay any taxation whatever on the people here — " Fleming paused to clear his throat, for he seemed to be afraid to pronounce the next words " — shall be deemed an enemy of His Majesty's colony." The burgess nodded once to Randolph, then sat down.

A very curious thing happened then: nothing. Hugh and the other members had been ready for a demonstration of outrage similar to that which greeted the fifth resolve yesterday. But, other than some expressions of restrained shock or distaste, none of the older members reacted during the reading or after it. Other than some whispered commentary among the spectators, the chamber was quiet.

Hugh was now convinced of two things: that the last two resolves were doomed, and that Randolph and his allies had foreknowledge of them. Nothing else could explain their odd, passive behavior. He glanced at some of the members he had seen descending the stairs to the lobby, but then remembered the only other member with whom had been shared the texts of all seven resolves: Edgar Cullis.

"What say anyone to these resolutions?" asked Peyton Randolph.

George Wythe rose to be recognized. For five minutes he fulminated against not only the new resolves, but the ones already adopted by the

House. "They are all treacherous and treasonous, and I propose that this committee — this House — redeem itself and save itself and this colony much sorrow by first rejecting these last two pugnacious resolutions, and then by withdrawing the first five." Even his manner was out of character, noted Hugh. He sounded as though he was calmly prescribing an herb for a mosquito bite.

George Johnston rose to reply, and for the next two hours the House was locked in a debate more acrimonious than yesterday's. Johnston began with, "This House may redeem itself, sir, by asserting the liberty that is threatened by the Stamp Act! If we do not make that effort, then *we* may be stained with the blots of treachery, treason, and cowardice!"

Richard Bland rose and proclaimed, "In regard to the sixth resolution, I must remind this body that we are obliged to obey Crown law until any injustices contained in any of its parts have been corrected! In that manner, we may preserve our liberty! That is not cowardice, sir, but the way of prudent wisdom!"

Colonel Munford rose and replied, "What is to move Parliament to rectify or correct those injustices, sir?" He remembered something of Henry's speech from the day before. "Have you knowledge of a motion to be made in the Commons to restage, on the floor of that House, Mr. Addison's *Cato*, so that the members there will be filled with remorse and shame, and rush to beg our pardon?"

Landon Carter rose and said, "The seventh resolve, by brazen implication, casts the authors of the Stamp Act in the role of enemies! That is so bold an affront that I would not blame Parliament or His Majesty for believing that this colony is governed by renegades and brigands!"

Hugh rose and replied, "If this His Majesty's colony can be said to be a polity of liberty, then any man or body of men that threatens that liberty may be rightly cast as an enemy of this colony. And if His Majesty approves of such perfidy — and there on the Clerk's table is proof of his endorsement! — then he joins the company of the true rebels and brigands, and that action blots his station...and we must look upon him as an enemy of his own dominion!"

One of the older burgesses rose and shook his fist at Hugh. In the manner of a dare, he shouted across the aisle, "Long live King George the Third!" His face was livid and he looked ready for a fight.

"Long live George the Third!" shouted another burgess. "Retract your treasonous words, sir!" demanded another member. All the older members shot to their feet now, and hurled their loyalty at the men on the other side of the chamber. "Long live our gracious sovereign!" "Long may his empire bless our lives and fortunes!" "Long live George the Third!" "God save the king!"

Hugh felt the thrill of being alive. He raised and spread his arms and closed his hands into fists. He shouted above the din, "Long live Lady Liberty!"

John Randolph, in the meantime, was gaveling frantically to bring the House to order, but abruptly stopped when the first older burgess stepped away from his seat and began to cross the floor, striding straight for Hugh as he brandished his cane. Randolph dropped the gavel, jumped up, knocking over his own chair, and blocked his way. "Return to your seat, sir!" he said to the sputtering burgess. "Return to your seat, or I shall have the sergeant-at-arms escort you from the chamber! Please, sir!"

For a moment, the older burgess seemed ready to strike the Chief Clerk. But, with one last wicked look at Hugh, he snorted once, turned, and stalked back to his seat. Randolph breathed a sigh of relief, glanced at his brother Peyton, who was also on his feet, and sat back down at the table. His hands were shaking as he needlessly rearranged some articles on the cloth.

The Attorney-General also resumed his seat in the Speaker's chair, and with a silent, imperious look invited the still-standing members to follow suit. One by one, they obeyed. The chamber was quiet for a long moment, so quiet that the rustle of leaves on the trees outside and the laughter of far-away children could be heard. Everyone knew, even the spectators, that they had just witnessed an unprecedented event. For Peyton Randolph and his allies, it was a precedent they could neither have foreseen nor desired.

Hugh Kenrick was the last to take his seat. He felt an odd kind of purity now, almost one of redemption. Unbidden, memories of his defiance of the mob on the Charing Cross pillory came to his mind. He looked across the floor at the burgess who had intended to thrash him. He smiled kindly and gratefully at that man.

Peyton Randolph rose from the Speaker's chair and said calmly, "It is not for this Assembly to deem anyone a traitor to or an enemy of the Crown or of any of His Majesty's dominions. I speak now as the King's Attorney, and emphasize that to presume such a role would be to abrogate the prerogative of His Majesty and thus violate the ancient compact between him and Parliament, and so consequently leave us open to the charge that *we* are the traitors and enemies. This is a plain fact, sir, and I beg this House to entertain it with all the gravity its members are capable of." Then he sat down.

Richard Bland rose and said, "I must further remind this body that what liberty we enjoy in this His Majesty's dominion is granted to us by the king, and that when His Majesty engrosses a Parliamentary act, he does so as King-in-Parliament. It is not merely Parliament that we propose to charge with scandalous oversight, or whatever some others may call an action, but His Majesty! This, however, is not a point that can be properly addressed in so short a time."

Landon Carter then rose and moved that votes be conducted on the sixth and seventh resolutions. Wythe seconded the motion. Randolph ordered his brother to prepare to record the votes, and asked John Fleming to read the resolves again.

After each new resolve was read, and the 'Ayes' and 'Nays' were recorded, John Randolph read from his clerks' tallies: "For adoption, fifteen. For rejection, nineteen."

Peyton Randolph managed to contain a smile of satisfaction as he announced, "The aforesaid resolutions have been rejected by this committee, and therefore will neither be reported to the House, nor communicated to Parliament or the Board of Trade."

Munford, Fleming, and Johnston glanced at some of the younger members in disappointment, and wondered which of them Hugh had seen coming down from the committee room, and what had been said to them.

George Wythe thereupon rose and moved that Speaker Robinson retake the chair. Richard Bland seconded the motion. The golden mace was returned to its place on the Clerk's table. Robinson, when he was comfortably seated, waited for someone to rise. It was Peyton Randolph who did, and who moved that new votes be conducted by the House in formal assembly on all the adopted resolutions. Before George Wythe could rise to second the motion, the older burgess who was restrained by the Chief Clerk rose and said, "I second that motion, and hope with God's strength that those resolutions are all sent back to Hell whence they came!"

Everyone looked at the man, who seemed not to notice. Peyton Randolph and Speaker Robinson both blinked in surprise. Robinson said, "Well....Let the clerk read each resolution — "

But John Fleming rose to be recognized. Robinson nodded to him. This was to be expected, thought the Speaker.

Fleming said, "These resolves have already been adopted by the House, sir. What is the precedent for this...unique action?"

"There is none, sir," answered Robinson. "But in these circumstances, one must be made. And I may be in error. In the long and glorious history of this House, I am certain that a precedent may be found."

"Then I move that these votes be postponed until such a precedent can be found, sir."

Robinson shook his head. "Mr. Randolph's motion has already been carried, sir. And there is no time. This session is too near its end."

Fleming's eyes narrowed in obvious contempt. "It would seem, sir, that a new hand has been dealt here over these resolves, or a pair of weighted dice!"

The Speaker came out of his chair and took a step toward Fleming. His face shook in anger and he spoke with an emotion that the House had rarely heard him express. "You will withdraw that remark, sir, or I will move to have you censured and expelled from the House!"

"I will not withdraw it, sir," answered Fleming. "It is clear to me now —"

"Withdraw that remark, sir!" demanded Robinson. "Apologize to the chair!" He pointed to it with his cane.

Colonel Munford reached up, touched Fleming's sleeve, and whispered urgently, "Do it, John! It is nearly over!"

Robinson pointed his cane at Munford. "Silence, sir! There will be no more apologies by proxy! Let this man speak his own regrets!"

Fleming sighed, briefly closed his eyes, then nodded slightly to Robinson. "I...withdraw the remark, sir, and beg the chair to accept my apology."

Robinson grunted once, then said, "All right." He turned and plunked himself back in the chair. He glared at John Randolph. "Let the Clerk read the first resolution!"

Three hours later — again past the customary time for dinner recess — and after several hundred vituperative and grandiloquent words were exchanged between both sides of the House — Speaker Robinson, who by now looked close to a nervous collapse, ended the debates. The first four resolves survived the fury by diminishing margins of twenty to fourteen for the first, nineteen to fifteen for the second, eighteen to sixteen for the third and fourth, while the fifth resolve's fate hung in the balance.

Spectators and burgesses alike rode on each vote as the members stood to pronounce *Aye* or *Nay*. And everyone knew the result before John Randolph read it from the tally sheet. "On the fifth resolution adopted by this

House: fifteen for its retention, nineteen for its expunction. The fifth resolution is so abandoned, and will be erased from the record."

Speaker Robinson accepted a motion by Peyton Randolph and
appointed a committee to draft the four resolves into a formal document to
be sent to London. There being no more business for the House to pursue,
he ordered an adjournment.

This time it was many of the younger members who rose in a body and
first left the chamber. All the older members remained behind to chatter
about their victory.

Chapter 13: The Dissolution

"**A**bove all, let us correct the grammar."

"Yes. The grammar must be corrected, in all the resolutions. It is too sharp, and gaudy, and conceited. It must be planed and blunted."

George Wythe and Peyton Randolph were the speakers. With them stood Landon Carter, Richard Bland, and Robert Carter Nicholas, burgess for York County. They stood in the lobby of the House, hastily convened there in the rush by members and spectators alike to find a late dinner or early supper in the inns and taverns near the Capitol. They comprised the committee appointed by John Robinson to draft the resolves in a document to be sent to Edward Montague, the House's agent in London, whose duty it would be to see it introduced in the Commons. A copy would also be addressed to the Lords of Trade. They were in agreement that they should meet some time in the evening, and had only to agree on a place.

"The present grammar, I say, is an aspect of the author of these resolutions, reckless and vile. I do not envy you gentlemen the task of sweetening it." So opined Reverend William Robinson, Anglican Commissary of Virginia and a cousin of the Speaker. He had been among the spectators, and had joined the group on his way out. His company was not particularly welcomed by the burgesses, but he was the Speaker's cousin and had to be tolerated. He now shook his head gravely. "The violence of these last two days will remain in my memory to the end of my own days. And I am pained by the outcome. I had expected you gentlemen to extricate yourselves from Mr. Henry's trap and commence tarring him with his own fanfaronade."

"Managing the affairs of this House," replied Randolph with nearly offensive courtesy, "is more difficult work than you might appreciate."

"Oh, I don't doubt that, Mr. Randolph," said the Commissary with a short laugh. "And you are to be commended for your skills. Still, you must admit that, if there were any justice, Mr. Henry would not have had the opportunity to present you with the task of planing and blunting his mischief."

"What do you mean, sir?" asked Bland.

"Why, yesterday was the *second* instance that he has uttered chargeable treason," scoffed the Commissary, "the first being his offensive speech two Decembers ago in Hanover. I am quite certain that you gentlemen have knowledge of *that* affair! Everyone else has. It would account for so large a public interest. So it is amazing to me that he is tolerated here, allowed to tread the same floor as you gentlemen. It is *more* amazing to me that you have accommodated him! By the justice I speak of, he ought to be a guest in this city's jail, chained hand and foot to the wall of his cell, awaiting his fate."

George Wythe narrowed his eyes. "While we are all here loyal subjects of His Majesty, sir, and pledge our hearts and minds to England...there are some aspects of the mother country that we are happy are not to be found here."

Commissary Robinson raised his eyebrows at this rebuke, then shrugged. "Well," he said, "in all honesty, the events that have occurred here are so disturbing that I feel obligated to write the Bishop of London about them, and report to him my own observations. In point of fact, it is my *duty* to report them, and it is one I shall take pleasure in performing."

Peyton Randolph saw his chance, and replied with a mock smile, "Then, sir, pray attend to your duty, and allow us to attend to ours."

Commissary Robinson looked regretful. "Sultry weather we've had lately," he remarked. "I wonder if it will rain." He stepped back and bowed slightly. "Good day to you, sirs." He turned and left the lobby.

No one in the group doubted that Reverend Robinson would write the Bishop of London, Richard Terrick, who himself was a distant cousin of the Commissary's, and a Privy Councilor to boot.

"That man," said Robert Carter Nicholas in a low voice as he watched the man leave, "sees himself as the first bishop of New York and all the colonies."

"God save us from the duty of kissing his ring," said Randolph.

The group agreed to meet early in the evening in the upstairs committee room and to work until they had completed a draft of the resolves. They broke up and went their separate ways.

Outside, as they walked together across the Capitol grounds to Randolph's waiting carriage, the Attorney-General and Wythe came upon Thomas Jefferson, who noticed them approaching. His young brow was furled in thought.

"My congratulations to you," said Jefferson to the pair. "A most bloody contest. I hope it was worth the strife."

"Very bloody," agreed Randolph, who sensed that the young man was addressing him exclusively, "but very much worth the strife." He saw a strange look in Jefferson's eyes, one that made him feel apprehension. "Still, I suspect that the House has been divided in a unique and permanent way. And I hope you have learned something of the way of true politics."

Jefferson seemed to nod with difficulty, then asked in too casual a tone, "May I presume that you found the five hundred guineas with which to purchase a vote or two, sir? I did not know there were so many to be found in the colonies. Guineas, that is."

Wythe gasped, then blushed in supreme embarrassment. Randolph exclaimed, "*What?*" and stared incredulously at his distant cousin. Wythe opened his mouth to upbraid his protégé, but Randolph, roused to fury by the comment, leaned closer to Jefferson's face and spat into it, "No, sir! Say, rather, one hundred guineas! Ask me another indecorous question, my fine, untrained puppy, and I shall have *you* banished from the House! Out of my way!" He pushed past Jefferson and stormed off to his waiting carriage.

Before Wythe followed hurriedly in his wake, he stopped to jab a finger on Jefferson's chest several times. "You, sir, have insulted a great man! I will speak with you later!"

Inside the carriage, which would take them a short distance to Randolph's home a half mile from the Capitol, Randolph said, "By God, Mr. Wythe! What are things coming to? What confounded brass! He is a decent fellow, that lad, but have you neglected to instruct him in manners and discretion? Has he allowed Mr. Henry's fever to addle his noggin?"

"I shall speak with him, sir," said Wythe.

They were quiet for a moment as the carriage bumped along the road that led to Randolph's spacious home. Then Randolph said, "The Governor will dissolve us over this affair. I believe you promised him defeat of the resolves."

Wythe shook his head, and sighed. "He will surely dissolve us, sir, no matter how well we correct the grammar."

* * *

Meanwhile, on the other side of the Capitol, the advocates of the resolves held a hasty conference of their own. "Well," said George Johnston, "at least there are four resolves, where before there had been none."

John Fleming grunted in disgust. "They are but a cart without a horse, Mr. Johnston, and by the time that committee have finished with them, they will be a cart without wheels!"

Colonel Munford remarked with bright sarcasm, "Why the despair, sirs? Mr. Robinson's party was obliged to adopt some of them! By next session, they may be persuaded that five shillings make a crown! That is some progress!"

Hugh Kenrick said, "I do not doubt the effect *all* the resolves will have here, and throughout all the colonies, sirs. It is unfortunate, however, that those who fought so stubbornly against them may in half a year's time be credited with their adoption, and perhaps even with their authorship."

Munford nodded in agreement. "And they will accept that credit, and very likely author their own little pamphlets to support their new-found patriotism!"

Johnston looked thoughtful, and said, "I confess I am a mite uncomfortable now with our project, sirs. After all, only four of the resolves were adopted, yet Mr. Kenrick's friend will print and post all seven to the four corners of the empire. Parliament and the king and everyone on these shores will believe that these resolves are the accomplishment of the House." He paused. "Is this not an exercise in *deceit*?"

Hugh scoffed. "No, sir. The resolves, all of them, are what ought to have been adopted. I do not see our project as an exercise in deceit. Rather, it is an effort to proclaim a truth, and every one of those resolves states a truth." Hugh chuckled in dark irony. "And among other effects the dissemination of the resolves will have, will be some compensation for our apologies." He shook his head again. "Let those who opposed the resolves write their fragments. They must, in time, come to agree with all seven resolves. We will have sown justice in the wind, sirs, and I am certain we will see a great harvest."

"So we may," remarked Johnston. "We may also see Governor Fauquier dissolve the Assembly before its time. I do believe that Mr. Wythe pledged him our defeat."

*　*　*

After he had exchanged farewells with his companions, Hugh walked alone down Duke of Gloucester Street. He had promised Jack Frake and his party that he would meet them at Mary Gandy's house, from which Jack,

Etáin, Ramshaw, and Proudlocks would begin their journey back to Caxton. As he was passing Raleigh Tavern, he heard someone call after him. He turned and saw Thomas Jefferson hurrying down the sidewalk. "Mr. Kenrick! I was afraid I missed you!"

Jefferson rushed up, took one of Hugh's hands, and shook it, this time without any hesitation. "I wished to thank you, sir, for your...inspiration, and for your words...and for everything else I have witnessed these last two days."

Hugh shook his head. "Do not thank me, sir. Thank...necessity."

"You, and Mr. Henry, and the others," protested Jefferson, "even those who opposed you so vigorously, have caused me to stand back and see a broader vista of matters." He smiled. "I own that I am in your debt."

Hugh grinned. "You may consider that debt repaid, Mr. Jefferson, when your mentor, Mr. Wythe, openly and with rock-hard conviction agrees with Mr. Henry and me and with everything that was said by us these last two days. You are the one for that task. I failed, as you saw. You may not."

Jefferson laughed. "What a Herculean labor you assign me! Perhaps even a Sisyphean one! He is a very crafty fellow in cool argument, you know, who allows one to believe that one has convinced him on a certain legal point, only to have him assail one with a barrage from Coke or Kames."

"I am certain that you will someday become his equal," said Hugh.

"Thank you," said Jefferson. He glanced up at the gray roof of clouds that had gathered over Williamsburg. "Well, it is time I took up no more of your own," he said. "I must prepare to leave for Shadwell and my duties there, now that the Assembly has concluded its business, and," he added in a lower voice, "has so displeased Governor Fauquier that he will certainly dissolve it some days before its natural conclusion. I have farewells to say to friends, including his honor." Jefferson's expression now became serious. "I remember our talk of a while ago, Mr. Kenrick, last December, I believe, and something you said to me. I promise you here that, if there is no honor now in the lawyer's profession, I shall work in the future to imbue it with some." He paused. "And perhaps you and I shall someday share a bench in the House."

"I would like to see that day," said Hugh.

After they had said their final goodbyes, Hugh continued down Duke of Gloucester. Something Jefferson said tickled an old memory. Then he smiled, for he remembered the day, long ago, when he had remarked to his tutor in Danvers that he would bring honor to the family name.

He was passing another tavern, lost in this pleasant memory, and won-dering about the implacability of justice, when he noticed John Proudlocks in the distance, coming toward him. He saw the man frown then, just as he heard someone behind him roar, "*You! You traitor! You regicide!*"

Hugh turned in time to hear more than see an object swoop down, then hear more than feel the object strike him on the head with an ear-splitting crack. As his knees buckled and he felt himself falling, he caught a glimpse of the face of the older burgess who had tried to attack him in the House. He had only enough time to note the flesh-distorting malice on that face before he lost consciousness.

But he was unconscious for only a moment. When he opened his eyes again, the man was still there, hovering over him, but being held by three men, one of them Thomas Jefferson, who had apparently rushed back across the boulevard when he heard the fracas. The burgess struggled against his captors, yelling oaths in a drunken slur. He had emerged from the tavern just as Hugh was passing it. He still held his cane, and his eyes never left Hugh.

As Hugh propped himself upon his elbows, he saw Proudlocks snatch the cane from the man's grip, raise it in the air with both hands, then bring it down and break it in half over his upraised knee.

"You!" yelled the burgess. "You blackamoor! Give me a sword! I'll teach you — " Then he stopped ranting, and seemed to realize where he was and what he had done. Proudlocks stared hard at the man, and offered him in one hand the two halves of the broken cane. The burgess sneered at him, and with his free hand knocked them from Proudlocks' grip. The silver-tipped halves clattered to the ground.

Proudlocks shrugged, then bent to help Hugh to his feet. A crowd of men, women, children, and slaves had gathered around the scene. One of the men holding the burgess asked Hugh, "Sir, do you wish him arrested? You won't lack for witnesses! I saw him strike you without provocation! So did others here!"

One of the onlookers stepped forward. "You can't arrest him, as well he might be! This is John Chiswell, a burgess of the city! He is immune from charges while the Assembly sits!"

Hugh began to feel a throbbing pain not only on his head, but in his ribs and shoulder. The burgess had struck him several times before he was restrained. He studied his assailant for a moment. The malice in the man's eyes had softened a little, but not much. He was breathing hard, as a drunken man will after a tremendous exertion. Hugh imagined he saw a glimmer of hope in the man's eyes.

He felt something warm slither down one side of his face, and put a finger to it. It was blood. He grimaced in disgust, then said, "Then he is fortunate on two counts: he is immune, and I do not carry my own sword. Let him go."

Jefferson and the two men released Chiswell from their holds, and warily stepped away. Chiswell stared at Hugh for a moment, then at the crowd, his expression communicating nothing. He grunted once, straightened his frock coat, spat on the ground, then turned and strode away across the boulevard, weaving as he went, muttering more oaths.

Proudlocks handed Hugh his hat. Hugh expressed his thanks to his rescuers, and the crowd dispersed. Jefferson remained behind, shaking his head in disbelief.

"Who is that man?" asked Proudlocks. His eyes had not left the burgess until the figure meandered onto a side street and disappeared behind a house.

"That," said Hugh, stepping over to one of the cane halves and kicking it into the boulevard, "was the father-in-law of the Speaker of the House." He saw the look of incomprehension in Proudlocks's face. "Mr. Robinson married that man's daughter."

Proudlocks's face brightened. "Ah! I understand now! That is why Mr. Robinson turned away in shame when that man tried to strike you in the House!"

"I had not noticed," remarked Hugh. "That is one more thing he should be ashamed of."

Jefferson said, "Well, I would not wager on Mr. Chiswell's reelection to the next Assembly, not even with Mr. Robinson's support."

Proudlocks narrowed his eyes in thought. "Mr. Kenrick, do you think he was told to hurt you? I saw also that Mr. Robinson is not your friend, either."

Hugh smiled in spite of his pain, and shook his head. "No, John. He was drunk and acting alone. You will have observed that there is not much difference between his sobriety and his drunken state. No, I don't believe Mr. Robinson or anyone else put him up to it." He paused, though, when he realized what Proudlocks had confessed in his query. "You are but half right in your observation, my friend. Intrigue there was — shameless intrigue — but what happened here was not a part of it. I shall put this incident out of my mind."

"I will not," said Proudlocks with finality.

"Why are you here?" asked Hugh. "I was to meet you and Mr. Frake and the others at Miss Gandy's for supper, and then see you off back to Caxton."

Proudlocks smiled. "I asked for Mr. Frake's leave to search for you. The supper was nearly ready."

Hugh noticed Jefferson listening to them with curiosity. "Where are my manners?" he said. "Allow me to introduce you to a future lawyer and burgess, Mr. Thomas Jefferson. Mr. Jefferson, may I present Mr. John Proudlocks, perhaps a future speculist and a rival of Mr. Bland...."

Half an hour later, Hugh was sitting in Mary Gandy's kitchen while the hostess and Etáin fussed over him and treated his head injury with ointment. Jack Frake sat with a mug of ale and a pipe and watched the ministrations with amusement. Hugh's story, however, had not amused him. "I suspected that fellow hadn't finished with you," he said. "But after the last vote on the fifth resolve, well...I thought he would have been satisfied with that." He paused. "How long will you remain here?"

Hugh said, "Until Governor Fauquier dissolves the Assembly. Until tomorrow, I should think. I want to be here when it happens." He reached over and picked up one of the cards of the caricature that Dogmael Jones had sent him. This one came from the door of one of the shops he passed on his way back with Proudlocks. "All will be quiet for a while," he mused with a smile. He waved the caricature once, then set it down. "Then we shall see some consequence. I am certain of it."

John Ramshaw, sitting at another corner of the table, grinned. "Sir, if what happened today to you — if what I witnessed the last two days — is any measure of the matter, I would say that the colonies and England are in for a patch of very nasty weather." He raised his mug of ale in salute. "Here's to you, son."

* * *

Late the next morning, as the remaining burgesses filed into the chamber — only thirty-two now, one having gone home, and John Chiswell not daring to attend, for he feared a public reprimand by his son-in-law the Speaker — an usher from the other side of the Capitol appeared and handed Robinson a summons from Lieutenant-Governor Fauquier to appear before him with the rest of the House in the Council chamber. Robinson informed the House of the summons, and the body filed back out again, crossed through the connecting committee rooms upstairs, and into the Council chamber. This large, richly appointed room was dominated by a vast oaken table covered with an exquisite purple cloth. At its head sat the Lieutenant-Governor, and around it seven members of his Council.

When all the burgesses were assembled around the table, standing with hats in hand, just as members of the Commons did when they attended a conference with the Lords in London, Fauquier welcomed them and announced that he had given his assent to the remaining legislation and that he was satisfied that the House had discharged its duties.

But when he came to the subject of the Stamp Act, he stared into the space ahead of him, and fixed his sight on some white object. "Gentlemen of the House," he began, "it has come to my attention that some very inelegant and offensive resolutions were passed by you concerning the late act, and that in the course of approving these inappropriate disputations, some altercations occurred unbefitting the dignity of the venue. Also, I have heard that some indecent language was employed on the same occasions. The altercations and language alone prompt me to reproach you. Further, while I concede that delinquency is not within Mr. Speaker's power to obviate, I believe that, had more of your fellows seen fit to attend this session until its natural expiration, neither the resolutions nor the altercations would have given me cause to advise you of the Crown's displeasure, for they would have...not happened." The Lieutenant-Governor flicked a wrist to make his point. "The resolutions, however, are a greater violation of my sensibilities, and I am certain they will have a similar effect on the parties to whom they are addressed, and perhaps move those parties to contemplate actions that can only abuse your own sense of propriety, moderation, and justice."

Fauquier's sight focused then on the white object; it was a small bandage fixed above Hugh Kenrick's brow. He frowned and interrupted his address. "Sir, you have suffered some mishap. Did your horse throw you, or you fall from it?"

"No, your honor," replied Hugh. "I will only say that a man fell from his grace as a rational being, or at least demonstrated that he had never attained that state."

Fauquier blinked once at this reply, and saw that Hugh would not elaborate or explain his answer. "I see," said the Lieutenant-Governor. "My sympathies, sir. May you heal quickly."

John Robinson, standing in the center of the burgesses, would not look at Hugh, for he now regretted having dismissed the necessity of apologizing to this young man for his father-in-law's criminal behavior, both in the House and outside it. His glance fell in the discomfiture of shame.

Hugh Kenrick did not look in his direction. Many of the other burgesses did, in critical appraisal, for news of the assault had spread around the town. They wondered now if the Speaker would try to make amends.

Fauquier shook the incident from his mind, and continued, looking briefly at George Wythe, Peyton Randolph, and the Speaker with ironic disappointment. "I had hoped that wisdom and prudence would prevail in the House over these resolutions. Instead, rash anger and thoughtless bravado seem to have triumphed. So, on that regretful note, and because the House has completed its chores, it is my duty to dissolve the Assembly until November first next, and you are so dissolved. Let us pray that the next Assembly is a more...pacific one. Good morning to you, gentlemen, and Godspeed you back to your homes."

Fauquier rose, and the seven Council members rose with him. The Lieutenant-Governor said, "God save the King!"

"God save the King!" answered the burgesses and Council members in unison.

Chapter 14: The Solecisms

That evening, in the solitude of his Palace annex office, to the steady, soothing patter of rainfall beyond his open window, Francis Fauquier labored over the draft of a report to the Board of Trade about the state of the colony, new legislation he had signed, and other matters of special interest to the Lords. Among those other matters were the trouble over the murdered Cherokees, the resolutions passed by the House, and the question of John Robinson's reelection as burgess for King and Queen County, which virtually guaranteed his reappointment as Speaker and Treasurer. The continued union of those two offices was a situation frowned upon by the Lords of Trade, and one they had been for some time hinting that Fauquier move to correct. He hoped that the Lords would allow his stalwart, loyal friend to continue in that dual role.

Robinson's reelection, though, never before in doubt, was now doubtful, because of the dramatic — and for Fauquier, the near-traumatic — actions taken by the House over the Stamp Act. The Governor dipped his quill and wrote, "There having happened a small altercation" — he paused here, then struck out "altercation" and substituted "alteration," for he did not wish to overly alarm the Lords — "alteration in the House, there was an attempt to strike all the resolutions off the Journals. The fifth, which was thought the most offensive, was accordingly struck off, but it did not succeed as to the other four."

He recalled with some irony the ardent assurances by George Wythe and John Robinson in a private audience that the resolves could and would be defeated. He would not blame them now for failing to keep that promise. "I am informed," he wrote, recalling the brief meeting he had with Wythe, Randolph, and Robinson early this morning before the burgesses began to appear in the House, "the gentlemen had two more resolutions in their pocket, but finding the difficulty they had in carrying the fifth, which was by a single vote, they did not produce them. The more strenuous opposers of this rash heat were the Speaker, the King's Attorney, and Mr. Wythe, but they were overpowered by the young, hot, and giddy members. In the course of the debates, I have heard that very indecent language was used by a Mr. Henry...."

Fauquier glanced at a sheet of paper that was on a corner of his desk. A flickering candle near it allowed him to read some of the words on it. It was a copy of the four resolves that Mr. Randolph's committee had striven to recast in less offensive language. They had tried, he knew, to accommodate him and the Crown. But, he thought, how much could one tamper with and modify the features and purpose of a musket, and at the end of the experiment still be able to call the thing a musket? They had even, for some reason unfathomable to him, inserted the words "liberties" and "franchises" in the body of the first resolve, where they had not originally occurred, according to Mr. Wythe. Fauquier could only conclude that these conscientious, able men were exhausted by the time they had completed their joint effort. Mr. Randolph had further volunteered this morning that, concerned about the legal ramifications of the resolves and the evidence of their adoption in the House Journal, he had arranged to have removed from it the page that contained the talleys of yesterday's votes and all mention of debate on the Stamp Act. What loyalty! thought Fauquier. What caution! What prudence!

Fauquier completed the draft to the Board, and after a glass of brandy, turned to the slightly pleasanter task of writing to his friend George Montagu Dunk, Earl of Halifax, president of the Board of Trade when Fauquier was appointed Lieutenant-Governor. His friend was now Secretary of State for the Southern Department. In this report he opined that the resolves did not reflect the "sullen mood" of the colony, but rather that the obdurate character of its citizens was due instead to the post-war depression, the ever-growing debt to British creditors, and the scarcity of specie with which to pay those debts and any within the colony itself. This situation, he wrote, "renders them uneasy, peevish, and ready to murmur at every occurrence."

Because his office did not permit him to attend the House when it was in session — he could set foot in it only on the House's invitation — the Governor relied almost exclusively on verbal reports of its actions and behavior from Wythe, Robinson, and Randolph. If he had been able to sit with the spectators over the past two days, he might have seen a link between the reaction of the public to the debates over the resolves and all those other attributed causes of disaffection. It never occurred to him that perhaps the information on which he based many of his own observations was skewed, biased, and even false. He had implicit faith in the veracity of all that was told him by his esteemed informants. If they claimed that the last two resolves had never been introduced, he would never doubt the truthfulness of the claim. And this particular truth meshed harmoniously with his desire to impress the Board and Lord Halifax with the loyalty of the House's leadership. He was fearful of many things: the wrath of the Board, of George Grenville, of the Privy Council, and of Parliament, when the resolutions at last came into their hands; of the retribution that the colony of Virginia might suffer as a result of that wrath; of the blame that would likely be attached to him for the whole affair.

And so he softened in his reports the harsh news he had for all those powers in faraway London. It was absolutely imperative that he attempt to assuage his own doubts, fears, and reservations. He toyed with the idea of appending to his report to the Board a request to take a leave of absence so that he could return to England for his health and personal business, but decided to delay that plea until he received an answer to the reports.

A question popped unexpectedly into his mind just as the floor clock struck one-thirty in the morning and prompted him, with a yawn and a stretch, to decide to end his labors for the day: What the devil had Hugh Kenrick meant by that cryptic explanation of his injury? He shook his head once to rid his mind of the fuzz that seemed to be accumulating in it. But it was no use; the thought-clogging fuzz simply remained. He rose, extinguished all the candles and sconces, closed the window, and left his office.

* * *

A few days later, while the Governor's secretary was putting the final touches on the Lieutenant-Governor's reports to the Board of Trade and Lord Halifax, the Chevalier d'Annemours, who had left Williamsburg to continue on his tour, stopped with some other travelers at a tavern in Newcastle on the Pamunkey River to escape a downpour. Already tired of the constant talk of the Stamp Act, of Patrick Henry, of how none of them would pay a farthing for a stamp, of how each of them would give his life to protect Henry should he be threatened by the Crown — and also because he did not want to chance being invited to join another card or dice game — he excused himself from his itinerant company and took a table by himself in the crowded, noisy tavern and began to transcribe his hastily taken notes into his diary.

His three days in Williamsburg were the chief subject, and his memory of the sequence of events and the particulars of those events was by now a little foggy, for there was so much to remember and he did not understand the half of it. He expanded his notes and recorded, as best he could in his imperfect English, his impressions of the debates and the moods of the men who participated in them, getting some things wrong, and often, without knowing it, contradicting what was being asserted as fact in the Lieutenant-Governor's official reports.

He recorded, among other things, that Henry apologized for having insinuated that George the Third was, or could become, a tyrant, while Francis Fauquier made no mention of an apology, for either he was not informed that Henry or anyone else had made one; or, he was informed, and thought it wiser to omit mention of the whole incident. Treason and murder were capital offenses under Crown law, and Fauquier, as viceroy and chief justice of the colony, would certainly have felt it his duty to exercise his authority to rule that, in this instance, Henry was not protected by House immunity from immediate arrest.

So, given that the Board of Trade invariably found fault with Fauquier's performance, and that Fauquier himself was always alert to ways in which to ingratiate himself with the Lords of Trade, it is a paradox that he did not pursue this serious matter — and pursuing it would assuredly have earned him applause from the Lords of Trade, and perhaps even a special acknowledgment from the king — and limited himself in the report to an oblique reference to the incident, naming "Mr. Henry," but neither reporting the content of his "indecent language" nor mentioning that he had apologized by proxy for employing it. Perhaps the John Wilkes affair in the Commons over *The North Briton* left a bad taste in his mind, and he did not wish to repeat such a tumult here. Or perhaps one or all of his informants — Wythe, Randolph, and Robinson — chose to keep him in the dark concerning the details, unsure about how their otherwise amiable Governor might react to them.

It is more than likely that the details of Henry's transgression were withheld from him. The Chevalier also noted in his diary that the seventh resolve was the subject of "very hot debates"; the knowledgeable Governor reported to the Board that it and the sixth were never introduced. The Chevalier harbored no animus for Patrick Henry, nor any for that man's enemies; their politics fascinated him only in the abstract. He had nothing to gain by lying or misrepresenting what he had witnessed. He recorded

Henry's apology, or what he believed was his apology, in the spirit of a neutral observer. And the Governor, who either feared telling the whole truth, or did not have the whole truth to tell, merely reported, from a severely abridged perspective, what had been told him by trusted informants and loyal advocates of the status quo.

Had Fauquier and the Chevalier been given the opportunity to compare each other's reports, they would undoubtedly have noted these and other discrepancies, and wondered how to account for them. On one hand, they might have ended their meeting by trading epithets of *liar, fool,* and *imbecile*; on the other, the friendly jousts of faro and loo between Fauquier and Wythe over brandy and good conversation might have altogether ceased, and the Frenchman have left Williamsburg with jolly contempt for the English.

"Alphonse Croisset" completed his tardy diary entries that evening, having courteously rebuffed invitations to cards, and retired to his paid quarters in the tavern. In the morning, after a sleep made fitful by the loud gambling and carousing of the Virginians downstairs, he continued his journey through the dampened countryside, trading mounts and hitching rides on wagons and sulkies as he went, and crossing innumerable streams and rivers. So much of Virginia reminded him of rural France; so many of the great planter estates reminded him of rural England.

Days later, he stopped for a while in the charming capital of Annapolis, Maryland, to note the customs and temper of the people there, and to observe the legislature, which he noted was more rowdy and less beholden to form and dignity than was that of Virginia. In his hurry, though, to catch a ferry across the Bay and to make his way to Philadelphia, he left behind in his lodgings his diary, and did not miss it until days later he searched for it in his traveling bag in order to record his impressions of the most populous city in the colonies. He slapped his forehead first in astonishment for his oversight, again with a sense of loss, and a third time in anger. *"Enfer et damnation! Je suis un idiot!"*

* * *

"I shall want a few for Mr. Talbot in Philadelphia," said Hugh. "And a few for Mr. Easley there, also."

He stood in Wendel Barret's shop in Caxton, holding a sheet of paper in his hand, and read again with a smile the banner above the seven neatly printed resolves: *Resolves Adopted by the Virginia House on May 31, 1765, in*

Answer to the Recent Stamp Act. Above him, pinned to and dangling from a length of twine strung across the room, were a dozen copies of the document, hung out to dry and wafting in a breeze from an open window. Barret and his apprentices, their faces and aprons smeared with ink, worked feverishly on the press as they printed more copies. One of the apprentices, who was his orphaned grandson, would insert a blank sheet of paper in the bed, Barret would pull on the lever to press the assembled type over and onto it, then lever the press back so that the second apprentice, a younger black slave boy, could remove it and add it to the twine.

Hugh glanced again at the first resolve, searched his memory, then said to the *Courier*'s publisher, "Mr. Barret, there is a discrepancy in the first resolve. Not a serious one. 'Liberties' and 'franchises' have been inserted in your version here. They do not occur in the copy I gave you."

Barret paused long enough to reply, "After I had pressed the first twenty copies, I noted an inconsistency, sir. The words you cite occur in the second resolve, but not in the first. So, I took the *liberty* of restoring them to their proper place. 'Tis my *privilege* and *franchise* as an editor, sir, and I challenge you to contest the inconsistency I have corrected. The first and second resolves are now married!"

Hugh regarded the printer for a moment, then burst out laughing. He shook his head and replied, "You are forgiven the liberty, Mr. Barret, and please forgive me for sounding now like the king. You were right to correct the oversight."

Barret beamed in triumph, and renewed his task on the press.

Chapter 15: The Soldiers

Hugh Kenrick returned to Meum Hall. He had not liked leaving it for so long a period, and so managed it from Williamsburg with all the attention to detail he exhibited when he inspected his fields.

For a while after his return, however, he was barely aware of Meum Hall, barely aware of his staff as they went about their duties. It was not until he had completed every task associated with the Stamp Act resolves — posting Barret's copies of the resolves to Talbot and Easley in Philadelphia and copies to his father and Dogmael Jones in England, bidding Captain Ramshaw a safe voyage on the *Sparrowhawk* when it left Caxton and sailed back down the York River, and finishing his transcriptions of the key speeches in the House — that he felt free to devote his full attention to Meum Hall. And it was only then, when he stopped to rest for a moment before moving on to the next task, and realized that there was no more to do, that he felt the odd feeling that he was in a strange and alien place. He emerged from his obsession to wonder who was the Hugh Kenrick who lived here and commanded the staff.

He dismissed the feeling, attributing it to tiredness, and inspected Meum Hall from top to bottom, from the water tower to Hove Stream. The gutters along the roof had been cleaned, and the branches of the trees near them trimmed. The lead pipes to the kitchen and some of the rooms in the great house from the water tower had been installed and tested, and basins for them built and put in place. The water tower itself was now virtually leak-free.

In the fields, the tobacco was nearly a foot high, the rye and wheat were nearly ready to be cradled, the corn and oats were coming up, and the patch crops of hemp and flax were doing well. Henry Zouch had almost completed the order for bricks for the merchant's warehouse near Richmond; several neat piles of them lined the sides of the brickyard. The conduit had been repaired and assembled, and sat in the fields waiting to be used; the ground was still damp from the most recent rain.

Meum Hall was in better condition than he had expected. Every order and instruction he had given from afar had been carried out. He began the long day of inspection with the confidence that, by day's end, he would reclaim his sense of ownership of the place. But before Mrs. Chance served him his favorite meal in the supper room that evening, he still felt that something was missing. He felt uneasy about himself, and, at the same time, at peace. He remembered now that the staff and tenants had welcomed him back with some enthusiasm; it was only now that he felt touched by the reception. They had all heard that he played an important role in some great event in the General Assembly; he did not know that they had observed his obsession, and were refraining from asking him questions about the session until they felt it was proper to ask them.

He happened to glance up from the supper table at the group portrait of his family on the wall, and for a moment did not recognize his father, mother, sister, and their servants. In anger with the phenomenon, he pounded the table once with a fist. This should not be, he thought. What is wrong with me?

He went to the library to unpack the crate of books, clothing, and other things that had arrived before he journeyed to Piney Slash to see Patrick Henry. He noticed only now that the crate was gone. He rang for Spears, his valet, and asked him for an explanation. Spears replied that the books had been put up on the shelves, the clothing added to the wardrobe and clothes press, and the plate and silverware stocked in the kitchen.

Hugh smiled in apology. "Thank you, Spears. You will please excuse my…lapse in memory. Part of me, it seems, is still in Williamsburg."

"Yes, sir," replied the valet. "We had all come to that conclusion."

"Is it so noticeable?"

Spears nodded. "We would not have said so to you, sir, but we will acknowledge it. I own that we had occasion to remark among ourselves on your…condition." After a brief pause, he added, "We had heard that you made a great victory in the Assembly, sir, and were wondering why you were so, well, angry."

"Angry?" laughed Hugh. "Did I seem that? Well, I can assure you, I was not. I am very pleased with the state of things here. My compliments, Spears."

"Thank you, sir."

It was only a little after nine in the evening, but Hugh said, "I think I shall retire early tonight. Perhaps after a good night's rest, that other part of me will have come home by morning." Then, he thought, he would awaken refreshed and in full possession of himself and of Meum Hall. "Rouse me at your own peril, Spears."

The valet grinned. "As you wish, sir."

But Hugh opened his eyes the next morning just after dawn, only a little later than his regular hour. He was up before even Spears, and had fixed himself some coffee in the kitchen before Mrs. Chance appeared. The rest had helped, but he still felt uneasy.

That morning, while he was busy rearranging the business on his desk, and putting his new books in their proper places on the shelves, Thomas Reisdale, the attorney and vestryman, called. He had been away seeing clients in Norfolk and Elizabeth City across the James River the last two weeks, and unable to attend the House's deliberations. "Forgive me for intruding, Mr. Kenrick," he said, "but I am informed that I have missed some epochal event. I regret now having so many prosperous clients who take up my time. What happened?"

Hugh answered by simply handing the attorney a copy of the printed resolves. Reisdale read them and emitted a slow gasp. He glanced at his host with new interest. "Oh, my! This is *provocative!*" He frowned. "And *you* had a part in this, sir?"

Hugh nodded. "They are Mr. Henry's resolutions, though only the first four were adopted by the House, and those four with great reluctance."

Reisdale stared at Hugh for a moment. "Why...the chamber must have been filled with the smoke of volleys from both sides!" He shook his head in confusion. "Were there so many of you that even the four had a chance to pass?"

Hugh briefly described the last two days of the session.

Reisdale grunted in appreciation. He held up the broadside and pointed to the resolves. "These read as though they might have been composed by Mr. Bland."

Hugh said, "Colonel Bland was a chief and very vocal opponent, Mr. Reisdale. I must say that I am disappointed that he did not endorse them." He paused. "Copies of those resolves are now on their way to every colony and even to England." He smiled. "Mr. Barret did us the service. He was there."

Reisdale sighed. "I am surprised that the good Colonel opposed these. They are very much in his style."

Hugh shrugged. "He advised caution," he remarked. "But there is always a time when it is advisable to throw it to the winds."

"That you have done," said Reisdale. "I shall write Mr. Bland about this." He rose to leave. "I must study these resolves. When these reach England, we shall never hear the end of it!"

Hugh looked grave. "Or nothing at all."

Some time after Reisdale left, Hugh sat at his desk and reread his transcriptions to make certain he had not missed anything. Later, he would assign Mr. Beecroft the task of copying the speeches so that they could be sent to his father and Dogmael Jones. He twirled his brass top as he read; its hum seemed to soothe his nerves.

Then a remark of Reisdale's came to mind, about the volleys from both sides of the House. It caused him to look up at his sketch of Reverdy Brune, and recall something he had said to her long ago, about the gorget of his mind. *"There are battles of the intellect to be fought, Reverdy,"* he said to her that precious day, *"for king, country, and liberty....A mind can accrue honor, too, and carry its own colors....I am an ensign in our country's most important standing army...."* A battle had indeed been fought over the course of those days in the House, he thought. And while I was an ensign in that conflict, Mr. Henry was our captain.

Even John Ramshaw, when he stopped by Meum Hall on his way to the *Sparrowhawk*, had acknowledged the violence of the conflict, and remarked, "It was not a soldier's wind that sailed your resolves through, my lad. You were beating to windward all the time you were taking and giving shot, and hazarding a wreck close to some killer rocks."

Hugh found himself wishing that his friend Roger Tallmadge was here, so he could ask him what he felt after a battle, and if it was natural for a man to feel drained and lifeless, even in victory. Because, he thought, while he was engaged in that battle, he had felt exaltation.

Then a smile began to grow on Hugh's mouth as he identified the thing that was troubling him: *I felt then that I had not only been defending an important hill, but attacking it, as well, and that the struggle was terrific, and merciless, and deafening, one side crashing repeatedly against the ramparts and parapets of the other, and thrown back. It was a steep slope to charge up, and a precarious one to hold, but both sides were determined, fearless, and courageous, and they thought it would never cease....The enemy?* wondered Hugh. *He was nameless, faceless, almost irrelevant...."*

Hugh's completed smile was one of enlightened irony and contentment. It is no wonder you are tired, he thought. You were fighting yourself.

And you were victorious.

His eyes wandered back to the picture of Reverdy Brune. *But I know what is missing here,* he thought. *A pair of lonely, grateful, hungry arms holding me to her, and my cheek resting on her scented hair....That special soldier's homecoming, that intangible recognition of valor that only a woman can bestow....*

Hugh shut his eyes against the longing. Well, he thought, pushing himself away from his desk. Enough of that. It is early in the day, and there are things to be done.

*   *   *

Jack Frake was not troubled. He was in the fields today, as usual, appraising his own crops. But he turned in his saddle now and then to look at the great house of Morland in the distance, and then let his sight roam over the expanse of fields that spread just south of it. Even though he knew that none of it had ever been in jeopardy, he felt now that somehow a great cloud of doubt and uncertainty was lifted from over it. He felt somehow released from that doubt and uncertainty, freer than ever before. The great event in Williamsburg had happened. He had been fortunate enough to witness it. He would have believed it, even had he not witnessed it. A copy of the resolves lay on his desk in the library.

Men were emerging from the caves of servitude, he thought; some boldly, some tentatively, still others darting back at the first touch of sunlight on their foreheads. He wondered for a moment where he had heard that analogy, other than in Redmagne's *Hyperborea*. Oh, yes! he recalled; during that long-forgotten encounter with Plato's *Republic*, when he was a youth being tutored in the very house he now owned. Yes: Men were emerging from those caves to see with their own eyes; beginning to doubt the necessity of guardians and messengers to tell them what the upperworld was and meant; beginning to question the assumption that such knowledge was impossible to them, or too special to acquire by their own efforts; beginning to suspect that the intermediaries and guardians were hostile obstacles who had a powerful interest in keeping the cave-dwellers ignorant, dependent on them, and chained to their tasks.

Jack Frake had never dwelt in those caves; he knew of them only as an external observer. He had always viewed it as a tragic paradox that other men remained in them, either from ignorance or indifference, or by educated choice. He was glad, however, that he had known some men who were much like himself, men who had never needed to ascend the darkened, jagged, perilous heights to reach the light that shone through the entrances to the caves, men who had refused to allow themselves to be herded at the birth of their consciousnesses to the depths of those caves. Patrick Henry was certainly one of those men, he thought. And Hugh Kenrick.

He heard the jingle of reins and the thud of hooves near him, and turned to see John Proudlocks approach and ride up to his side. And this man, he added.

"You are looking...philosophical, Jack," said the Indian, "when you should be concerned about the corn." He waved a hand to indicate the broad square of cornstalks before them. "Worms and birds have been fattening themselves on this crop. I do not know why they are so...numerous, this year. Our people pick off the worms and chase off the birds, but it is useless. The...vermin always return."

"I know," said Jack. "This year, we will be lucky to harvest enough fodder for ourselves." In the past, Morland had been able to sell about half its corn crop to merchants and ship captains for resale to farmers and planters throughout the Tidewater.

After a moment, Proudlocks asked, "What were you thinking?" He was intimate enough with his friend's manner and bearing that he knew that the corn crop had not been on Jack's mind.

Jack smiled. "How wonderful this place is, John, now that what must be said has been said." He related his thoughts on the caves to Proudlocks, who listened with great interest.

Proudlocks nodded sagely when Jack had finished. "Oh? Plato and his guardians and philosopher-kings? I have read that parable. It was quite silly, and without purpose." He pointed to the sky. "There is the sun," he said, "and there is the house, and the fields, and Mr. Hurry on his horse, and the river beyond. Where is the messenger to tell me those things?" He pointed to his eyes and forehead, wagging a finger a few times to stress that he made no distinction between them. "Here. They are truth-tellers, not tale-tellers of shadows and forms, or philosopher-kings who deal false cards to their subjects." He shrugged. "*They* are...more little men, that is all." He paused. "What happened in the Assembly — that is the beginning of a march from the caves, as you say, is it not?"

Jack shook his head. "For others," he said. "They have not yet begun their march. They are only just gathering at the entrance, so to speak."

Proudlocks nodded to another figure in the distance. "Look. It is Mr. Kenrick."

Hugh Kenrick walked his mount through the fields, then urged it into a canter for the last fifty yards. As he approached, Jack doffed his hat in salute and greeting.

Hugh smiled and touched the brim of his hat. "Good afternoon, sirs. May I invite myself to supper, Jack?" he asked. "And perhaps persuade Etáin to give us a round on her harp?"

Jack saw by a subtle, unintentional set of Hugh's face that it was not merely company that he was seeking. He was certain that Hugh was still trying to close the wound he had suffered in the House over the apology, that he was in the final stage of recovery, and that he simply needed some kind of reminder that there were men he did not need to persuade, fight, or oppose. Nor apologize to. He needed some time in *Hyperborea.* "You are welcome to stay, Hugh," said Jack. "And I believe Etáin would oblige us with a private concert."

"Thank you," said Hugh. He accompanied Jack and Proudlocks as they inspected Morland's fields. At the end of the tour, they rode back to the great house. Etáin was sitting in a chair on the veranda. She rose and said, "Here are my soldiers!"

Hugh grinned, but laughed inwardly to himself. Jack said, as he dismounted. "And hungry ones, too. Ask Mrs. Beck to set another place for Hugh. He is staying to supper."

Etáin nodded. "I saw you three in the fields, and have already instructed her." Israel Beck, husband of the cook and servant and assistant bookkeeper for Mr. Robins, the business agent, came out and led the mounts to the stables. Etáin bussed her husband first when he stepped onto the veranda, then Hugh. Hugh said to her, "I am hoping also that you will charm us with some music. My head, at least, is still staggered by the excess of words I have spoken and heard these last few days, and I believe that a dose of your talent will clear them away."

"Of course," laughed Etáin. "I have tamed Mr. Bach, and have been wanting you to hear how."

"Ah!" laughed Hugh. "I cannot bear him on the organ, but on your harp, he is quite heavenly!"

That evening, over supper, together with Mr. Robins and William Hurry, they talked about everything but politics. Jack, Hugh, Etáin, and Proudlocks laughed more than they had ever before. And later, Etáin performed on her harp in the music room, playing her own transcriptions of Bach and several Continental composers.

Far into the evening, at Hugh's request, she played "Over the Hills and Far Away," and ended with "Westering Home." Near the end of the latter, Jack happened to glance at Hugh because his guest had not moved in a while. He saw that Hugh's eyes were shut. Hugh sat in his armchair in too relaxed a manner, his head lolling to one side.

Etáin completed the melody, and noticed it, too. She whispered, "He called it a soldier's lullaby, and indeed it put him to sleep!" Proudlocks rose and made to rouse Hugh, but Jack put up a hand. "No. Let him sleep. We'll get him a pillow and a blanket." He paused. "He is tired, and ought to awaken here."

After they had made Hugh comfortable, and Robins, Hurry, and Proudlocks had gone to their quarters, Jack and Etáin sat on the steps of the veranda for a while before they, too, retired. "When I was in town today," said Jack, "I met Mr. Stannard, who has somehow procured a copy of the resolves. He promised they would cause trouble. I replied that when one purchases a bull, its horns are natural and inevitable appendages."

Etáin laughed. "What did he say?"

Jack chuckled and drew on his pipe. "Nothing. He made a face, as though he had just tasted some wrong beer. Reverend Acland was about, too. He crossed the street to avoid me."

"I never liked that man," remarked Etáin. "Not as a man, not as a minister."

"Hugh said today that the resolves will have a greater effect and consequence than did Martin Luther's ninety-five theses when they were nailed to a church door in Wittenberg. I agreed. He also said that he had half a mind to nail a copy of the resolves to the door of Stepney Church."

"That would be prankish and beneath him," said Etáin, "though I think that Reverend Acland has deserved to have such a trick played on him."

Jack sighed and shook his head. "Hugh doesn't quite realize what he's done, Etáin, or, at least, what he's helped Mr. Henry and the others to do. He has advanced my own thesis, and shattered his own." He paused. "A part of him is still captive in Plato's caves."

"How can he not know, Jack?"

"Because…he has not yet found the words."

"What words?"

"The words his friend Glorious Swain told him he would find someday."

Jack paused again. "The words Skelly told me once I would find." He shook his head. "I am closer to finding them than is Hugh. They are simple words, words we use every day, words I sometimes think I am about to pronounce that particular way. But they elude me. They are simple words, Etáin, but they are at the peak of a great complexity. I cannot fathom their source." He smiled. "They are the crest of Hugh's Mount Olympus…the spirit that envelops and animates and protects *Hyperborea*."

Etáin leaned over and rested her head on Jack's shoulder. "Have you told Hugh what you plan to do in November?"

"No, not yet."

"He will approve. He will join you."

"We'll see." Jack and Etáin had discussed it between themselves, and then with John Proudlocks. For on the day they returned from Williamsburg, Jack had announced, "I have made my own resolution — that not a single stamp will be landed in this county."

Etáin sat up and gazed at the profile of her husband's face in the light of the lantern that hung from a hook on the veranda above them, then passed a loving, possessive hand over his hair. "If this is *Hyperborea*, then you are my Drury Trantham."

* * *

Hugh Kenrick did not attach any significance to dreams. He once wrote to his mother that they were "but the skewed, tilted, involuntary recollections of one's experiences and thoughts." Tonight, however, he had one of his infrequent dreams, and if he had been able to remember it, he might have seen some relationship in it between its events and those of the last month.

He saw himself wandering among the stalls and carts of the booksellers in St. Paul's Churchyard in London, then picking up an ancient tome, and wondering of a sudden how he was going to announce that he had just discovered a lost play by Shakespeare, *The Tragedy of King Henry the Second*. In the dream, he recognized it instantly. It was about Thomas á Becket's clash with Henry over whether the Church was going to punish a pair of murderous priests, or the Crown. Then he saw himself sitting in a theater, watching Garrick in the role of Becket, delivering a glorious soliloquy, and then the actor Samuel Foote as Henry speaking a hand-wringing answer. Then, with unaccountable abruptness, the stage figures merged, and Hugh imagined himself, at times with Patrick Henry, and, oddly enough at times,

with an older Thomas Jefferson, delivering speeches on liberty to a mal-
odorous assembly of men of Becket's time. Somehow he knew that his
scruffy audience understood every word he spoke, but also that what he
was saying was unintelligible to every man in it. The serfs, the knights, the
tradesmen, the princes all gaped up at him with cows' and sheep's eyes. He
was standing on a dais with Patrick Henry and Jefferson, and turned to
them to remark, "We may as well be speaking Dutch, or Algonquian, or
court German, sirs. Ought we to go on, before they take us for sorcerers,
and burn us at the stake?"

At this point, Hugh awoke with a start, shook his head, opened his eyes,
and saw the darkness around him and heard the crickets and tree frogs
beyond a window. Then, with a fleeting, half-conscious awareness that he
had been dreaming, he fell back on the divan and resumed his interrupted
sleep.

Epilogue: The Sparrowhawk

Young Thomas Jefferson, two mornings after Lieutenant-Governor Francis Fauquier dissolved the General Assembly, left a New Kent ordinary and resumed his journey by cart north to Albemarle County and his Shadwell estate in the company of his friend and slave servant, Cupid, a black youth only slightly younger than his master. The latter noted that his master had been pensive and taciturn ever since they left Williamsburg, not his usual gay and talkative self. He ventured to ask, as they sat together on the board as the cart bumped and rocked over a dirt road rutted with the passage of innumerable wagons and coaches, "What troubles thee, Master Tom?"

"*Troubles* me?" scoffed Jefferson with astonishment. "Ask, rather, what *excites* me! Back there in the Capitol, my friend, I witnessed a battle of the Titans for possession of the earth and of our future on it! I regret not having had a hand in its outcome! Oh, how I ached to enter the fray and support Mr. Henry and the others! I would have gladly suffered a mortal wound in that contest, knowing as I died that I had helped to advance a great cause!" He chuckled and shook his head. "Well, I was grazed nonetheless, by Mr. Randolph, and was given a thorough dressing down by Mr. Wythe for having reminded my mother's cousin of his wishful venality. You heard him ranting at me that very evening!"

"Mr. Wythe was very angry with you, sir," agreed Cupid with amused irony. "I thought he would strike you."

Jefferson laughed again. "Well, no matter! What happened back there, my friend, has enriched us all. A few well-chosen, well-spoken words have cracked a wall groaning with the ivy of slothful ignorance, and that wall must someday tumble down from the rot! And through the widening cracks shines a magnificent, incalescent light, one that shows what is possible to us, a light that cannot but warm the brow of any man who chooses to contemplate it! It is a sobering experience, to see such a light. It gives one pause to think of which course in life one must choose to take — to show one's back to the world and its ways and remain a mere spectator, or to face them and say '*No!*'"

Jefferson felt the worried scrutiny of his companion on him, and turned to bestow a reassuring smile on him. "Never mind my ramblings, my friend. I am burning bright myself." He cocked his head once in appreciation. "That Kenrick chap was right. I have overlooked myself, all these years. I have neglected to raise my head and see the broader vista. The fire is in me, and shall ever burn from this day forward. I have a greater ambition now, a new direction. Law is in jeopardy, and it is law I shall study and uphold...come what may...."

He glanced back at the baggage piled in the bed of the cart. Among his things was a worn and marked-up copy of Sir Edward Coke's *Institutes of the Laws of England*, which, together with other treatises on law, he had been studying for a time under George Wythe's direction. "What irony, my friend! In back of us is Coke, our greatest jurist and an enemy of royal tyranny. Yet, there was a man who, in one damning instance, ignored his own reason and rules of evidence, and charged Walter Raleigh, a patriot and benefactor of his country, with treason on the most specious of testimony. Inconstancy is a great enemy of virtue, even among sages, my friend. And it is at work again! We must work hard and be constant in our principles, to ensure that we are virtuous enough that such history does not repeat itself in our own conduct...."

Cupid's attention was diverted then by some motion in the blue sky ahead of them. "Look!" he exclaimed, pointing to a black spot that hovered high over a field. Even as he spoke and as Jefferson lifted his head to watch, a sparrowhawk circled once, then folded its wings and plummeted to the earth. At the last moment it spread its wings again over a pair of doves that had just risen from the field. Too late did the doves become alert to the menace. In an instant the sparrowhawk seized one of the doves, then soared off into the sky, its prey clenched firmly in its talons. The second dove fled in another direction.

Jefferson laughed. "There goes Mr. Henry, making off with Mr. Randolph!"